COLD
MOURNING

Stonechild and Rouleau Mysteries

Cold Mourning
Butterfly Kills
Tumbled Graves
Shallow End
Bleeding Darkness
Turning Secrets
Closing Time

BRENDA CHAPMAN

COLD MOURNING

A **STONECHILD AND ROULEAU** MYSTERY

DUNDURN
PRESS

Publisher: Kwame Scott Fraser | Editor: Jennifer McKnight
Cover designer: Laura Boyle
Cover image: unsplash/ Milada Vigerova; unsplash/ Osman Rana

Library and Archives Canada Cataloguing in Publication

Title: Cold mourning : a Stonechild and Rouleau mystery / Brenda Chapman.
Names: Chapman, Brenda, 1955- author.
Description: 2nd edition.
Identifiers: Canadiana 20230160794 | ISBN 9781459752580 (softcover)
Classification: LCC PS8605.H36 C65 2023 | DDC C813/.6—dc23

This book is also available in ebook and audio.

We acknowledge the support of the Canada Council for the Arts and the Ontario Arts Council for our publishing program. We also acknowledge the financial support of the Government of Ontario, through the Ontario Book Publishing Tax Credit and Ontario Creates, and the Government of Canada.

Care has been taken to trace the ownership of copyright material used in this book. The author and the publisher welcome any information enabling them to rectify any references or credits in subsequent editions.

The publisher is not responsible for websites or their content unless they are owned by the publisher.

Printed and bound in Canada.

Dundurn Press
1382 Queen Street East
Toronto, Ontario, Canada M4L 1C9
dundurn.com, @dundurnpress 🐦 f 📷

For Ted Weagle — Love Always

1995

SUNNY HAD BEEN crouching in the tall grass for what felt like a very long time. After Lily left, she'd flattened out a little burrow and huddled into the dank earth that smelled of earthworms and rotting leaves, turning around and round like her dog Rascal getting his bed ready for a long sleep. Finally satisfied, she'd squirmed into herself, knees tucked under her chin, arms wrapped around her skinny legs. She'd kept motionless while the wind rustled the grass around her like garter snakes slithering through the underbrush. She'd crouched there long enough for the sunlight to fade from dazzling hot to a pale golden yellow. Long enough for her legs to go from tingly to numb.

But still Lily did not come.

What was it Lily had whispered to her just before she stood to face the woods at the far end of the field? "Don't stand up and don't make a sound. Do *not* move until I come back for you. I will come back for you, Sun." The last words were a hot breath of promise against her cheek.

She'd nodded and felt the warm pressure of Lily's hand on her head. Lily's fingers had tangled in her hair, but she hadn't made a peep, not even when Lily pulled her hand too quickly away, yanking with it several strands. She'd listened to Lily pushing her way through the thick reeds until the sound of her feet squelching through the mucky dirt had faded, leaving only the soft *whoosh* of the wind through the grass and the water tumbling over rocks on its way downstream. She'd fought back the panic, the need to stand up and scream at the top of her lungs for Lily to come back, not to leave her behind. She was really alone then, with her thudding heart and burning lungs — reminders of their frantic run through the brush along the slippery riverbank.

Almost instantly, mosquitoes had buzzed around her head and tracked their way to her arms, getting worse later as the sun started to go down. Her sweater had kept most of them from biting, but not all. She'd tucked her hands between her knees and pulled her jeans lower over bare ankles, keeping her eyes tightly shut, face pressed into her pant leg. From time to time, she'd lifted her head just enough to see the edge of the sky above the grass. Then she'd lowered her forehead back onto her pant leg and squeezed her eyes shut. Even when sharp stalks of grass had rubbed against her face, she'd stayed motionless, letting the fear buzz unchecked in her stomach like the flies circling her head.

She could only guess at the time as the afternoon emptied into early evening. Her belly had grumbled in hunger. She'd needed to pee, but she'd stayed in place. At some point, she dozed.

The sun was just above the tree line when she opened her eyes again, not sure at first where she was or why she was there. She'd been dreaming that her mother's arms were tight around her. Safe, warm arms with gentle hands attached that rubbed up and down her back. She'd known it was just a dream though, even half-asleep. She could barely remember having a mother let alone the feel of gentle hands on her back.

A noise ricocheted across the field above the sound of the river and the wind in the trees. It was the crack of a tree branch farther up the bank and off to her right. Sleep disappeared and her senses screeched onto high alert. Questions jumbled in her head. Was someone coming through the tall grass toward her? Was Lily on her way to find her? Hope filled her, but only for a moment.

Lily should be coming from the other direction. She'd be walking silent as a cat, never giving herself away. It couldn't be Lily.

The girl lifted her head just enough to see the sky above the grass and listened, testing the air like a frightened rabbit. Then she dropped her chin again and pulled herself into a tighter ball. Footsteps were coming closer, crunching through the grass like a monster in a bad dream. A whimper rose up her throat but she held it in, squeezing her eyes tighter.

He'd followed them. The man with the unblinking eyes that had looked at her and Lily like they were garbage. She'd known he would come. Lily had said he wouldn't give up easily. *Lily*, she screamed in her head. *Lily, come save me!* She scrunched her face harder into the rough denim of her jeans.

The footsteps stopped above on the incline, not far from her hiding place. She imagined him raising his head and sniffing the air like one of those hunting dogs, trying to smell out her and Lily. He'd be even angrier now. He'd be thinking of all those unspeakable things he'd promised when he'd had them in the back of his van. She squeezed her eyes tighter, willing him to follow Lily's trail up through the field to the forest.

If only they hadn't taken his offer of a ride. If only she hadn't leapt ahead of Lily into the open door to sit in the back seat. She'd known it was wrong to ignore Lily when she shook her head not to get in the van, but she'd been angry with Lily for bossing her around all afternoon. Doing what she wanted for once was a little victory, and for a few minutes it had felt good to sit and not have to walk one more step in her cheap, too tight shoes.

Lily's eyes had darted between her and the man and he'd smiled at her hesitation before he shrugged and started to slide the door shut. That was when Lily had pushed her way past him and into the back seat next to her, landing with a flounce and sigh that was all Lily. She'd reached across the space between them into Sunny's bag of jujubes and taken a handful, stuffing them into her mouth and chewing slowly, all the while pinning her with accusing eyes.

"I'm tired, Lil," she'd said by way of explanation. Already she regretted her weakness that brought them into the back seat. Her stomach was filled with a hum of worry she couldn't still. "My feet hurt." The last sentence came out grumpy.

"We could have called Roger to come get us," Lily said. Her voice was soft, without blame. It would have been better if Lily had been angry. This quiet Lily was unsettling.

"I'm sorry, Lil." She passed her bag of jujubes over to Lily to take the last. She'd saved the black ones but didn't feel right eating them now. Lily took two and handed the bag back to her.

"Just don't tell Roger we took this ride. He won't like it."

Their attention was drawn to the front seat. The man cleared his throat loudly as he pulled onto the highway. He reached over and fiddled with the radio until he found a country station. Then he lit a cigarette and started humming along to the music. Every so often, his eyes would be looking at them in the rear-view mirror.

She could feel Lily hunching down lower in the seat beside her. The ride hadn't been too bad so far, and she'd relaxed, turning her head to look out the window at the houses flying past. It would be okay. They were going to be home soon and Lily would forgive her.

That was before the man started talking.

"You little girls like to go riding with strangers?" he asked.

His voice was fake friendly like the people in the last home Sunny had lived in. She swivelled her head slowly around to look at Lily. Lily had lowered her head and tucked her chin into the fabric of her shirt. Neither of them said anything. They sat very still. The man lit another cigarette. It bobbed up and down between his lips as he spoke, the smoke drifting into the back seat in a white haze.

"I mean, look at the two of you. No sense between you. Why, a man might think you were asking to get fucked. I just don't know what it is with sweet young things these days. Leading a man on. Jumping into his van. Good girls woulda known better."

She'd stopped understanding then. His words got uglier and faster and Lily reached for her hand until she couldn't tell who was squeezing harder. They were driving out of town the right way and then the man turned onto a road she didn't know. She didn't recognize the last of the houses they passed before the woods and the brilliant blue glimpses of river that replaced them. The man's eyes in the mirror were long past friendly.

"You're going the wrong way." Lily's voice, small but defiant. She'd got back some of the anger she carried around and for a moment, it felt like they might just get out of the van okay. Lily was no match for the man though.

He inhaled deeply on his cigarette and then smiled at them in the mirror. His humming was as bad as all the awful things he'd been saying. The car started to slow and he was leaning into the windshield, looking off to the right side of the road. "You girls don't mind a little detour, now do you?" he asked. He turned the wheel suddenly onto a dirt road that she wouldn't have noticed. "It'll give us a chance to get to know each other better."

The car jolted through potholes, blowing a billow of dust skyward. Shadows whipped in bands across the car from the trees that lined the road. Lily let go of her hand and sunk lower in the seat with her face tucked into her shirt. They drove deeper into the brush. The man opened his window a few inches and she could hear the sound of the river getting louder. She turned her face toward Lily, silently begging her to come up with a plan. Lily kept her face hidden and for a moment, Sunny thought she might be sleeping but knew this was impossible.

The car drove around a long curve and she could see the river sparkling in patches through the trees. She'd never been on this road before but knew this was the same river that went past their reserve. The car slowed and the man eased it into a clearing carved out between the road and the river bank. He shut off the engine and flung one arm across the seat back as he turned to face them. His mouth formed a straight, hard line. His pale blue eyes were shiny.

"Which one of you cunts wants to play first?" he asked. His eyes shifted between her and Lily. "May as well start with the big one and work my way down." He chuckled and pointed to Sunny. "You stay in the car and wait your turn." He got out of the van and came around to slide open Lily's door. "Out," he said.

Lily shook her head.

"I said out!" He grabbed hold of Lily's arm and yanked her from the seat. Her feet twisted backwards like a rag doll, but he kept pulling her, dragging her from the floor of the van until she was half-lying in the dirt. He picked her up from behind, arms around her waist, and dragged her farther behind the van until they were out of sight. Lily screamed and kicked at the empty air the whole way.

The noises didn't stop even though Sunny couldn't see them. Scuffling and a slap that echoed back to her in the van. She jammed the knuckles of one hand into her mouth to keep from crying out. Lily was in trouble and she had to do something. She couldn't just sit and wait like the man had told her. She had to help Lily.

She reached across the front seat and grabbed the keys from the ignition. A little metal bottle opener hung from a silver chain with five keys on the ring. She couldn't see anything else in the van to use as a weapon. She'd jab the man with the keys so Lily could get away.

She slid the van door open and jumped onto the ground. Crouching low, she crept the length of it until she reached the tail light. The man had his back to her. She stood and took a few steps toward him.

Lily was on her knees and the man was standing in front of her with his back to the van. He had his hand in Lily's hair and was pushing her face back and forth, back and forth in front of him like a yoyo. His head was thrown back so that he faced the sky and his eyes were closed. A moan came out of his mouth as if he was in pain except he was smiling. Sunny moved closer. Lily had her mouth around the man and she was making gagging sounds as he thrust himself into her. Her eyes were wide open and the whites reminded Sunny of a wild horse.

"Harder," the man said and he growled in his throat like an animal. "This is the only thing you Injun girls are good for. Harder, girl."

Sunny stepped closer, ready to lunge, the keys clutched between her fingers and her hand raised to strike. She would do it even if it made the man mad. If he hit her, Lily would have a chance of getting away. Another step and Lily's crazed eyes found her. Her right eye, which had been partially turned from Sunny, was now visible in all its horror. The blackened socket was swelling up like a burnt marshmallow. Lily tried to shake her head but the man yanked her face forward. Sunny took another step. She scanned the ground for something to hit him with. There were only leaves and twigs. She started to run toward the man's back, her hand with the keys stretched out in front of her.

Without warning, the man dropped to the ground, screaming like he was on fire. He rolled himself into a ball, his back arched and his legs tucked into his chest. Lily scrambled away from him on her hands and knees. She kept her eyes on him writhing in the dirt as if he were a rattlesnake that wasn't done striking. Her mouth was sticky with saliva and she wiped her mouth on the sleeve of her shirt, never taking her eyes off the man screeching on the ground.

Sunny swerved past him to get to Lily, who was staring at the man, frozen in place. Sunny tugged hard on her arm, frantically pulling Lily back from the panic that filled her face. Lily shifted her eyes from the man and looked down at Sunny as if she didn't recognize her. Sunny grabbed on to Lily's hand and tugged. They backed away, their feet feeling for footholds in the uneven ground until it felt safe enough to turn their back on him to face the brush and trees. They ran toward the riverbank. The man's crazed screaming chased them as they scrambled through the bushes, but his footsteps did not.

They half tumbled down the embankment, stumbling and holding on to each other, their limbs rubbery and out of control. They slid on their bums the last way down and regained their footing just before the water. The shoreline was pitted with tree roots and large rocks that they dodged past in their frantic scramble to escape. Sunny held fast to Lily's hand, twice falling to her knees in the muck and water.

Lily wailed deep in her throat, a keening sound of anguish. She half dragged Sunny through the weeds and water while Sunny struggled to keep her feet from slipping from under her again. They rounded the bend in the river. A stretch of beach and open water sparkled before them. Lily moved deeper into the river. She sank to her knees and plunged her face into the cold water, spitting out a long stream when she surfaced. Her black hair hung in dripping strands across her face. She staggered to her feet, crying and panting at the same time. Her legs were wobbly and the current pushed her off balance so that she rocked back on her heels, nearly falling into the faster moving water. Somehow, she stayed upright. She turned away from the shore and wrapped her arms around her stomach before hunching forward and throwing up. The sound of retching was deadened by the water rushing over rocks deeper into the river.

Sunny didn't move, too frightened by this Lily she had never seen before. The Lily who never backed down from a fight. The Lily who never cried. "Come back!" Sunny wailed above the sound of rushing water. "Lily, come back!"

Lily straightened from the waist and squared her shoulders. She wiped her face one more time with the back of her hand while looking downstream from where they'd come.

Then, she turned back toward Sunny and took careful steps through the water to where she stood waiting on the sandy edge. Lily's face had settled back into its normal flat mask and Sunny felt the fear lessening. Lily took her hand. Her mouth was set.

"Time to go."

"Why did he fall like that?" Sunny asked as they crossed the little stretch of sand and stone. "I didn't even touch him."

"Because I bit him," Lily said. "I would have bitten him in two if I could have gotten my mouth open wider." She pushed the hair from her face and stopped in front of Sunny. Her right eye was nearly swollen shut. "You still have his keys?"

Sunny looked down at her hand. She didn't remember clutching on to them. She nodded.

"Give them to me." Lily reached out her hand and tucked them into the pocket of her jeans. "Come on, let's get out of here."

They started up the side of the river bank. Sunny kept looking back as they climbed, imagining the man close behind them. She was starting to tire but didn't complain. Her cheap black shoes were cutting into her feet. Lily stopped a few times and waited for her to catch up.

"Why'd you wear those shoes today? Your runners would have been better," said Lily.

"I wanted to look pretty for going into town," said Sunny. "These are my dress-up shoes."

"You've started limping. Maybe you should take them off."

"I think I twisted my foot on a rock," Sunny admitted. She hadn't wanted to tell Lily but it hurt when she stepped on her right foot. Lily frowned.

They'd reached the crest of the hill and a long field of grass stretched in front of them. The ground was muddy under their feet and water pooled in their footprints. Lily looked around until she found a dry place in the grass closer to some pin cherry bushes near the marshy edge just where the land rose up from the riverbank.

"I'm going to go ahead and lay a trail for him to follow if he gets this far," said Lily. "He didn't strike me as someone who gives up easy. Plus, we have his car keys. He can't very well drive away without them. You stay here and I'll double back after I leave enough clues to make him think we're in the woods over there." She squinted into the sun with her good eye and pointed across the field.

"I want to stay with you, Lil."

Lily looked down at her. "Your legs aren't as fast as mine, Sun. It's better if you can hide here until I come for you. We have to outsmart him. I won't let him catch us again." She spit into the dirt and used the tip of her shoe to spread the gob of phlegm around. She took Sunny's hand again. "Here's a spot where you'll be out of sight. It's our best chance, Sun. You're not going to go all baby on me, I hope."

Sunny shook her head.

"Good because you know what I think about babies."

———

Sunny thought the man was gone. She'd heard him circling around, but there hadn't been any sounds for several minutes. It would be good to stand and stretch but Lily said not to move. She would stay hidden until Lily came for her. A noise in the grass somewhere off to her right and Sunny strained her ears to hear. Was it a mouse scampering closer to her hiding place?

A flock of birds rose in unison from a nearby tree, their wings flapping in the air above her head. Sunny tucked her head lower to the ground. Another movement in the grass, but this time she couldn't pretend it was a harmless rodent. It was the sound of someone getting closer, pushing through the stalks of grass, tramping through the wet earth toward her.

She heard him laugh.

She turned her head slightly and opened her eyes a slit. His shadow blocked out the sun above her. Before she could move, his hand pulled the back of her sweater into a clump, yanking her from her hiding place and pitching her like a ragdoll onto her stomach in the grass. She scrambled forward on her hands and knees, but he was on her before she got far.

"Where's your friend?" he hissed in her ear, the weight of him making it hard for her to breathe. He eased off his bulk and a hand reached under her and flipped her over so his face was inches from hers. He used his hands to pin down her arms on either side of her head. His eyes bore into her. "You didn't think I'd see your footprints in the mud? Where is she?" he asked, louder this time. Spittle sprayed her face. "I owe her."

Sunny turned her head sideways, trying to avoid his unblinking stare. She wouldn't answer. Lily had gotten away and she would say nothing.

He ran his fingertips up and down her cheek. She closed her eyes. When his mouth was on hers, she started screaming inside her head. She tried to fight him off, but she was no match for his size and strength. The hand he'd used to touch her face was now sliding down her stomach. His breath was coming harder and he'd begun moaning. Sunny was frantic to get away but she couldn't move. She couldn't stop his hand from sliding between her legs.

Neither of them heard Lily's angry lunge across the field until she was upon them. Sunny felt the man's pressure lift from her as he heaved himself sideways. She could see Lily behind him. Her face was contorted in rage, the rock she held in her hand pounding again and again on the back of the man's head until the weapon and her hand were both sticky with dark red blood, and still she would not stop. The man's arms took the full brunt of his weight while the blows reigned down, but he was too late to protect himself from Lily's fury. Finally, his breath escaped in a final whoosh as he collapsed onto Sunny like a sack of cement.

Sunny's screams pierced the stillness of the afternoon, echoing across the water and filling every crevice and burrow in the grassy field. They penetrated Lily's anger bringing her back to earth and out of the terrible place she'd disappeared. Lily lowered her head and looked down at what she'd done. She dropped the rock like a burning pan onto the ground and wiped her hand on the earth and leaves. Then she knelt into the grass next to Sunny, using all her strength to shove the man off her. She gathered Sunny weeping into her arms.

"It's done," Lily said. "Shush. Shush. He can't hurt you." She looked at the man's still bulk next to them covered in blood. "I killed him." She tossed the words into the wind as if waiting for them to come back. Her shoulders slumped forward as she hunched in on herself.

Sunny's sobs lessened. She straightened and looked at the man lying on his side, his face turned toward them, his eyes open and blood pooling around him like a hood. She was glad she didn't have to see the back of his head where Lily had bashed it in with the rock. "I was so scared, Lil."

"I know," Lily spoke gruffly. "I was scared too."

"We'll tell them what he did to us. They won't blame us." Sunny saw the worry in Lily's frown, the hesitation in her eyes.

"We can't tell anyone what I've done," Lily said. "They'll put me in juvie again, or worse."

"I'll tell them what he did."

"No! Don't you get it? They'll never believe two Indian girls didn't deserve what we got, especially us in foster care and me with a record. They won't believe I had to kill him."

"I'll tell them, Lil. They'll have to believe me."

Lily stood up and looked down on her. "They won't do nothing to you since you're just ten, but I'm almost fifteen. They'll lock me up again, and I would rather die than have them tell me when I have to get up and what I can eat and when I can leave my room. I ain't doing that again. I'll kill myself first."

"Then what'll we do?"

Lily blinked her good eye. "We'll put rocks in his pockets and roll him into the river. The rocks will weigh him down, and if we're lucky they'll never find him. Nobody knows he took us out here. We'll wash his blood out of your shirt and where it splattered your face."

Tears dripped onto Sunny's hand. She lowered her head.

"If you don't want to help me, just say it," said Lily. "You won't be the first one or the last." She squatted next to the body and reached into the dead man's pockets. A brown leather wallet was tucked inside his nylon jacket. She scooped it out and flipped through the credit cards and bits of paper until she found his driver's licence. She held it up to her good eye. "David Williams from Toronto. Look, Sun. Do you figure this is his wife and kids?" She held out a photo of the man with a blond woman and a boy and girl in their early teens.

Sunny glanced at the photo. "Probably. I wonder if they'll miss him."

Lily shrugged. "They might be glad to be rid of the dirty old bastard." She picked up the bloody rock and started walking toward the river.

The fear started up again as Sunny watched Lily walk away from her. Lily was angry and shutting her out. Sunny felt a wave of loneliness and panic fill her. She couldn't bear to have Lily mad at her. She stood and ran toward her.

"Okay, I'll do it," she called. "I'll help you push him into the river."

Lily stopped walking. She turned and faced Sunny. She looked at her for a few seconds as if weighing something. Finally, she nodded. "Then help me find some rocks. After we get rid of him and clean you up, I'll drive his van back to town, dump it somewhere, and call Roger to come get us. I'll just have to hope the cops don't pull us over and figure out I'm underage. But first, I'm going to throw this rock that I hit him with as far into the river as I can where nobody will ever find it."

———

Lily was waiting for Sunny when she stepped off the school bus that brought her back to Birdtail Creek reserve. It had been a month since the man's death, and they'd kept away from each other, not wanting to draw attention to themselves or say something by mistake. Lily was dressed in a buckskin jacket and ripped blue jeans. She'd braided her hair and a beaded band encircled her head, resting low on her forehead. She flicked a glowing cigarette into the dirt as

Sunny approached. They started walking toward the house, not speaking.

Lily pulled Sunny into the trees partway up the property. There'd been a cold snap on the weekend and the leaves were starting to turn colour. Sunny craned her neck back to look at the shades of yellow in the alders and the blue sky overhead. A string of Canada geese was honking its way to the marshes south of the reserve. She waited for Lily to start talking.

Lily leaned against a pine tree. "You okay?"

Sunny nodded. "You?"

Lily shrugged. "I'm not sleeping so good. Nightmares."

"Is Roger still mad about us being out so late and your black eye?"

"He got over it. He wanted to track down the girls I told him I'd had the fight with. Took a while to keep him from charging back to town to start hunting them down. Luckily my story kept him from figuring out we were with the city man who disappeared. Did you get into trouble coming home late?"

"I don't think they noticed. The police still looking for that man?"

"Big mystery. They can't figure out why he left his van and nobody's seen him. He grew up near here. His parents still live in Miniota. Roger and I were in town two days ago and I saw that guy's, you know that David Williams, I saw his wife yesterday sitting in the coffee shop. Well, the same woman as in that picture. She was sitting all alone having lunch."

Sunny shivered inside her down vest. She'd tried to forget about that day and already bits of it were getting fuzzy. She wasn't too happy to have Lily show up and remind her even if she was glad to see her.

"Anyhow," Lily said, "the reason I'm here is because I wanted to tell you that I'm leaving. They've decided I need to get me a real education so I'm flying out tomorrow for Winnipeg. Some family is putting me up while I get my grade eight. It's all arranged."

"You never let them take you off the rez before," Sunny said. Tears came to her eyes. She lowered her head and blinked hard so Lily wouldn't see.

"Well, I never killed nobody before neither," said Lily. "Things change."

"I wish I could come with you."

Lily's voice softened. "Are they still treating you okay?"

Sunny shrugged. "They have six other kids. Half the time we don't have much to eat. I think they've already asked for me to be moved." She tried to smile, but it didn't work. "If you go, I won't have any family left."

"I'll always be your family, Sun. No matter where I live. I just can't …" Lily took a deep breath, "I just got to get away from here. I can't take knowing what I did."

"You had to. He wasn't going to let us go." Sunny let her mind flit to an image of the man on the ground and all the dark blood coming from his head before she closed it off. She couldn't think about it because thinking about it made her stomach hurt and her head fill with screams that wanted to get out. Sometimes, she woke up in the night crying. She knew she couldn't tell anyone, especially not Lily. Lily had her own nightmares.

"Does Roger want you to go?"

Lily shrugged. "I think he hoped that if I stayed, my mother would come back. Maybe he's starting to wake up to reality. She was only with him two years. It's not like he owes me nothing."

"We'll be together again one day, won't we Lil? You'll get me when we're old enough to live on our own?" Sunny moved closer until she leaned against Lily. She rested her head on Lily's shoulder. Lily stiffened for a moment before she wrapped an arm around Sunny.

"Yeah, we'll be together again little one. We'll have our own house and nobody will do nothing to us that we don't want. We'll have good jobs and money and lots to eat."

"And I won't have to keep Rascal tied up outside and I'll have my own bed."

"Yeah, your own bed. You won't have to share with the other kids." Lily laughed. "Can you imagine, Sun? We'll have real lives and people will envy us."

"Let's promise to find each other. Promise we'll be together again."

"I promise, Sunny. So help me God, I promise."

"And I promise too."

I

Tuesday, December 20, 10:45 p.m.

TOM UNDERWOOD LOOKED across the room at his wife and wondered how it would feel to place his hands around her slender neck and throttle the life out of her. He imagined her sinewy veins under his fingers and the satisfaction of hearing the bones crack as he twisted in a quick motion — like putting his hand around a jar lid and applying pressure in one glorious snap. Her red lips would form a soft O of comprehension as he tightened his hold and her eyes would widen before freezing open in death. He'd seen people murdered in enough films to know the drill. Would it be better to get rid of her before or after Christmas? He could return the gifts he'd bought her on Boxing Day if she were to die within the week. That could be the deciding factor. The gold link bracelet he'd bought her was overpriced. He took a long swallow of Scotch, and kept his eyes on her, then blinked back the dream.

Laurel lifted her head and tossed back her ironed veil of red hair. She'd lined her violet eyes in kohl and filled in the lids with gold shadow that shimmered in the light from the chandelier. She'd seen him looking at her. Her full lips curved into an amused smile as she trailed the fingers of one hand up and down between the V of her breasts as if rubbing an ice cube across her skin to cool off her hot flesh. Her lips parted in a suggestive smile before she turned her attention back to the man standing next to her.

Tom imagined the man eying Laurel's breasts, poor bastard probably wondering if he stood a chance of getting her somewhere alone so he could run his own hands up and down the curves outlined by her black form-fitting gown that dipped like a crescent moon in front. The thought of plunging one's face between those twin mounds could drive a man crazy if he let it. Tom knew all about that. He felt the familiar heat in his groin and cursed himself for being weak, for still wanting her.

"You meeting Archambault tomorrow?"

Tom dropped his eyes to look down at the man in front of him. J.P. Belliveau. He couldn't be in the same room as his partner anymore without thinking of bullfrogs — squat, round toads with oversized cheeks and bulbous eyes under heavy lids. He forced his face to relax, as if he had nothing on his mind but the deal.

"I have a call scheduled with him when I get into the office tomorrow. I'm going to fax him the contract before lunch and then head to his office in Montreal right after Christmas to finalize and pick up the signed papers."

"For less than we offered last month?"

Tom nodded.

"How did you manage to talk Archambault down?"

"I told him we would only assume the risk if he came down in price. I knew we were his only real hope so he had to drop his bottom line."

"I thought an American company expressed interest."

"They didn't have the capital to take it on this quarter. I might have also planted a seed with their point man that the design was flawed." Tom shrugged and smiled.

"You impress me. If I didn't know any better, I'd think we were separated at birth."

Tom nodded again but something burned in his guts like bile on a barbecue. He'd forgotten to bring antacid tablets and would be in rolling pain by the time he pried Laurel away from the party. Maybe he would make time for the doctor's appointment tomorrow. He'd cancelled the last two times but this ulcer was getting worse.

He felt an arm slip through his and flinched involuntarily until he looked down and saw that it was his daughter. He let his arm relax against hers. Geraldine tilted her shiny blond head and smiled up at him, a smile that softened her long, narrow face and plain features.

"Max and I are just heading out, Daddy. He's got an early day tomorrow and I'm a bit whacked." She patted her rounded belly for emphasis. "This baby is sapping my energy."

"I'll walk you out then," said Tom. He noticed Max standing behind Geraldine, checking his BlackBerry and punching keys with his thumbs. "Something in the hopper?" Tom asked over Geraldine's head, not sure why Max's fiddling with the contraption unsettled him. It might have had something to do with the focused look on Max's face that shut out everybody around him, including his pregnant wife.

Max glanced up. "Just a question about a meeting tomorrow. It could have waited until morning but you know Benny. He's a bulldog when it comes to nailing down the details."

"Sure." Tom looked closer at his son-in-law. When had he added the blond streaks to his hair? His grey pinstriped suit looked tailor-made and his shoes brand new. Tom grimaced.

If Geraldine hadn't begged him to give Max Oliver a job, he never would have let the guy through the front door. Tom had Max's number at hello — as deep as a puddle and as vain as a show horse — but Geraldine couldn't live without him, and he couldn't deny her. Tom felt a stab of indigestion below his rib cage. It was worse than normal tonight and that was saying a lot. At this rate, he'd have to find somewhere to lie down and curl into a ball until the pain lessened to something approaching bearable.

"You okay, Daddy?" Geraldine squeezed his forearm as they walked. "You've turned pale all of a sudden."

"Just tired. I think I'll leave right after you."

"What about Laurel?" Geraldine's eyes narrowed as she looked toward his wife holding court. "She doesn't look like she's ready to leave."

"Don't worry about Laurel," Tom said. He gently steered Geraldine toward the coatroom. He didn't feel like another scene tonight. He hoped Geraldine didn't feel his weight on her arm. The spasm of pain had nearly made him double over.

He forced himself to walk upright as they stepped outside into the welcome cold of the winter evening. The air chilled the sweat on his forehead and he felt like he might just make it home. He handed the doorman in the heavy red overcoat their two tags and watched him speak into a radio to have their cars brought around. Tom looked past him at the blue-and-green Christmas lights swaying on the tops of the trees in the square across from the Château Laurier.

"Looks like I have to go back to the office," Max said stepping close behind them. Tom and Geraldine turned in unison to face him.

"No!" Geraldine wailed. "You promised me not tonight."

Max frowned and his shoulders rose in a quick shrug. "Sorry angel, but it can't be helped. Benny's found a problem with one of the contracts. If I deal with this now, I might avoid a trip east. God knows, I have no desire to head to the coast this time of year."

Geraldine began to say something, but whoever was driving their car approached a little too fast and it skirted to a stop, fishtailing slightly so they all took a step backwards. Her voice trailed away.

"What the hell?" said Max. He raised a fist toward the car.

A kid in his early twenties wearing a red toque and an iPod jumped out and grinned at them before he headed back to the parking lot. Max lowered his hand and cursed again. He took Geraldine by the arm and guided her to the other side of the car, walking slowly so she didn't slip on the ice. He opened the door and lowered her onto the seat. Whatever he whispered into her ear must have been amusing because when he straightened she was smiling up at him, her eyes luminous in the overhead light of the car.

———

Tom motioned Laurel over. He'd left his overcoat on and didn't want J.P. to see that he was leaving early. Laurel said something to one of the men and he laughed as she stepped away from them. She made her slow way toward him, her hips swaying in time to the music like a stripper crossing the stage. Tom pulled her into the hallway.

"I'm heading home," he said. "I'm a bit done in."

"I can come with you. I don't mind leaving."

Her eyes said otherwise. He could see the wine glow on her face and knew she was just warming up to the evening. He'd long since stopped worrying about trying to keep up with her. Their twenty-seven-year age difference had become an insurmountable chasm.

"You should stay. If J.P. sees us all cutting out early, I'll never hear the end of it."

"If you're sure." Her eyes slid past him, back into the glitter of the party room. The DJ had replaced Bing Crosby with Beyoncé and couples were dancing in the centre of the gilt ballroom.

"Will you manage to get home okay if I take the car?"

"I have cab money if nobody is going my way."

"I'll kiss Charlotte goodnight for you then," he said.

"She'll be long asleep." Laurel leaned forward and for a second he thought she might kiss him on the mouth. He felt her lips brush his cheek and the disappointment was more than it should have been. "Don't wait up."

"I never do," he mouthed at her retreating back. The musky smell of her stayed on his skin, like a memory that would not leave him alone.

———

This time, it was an older bald man who delivered Tom's silver Mercedes to the front of the hotel. Tom tipped him generously before slipping behind the wheel and pulling away, careful not to spin the tires on the patches of black ice. The doorman was spreading salt from a bag onto the driveway when Tom glanced into the rear-view mirror. The temperature had risen since they'd driven to the hotel some four hours earlier, but it was still a cold night. He was glad for the blasts of dry heat coming out of the vents on either side of the dashboard.

He drove toward the Rideau Centre and made a right onto the Canal driveway, following its curved length to the Pretoria Bridge. He stayed to the same side of the canal and continued south through the Central Experimental Farm. The blackness of the sky sequined in stars and the reassuring hum of the car's powerful engine gave him the feeling of driving in the country, even though the farm was surrounded by subdivisions and commercial buildings. Turning onto Prince of Wales, he passed a string of bungalows with Christmas trees lit up inside their living rooms. He continued on to what used to be the country but was now a series of new subdivisions that had sprung up along the Rideau River. Winding Way, where his six bedroom grey stone with the three-car garage nestled, was another ten minutes away. The thought of going home to his mausoleum of a house was suddenly depressing.

Tom stopped at a light and watched a woman and a boy around ten years old walking along the other side of the road. It was late for the kid to be up. At that age, he'd have been long asleep no matter holiday or school night. The kid hung back, dragging his feet.

For a moment, Tom flashed to the boy he'd been and the parents who'd tried to cocoon him from the world's worst. They'd been lower middle class with strong Catholic values in a more innocent time. They'd be appalled at today's youth if they were still alive. The world had changed drastically even between the short years raising Geraldine and Hunter and now Charlotte. He shuddered to think what lay ahead for his youngest daughter. Sometimes it felt like too much to deal with. He saw himself now, a man approaching sixty with more money than he would ever spend and no ability to keep the women in his life happy. He was running on empty, drained of conviction, an utter failure in anything that mattered. The innocent, hopeful boy he'd once been was long gone.

But maybe, just maybe, there was still hope.

The light turned green. Tom released his grip on the steering wheel and pressed his foot on the gas pedal. The car powered forward while he rummaged inside his coat until he grasped his cellphone in his suit jacket pocket. He held it for a moment, debating with his inner voice that told him to just go home. Loneliness won out in the end. He kept one hand on the wheel as he looked down and punched in the familiar number. Two rings and her voice like warm honey in his ear.

"Tom? Is that you?" He could tell he'd woken her. He smiled to think of her tousled hair and bleary eyes.

"Yeah. Would now be a bad time …?" He hesitated, not sure he could get the words out. Her breath exhaled stronger in his ear but she didn't speak. He knew she was weighing what his call could mean and whether she should let him in. "I shouldn't have called," he said, now sorry that he had. He shouldn't have put her in this position. They'd agreed last time that it should be just that until they'd both made some changes.

"I'll leave the back door unlocked," she said at last. Her voice was stronger as if she'd shaken away the sleep.

"I have a bottle of Grand Marnier with me," he said. "I'll pick up a few glasses from the hutch on my way to your bedroom."

"I'll be waiting."

She hung up before he did, but the night seemed less empty than it had a moment before.

—

It was three a.m. when Tom pulled into his own driveway on Winding Way. The outside lights were on but the interior was in darkness except for a light in Winnie's room on the far side of the house. She'd probably put Charlotte to bed and then fallen asleep reading. He turned off the engine and sat with his arms resting on the steering wheel, looking at his fortress until the car cooled and the chill began seeping into his bones. Only then did he stir himself to step outside the car into the winter night. Snow had begun to fall and it wet his face when he lifted his eyes to the sky. A bank of clouds had blown in to hide the stars.

The ticking grandfather clock marked time as he padded upstairs in his socked feet. He'd left the lights off and the branches of the oak tree made dark patterns on the wall through the windows that lined the staircase. Laurel's bedroom door was closed. He hesitated for a moment standing next to it, listening to hear her inside. At last he turned the knob and pushed the door open. Her bed was empty, the covers folded neatly over the pillows.

He quietly closed the door and continued on to Charlotte's bedroom. Her door was partially closed. He pushed it fully open and stepped inside. The one bright spot in his marriage was sleeping on her back, one arm wrapped around her favourite teddy and the other flopped over the side of the bed. He moved closer and gently lifted her arm to place it under the covers. She stirred and mumbled something but didn't wake up. He straightened and looked down on her. Charlotte had inherited Laurel's thick mane of hair. If her eyes had been open, he'd be staring into the same violet ones that had made him throw away his twenty-year marriage to Pauline. He reached out a hand to push the lock of hair that had fallen across Charlotte's face but pulled back his hand before he touched her silken hair. *Leave her*, he thought. *Don't chance disturbing her sleep.*

He raised his hand to his lips and blew a kiss toward his sleeping daughter before backing as quietly as he could from her room. It was time to find his bed. Maybe tonight he'd had enough to drink so that his sleep would be long and dreamless. It would be the first time in a long time and his body could use the rest. His mind could use the oblivion.

2

KALA STONECHILD SAT in her Ford pickup in the parking lot of the Ottawa Police Station just west of Elgin Street. She'd spent the better part of the night driving and could have done with a shower and a good night's sleep. Instead, she had ten minutes to make it inside or risk starting off on the wrong foot. It might be better if she restarted the truck and pointed it north. If she hadn't been so tired, she might have done just that. She grimaced at herself in the rear-view mirror and tucked stray strands of black hair behind her ears. She rubbed the grit out of her eyes with the backs of her hands.

Ready or not.

Stepping out of the truck was a pleasure after fourteen hours of driving. Her right leg had cramped and she winced as pain shot up from her calf. She took an extra turn around the lot to get the circulation flowing before heading toward Elgin Street and the front door of the station. The building was three storeys and flat grey, taking up a city block. The entrance was glassed in windows with a view of a giant mural painted the width of the far wall. Police officers in the community stared down at her in frozen stances. The uniformed cop on the front desk had probably been watching her on a television screen the whole time, but he barely glanced at her as she stepped up to the desk.

"I'm here to see Staff Sergeant Jacques Rouleau," she said, looking around the foyer, taking in the layout. His voice drew her back.

"And who should I tell him is here to see him?" His nametag said Cooper.

She forced a smile. "He's expecting me — Officer Kala Stonechild. I'm reporting for duty."

Cooper lifted a clipboard and ran a finger down the list of names. "Here you are. Stonechild." He looked at her directly for the first time. "I'll just call Sergeant Rouleau to come get you. Have a seat if you like."

"Thanks, I'll stand."

"Suit yourself."

Ten minutes ticked by before a man in a grey suit walked toward her. He looked to be early fifties, but it was hard to tell because of his shaved head and lean body. Up close, his eyes were a startling green with tiny laugh lines etched into his skin.

"Sergeant Rouleau," he said, extending a hand. "Welcome Officer Stonechild. How was the trip down?" They started walking toward his office. His voice had the faintest trace of a French accent that she wouldn't have detected unless she'd been listening for it.

"There was a snowstorm outside Sudbury and I had to spend an extra day waiting it out. Other than that, the trip was uneventful."

Rouleau glanced sideways at her. "Did you find a place to stay in Ottawa?"

She nodded. She hadn't yet, but it wouldn't take much to find one.

They passed a room with several desks and officers talking on the phone and then turned right into another room. It was a little more cramped with six desks and a closed office directly ahead. The fluorescent lighting hurt her tired eyes. Three men stood next to a coffee machine, each one holding a full mug. They stopped talking and turned in unison when she and Rouleau walked in. Kala met their stares square on. An East Indian with darker skin than hers, a red-headed stocky Irishman, and a sandy-haired looker with brown eyes and wavy hair. She hoped he wouldn't be her partner. All four men stood close to six feet tall; she'd be the short one on the team at five seven.

Rouleau made introductions and each shook her hand. Sandeep Malik, Clarence Whelan, and Philip Grayson. "Whelan will show you around. You two will be working together."

The heavy-set, red-headed man gave her a nod. She was happy to see the wedding ring on his left hand. He had the look of a well-fed man happy with his lot. No complications. That's all she wanted in a partner. No suggestive looks or subtle innuendos. No avoiding late-night drinks and pretending his hand on her leg wasn't an invitation. She looked past him to the good-looking one, who by process of elimination had to be Grayson. He'd looked her over when she first came in, but now he was deep in conversation with Sandeep Malik. She turned to Whelan and held out her hand. He didn't hesitate and reached out his own. His grip was warm and strong.

"Good to have you on board, Kala."

"Thanks. Good to be here."

Rouleau was heading to his office. "Take Stonechild with you on that assault call. When you get back, she can get her paperwork over with." He said it without turning and continued walking without waiting for a response.

"Nothing like jumping right in," said Whelan. "Your desk is there, facing mine. Sorry you won't get a chance to warm the chair."

"Lots of time for that."

"Have you got a gun?" he asked. "Not that we're going to need it on this call."

She patted her jacket. "Side arm. Don't worry. I've got the carrying permit." They started walking toward the door and out of the building. "It's nice not having to wear a uniform."

They reached a black four-door Chevy and he motioned for her to get in the passenger side. "Good thing we have indoor parking," he said, starting the engine and turning the heater up high, "because it's as cold as a witch's tit out there."

Cold air blasted into their faces. He backed the un-marked car out of his space and turned it to face the exit. They merged with the traffic onto Elgin and kept going south to the Queensway on-ramp heading west. He cut across two lanes to the show-off lane.

Whelan glanced at her after they passed the Bronson exit. "There's some perv in the west end who gets into apartment buildings and jumps women in the lobby. He likes to grab them from behind and fondles them through their clothes. Then he gives them a shove into the wall and runs off."

"Lovely. How many times has he done it?"

"Five so far. This latest woman called it in twenty min-utes before you arrived. She's in her apartment and shaken up but says she's not hurt. None of the women has given us a great description of the guy and we're hoping this time we get more to go on."

"Is he escalating?"

"Rouleau's worried enough that he wants this nipped in the bud, so to speak." Whelan flashed a smile. "Welcome to the big bad city. Our investigations unit is an offshoot of Major Crimes. It was formed to prevent crime from happening and to take over tricky homicide and major crime cases after a certain time period from Major Crimes. We're the latest trial balloon. If we end up proving good value, we could be the way of the future, that is, if we get the chance to show our stuff."

"Some would say policing needs to start thinking outside the box."

"Or it just comes down to resources. Hard to keep a handle on crime if there aren't enough cops on the street. So what brings you to Ottawa anyway?"

"Just wanted a change."

"You were with the OPP up north?"

"Yeah. Out of Red Rock. Before that, I worked a reserve in the far North. When this job came up, I thought it would be a chance to try city policing." It was the story she'd decided on as she drove south. It was as good as any.

Whelan glanced at her. "Where you staying?"

"Not sure yet. I thought I'd bunk at the Y until I have a chance to look at apartments."

"I'd take you home but we have a one-month-old with colic. You'll thank me later for not offering."

"That's okay. Your first?"

"Second. Harry's three and gotten wild since baby Logan showed up. Meghan is sending me for a vasectomy as soon as she can get me into a clinic. Either that, or separate bedrooms."

"More information than I need," said Kala. "Really." She pretended to cover her ears.

Whelan laughed. "We're going to be spending a lot of time and I like to lay my cards on the table."

"Well that makes one of us." Kala smiled but she kept her eyes straight ahead. Traffic was light and they'd crossed the city in no time. Whelan eased the car across the lanes to the Woodroffe off-ramp.

Rouleau filled his coffee cup for the third time that morning and wandered over to look at the photos of murder victims posted on the wall in their meeting area: a homeless man, two gang members, and a cab driver. They'd been handed the cases from homicide after his team formed – newly cold cases with little to go on. He wasn't convinced his team would uncover enough evidence to solve any of them, but that wouldn't stop them from painstakingly building the files. Solving any one of them would validate the unit's existence.

His heard his phone and made it back to his office by the third ring. He said his name automatically before he checked the incoming caller. *Frances.* It was a shock to hear his ex-wife's voice.

"Jacques."

The same breathy way she'd always exhaled his name when they were together, a honeyed combination of warmth and exasperation. He smiled to hear her say it again. His heart beat faster. "To what do I owe this pleasure?" he asked.

"I thought it was time, that's all. We promised each other we wouldn't end up hating, remember?"

He closed his eyes. "I remember."

"I wonder … do you think we could meet for coffee or a drink maybe?"

All the times he'd longed to hear her voice. For months she'd avoided contact, and now she was offering him … what? He had no way of knowing. "When?"

"Tonight, if you've time. I know it's short notice."

"I can make it tonight. Should I pick you up?"

"No. I'll meet you at the Royal Oak on the Canal at eight thirty. Just for a drink though. I'll have already eaten. Is that okay?"

"That's fine."

He hung up the phone and pictured his ex-wife the last time he'd seen her. She'd just come from the hairdresser's and her naturally brown hair had been cut short and streaked with blond highlights that made her face pale and her eyes darker. She'd lost weight and walked with a new confidence, but he'd liked it better when she was a curvier size twelve. They'd just signed the divorce papers and she was in a hurry to cross the street and catch a bus to her apartment in Sandy Hill. She was wearing a new olive-green pantsuit with a gold scarf knotted around her neck and it had struck him sad at her need to remake herself. She'd tilted her chin up and out like she did when she'd made up her mind about something and wouldn't hold his eyes as he said goodbye. He'd wanted to hug her but knew she wouldn't welcome his touch. He'd made it the three blocks to his car before he'd crumpled into the front seat and wept.

Grayson poked his head around the doorway to Rouleau's office. "Got a minute?"

Rouleau glanced at the photo of a murdered cab driver named Abul-Jabbar Amin on his desk. Whoever had attacked him that January night a year ago had pummelled his face into a bloody pulp, crushing his nose and bludgeoning the right side of his face with a weapon that was never re-covered. Rouleau closed the folder. "Sure. Come in."

He watched Grayson cross the room and flop down in the chair on the other side of his desk. Rouleau glanced at his watch and mentally kept track. Five minutes in, Grayson got down to it.

"About Stonechild. Are you sure she's a fit for our team?"

"She's young but comes highly recommended."

"She doesn't have experience in major crimes and isn't familiar with Ottawa. I think she'll have a hard time."

"I'm willing to give her a chance."

Grayson spread his hands upward. "I just wanted to let you know the team isn't opposed to her working with us, but we have concerns about her experience."

"Point taken. I know I can count on you to help her settle in."

Grayson stood to leave. "Sandeep and I are heading to the Rideau Centre to track down the missing homeless woman Annie Littlewolf and then we'll call it a day."

"Nobody at the women's shelter phone in yet?"

"I checked and they haven't seen her. They're worried because she and Claude were always together and now that he's dead, they're not sure what she'll do to herself."

Rouleau sighed. "Or maybe she saw whoever left him dead in the alley and she's gone into hiding. Find out what you can and I'll see you tomorrow."

"You should call it a night too."

"Soon."

Grayson turned at the door. "I just want you to know it's not because Stonechild's …"

"Descended from the original inhabitants of this great land?" asked Rouleau with his head down.

"Yeah. That."

Rouleau lifted his eyes and shook his head at Grayson's retreating back. *Don't cause me any grief,* he thought. *The team can't take any more pressure.*

He reopened the Amin file to sift through it again with Grayson and his prejudices filed away but not forgotten. He picked up the photo of the murdered cabbie. There had to be some detail he'd missed that would lead them to a new line of enquiry. Nobody should get away with what they did to this man.

———

At six thirty Rouleau put on his overcoat and boots to grab some supper at the Oak before Frances arrived. Maybe the lamb stew and hunks of crusty bread. It had been their favourite pub when they were together, even though it changed hands now and then. It was conveniently located halfway between his office and their first home off Main Street in Ottawa South. Could there be any significance in her choosing it as their meeting place? He told himself not to read anything into the flicker of hope that started in his chest. It could be a dangerous thing if allowed to take hold. He hadn't seen her since November a year ago. She'd started a new life and hadn't wanted him to be a part of it.

Once he thought he'd seen her in the ByWard Market picking out a pumpkin for Halloween, but when the woman straightened up, it wasn't Frances at all. The woman who turned to face him was thirty years younger. Then he noticed the children trailing behind her as they searched for the perfect pumpkin. He watched them for a while, trying to capture the feeling he'd had when he thought the woman was Frances.

He glanced through the door into the main office. Stonechild was clicking with one hand on her keyboard and talking into her phone. There was something unnerving about her. Something about her watchful black eyes — eyes that looked tired when she glanced his way. Whelan had long since gone home. She lowered the receiver as the desk sergeant Cleese approached, waving a piece of paper. She covered the mouthpiece with one hand and pointed toward Rouleau's office with the other. Cleese spun around and changed direction.

"The Chief wants you to look into this ASAP," he said, handing Rouleau the paper. "A businessman named Tom Underwood hasn't been seen since last night. He didn't show up at work today and his wife hasn't heard from him. She's the one called it in. Sounded worried. Says he's never done anything like this before. Always keeps in touch and would never miss work."

"This should go to Missing Persons. She can fill out the form, but it's a bit early to start anything else."

"Chief says this one is ours. We're to give her the star treatment, he said. He specifically asked that you handle it. After we give her the priority treatment, he wants you to hand it over to Missing Persons and they can take it from there."

"Great, and everyone's gone for the day. I guess it wouldn't hurt to take a run out to see her, politics being what they are." He called across the room to Kala, who was still talking into the phone. "We've got one more call. Are you free to come with me?"

Stonechild nodded.

"We'll take my car," he said.

3

"SO HOW DID the interview go with the woman who was attacked earlier today?" Rouleau asked as they pulled out of the parking garage.

Kala leaned her head back against the headrest and turned slightly so she was facing him. She'd wrapped her arms around herself since the heater hadn't yet warmed the interior.

"Glenda Martin was shaken up but getting angry by the time she told us what happened. She's an assistant deputy minister in the federal government and not used to being pushed around."

"I thought all government workers got accustomed to being on the receiving end." Rouleau took his eyes off the road long enough to smile at her.

The corners of Kala's mouth lifted briefly. "Seems Glenda's high enough up in the food chain to be the one doing the pushing. Anyhow, she was quick enough to get a glimpse of the guy after he threw her head first toward the wall. She elbowed him in the stomach after he grabbed her breast through her coat. He had his other arm wrapped around her neck and was tightening his hold. She heard him say 'bitch' just before he heaved her forward. She got her hands out in front of her and managed not to hit her head. Her hands and neck were bruised but she didn't want to go to the hospital. Her injuries were worse than she let on."

"I don't like the sound of him getting her in a strangle hold. He's escalating."

"She said the perp had on black army-type boots, black pants, and a black ski jacket. He was husky but not too tall. The angle she saw him from lying on the floor wasn't the best for getting all the details."

"Anything else?"

"She thought she saw white hair under a black toque but didn't see his face because he'd turned to run by the time she got herself twisted back around. Luckily the front door sticks and that gave her a chance to see him."

"It's not much, but beats what we had so far. He likes wearing black, might be a strong, old guy, and has a limited but colourful vocabulary."

"I'd say we've almost got him then." It was Kala's turn to smile in his direction.

"Gabriel Marleau might be useful in getting a read on what type of person we're dealing with. Marleau is our staff psychologist and does profiling."

Kala took a notepad out of her pocket and made a note. "Anything else?"

Rouleau glanced at her. "Just that I won't expect you in until noon tomorrow. When this interview is over, you can take off and get some sleep. You've done more than enough for a first day on the job after a long drive to get here. Go get settled in."

"I'm okay," she mumbled before turning to look out the side window.

She angled her body away from him, and Rouleau felt the distance she'd put between them, even in such a confined space. He turned on the windshield wipers to clear away the softly falling snow. He didn't attempt to talk to her the rest of the way to Tom Underwood's mansion south of town in the ritzy Winding Way subdivision on the Rideau River.

———

Rouleau wasn't a man who put much stock in looks, but Laurel Underwood was the kind of woman to make a man want to leave home, to paraphrase a Bonnie Raitt song. If a person could be taught to slink seductively across a room, Laurel would be the one giving lessons. She'd led him and Stonechild into the kitchen and set about pouring tea in white porcelain cups rimmed in gold. An equally arresting red-haired girl about six years old kneeled on the carpet in the family room two steps down from the kitchen. She was in front of the wide-screen television, colouring in a book that rested on the coffee table. She'd glanced at them when they first entered, but immediately lowered her head to complete her work with a blue crayon. A naked evergreen tree stood in the corner, boxes of tinsel and decorations stacked in boxes on the floor.

Milk and sugar delivered, Laurel sat and leaned her elbows onto the counter between them. Her glossy red hair, several shades darker than her daughter's, trailed past her shoulders and down her back. Pink gloss emphasized her lips and black eyeliner defined her violet eyes. Their heather colour was a freak of nature not unlike Elizabeth Taylor's eyes. Rouleau searched her irises to see if she was wearing tinted contact lenses, but the eye colour looked real enough.

Her gauzy white top clung to her, the top buttons undone to show off her cleavage.

"Tom never stays away without telling me. *Never*." Laurel gazed at Rouleau as if defying him to contradict her. Unbelievably, her eyes had darkened to a richer shade of violet.

"When did you last see or hear from him?" Rouleau asked. He motioned for Stonechild to begin taking notes.

"We were at a Christmas party last night at the Château. It was his company party and I know this might sound odd, but he left early and I stayed. Tom hates parties so he left me to keep the public face. It wasn't unusual."

"You didn't see him at all after the party?"

"No."

"What time did you come home?"

"It was close to four a.m. Tom's car was in the driveway. His bed was slept in when I checked this morning."

Kala raised her head but looked down again. The implication was obvious and Rouleau didn't pursue the Underwoods' sleeping arrangements, not yet anyhow. "Did anybody see him before he left the house this morning?"

Laurel nodded. Her voice softened. "Charlotte, our daughter." She motioned to the child hunched over the colouring book. "Tom kissed her goodbye on his way out. She has no idea of the time but said it was still dark in her room."

"Did he say anything to her?"

"No. Charlotte doesn't know yet that he's missing. I'd rather you didn't ask her any questions now. They're very close and it would upset her. She's waiting for him to come home to decorate the tree."

"No need," said Rouleau. "What was your husband's frame of mind? Was business going well? Were things good between you?"

"You're asking me if he was depressed, aren't you, like you think he would do something to himself. *Tom would never* ..." Her voice rose.

"Mommy?" Charlotte lifted her head like a rabbit sensing danger. She held the crayon in her fist, her eyes wide and frightened.

Laurel looked across at her daughter. Her features relaxed. "Nothing, darling. Nothing to worry about. Finish your picture for me. It looks so lovely already."

"It's for you *and* Daddy," said Charlotte, her face puckered in seriousness, picking up an emerald-green crayon and turning back to her task.

Laurel studied her daughter for a moment more. When she spoke again, her voice had returned to its normal huskiness. "I phoned his partner, J.P. Belliveau, and he said Tom didn't come into the office this morning or phone that he wouldn't be in. Tom missed two meetings. He would never do that without a reason. One of the meetings was important."

"Is there anyone else he might have gone to visit? Family? A friend?"

"I checked already. Tom has two children from a previous marriage." She choked out a laugh. "I was so desperate, I even called his ex-wife Pauline. Nobody has heard from him."

Kala said, "I'll need their names and addresses."

"I thought you might and wrote them down. I left the paper upstairs in the study with a recent photo. I'll go get them."

Rouleau sipped his tea after she'd gone, then lowered his cup, "What do you think?"

"That she's very worried."

"I wonder why. Her husband hasn't been gone a full day yet."

"Sometimes women know. They have a sense when their partner's in trouble."

"Well as far as I can see, no crime has been committed yet and it's too early to tell. He might be on a bender or gone somewhere and forgotten to call."

"As you say," Kala's voice trailed away and she lifted her teacup. She lowered it without drinking and pushed herself to her feet, then crossed the floor to squat down next to Charlotte, resting back on her heels as she murmured something that caught the child's attention. Charlotte responded and Kala picked up the picture, leaning close and talking into Charlotte's ear until the child laughed and took the picture back.

By the time Laurel returned with the list of names, Kala was standing next to Rouleau. They left the kitchen without another word to the child.

———

Rouleau dropped Kala at the station and continued on to the Royal Oak, crossing the Pretoria Bridge over the Canal to where the pub sat on the corner of Echo Drive, directly across from the waterway. He was a few minutes late and felt the familiar tightening in his stomach that had been the norm at the end of his marriage whenever he'd stood up Frances for work. Luckily, she was just hanging up her coat inside the doorway when he arrived. She turned and smiled at him without the anger that had punctuated the final months when she'd begun freezing him out. They hugged lightly before a waitress led them to a table near the gas fireplace in the corner of the room.

Rouleau scanned the room as he walked behind Frances. The same oak decor and flowered seat cushions, a little more frayed and faded, with Irish music playing from overhead speakers — The Irish Rovers' rendition of "Danny Boy." Time really could stand still. The place was proof. They sat next to the window. He ordered a tall Keith's for himself and gin and tonic for Frances, suddenly not hungry for food.

"It was good to hear your voice after all this time," he said, leaning back. The lines had deepened around her eyes and the pale pink blouse washed out the colour in her face. She'd always had pale skin but it seemed more translucent somehow. Her hair was cropped shorter than he'd ever seen. When he complimented her on it, she absent-mindedly lifted a hand to touch the exposed nape of her neck.

"I know this must seem awkward, Jacques, after all this time."

"Your call was unexpected, yes." He took a long drink from his glass. "But expected at the same time. It's not like I haven't wanted to hear from you. When you didn't answer my emails, I figured it was in your court. That you would contact me when you were ready."

"I'm sorry. I should have been in touch before now." She lowered her head to study her hands clasped together on the table.

He hadn't meant to put her on the defensive, but normal conversation was eluding him. Just how did you greet an ex-wife when it had ended badly? What was the trick for pretending they hadn't been intimate and best friends for sixteen years?

"So what have you been up to? Have you had a good year?" he asked. *Have you left Gordon?*

Frances picked up her glass and drank. "Time was I'd be lighting a cigarette to go with this G and T," she said wistfully. "Those were the days." She set the glass down carefully on a clover-shaped green coaster. "Remember that day in grade twelve when we skipped school and you borrowed your father's car and we spent the afternoon at Constance Bay?"

"Do I? My father gave me royal hell when I got home after dark, but it was worth every minute. It was the first time we ever ..."

"That's the memory I've kept coming back to," she smiled. "That first time and how young and free we were back then. If only we could go back."

Rouleau found her eyes and wouldn't let her look away. "What's wrong then, Fran? Why did you call me here after all this time?"

"Am I that obvious? I was planning to have a pleasant catch up over drinks and tell you my sad news as we got ready to leave. You know, when I went through all those rounds of chemo, I kept thinking that it wasn't so long ago I was happy. I mean really happy. I can't believe how quickly it all went away."

His stomach lurched like a hand had reached inside and squeezed his large intestine. "Cancer?"

She nodded. "It began in my breast and I thought it was nothing serious. You know, just a benign cyst or something easily explained away. The doctor said I was very unlucky." Her gaze didn't falter. "I have a few months they think. Maybe as many as six. I wanted you to hear it from me."

"God, no. Are they sure? Can't anything be done? There are so many new treatments. Have you tried another doctor?" He heard his voice rising and struggled to bring it down to normal pitch.

"God hasn't had much to do with this, I'm afraid. No miracles or answering of prayers. He's been strangely silent as I contemplate the final chapter."

He reached across the table and placed his hand on hers. She turned her hand over and twined her fingers through his. "Is there anything I can do? Anything you need?"

This time, she shook her head. "It's under control. Gordon took it badly at first, but he's stepping up." She laughed. "He wants to marry me. Can you believe it?"

"In a heartbeat."

Her eyes filled with tears. "I'm so sorry, Jacques." Her voice was a whisper. "I screwed up our lives. I'm trying very hard not to screw up my death."

He reached across the table and took her hand between both of his. Her skin was cool to the touch, her palm papery dry. "I'm as much to blame for what happened to us as you are. More so, in fact. I'm still here for you, Fran. Anytime, anywhere. You've got to know that."

She gently squeezed his hand before withdrawing hers. "Thank you, Jacques. It's good to know that we're still friends. That's something anyway." She folded her hands in her lap and lowered her head.

He looked at the bony curve of her jaw and her eyes nearly black in the dim light of the bar. She'd lost a lot of weight. "I think you should marry Gordon."

She lifted her head and studied him, her eyes amused. "Really? You wouldn't mind too much?"

The familiar smile on her lips twisted his heart. He swallowed before speaking. "No. Do what feels right, what makes you happy."

"I don't know quite what that would be anymore. A call from the hospital saying that they'd gotten it all wrong. It was a screw-up in the lab and my real test results were hiding in somebody else's file." She tilted her head and shrugged as if dismissing the possibility. "But maybe for Gordon, getting married would mean something."

"Then do it." She wouldn't marry again without his blessing he knew. He could see it in her eyes. "You shouldn't have any regrets."

She reached for her glass. "I'm not sure what I'll do yet, but thank you, Jacques. As for regrets, I have many but it's past the time when I can do anything about them." The glass shook as she brought it to her lips and drank, her eyes meeting his and saying everything.

He raised his glass and drank too, not stopping until it was empty. The long draught of bitter beer wasn't nearly enough to clear the pain clawing at his throat. It couldn't even begin to dull the impact her words had made on the rest of his life.

4

KALA GRABBED HER duffel bag from the cab of the truck and walked two blocks through the snowy streets to the YMCA-YWCA. The night duty cop had given her directions to the tallest building in the neighbourhood. He said it was impossible to miss. She decided to leave her truck in the police lot until somebody told her otherwise.

An empty gym stood illuminated in the tall windows on the south side. She rounded the corner to find the main entrance. Up stone steps was a bright foyer with posters of flowers and art hanging on concrete block walls and a leaning silver Christmas tree in the centre of the space. The teenage girl on the desk had a bad case of acne but a friendly smile. She handed Kala a pen and clipboard to sign in. "How long will you be staying?"

"End of the week probably." Kala couldn't think beyond that. She felt no connection to this job or city. She could see herself getting in her truck and heading back north without much regret. She wouldn't allow herself to give in yet. "I'll pay for a week in advance."

"Tenth floor to the right of the elevator," the girl said, taking Kala's credit card before handing over a key.

"Thanks." Kala picked up her bag and headed toward the elevators.

The Spartan blandness of the room and the cramped space were what she'd expected. A single bed with a greyish bedspread was set against the wall with just enough room for a bedside table and chest of drawers scarred by cigarette burns and rings from hot drinks. The overhead lamp cast harsh yellow light that hurt her eyes. She flicked off the switch and crossed the room in the dark to turn on the desk lamp. The bathroom and showers were down the hallway but she was sick with tiredness and stretched out on the bed. She promised herself a five-minute rest before going to clean up. In the room overhead, a radio was playing music that thump-thumped like a heartbeat through the ceiling. Women's voices grew louder in the hallway, one of them laughing as they moved past her door. Kala closed her eyes and let her mind drift.

She wasn't sure what woke her — perhaps the elevator rumbling to a stop across the hall or somebody in the corridor — but whatever it was, her eyes snapped open and it took her a moment to recognize the room and its contents. The lamp was still burning. She raised her left arm and looked at her watch. One a.m. She'd slept nearly four hours, as if somebody had knocked her unconscious.

She lay for a moment longer, imagining Jordan's face and wondering if he was sleeping, if he knew she was gone for good. He probably had an inkling by now because she'd left Nipigon two days before. One day without seeing her wouldn't have had him overly concerned, but she knew he'd be dropping by the station today to talk to her. He'd be puzzled when he found out that she wasn't working the shift. Then he'd seek out Shannon, who worked the phones in the office. Shannon would tell him that Kala had gone away for a while, but not where. They'd worked the story out together.

Kala stood and stepped out of her clothes, tossing them onto the chest of drawers. She pulled back the covers and slipped naked between the cotton sheets, reaching to turn off the lamp. Wind whistled through the window pane and rattled the glass. She'd forgotten to close the curtains and the light from a street lamp cast silvery light across the floor. Snow streaked down the glass in wind-blown swirls. She thought about getting up to shut out the night, but closed her eyes instead, snuggling deeper under the covers.

Her mind wandered back over the day. Rouleau looked like someone who kept his cards close to his chest. Better this than a fake bastard who said a lot and meant nothing. She wasn't sure about having a partner. She liked working alone and avoided teaming up as a rule. Whelan seemed sturdy enough though, if she had to have one.

What would she be doing now if she was back in the North? Maybe finishing her tour of the town and starting down the beach road to check on the spots where kids liked to park and drink or make out in their cars with the heaters on full. She'd signal them with her headlights to pack it in for the night, making sure none got stranded in the drifting snow. She'd always liked the early morning hours of the night shift: the stillness of the woods, the night sky, the stars sparkling in the blackness that swallowed the earth.

A feeling of loss tore through her. She breathed deeply, in and out, slowing her breathing and forcing herself to relax. For a moment, she was back in her little house on the edge of town with her black lab Taiku sleeping on the floor in his spot next to her bed. The same wind rattling against her window in Ottawa became the northern wind off Lake

Superior, sweeping through the pine trees and whistling down her chimney.

She rolled onto her side and tried to find a comfortable position on the lumpy mattress. If she found a place to live in this city that allowed dogs, she would drive home and get him from Shannon. The hell with the upheaval and the asphalt, the reasons she had left him behind. If she could adjust to a city, so could Taiku. Already she regretted leaving him, with more pain than she would have imagined.

———

Geraldine's legs throbbed like a couple of toothaches. The rest of her didn't feel much better. She lay next to Max and listened to him snore while she slowly stretched out her legs to try to ease the ache running up her calves. Her body was running on empty while her mind wouldn't shut off. Where could her father be and why hadn't he been in touch? Why was Laurel so quick to think something awful had happened to him?

If her dad and Laurel were having marriage problems, as she suspected they were, her dad was capable of changing his life in an instant. He'd left her mother for Laurel without warning. Maybe Laurel was about to find out what this felt like from the other end.

Geraldine rolled closer to the edge of the king-sized bed and swung her legs over the side, careful not to wake Max. Warm milk might help her relax — her and the baby both if she was lucky. The little guy had been kicking and rolling around in her stomach the better part of an hour. She felt for her slippers in the darkness and grabbed her housecoat from the chair where she'd thrown it after her shower, then made her way downstairs to the kitchen. She quietly heated up a saucepan of milk and sliced the leftover apple pie. She'd skip the ice cream though. Her doctor had warned against putting on much more weight on her last visit. Max had probably put him up to it. If she believed the doctor, she was calories away from diabetes.

She chewed the pie slowly and sipped her milk at the kitchen table, fatigue making each bite an effort. Only four days to Christmas and she couldn't have cared less. Max said it was her hormones acting up, but she didn't think so. The malaise had started months before she got pregnant. It had begun when her best friend Karen Walters moved to the East Coast to open a seafood restaurant and she realized that she wasn't free to do anything so daring. Her life map was drawn the day she married Max.

Being his wife was what she'd wanted from the moment he'd sat next to her in the university cafeteria and started talking to her as if she was one of the pretty girls and not the plain one she knew herself to be. When he'd started seeking her out every day and then asking her to meet him after class, she'd felt such a glow inside. It wasn't long before he'd consumed her every waking moment. She'd gone a little bit crazy. She knew that now.

She looked around the renovated kitchen and studied the pine cupboards she'd chosen after visiting every kitchen store in the city. For something that had seemed so important to get right at the time, they hardly seemed worth the effort. She'd thought once that a welcoming home would make a difference, but Max wasn't interested in the house or spending time in it. He had to be in the middle of things, wheeling and dealing. As long as he had access to the Internet, he could be anywhere: the office, a coffee shop, a bar. He used the house as a place to sleep and launch out of in the morning.

She heard footsteps in the hallway, and as if he'd known she was thinking about him, Max appeared in the doorway. He was as dressed down as he ever got in a white undershirt and navy silk pajama bottoms. He ran a hand through his thick hair and grinned at her with sleepy eyes. Her heart still leapt at the sight of him and she wondered how her body could want him while her mind was revolted. Maybe it all came down to hormones as he'd suggested. He slid into the seat next to her and leaned his arm against hers. His smile was the same one that used to charm her. "Can't sleep?"

"No. Baby's kicking. Plus I can't stop wondering where Dad has gotten to. Did he say anything to you about taking off for the day?"

"Not a word. His office door was closed when I got in so I just assumed he didn't want to be bothered. I had no idea he wasn't in there. Any apple pie left?"

"In the fridge. Maybe I should call Hunter."

Max crossed the kitchen and opened the fridge door. He pulled out the pie plate, then cut a large slice and sat down next to her. "What good would that do? Hunter hasn't spoken to your dad in months."

"I think Dad visited him lately. Besides, Hunter has a right to know our father's gone missing."

"I sincerely doubt your brother'll care all that much."

"I just can't imagine Dad leaving Charlotte this close to Christmas. He told me once that if Laurel ever tried to divorce him, she'd never get custody of Charlotte." She forced herself to stop talking. Max didn't like it when she went on about her family.

"Did he think Laurel would leave him?"

"Dad was beginning to see her for the opportunist she is. It took long enough, but he was starting to make plans."

"Plans?"

"When Daddy makes up his mind, he doesn't wait for things to happen. He takes charge. It's what makes him so good in the business world."

Max cut hard through the pie crust with the side of his fork before turning his head to look at her. He wasn't smiling. "You call the way he manipulates people 'taking charge'?"

"What do you mean 'manipulates'?"

"Everyone your father comes into contact with either bends to his will or gets trampled on. Look at your mother. He discarded her like an old shoe as soon as he'd used up all her money. Now you tell me he was prepared to destroy Laurel."

"You make him sound like a monster. He's not like that at all."

"What I can't figure out is why you defend a man that everyone else in the world considers the biggest self-serving prick they ever had the bad fortune to come across. He has a way of making us all feel like something under his boot, you included. You take his bad qualities and make them seem like attributes."

Max threw the fork onto the table and pushed his chair back. "The way he treats you over and over and you take it like a lump. At least Hunter had the balls to get away. You don't see any of this, do you? Oh, what's the use. I'm going back to bed."

Long after Max left her, Geraldine sat at the kitchen table, immobilized by his words. The cold anger in his eyes was beyond anything she'd seen before. This was not the same man who'd courted her with flowers and undying love; the man she'd tied her future to, for better or worse. His ugly words replayed in her head, spreading like indelible ink through her brain. She knew now that she hadn't been imagining his dislike.

Maybe it would get better if he said what he was thinking instead of giving her the wall. That's what she'd come to think of his silence — a thick wall that came up whenever he looked at her. She had to change whatever it was about herself that made him look at her that way. She just needed him to tell her what it was. She would change and make him love her again.

God, she needed a drink. Not for the first time, she regretted having thrown out all the alcohol in the house when she'd found out she was pregnant. Cold turkey, they called it. She'd called it torture. All the nights sitting home alone before she was pregnant while Max worked, easing the time away with a bottle of wine that eventually stretched into two and a drinking time that started closer and closer to lunch. She'd hidden the empties from Max, driving to different liquor stores on Monday mornings to return them and replenish her stock for the week. She hadn't had to hide her drunkenness since he usually turned up after she'd crawled into bed. That time seemed like a dream to her now. The evenings had been hazy and the mornings were just something to get through until she could pop the next cork. What she'd give for a cold glass of pinot now.

She looked down at her swollen belly. Perhaps she was far enough along that a glass wouldn't hurt the baby. It might even help them both relax. Having a drink might be a kindness. She pushed herself to her feet. First thing in the morning, she'd take a drive into the city and pick up a bottle. She'd tell the cashier it was a gift for a friend's birthday. It wasn't really that far off from the truth.

5

ROULEAU LEANED ON the kitchen counter and looked out the window rimmed in frost. The darkness had lifted enough that he could see chickadees eating birdseed from the feeder that Frances had hung on a low hanging pine bough, now covered in a thick coat of snow. He'd kept the feeder replenished even after she left.

He filled his mug from the coffee machine and took a sip while he looked at all the work he'd been putting off. When he and Frances had moved in five years ago, he'd planned to redo the kitchen and get rid of the blue cupboards and the green and grey tiled floor that puckered in places like a wizened apple. After that, he'd wanted to tackle the fake oak panelling in the front room and rip out the gold shag carpet and spring for new windows and doors. That had been the plan when he put in an offer on the fifties bungalow on a dead end street that ran alongside a bike path. So far all he'd accomplished was contracting out the new roof the summer before.

He ran his hand along the jagged edge of the counter. Time to start getting organized and clean the place up. Might be a good idea if he decided to sell.

He took a final swallow of coffee and dumped the rest
into the sink, then grabbed his parka from the back of the
kitchen chair on his way to the front door. He checked his
cellphone as he walked. One message waiting. He punched
in his password and listened to Vermette telling him to be in
his office at nine for a briefing. No time to stop for breakfast
like he'd planned.

He bent to put on his boots, then stood and closed his
eyes, letting the rush of grief fill him. *Frances.* He wrapped
an arm around his stomach, clenching back the pain that
rose from somewhere deep in his guts. He let the sick feeling overwhelm him for a few moments before straightening
and taking a deep breath. The intensity lessened. She hadn't
looked ill. Perhaps it was a misdiagnosis after all? Maybe
she'd be one of the lucky few to beat the odds. She couldn't
give in yet. She'd always been strong. *Do not go gentle into
that good night.* Dylan Thomas, if he remembered his high
school English. Frances would know the whole poem by
heart. She had an amazing memory when it came to words
on paper.

He used to come home unexpectedly to find her in the
kitchen reading from a poetry book she'd picked up at the
Sunnyside branch of the public library. Her lips would be
moving and her forehead would be fine lines of concentra-
tion as she stirred the pot on the stove with her free hand.
He'd stand and watch, drinking in the sight of her, the
white curve of her neck as she bent over the pages, sliding his eyes down to her full hips, long legs, and bare feet.
She'd look up to find him there, her eyes lost in a world
he could never follow, then lighting with happiness as she
took him in. If he was lucky, she'd read those same lines
to him after they made love while the meal simmered on
the stove and the afternoon light shifted from lemon yellow

to pale pink and grey in the gathering dusk, his head resting on her breast, his arm wrapped loosely around her stomach.

———

Vermette was talking on the phone when Rouleau entered his office and dropped into the chair across from him. The conversation on Vermette's part consisted of a lot of head nodding and murmured agreement. Rouleau searched his face. Vermette wouldn't be happy to be forced into the obsequious end of whatever was being discussed.

He took the time to look at the man across the desk. Early fifties, wiry build, and slightly oversized head, glistening like a soft-boiled egg. Vermette's pale blue eyes were framed by incongruous long, black lashes that looked as if they'd been combed through with mascara. He favoured tight dark suits and different coloured turtlenecks. Today's was white with a coffee stain approximately where his navel should be. A man who grew up in the tough east end of the city, he'd broken free of his family and neighbourhood and beaten the odds. By all rights, he should be in jail, not heading up the city's police force. He should have been someone to admire.

Vermette thrust the phone back into its cradle. He scowled first at the phone and then at Rouleau. "Fuckin board member. Think they know everything. Brains so far up their arses, you have to dig with a shovel to get a coherent thought." He ran a hand across his forehead, wiping away tiny beads of sweat. "So, where are you with the Tom Underwood business?"

"We met with his wife yesterday. She gave us a photo that Kala passed on to Missing Persons like you asked."

"I know, but now I want a couple of your team on this one full time."

"Any particular reason?" Rouleau studied Vermette's face. A purplish vein pulsated like a turn signal in his right temple.

"Underwood's got business contacts. Somebody with strings to pull is putting pressure on us to find him."

"We don't know that anything has happened to him. It's been just twenty-four hours since he didn't show up at work. I admit it looks less good as time passes, but …"

"Until the man is back in the bosom of his loving family," Vermette interrupted, "finding him has just become your number one priority. Do good work on this one and your unit could get some recognition. It'll please the board if their inane pet project succeeds at something."

"Underwood's company website says they make military equipment, amongst other things. They have contracts with National Defence and some overseas."

"We don't need to start dreaming up some lame-brained government conspiracy. Just start tracking down his movements and talk to his family and co-workers. If he really is missing … well, we'll deal with it when the time comes."

Uncertainty had entered Vermette's voice and it made Rouleau curious. Vermette had argued strenuously against the special unit, saying it would dilute investigations of Major Crimes if his officers were torn in too many directions.

Rouleau stood. "I'll get on it then."

He was halfway to the door when Vermette said, "How's that Native woman working out? Stonechild, is it?"

"Kala Stonechild. Should be fine. She's a quick study."

"I hear she's easy on the eyes. See she gets some media training. We may as well make use of her appearance."

"I'll ask Kala if she wants to be a media spokes."

"She doesn't need to be asked. Either she does as she's told or we send her back to the reserve where she can spend her days locking up drunk relatives."

Rouleau took a step toward him. "I can't believe you just said that."

Vermette tilted his head and met Rouleau's narrowed eyes before his slid away. He smiled. "Just kidding."

Rouleau thought about telling Vermette what he thought about him before walking out the door and into early retirement. He'd leave this crap behind and sell the house and go somewhere warm. Australia was a place he'd always wanted to visit. He could stay a year and see if it suited him. Find a little house with wide windows that looked out on the sea and let the seasons slip by. Learn to appreciate Australian beer and grow a beard.

His feet moved toward the door without conscious effort. His hand encircled the brass doorknob and he pulled the door open and stepped through. Screw Vermette. He'd go when he was ready, at a moment of his own choosing. When the time was right.

———

Whelan watched his new partner Stonechild step into the office as if she was walking into a crime scene. She'd stopped just inside the doorway and checked to her left and right, her black eyes sweeping the entire room before she seemed satisfied and started toward their desks. He could picture her walking through the woods, silent, sure-footed, and alert. Something in her eyes made him wonder what she'd seen in her life that brought her here. *Haunted.* He didn't know why that word popped into his mind. He wasn't a fanciful man, preferring a night of football and the sports section of the paper, but there was something about her.

She sat down in the chair facing him and stretched out her long legs. She was wearing Cougar winter boots, black cords, a black sweater, and grey jacket. Green-stoned earrings sparkled from her ears, the only bit of colour. "Sorry I'm late. I had trouble falling asleep."

He checked his watch. "Fifteen minutes isn't a major crime. Have you eaten?"

She shook her head. "No time."

"There's a cafeteria upstairs. Let's go."

"You sure?"

"Rouleau's in a meeting so we have half an hour I figure. May as well make use of it."

"You don't have to ask twice. My stomach's been grumbling like a grizzly bear since I got up."

"Then let's go feed the beast."

They got coffee and the breakfast special — scrambled eggs with sausage, hash browns, and whole wheat toast. Whelan spotted Malik and Grayson near the back wall and turned, motioning for Kala to follow him. She hesitated but then nodded. The two men had had their heads together and were laughing until their eyes moved past Whelan to Kala. Malik saluted her before looking away. Grayson focused on his cup of coffee, raising it to his lips and draining the last.

"Shit, snow's started again," said Grayson, his eyes swerving toward the line of windows. "Should have bought a snowblower."

"Three days till Christmas. Looks like it'll be a white one." Malik smiled at Kala. "So how was your first day?"

"Good."

"You've arrived in time for our annual Christmas party. Did you tell her about it Whelan?"

Whelan hit a palm to his forehead. "Is that tonight?"

"Yeah, it's tonight." Malik looked back at Kala. "The whole force should be there, or at least those off shift. Dinner and drinks in the San Marco Hall on Preston Street. Gets underway around seven."

Whelan groaned. "I promised Meghan I'd watch the kids while she goes for a haircut. I'm going to have to show up late."

"Tell her to change her appointment," said Grayson.

"Not if I want to sleep in my own bed tonight. She's been talking about this all week. I'll have to give you directions, Kala. It's just outside downtown."

"Little Italy, right?" asked Kala.

"I can drive you," said Grayson looking across at her for the first time. "Where're you staying?"

Kala glanced up at him. "I can make it on my own steam. I've got to figure the city out sooner or later."

"Well, if you change your mind."

"Thanks."

The silence stretched awkwardly. Whelan smiled to himself. Rejection looked good on Grayson, who prided himself on his female conquests. Whelan reached inside his jacket and pulled out his phone that was vibrating against his chest. He glanced at the screen. "Rouleau's looking for us. I'll just send him a message to meet us here."

"Wonder how it went with the big F.U.," said Malik. "The Chief's nickname," he explained in answer to Kala's questioning stare. "When you hear Vermette talk, you'll understand why."

"Rouleau handles him okay," said Whelan. "Don't envy him that job."

"That's because no matter how hard the big F.U. pushes Rouleau, he doesn't react. If it were me, I'd probably be up on aggravated assault charges by now." Grayson stood. "Anyone want a refill while I'm up?"

Sandeep handed over his cup. "With cream, thanks."

Whelan watched Grayson cross the room and spotted Rouleau. He'd entered while they were talking and was ordering food from the woman behind the counter. He might have believed Grayson's bravado about Vermette if he hadn't seen them all chummy in the bar recently.

Sandeep turned back to Kala. "I imagine you didn't have to deal with the chain of command where you came from."

"We still had to report up."

"Why'd you leave?"

"Wanted more experience in a different unit. I heard about this opening and the timing was right."

Whelan nodded. "My partner followed his wife to Germany. She's got some high tech job."

Sandeep looked at Kala again. "Many murders up north?"

Kala smiled. "We had a murder once. Fellow killed his best friend in a hunting accident. Turned out the best friend was sleeping with this guy's wife and he wasn't too pleased. Other than that, we've got the usual drunk driving, B and Es, people lost in the woods. Bears chasing people up trees."

"You're joking."

"Yeah, bears can climb trees faster than most people so you'd have to be an idiot to think climbing a tree was going to save your hide. Maybe you should try a northern placement."

"Not sure my wife would take to living in the wilds. She might be a match for the bears though."

Whelan hoisted a forkful of egg into his mouth, then wiped his mouth on his sleeve. "Probably for the moose too."

Rouleau slid into the seat next to Kala and took a bite of his fried egg sandwich. Grayson set down the coffee mugs and sat across from her. Rouleau drank from his coffee cup then looked around the table.

"So, today Whelan and Stonechild are going to find Tom Underwood. His welfare has become your raison d'être."

"Ahead of finding who killed buddy homeless man?" asked Sandeep.

"Ahead of every case we've got on the go."

"Since Underwood hasn't been missing more than a day, I can only assume Vermette's lost it completely," said Grayson.

Rouleau grinned. "Not ours to question why my young friends." He looked at Whelan and Stonechild. "Check in as you go. Keep good notes because this case seems important to Vermette. Let's see if you can bring Tom Underwood home where he belongs in time for Christmas."

6

KALA RANG THE bell for the second time on the front door of the detached brick house and listened to it chime inside the house. They were deep in the new subdivision named Chapman Mills on Haileybury Street. The homes were so close together, people had to walk single file to get between them. It was hard to believe anyone liked living in a place where they couldn't see the stars at night.

While she waited, she mapped out the area in her mind. Prince of Wales Drive, a major thoroughfare, separated Pauline Underwood's Chapman Mills subdivision from the Rideau River and the wealthier homes where Pauline's ex Tom and his new wife Laurel lived on Winding Way. It was about a ten-minute drive between the two subdivisions. She glanced toward the street. No car parked in the driveway, so it was either in the attached garage that took up half of the house's frontage or Pauline was away.

Through the thickness of the door, she heard footsteps coming down the hallway toward her. Kala motioned for Whelan to join her on the steps. Whelan snapped his cell-phone shut and just made it to the top step as the door swung open. His eyes were worried.

"Everything okay?" Kala asked over her shoulder.

"Baby has a cold and now a fever. Meghan's going to take him to the doctor if it goes any higher."

The door swung halfway open. A tall woman with white hair to her shoulders looked out, one hand resting on the door frame. Her brown eyes peered at them over half-moon glasses. She wore designer blue jeans and a grey sweatshirt sprinkled in red paint splatter.

"Yes, may I help you?"

Whelan held up his badge. "We're from the Ottawa Police and would just like to ask you a few questions about the disappearance of your ex-husband."

The former Mrs. Underwood raised a hand to her chest. "Thank God. He's still just missing … I thought you were going to tell me something horrible. Come in. Come in, please." She swung the door open and stepped down the hallway. "We can sit in the kitchen if you don't mind. The living room is in a state."

Kala glanced into the living room on the way by. Drop cloths covered the furniture. The smell of fresh paint was strong. The fireplace wall was cranberry red and the rest of the walls were beige.

The hallway was lined with framed photographs of flowers, leading into a large, sunny kitchen with glass doors along one wall and a pine table directly in front. The oak cupboards and stainless steel appliances looked new. Several watercolour paintings filled one wall. Lake scenes and flowers. They gave the room a homey feel.

"Coffee?" asked Pauline Underwood, already crossing the space to the coffee maker. "I just put on a pot. I'm not sure why I made so much." Her voice trailed away.

Kala met Whelan's eyes. "Sure, that would be nice. Thank you," she said.

They took seats at the table, Whelan at one end and Kala facing the window. The backyard was small and half-filled by a raised cedar deck. Birdfeeders hung from the only tree. Pauline carried over a tray with mugs of coffee, cream, and sugar in a matching blue pottery pattern. She slid into a seat across from Kala.

"I know Tom's missing. Our daughter Geraldine called me yesterday to find out if I'd heard from him. Laurel called earlier as well. We don't talk on the phone as a rule."

As agreed before they got out of the police car, Kala took the lead. "When was the last time you saw Tom?"

"Oh my, let me think. I'd have to say a month ago. I cooked a birthday dinner for Geraldine, and Tom came by for cake. Laurel had a headache and stayed home." Pauline's eyes met Kala's before she looked down. The dark smudging under her eyes spoke of unquiet nights.

"How did Tom seem? Was he upset about anything?"

"Tom wasn't a man who showed emotion. The stock market could have crashed and burned and he wouldn't have let on anything was wrong."

"Did he talk about any problems at work or in his life?"

"Well, he worked too much and business was stressful. His diet was terrible after our divorce. I'm not sure Laurel knew how to cook." Pauline lifted her mug and held it in front of the tight line of her mouth.

"It couldn't have been easy for you." Kala watched Pauline's eyes.

Pauline slowly lowered the cup. "No, but our marriage ended ten years ago when Tom hit the mid-life crisis. I've long forgiven him. We're friends again, although I'm not particularly fond of Laurel." She shrugged. "I'm sure you can understand."

"Do you have any idea where Tom might have gone?"

"No. I'm not privy to his comings and goings. If he and Laurel were having trouble, he might be somewhere clearing his head. When we were married, he was gone a week before he got in touch with me to tell me that he was leaving."

"You must have been frantic."

"No. I knew he was having an affair. I was hoping … well, that he'd get her out of his system and come home. I thought he just needed some time. I knew it would devastate Geraldine and Hunter if we separated. Unfortunately, Hunter still doesn't have a good relationship with his father."

"It seems like a long time not to get over a parents' divorce."

"They're both strong-willed men."

Kala took a drink of coffee and signalled Whelan with her eyes.

He handed Pauline a card. "Call any time and leave a message if you think of anything. One of us will be back to you as soon as we can."

"Thank you, I will."

They stood. "Nice paintings," commented Whelan, moving toward them. "Is that your signature at the bottom?"

"Why, yes. I dabble and also teach at two youth centres twice a week. It's something to do."

"You should sell some. They're very good."

"I mostly give them to family and friends. I've sold a few."

They started down the hallway to the front door just as the doorbell rang.

"It's probably my friend Susan Halliday, who's come for our morning walk." Pauline stepped past them and opened the door.

The woman standing on the top step was about the same age as Pauline but her hair was a chestnut brown and pulled back into a ponytail, making her seem younger than a woman approaching sixty. Both women were in good shape and wore their clothes well. Susan Halliday had on a red ski jacket, black gortex pants, and runners. Her smile disappeared when she saw Pauline's visitors.

"I didn't realize. If you'd rather run later, I can come back," She turned and started down the steps.

"We were just leaving," said Whelan. "No need to go on our account." He passed her on the stairs, doing up his jacket as he went.

"Come in, Susan," Pauline called over Kala's head. "I'll just be a few secs."

Susan hesitated and waved toward her Mazda. "I'll just get my water bottle and will be right back."

Kala looked back at Pauline. "Thank you for your time."

Pauline blinked as if being pulled back from somewhere far away. The tight line of her mouth relaxed and a hand came up to brush back the hair from her forehead. "I hope you find Tom soon," she said as she started to close the door. "Christmas is when a family should be together."

Whelan started the car as Kala climbed in the passenger side. He leaned forward and scraped at some frost from the inside front window while they waited for the engine to warm up. "What did you think of Tom's ex?" he asked.

"I know why Laurel avoids family get-togethers with the clan. I'd have a headache too."

"What you find out about families. Makes me satisfied with my own lot."

"Where to next?"

"We can swing east and talk to the son before we head downtown to Underwood's office."

"Works," said Kala. She checked her notepad. "Looks like a bit of a drive. Hunter lives just off Highway 417 near Carlsbad Springs."

"A country boy. Should take forty-five minutes or so to get there."

Kala looked out the side window. Snow had begun lightly falling and flakes were landing on the glass like confetti. She glanced into the side mirror as they pulled away. The friend, Susan Halliday, stood behind her vehicle watching them. Kala kept herself from turning around to stare.

"You know what's odd?" she said to Whelan.

"What's that?" He looked over at her.

"Her friend, that Halliday woman, went for a water bottle but I could see the shape of one inside her jacket."

"Maybe she just forgot she already had it."

"Maybe," said Kala. *Or maybe she was just trying to avoid talking to us.*

She kept the thought to herself.

———

An hour and a half later, Whelan was driving at a snail's pace the length of the country road for the third time. The snow had picked up speed and was making visibility difficult. Kala squinted toward an opening in the jagged line of snowbanks.

"This has to be his driveway. I can't see anything else."

"What, is the guy in the witness protection program?" asked Whelan. "Where the hell is his mailbox?"

He turned the car slowly and started up the unplowed side road, which wound to the right through pine trees and bushes frozen in ice. It was icy, slow going. Half a kilometre on, a black and tan dog the size of a Rottweiler bolted out of the woods and began loping alongside their car. Kala could see its head bobbing up and down outside her window.

"Careful," she said to Whelan. "The dog could slip under the tire."

Whelan muttered under his breath and scowled but slowed the car to a crawl. Finally, he pulled into a clearing and parked next to a green Cherokee Jeep. A small cabin was set back into the trees. Smoke billowed from the chimney and disappeared skyward into the falling snow.

"What do you think our chances are with the dog?" asked Whelan, leaning his arms on the steering wheel and turning to face her.

"Scared?"

"Let's say I have a healthy respect."

"I'll go first," said Kala already opening her door. "Hey boy," she called. The dog's tail wagged. "How are you boy? You protecting your property?" She reached down her hand to let him smell before scratching his head. She stepped out of the car and looked back at Whelan. "The danger has been neutralized."

She straightened and looked over at the cabin. A man stood in the open doorway holding a cup of coffee. He whistled through his fingers and the dog ran toward him. Kala and Whelan followed at a slower pace. They stopped a few yards away.

"Hunter Underwood?" asked Kala. She blinked as his eyes stared into hers. His were a riveting deep grey, lined in dark lashes. "We're with the Ottawa Police. We've come to speak with you about your father."

"Come in," he said, turning abruptly and disappearing inside.

Whelan looked at Kala and shrugged before he led the way up the stairs.

The living room was sparsely furnished. A battered leather recliner sat near the window with a floor lamp next to it. Bookcases lined two walls. The only other piece was a roll-top desk with a laptop set on top. She followed the men into the kitchen. It was a long, narrow galley with a small table and two chairs at the far end. Tall, lead-paned windows let in greyish light.

"Have a chair," said Hunter pointing to the two at the table. "Coffee?"

The dog padded silently across the floor and flopped down at Kala's feet. She felt its head rest against her leg and shifted so that there was more room for the dog between her foot and the chair leg. She imagined Taiku's weight pressed against her and felt an overwhelming longing for home. The cabin resembled her own small place not far from Lake Superior.

She moved her head to study Hunter as he poured them each a cup. He hadn't shaved and was dressed in faded jeans and a checked shirt with sleeves rolled up to his elbows. He looked to be five eleven, a hundred and sixty pounds, with wide shoulders, lean physique, and curly brown hair that brushed his collar. After he set the coffee cups and the milk container on the table, he leaned up against the counter and sipped from his cup. He didn't appear disturbed by their presence. She wondered if his calmness was an act.

Whelan cleared his throat. "You know who we are I gather?"

"Since I heard my father is missing, I figure you've come to find out if I know anything."

"And do you?"

"No."

"Have you seen your father recently?"

"He came by a week ago."

Whelan looked down at his notes. "We were informed that you and your father are estranged."

"We are, more or less."

"Then why the visit?"

"I've been asking myself the same thing. He said it was time to mend fences."

Kala said, "I imagine you found that odd after ten years of not being on speaking terms."

Hunter looked at her and then at his dog lying with its jaw on her boot. "You've made friends with Fabio. Not many do."

Kala looked down and smiled. She reached a hand to pet the dog's massive head before looking up at Hunter. He was still watching her, his grey eyes observant, taking in more than she would have liked.

Whelan cleared his throat again. "So how'd the visit with your father go?"

"Okay. He came into my shop and we talked while I worked on a painting. He seemed at ease. I got the feeling he just wanted to get away from his life for an hour."

"Was something making him unhappy or depressed?"

"We didn't talk long enough for me to find out anything personal. He asked if he could visit me again soon. I told him to do as he liked. If I had to say my impression of his state of mind, I'd say regretful."

"He didn't give any indication why?" Whelan asked.

Hunter grinned as if Whelan had said something funny. "He had lots to regret, let's just put it that way."

"Do you know of anybody who would want to harm your father?"

"I'm really not part of his world so I couldn't say. Did you ask my brother-in-law Max Oliver? He'd know more about Dad's life than I do since they work together."

"We'll be sure to raise it with him." Whelan jotted in his notebook.

"I don't suppose you have any idea where he could have gone," said Kala.

"Not a clue."

Whelan took his time pulling a card out of his pocket. "If you hear from your dad …"

"I'll be sure to let you know," finished Hunter.

They stood to leave. The dog followed them out of the kitchen and down the hall.

Kala stopped near the front door and turned toward Hunter. "You said you were painting. Is that your profession?"

"I paint portraits on commission, but my main line of work is sculpting."

"You must get your art gene from your mother. We were just admiring her paintings."

"She taught me when I was young and she still works with inner city kids in the after-school programs. My studio's out back if you'd like a tour."

"We're due back at the station."

"Well, another time."

She didn't respond. There was something about Hunter and the piercing way he looked at her that put her off-balance. His eyes made her want to keep looking back. A family with all that money, and he chose to live like a hermit. His home wasn't much different than hers, although their lives were separated by culture and financial gaps so wide it was unthinkable that they would have anything in common.

Kala and Whelan walked back to their car and got in. Whelan turned the key in the ignition and looked over at her.

"I'm beginning to think Tom Underwood just left to get his head straight. He might have come to see his son because he was planning to leave and wanted to make amends for whatever went on in the past."

Kala thought it over. "Maybe."

"You don't sound convinced."

"He asked if he could come visit again. That doesn't sound like a man getting ready to leave town."

"You could be right." Whelan backed the car into an opening where he could turn around. "It's late to go to Underwood's office now. We wasted a lot of time looking for this guy. We have to fill in our reports on the two interviews and still have a half-hour drive to get back to Ottawa."

"We could do the reports tomorrow."

Whelan shook his head. "Doesn't work that way. Reports have to be filed the same day. Vermette's rules. We'll be at the office half the night if we make another stop. I'm going to head back to the station and we'll get the paperwork done. We can visit Underwood's workplace tomorrow. We also have the party tonight and Meghan has that hair appointment."

"Okay," said Kala. She didn't see the rush to fill in paperwork, but no crime had been committed yet, so they weren't exactly racing against time.

7

ROULEAU SET DOWN his pen and stretched. It had been a day spent in meetings and filling in paperwork. He was ready to go home and watch the Senators hockey game on TV. The Maple Leafs were in town and there was always good rivalry. Then he remembered the Christmas party. It would be impossible to skip it even if he was so inclined. Could Christmas Eve really be just two days away? The years sure spun around the calendar with increasing speed. Christmas morning, he'd travel to Kingston to visit his father and take him to lunch as he did every year. He still hadn't picked out his father's gift and the clock was ticking. It would have been a good night to poke around the eclectic shops in the Glebe, if not for the staff party.

He picked up his pen as Whelan poked his head around the corner while tapping on the door. Whelan was wearing his winter jacket unbuttoned. "We're about done typing our notes and set to leave unless there's anything else."

"You bringing Stonechild to the party?"

"I'm going to be a bit late so she said she'd make it on her own."

"See you when you get there."

Rouleau shut off his computer. He'd go home and have a shower before the evening's festivities. He rubbed a hand across his chin. A shave was in order too.

It took him a few minutes to lock up his files and put on his coat. By the time he entered the main office, Stonechild and Whelan were gone. Malik and Grayson had knocked off earlier. He stood motionless in the centre of the room and looked at the six desks — only four were occupied. It was all the manpower Vermette would agree to on this special project.

They were to have been an elite squad that prevented crime before it happened and took over some of the tougher-to-solve cases, giving Major Crimes some much needed support. An upsurge of gang activity and organized crime had all but overwhelmed the Ottawa force. Vermette had scuttled the trial balloon before it got started by insisting on a mountain of paperwork for every hour spent outside the office, and he continually tightened their budget. The team was now doubly weighted down in useless bureaucracy and a lack of resources. Vermette hovered like a buzzard on death watch. Rouleau understood the animosity. He'd turned down Inspector before the job was offered to Vermette. His decision had been made easy by the thought of endless meetings and political games, but considering it had made him feel like he was stagnating in Major Crimes. When the offer came a few months later to lead an elite trouble-shooting team, the challenge had appealed to him. It should have been a satisfying way to end his career. Unfortunately, Vermette found out he'd been second choice for Inspector, which unleashed a vindictive streak longer than the St. Lawrence River. He controlled the work that flowed Rouleau's way, keeping the team on the outside looking in. Rouleau had selected Stonechild, not because of her experience, but because nobody on the Ottawa force wanted to be part of a unit that was rumoured to be folding by the end of the fiscal.

Rouleau sighed and headed for the door, flicking off the lights as he walked by.

———

The chill hit Rouleau as soon as he stepped inside the house. He kept his coat on and clumped down the basement stairs to look at the oil furnace that was original to the house. It was completely shut down.

Rouleau returned to the kitchen and called the heating company. The guy who answered promised someone would come by the next morning and have a look. He assured Rouleau that he was lucky to get an appointment so close to Christmas. Rouleau really wanted to believe him.

He hung up the phone and stood looking around the kitchen, at all the work left to be done. There should have been new gleaming white cupboards and stainless steel appliances, a hardwood floor, track lighting, porcelain backsplash. He and Frances had gotten as far as hiring a designer. They'd laid out what they wanted … well, what Frances had wanted, and he'd been happy to see her face light up as she described her latest idea. But there'd come a day she'd stopped talking about the colour of the walls and the shape of the light fixtures. The plans she'd pored over with such hope were yellowing in a folder in his bedroom.

Frances. He closed his eyes. *What the hell was the point of it all?*

He took a beer glass from the cupboard and poured himself a cold one from the fridge. He'd begun drinking Scotch in the evenings after Frances left. Six months of fitful sleep and hangovers. Six months of mourning. Now, he was down to a couple of beers and often, not even that.

He climbed the stairs to the second floor, sipping from the glass as he went. A half hour of rest and then a shower and off to the west end. Maybe it was a good night not to be alone with his thoughts after all.

———

Kala drove her truck north on Elgin toward Parliament Hill, happy for a few hours to herself. It was her first opportunity to check out the address she'd tracked down three months before. It was nearly four thirty and dusk was already settling in. Stores and restaurants were decked out in twinkling Christmas lights and glitter while snow piled on the sidewalks gave the street a village feel. Pedestrian traffic was light.

She cruised past the war memorial and the Château Laurier and followed the swoop of road left onto Sussex into the part of town called the ByWard Market. Spindly trees lined the roadway, weighted down by glowing Christmas lights in blue, red, and green. She passed the Bay department store and a giant Chapters bookstore before turning right into a rabbit's warren of stores and restaurants that twined down the narrow side streets. People were walking purposefully down the snowy sidewalks and streaming across intersections on their way home from work or to meet friends in one of the many bars or restaurants. At a red light, she watched a man and woman meet and embrace in the middle of the crosswalk, his arms wrapping around her and her face turned up to his. They continued on their way, arms slung around each other, his face nuzzled into the collar of her coat.

She searched for street names printed on the city map as she drove slowly through the commercial district to low-rent apartment buildings on the outskirts. The building she was seeking turned out to be dirty yellow brick with rusted balconies and cheap curtains or sheets hanging in the windows. She cruised the block looking for a parking spot. Two streets over, she lucked into a space in front of a beer store. She locked the truck and trudged down the side of the snowy street back the way she came.

The apartment building had a small foyer with metal mailboxes lined in a crooked row. A telephone and directory were positioned next to the door, but the lock was broken and she didn't need to be buzzed in. She scanned the list of names and apartment numbers and frowned at the name next to apartment 301. She prayed the listing was a mistake.

She took the stairs rather than the claustrophobic elevator with the tarnished metal gate. A smell of stale beer and cigarettes reeked from the carpet in the hallway on the third floor. She surveyed the concrete corridor and counted six apartments. The one she was looking for was between the elevator and the garbage disposal. A faded bouquet of plastic flowers had been nailed on the door beneath the apartment number. Kala took a deep breath and lifted her hand to knock.

Disappointment coursed through her. The woman who peered out from behind the chain was not the person Kala was searching for. This woman was in her late twenties with bleached white hair springing from her head in frizzy coils and eyelashes caked in black mascara. A silk kimono with giant roses that climbed upwards from the hem wrapped around her skinny frame. The fabric gaped open above her waist to display a red bra and skin the colour of talcum powder.

"Yes?" The woman's voice was husky from cigarettes; suspicious from living in a Centretown slum high-rise.

Kala held up her hands to appear non-threatening. "I'm sorry to disturb you. I thought my friend lived here. It's the last address I have for her. I was hoping to get together over Christmas."

"I moved in last month." The woman's stance relaxed but she kept the chain on the door. "Don't know nothing about who lived here before me or where they've gone."

"Is there anybody who might know?"

The woman screwed up her face while she thought. "The lady across the hall has been here a long time. She might know."

"Thanks, and sorry again to have bothered you."

Kala turned and crossed the hallway. She knocked on the door to 302 and waited. She knocked again. She didn't hear any movement from within.

The woman from 301 called across to her. "Just remembered. She told me last week she was going away to visit her son."

Kala turned. "Do you know when she'll be back?"

"Maybe tomorrow?" It came out like a question.

"I'll come back then," said Kala.

She would have left the woman in 301 with a phone number to call when the neighbour arrived home, but something told her this woman would hang up if she got the police department. Kala wasn't sure the number of the YWCA and hadn't had time to get her cellphone number changed to local. It would be better just to follow up herself. She'd waited this long. Another day wouldn't matter.

—

The lobby was quiet when Kala returned to the Y to clean up for the party. The young girl behind the desk had been replaced by a white-haired man reading the *Ottawa Citizen*. He looked up and smiled as she walked by but didn't try to engage in conversation. She liked that about him.

Once inside her room, she settled in the desk chair and pulled out her cellphone. Shannon should just be arriving home from work. It would be good to hear a voice from home.

Shannon answered on the third ring. She sounded out of breath. "I just got in the door. I'm *so* glad you called."

"How are things in Nipigon?" *How is Jordan? Does he know I've left town?* She could hear Shannon settling into a chair, the sound of her boots clunking onto the floor.

"It is *so* lonely with you gone. How's it there?"

"Interesting. We're a small team of five, including the sergeant Jacques Rouleau. I have a partner, Clarence Whelan."

"Really? You with a partner? Why can't I picture that?" Shannon's laughter bubbled across the miles.

"Hey, I can be a team player," said Kala. "When I have to."

"They don't know you yet, do they, Kal?"

"Not so much. I'm still in the honeymoon stage. How's my boy?"

"Taiku is fine. He keeps watching for you, but Doug and I have been taking turns bringing him on long walks."

"I miss him too. I'm thinking of getting a place where I can have him live with me."

"You should. I hate to think of you there all alone." Shannon paused. "Jordan came by a few times. I told him you'd taken a job near Toronto. He looked about as dejected as Taiku."

"Thanks for covering for me, Shannon. I owe you."

"I saw Miriam shopping for groceries this afternoon. She's getting big."

Kala closed her eyes. Jordan would do the right thing with her gone. "I hope she has a healthy pregnancy."

"Yeah." said Shannon. "I still say she tricked him."

"Jordan's a big boy. He knew what could happen."

"Well, there's knowing and there's being tricked. He hasn't moved back in yet."

"Give him time. They'll work it out."

"So what're you doing for Christmas?"

Kala looked around the colourless, cramped room. "Not sure, but I'll think of something. Are you and Doug having the family for dinner?"

"Yeah, just fifteen this year. I wish we would be sixteen, but maybe you'll be home next Christmas. Call me if you need to talk. Christmas morning for sure."

"Thanks, Shannon. I'll let you go make supper."

"Love you."

"Same."

Kala hung up the phone and stood to look out the window at the night sky, visible above buildings and the glow of streetlights. A nearly full moon hung suspended like a giant Christmas tree ornament in the darkness. She imagined Shannon and Jordan a thousand miles away looking up at the same moon. The idea gave some comfort, but not nearly enough.

8

ROULEAU PAID FOR his beer at the bar and sauntered toward the main entrance. He stopped to talk along the way, always keeping one eye on the people coming into the hall. He'd dressed in charcoal-grey slacks and a black Nordic sweater. Most of the women wore party dresses but the men were on the casual side like him. The room was a hum of conversation. He calculated over three hundred officers and spouses all told. Stonechild finally walked in as they were being seated. He met her outside the cloakroom.

"I'd almost given up on you coming. I should have offered to pick you up, but it was too late by the time my old brain thought of it."

"No problem. Sorry I'm so late. It was hard to know what to wear." She looked down at her black jeans and silver blouse. "This is about as fancy as I have."

"Our colours match. You look great," said Rouleau. He should have filled her in on the dress code for the party. Another reason to feel like he'd neglected his duty.

She shrugged and smiled. "Even if I'd known it was fancy dress, I'd have worn this because I didn't bring anything else. Clothes aren't really my thing."

"I don't think I've ever met a woman who didn't care about clothes."

"Then say hello to your first."

He steered her around a group of officers. "Whelan called. The baby is sick and he can't make it. I've saved us a spot with Malik, his wife Annika, and Grayson over there by the exit sign. What would you like to drink?"

"A soda and lime."

"Grab a seat and I'll bring it to you."

"Thank you, Sir," said Kala.

"Call me Jacques."

He walked over and leaned on the bar while he waited for his order. He looked over at the table. She'd chosen the empty seat next to Malik and his wife, leaving the seat beside Grayson for him. He wondered if Grayson had managed to alienate her already.

———

The opening speech by the head of the Police Services Board was followed by carrot soup, salad, and plates of roast turkey, mashed potatoes, and vegetables. Dessert and coffee rounded out the meal. Rouleau finished the last forkful of Baked Alaska and looked across at Stonechild. She'd eaten as much and as quickly as him. Their eyes met and he could see the amusement in hers as she lowered her fork onto her empty dessert plate.

"I didn't realize how hungry I was," she said. She patted her stomach. "I really shouldn't have had that third dinner roll."

Malik looked over. "You tuck in better than Whelan. He's going to enjoy driving around with you."

"As long as he likes fast food, we should do okay."

Malik laughed. "Whelan cut his baby teeth on Big Macs and fries."

"So what happens now?" asked Kala.

"More speeches and then the DJ starts," said Malik.

Malik's wife Annika leaned across and touched Kala on the wrist. "Why don't we go to the washroom and freshen up before they start? It can be a long hour."

Kala nodded. She instinctively liked this elegant woman dressed in a gold sari with red and silver threads woven into a border at the neck and hem. Gold bangles slid up and down when Annika moved her long, graceful arms. Her liquid black eyes searched Kala's as if she could see inside to her core. When Annika leaned back, Kala could still smell the musk rising from her skin. Malik stood and helped his wife to her feet. He touched her back lightly with one hand before she stepped away to lead Kala toward the washroom.

The line was short and they didn't have long to wait. They met again in front of the mirrors. Annika was refastening a comb that held back her hair in a tight bun. "So how do you like the force so far?" she asked. Her Indian accent was soft and lilting. Their eyes met in the mirror.

"I think I'm still having culture shock. I miss my home." Kala surprised herself by this confession, but something about Annika reminded her of Shannon.

"I know what you mean. When I first arrived in Canada to marry Sandeep, I thought my heart would surely break. India has its problems, but it is still a most beautiful country. And Canada was so cold. It took me a long time to get used to the cold."

"You must have loved Sandeep a lot to move to a new country."

"On the contrary, I'd never met him before I came to Canada. Our families arranged our marriage." Annika

finished straightening her sari and turned to face Kala. "I've
learned to love him. He is a fine man." They started walking slowly toward the door. "Do you have anyone special?"
asked Annika. "Back north where you come from?"

Kala didn't want to talk about what she'd left behind,
but she'd opened the door for this question. "I had someone,
but it didn't work out."

Annika nodded, her eyes sad. "You've come at a tough
time for the team," she said. "Sandeep says you need to solve
a high profile case soon or everything will stop. He would be
sorry as he deeply respects Jacques Rouleau."

"Oh? I had no idea."

"Internal politics. I should say no more."

They entered the main hall. A man's voice boomed from
the front of the room. Kala looked toward the microphone
that had been set up on the makeshift stage. A bald, sharp-
featured man was giving the punch line to a joke and laughter rippled across the tables. He was short but muscular in a
hunter-green turtleneck and brown suit jacket. She saw him
looking in her direction.

"Inspector Vermette," Annika said over her shoulder.
"He tells dirty jokes, no matter the occasion."

Kala sat down next to Rouleau and looked toward
the stage then back at Rouleau. He leaned back in his
chair, not smiling. His eyes were fixed on Vermette.
She turned back, curious to watch the man everyone
seemed to dislike. After Vermette finished speaking, a female officer invited everyone to mingle until the music
started.

Rouleau stood. Kala looked in the direction of his gaze
and stood just as Vermette reached their table, his hand out-
stretched. His grip was vice-like around her own. She kept
herself from squeezing back as hard.

"Welcome to our little family. It's nice to soften up Rouleau's team with some femininity. Has Jacques organized your media training yet?"

She shifted her eyes to Rouleau. He shook his head very slightly. She looked back at Vermette. "I believe it's in the works, but has to wait until after Christmas."

"Of course," said Vermette. "The holidays really mess us up. Too bad criminals don't take the week off too. I'll leave you in Sergeant Rouleau's capable hands then. Enjoy the rest of the evening." His eyes slid up and over her head, abruptly dismissing her as he stepped around her to join another table of men.

Kala turned to Rouleau and waited for him to explain.

"Thanks for that," he said. "I meant to tell you about the training but the Underwood case took over."

"Am I to be the minority face of the force?" she asked. She lowered her eyes. "Sorry, that was out of line."

"No need to apologize. Let's say Vermette could set racial relations back fifty years. Male-female relations too, for that matter. I'll see about getting you signed up after the holiday."

———

Kala stepped outside onto Preston Street. The temperature had dropped. When she exhaled, her breath streamed in front of her in a white plume. She pulled the hood of her jacket over her head and started walking. She'd stayed later than she'd planned, but officers kept coming over to be introduced. She pulled up her sleeve and glanced at her watch. Nearly two a.m. No wonder she was exhausted.

She was almost at the corner when she heard her name being called. At first she thought it was a mistake. She turned around, waiting for the red light to change. She recognized Rouleau in a black duffel coat hurrying toward her, a cellphone at his ear. He raised his free hand toward her to wait as he listened to whoever was on the other end. He said something into the phone before disconnecting.

"They've found a man's body. The car is registered to Tom Underwood so looks like it's him. We can take my car."

"Where is he?"

"The Central Experimental Farm just south west of here. Should take us ten minutes. Somehow, his parked car missed detection all week. I hope you didn't have any plans. This is going to be a long night."

"No plans." Suddenly, she wasn't tired anymore. Adrenaline was kicking in. She trudged through the snow beside Rouleau and felt as close to alive as she'd felt since she pointed her truck toward Ottawa four days earlier.

9

GERALDINE OLIVER WOKE up before Max but pretended to be asleep. It was another hour before he shut off the alarm and finally got out of bed. Seven a.m. Forty minutes and he'd be gone for the day. The baby was heavy in her belly. For the past two months, she'd been forced to sleep on her side, her back to Max. She couldn't believe she had four more weeks of discomfort before the baby was due. Surely the kid was full size by now. Any bigger and it would come out riding a tricycle.

She heard Max rummaging around, getting his suit from the closet and searching for his shoes under the dresser. It was easy to keep her breathing deep and even. She even drifted off a few times. She sensed him standing over the bed looking down at her and slowed her breathing even more. What the hell was he doing? Did he think he could stare her into waking up? At long last she heard him cross the floor and start down the stairs. She let her breath out in a loud sigh when he reached the bottom.

She waited a good fifteen minutes after she heard the front door slam before she swung her aching legs over the side of the bed. It would have been catastrophic if he'd come back for something and caught her up and about. He'd have known she'd been faking sleep to avoid him.

She flicked on the flat screen on her way to the bathroom. Max had left it on CNN, and she didn't bother to change the channel. She just wanted to hear another voice. If she hadn't promised Hunter she'd drive to his place for lunch, she would have run a bath and spent the morning lying in bubbles and reading the Harlan Coben thriller she'd picked up at the library. She'd become good at idling away her days, but not today. A quick shower would do and then she'd eat something light and head off to the hairdresser's for a shampoo and cut. There'd be enough time to stop at the bakery for fresh bread and dessert before the drive to Hunter's.

She reached for a towel and facecloth in the cupboard. Her hand lingered, her fingers stretching to the back of the shelf and under a pile of towels. Her hand closed around one of the two bottles she'd hidden the day before. The glass was deliciously smooth to her touch and she ran her fingers up and down its curved length. She remembered the colour of the bottle was emerald green, her favourite colour. She forced her hand away from the temptation and traced her fingers across her bulging belly.

One day at a time. She could put off a drink one more day.

The bathroom tile was cool under her bare feet. She sat sideways on the edge of the bathtub, awkwardly bending over to turn on the taps. Her fingers opened wide under the rush of warm water. It felt soothing and she sat for a while longer. Then, she stood with a grunt and slipped out of her nightgown. It pooled around her feet in a silken heap. Her face reflected exhaustion in the mirror but her eyes were determined.

She stepped into the shower and raised her face to let the water pour over her in a steaming cascade, the drops hitting her skin like pin pricks. She kept her eyes closed and avoided looking down at her misshapen belly.

Max had said he could hardly stand to look at her anymore. He'd told her she'd have to start dieting right after the baby if she wanted him to be attracted to her again. He'd prepaid her gym membership, not even asking if she wanted it. She'd imagined herself beautiful when they first met because he'd looked at her like she was. Now, when she looked into his eyes she saw the homely woman she'd been all along. His disgust hurt like a knot twisting in her chest. It was the most horrible feeling she'd ever known. At times, taking another breath had been an effort, the pain threatening to strangle her.

———

Kala pressed Laurel Underwood's doorbell one more time. Rouleau had dropped her near her truck after she'd offered to make this call on her way home for a few hours of sleep. He'd continued on to the station to update Vermette. Whelan should have been with her, but he'd left some jumbled message on her cellphone around midnight and hadn't been reachable since. So far, she thought working with a partner wasn't much different than working alone.

It was the morning before Christmas Eve. She'd expected Laurel to be at home. A cheery evergreen wreath with a silver bow and red berries that hung on the door felt out of sync with the news Kala had come to break to Tom Underwood's wife. She didn't plan to give many details about the death. It would have done no good to talk about how they'd found her husband's stiff body crowded into the trunk of his Mercedes. The coroner, Grogan, estimated Underwood had been dead a few days, but it was hard to say when exactly because the freezing temperatures had kept him preserved like meat in a locker. Grogan said that Underwood was alive when he was locked inside the trunk. He'd found scratch marks inside the trunk and Underwood's nails were ripped and ragged, caked in dried blood. Underwood had definitely been alive and trying to get out. She thought about what he must have gone through when he realized the trunk would be his frigid tomb. The cruelty of somebody leaving him to freeze made her want to punch something.

She pulled out her cellphone and called Rouleau. "Nobody home at the Underwoods."

"How about Underwood's daughter, Geraldine Oliver? Are you okay to go over to her place?"

"Yeah. I could do that, but I've never met her. It'll be a shock, and didn't somebody say she's pregnant?"

"Right. It might be better if she heard from a family member."

"I can drive out to Hunter's. It won't take too long now that I know where he lives."

"Sure you're not too tired?"

"I can go a few days without sleep. Anyway, somebody in the family has to be told before word leaks out."

"We'll need him to identify his father, although there's no doubt based on the photo Laurel gave us. You sure you're okay to do this?"

"I'll be fine. I've broken the news of a sudden death to family members before. Any word from Whelan?"

"Nothing. When I reach him, I'll get him to meet you."

"I'm on my way then."

"Bring Hunter to the station."

"Will do."

"I'm pulling in Grayson and Malik. They'll be here within the hour. I need to sign off. I'm being paged."

Kala tucked her phone into her jacket pocket and walked back to her truck. She trod carefully on the icy driveway. It hadn't been plowed since the last light snowfall and drifts hid patches of black ice. The cab of the truck was still warm from her drive to the Underwoods. She turned the heater up high and pushed a John Hiatt CD into the player before starting down the circular driveway.

She stopped when she reached the road to look back at Underwood's grey stone mansion. It was an imposing residence. Too many rooms to be cozy and too much space for three people. It was a depressing contrast to the shacks she'd lived in growing up.

She checked both ways and pulled onto Winding Way.

All that money and what had it gotten him? Nothing that mattered much in the end.

———

This time, there was no dog to greet her. The property was silent and deserted. Kala stepped away from her truck and looked around. Hunter hadn't cleared the woods from his property or cut back the brush. His house nestled into the pines and snow as if it was posing for a Christmas card photo. Even the low cloud cover and first flakes of snow added to the effect. It left her homesick for her own woods and her own cabin.

Hunter didn't answer the door although his truck was in the driveway. She knocked a third time, jumping from foot to foot to keep the circulation moving. When he still didn't answer, she started walking toward the side of the house.

She reached the corner and heard music coming from the back of the property. A narrow path led her around the side of the house to a barnyard-grey workshop. Through the window, she spotted Hunter standing in front of an easel, dotting at his work with a paintbrush, totally absorbed while classical music filled the shop and spilled into the winter air. He wore a white denim shirt rolled up at the sleeves and tucked into black jeans, and he'd tied his hair back from his face with a red bandana. Kala watched him for a full minute before she knocked, thinking about how she would tell him that his father was dead.

Hunter opened the door and his eyes searched her face before he stepped aside to let her in. "Just give me a minute." He crossed the floor to turn down the stereo and then returned to his easel to close up the paints and soak his paintbrush in turpentine.

She took the time to look at the bronze statues. Two sat next to each other on a work table. The first was of a pigtailed girl in a leotard on a balance beam. The second was an older girl spinning on ice skates. Her hands were spread wide and her face turned upwards. The detail was exquisite. She turned to face him. "Your work is brilliant. I can feel the joy in each of these children. Are the pieces for sale? They are just so perfect … I'm not much of an art connoisseur, but these are magnificent."

Hunter tucked his head. When he looked up, he was smiling. "No, these were all done on commission. They're Christmas presents. The dad is coming to pick them up later today. He had them done for his wife."

"They're simply beautiful," she said.

"Thanks. I'm told I have my mother's eye."

"You're both very talented." Kala moved closer to the door. "I'm actually here on police business."

"I thought that might be the case." He waited, his grey eyes on hers.

"I'm afraid it's bad news. We found a man's body early this morning and we believe it is your father."

Hunter's brow furrowed. "You found his body? Where?"

"In his car. At the Central Experimental Farm."

"Are you sure it is my father? Was it … suicide?"

"I need you to come with me to make the official identification, but we believe it is him. The car is registered to your father. We couldn't find Laurel to tell her so you are the first of the family to know."

He rubbed his hand across his jaw. "I can't believe it." He looked up. "Geraldine doesn't know?"

She shook her head. "No. You're the first we've been able to reach."

"Shit."

She thought he was upset that she hadn't told Geraldine, but then she realized that his eyes were looking past her to the door. She heard a clumping noise outside. The door opened at the same time as she turned. A cold blast of air filled the room, bringing with it a hugely pregnant woman. Her smile disappeared when she looked from Kala to her brother.

"Hunter! I'm early. They got my hair appointment mixed up and I just kept driving. I'm sorry." She held a bag with a baguette sticking out the top and a cake box under her other arm. "I can just go up to the house and wait for you until your customer leaves." She turned to go but Hunter stopped her.

"No. It's fine, Geraldine. I was expecting you. Come in out of the cold. Here, let me help you." He reached for her packages and guided her gently by the arm.

Kala studied the two of them together. Geraldine had a long, narrow face with a wide nose that made her eyes look too close together. Her eyes were grey like her brother's, but a paler, washed-out shade. Hunter leaned into her as if protecting her from what was to come.

"I have to drive into town for an hour or so. Will you be able to get the soup on the stove and kick back until I return? I prepared it last night so it just needs heating up."

Geraldine looked up at him and smiled. "Of course. I'll read that book you keep meaning to lend me."

"In the bookcase on the right," said Hunter. "Fabio will keep you company. He's sleeping by the hot air vent in the kitchen."

"Don't worry about me then." Geraldine held out a hand. "I don't believe we've met. I'm Hunter's sister, Geraldine."

"Pleased to meet you. Kala Stonechild." She shook Geraldine's. She'd decided to play along with Hunter. His eyes had flashed a silent pleading for her to go easy. If Geraldine hadn't been so obviously pregnant, she would have asked some questions about her father. There'd be time enough after he identified the body.

Hunter took his coat from the hook by the door and followed them outside into the frigid morning. Kala took a moment to inhale the frosty air while she surveyed the dark line of woods that stretched to the east of Hunter's house. The sky was heavy with clouds and the snow was starting to pick up. She led the way on the narrow packed path back toward the house and continued to the driveway while Hunter helped Geraldine and her packages safely inside. He joined Kala in the driveway where she stood next to his Jeep.

"Thanks for that. Dad and Geraldine are close and I don't know how this is going to affect her. I want to make sure it really is Dad before we have to put her through a load of grief."

"Understood, but we'll need to speak with her afterward."

Hunter unlocked the Jeep and reached for the scraper. He started the engine to warm it up and began cleaning snow off the windshield as he talked. "I'll follow you." His hand stopped mid-motion like he'd just thought of something. He turned to face her. "You never said how he died."

Kala hesitated. "I think it best you identify him. Then we can talk about how he died."

He started to protest but stopped himself. Instead, he shrugged and raised the scraper to the windshield. "Fair enough. I guess waiting another hour won't make much difference, that is, if it really is my father."

10

ROULEAU WALKED WITH Kala and Hunter toward the room where Tom Underwood's body was waiting for identification. He'd tried to prepare Hunter for what he was about to see, but he knew it would still be a shock to see his father's body laid out on the table. Kala stood behind Hunter while he gave his recital, her face impassive. Surprisingly, she didn't look tired. In fact, she looked like she'd just started her day. She made Rouleau feel old. There'd been a time he could go a few days and still perform, but not anymore. Between briefing Vermette and bringing Malik and Grayson up to speed, he'd managed a fifteen-minute cat nap in his office chair. It had left him feeling worse, not better.

He led Hunter and Stonechild into the viewing room. They lined up next to him and he grabbed the sheet. "Ready?" he asked.

Hunter nodded and Rouleau rolled the sheet carefully down from Underwood's face and halfway down his chest.

Hunter took a step forward. His eyes swept the man on the table and then back to Rouleau. "That's my father. Tom Underwood."

"You're certain?"

Hunter nodded.

"I'm sorry. We'll do all we can to find who did this." Rouleau glanced at Kala who'd also taken a step forward. She shook her head just as Hunter turned his full gaze on her. Rouleau realized his mistake. "Let's step into the office next door. Perhaps you can answer a few questions and we'll tell you what we know."

Hunter nodded again and they filed into the coroner's office. It was Spartan clean with a desk, computer, and a wall of filing cabinets. Posters of the human anatomy covered two walls. Hunter lowered himself into the one chair and bent forward, his elbows on his knees and his forehead in his hands. Kala leaned on a filing cabinet and Rouleau stood in front of Hunter, waiting for him to collect himself. It didn't take long before Hunter looked up.

"Was my father murdered?"

Rouleau nodded. "He died in the trunk of his car. Preliminary findings are that he froze to death."

"My God."

"We're not exactly sure when, but probably a few days ago. We're running tests."

"This is like a bad dream. My father wasn't the easiest man to get along with, but for somebody to murder him in such a heinous way … it's unthinkable."

"You were estranged from your father until recently. Can you tell us why?"

Hunter slowly raised his head. "What you're really asking is if I could have murdered *my own father*? If I said I found that offensive, I don't suppose it would matter to you."

"We are a far cry from accusing anybody, but the sooner we start finding out the situation of everyone involved in your father's life, the sooner we can solve who left him to die."

"I see." A look crossed Hunter's face as if he was choosing what to reveal. Rouleau noticed and glanced over at Stonechild. The look in her black eyes signalled that she'd observed it too.

Hunter looked at a spot between them. "My father and I had a falling out about ten years ago. I didn't like the fact that he was fooling around on my mother and told him so. When he left her, I ended contact with him."

"You didn't talk for all this time?"

"I live far enough out of Ottawa that we didn't run into each other. I might have seen him leaving my mother's once or twice but that was it. We didn't seek each other out."

"It seems like a long time to be upset about his affair."

"I wasn't upset after the first while. It was more I didn't feel anything at all for him. He didn't matter to me one way or the other."

"Can you account for your movements over the last week?"

"I spent yesterday afternoon in town getting groceries and meeting friends at the pub. Other than that, I've been home working. I had a few pieces on commission to finish before Christmas." He glanced at Kala as if seeking confirmation.

"Did you see anybody over this time?"

"Just customers."

"We'll need everyone's name, including your pub friends. Jot down their addresses and phone numbers for me, would you?" Rouleau slid a pen and notepad across the desk.

Hunter complied, then tossed down the pen. "Is that all?"

"All for now."

Hunter stood and started for the door. Rouleau called to him.

"Do you have any idea where Laurel Underwood might have gone? We've been trying to reach her to let her know what's happened."

Hunter stopped, his hand on the doorknob. "No idea. Sorry." He didn't turn around as he pushed open the door and kept moving.

Rouleau and Stonechild followed him into the hallway and watched him get into the elevator. Rouleau turned to Kala.

"He's hiding something."

She nodded. "I have the same feeling. He'll be heading home now to tell his sister Geraldine what happened. She came by for lunch just before we left. I'm certain we can rule her out. She's so pregnant there's no way she could have gotten her father into the trunk."

"She might have hired somebody to do it, or managed it with somebody else's help. Maybe Hunter's."

"Hunter said that Geraldine and their father were close."

"That might mean nothing. I've seen close family members kill each other over the most insignificant things."

"You're saying to keep an open mind."

He smiled. "The first rule of investigation."

"Any word from Whelan?" Kala asked.

"No. I've asked a squad car to go by his place and check in. I hope to have an answer soon."

"There seem to be a few people missing. It's like Ottawa has a black hole that people keep dropping into."

He smiled again. "Sounds like the script for a science fiction movie. Let's hope not. Vermette has already let me know that we'll be running this investigation through Christmas season because staff in Major Crimes is at a minimum. One just had surgery, another two are off with the stomach flu, and of course there are the booked holidays. I've got Malik heading up a team at Tom Underwood's office and Grayson at his home. They're going through his things to see if there are any clues hidden in his effects. Underwood's laptop and computers are already in the lab being gone over. You should go home and get some sleep."

"If you need me, I'll have my cell close by. I can be here inside of ten minutes."

"Hopefully, we'll both get time to rest. I don't anticipate any news for a few hours at least. I'm going to stay down here for a bit."

"Okay."

He watched her walk down the corridor and get on the elevator. He'd meant to ask her where she was staying, but his mind was sluggish. There were several hotels in the city core not too far from the station. They'd start adding up if she stayed in one very long. Maybe he should offer her a spare room. It would save her some money until she got to know the city and found a permanent place. He'd ask her next time she was in.

———

Geraldine was angry. Angrier than she could remember being in her entire life. The car seemed an extension of the rage coursing through her body, barrelling down Highway 417 toward Ottawa like a bullet.

Hunter had wanted her to stay overnight. He'd kept studying her with that worried look on his face he reserved for lost animals until she wanted to push him away and scream like a mad woman. She'd eaten his homemade soup and drunk the sugary steeped tea, not shedding even one tear after he told her that their father was dead. She'd known all along how her father's disappearance would turn out. Hunter had just confirmed what she'd been expecting.

He'd tried to drive her into town but she'd told him not to be so ridiculous. She could drive herself. Their father had died. The world hadn't collapsed and neither would she. Still, Hunter had hovered, watching her with concerned eyes when he thought she wasn't looking. It was a relief to finally back her car out of his driveway and be alone with her thoughts — thoughts that kept her from looking her brother in the eyes because she didn't want him to see the suspicion in hers, and she sure didn't want to see the evasion in his.

She wouldn't blame him. Their father had set this into motion many years before when he'd put his self-interest before the good of his family. Hunter had been a victim and maybe now, he'd gotten revenge. He thought he'd escaped the ugliness by hiding out in this cabin for the past ten years, but he couldn't hide forever. It all started and ended with Laurel. She was to blame. She was the one who would have to pay.

Geraldine passed the St. Laurent exit in the passing lane. Slower traffic ahead forced her to brake and get a grip on her emotions. It wouldn't do to be in an accident now and hurt the baby growing in her stomach. The baby for whom she'd given up alcohol and barely formed thoughts of leaving Max. The growing fetus had become her excuse for inaction. It had seemed like a second chance.

She was coming up on the Bronson exit. Decision time. Would she take the off ramp and head to her father's home to confront Laurel with what she knew? Would it hurt her brother or help him? She gripped the wheel and changed into the middle lane. She put her turn signal on in preparation for pulling into the inside lane to take the exit.

One last shoulder check showed her the green Toyota riding in her blind spot. The sight of it made her gasp. She straightened the wheel as he pulled alongside, cutting off her chance to pull into the lane in time to make the off ramp. She realized how close she'd come to hitting the other car, and her heart beat hard inside her chest. If she hadn't done that last shoulder check, she'd have driven right into him.

She kept driving. Her anger had ebbed and a feeling of weariness was replacing it. Her arms felt heavy and her head was throbbing. All she wanted to do was go home, crawl into bed, and sleep for a dozen hours. Maybe the green Toyota had been a sign from above. She'd come too close to disaster to tempt fate now. She'd bide her time and confront Laurel when she felt stronger. Whatever it took, she'd bring Laurel down. She'd protect Hunter from himself.

By the time she reached the March Road exit in Kanata, the first of her tears were seeping out of the corners of her eyes. She'd begun shaking and was having trouble driving in a straight line. She slowed the car to below the speed limit and cruised down the ramp, turning left and left again before pulling over in a no parking zone in front of an elementary school.

The children were out for recess, chasing each other around the yard, their snowsuits and toques patches of brightness against the white snow and grey sky. She could hear their loud carefree voices through the windows of her car and their innocence made her weep. She watched them for a while until the tears blurred her vision and she couldn't see more than watery shapes in the distance. The salty tears dripped down her cheeks and onto her hands lying across the steering wheel. She slowly lowered her head until it rested on her hands.

Her life had been unravelling for months. Alcohol had been her salvation. Now she couldn't even turn to that for fear of hurting her child. The only one who'd come close to understanding was her father, and now he was dead. Her one safe harbour and she'd never see him again. She started to cry in earnest then, her shoulders shaking and sobs ripping up her throat until her pain and rage filled the car's confined space.

II

A LOUD BANG from the room above woke Kala from a deep sleep. For a few seconds, she lay confused, unable to place where she was. A heavy box was being dragged across the floor overhead. She stared at the brown-stained crack in the ceiling and it came flooding back. *The YWCA. Room 1005.* She sat up and looked at the clock on the nightstand. Five o'clock. She'd slept a solid six hours. It would be enough to keep her going. Time for a quick shower and then she'd venture out for a meal.

Twenty minutes later, she was trudging through the snow toward Elgin Street to find a restaurant. She'd seen several eating establishments on the drive earlier. The snow drifted down in large wet flakes, landing on her eyelashes and cheeks, filling the crevices of her coat and hat. The coolness felt good and she turned her face toward the sky. She reached Elgin and walked north.

It took no time to reach the Elgin Street Diner just past Gladstone. The windows were aglow with neon signs. One announced it was open twenty-four hours, a fact that would come in handy later. Inside, the decor was bright and unpretentious and Christmas tunes were playing from the speakers. If the food was any good, it might become her restaurant of choice. She ordered eggs over easy, bacon, and toast from a boy of university age. He promised to keep the coffee coming.

She kept her head down while she ate. She drained the last of her third cup of coffee after dragging the remaining toast crust through the smear of egg yolk. Satisfied, she pushed back her plate and looked around. The place was nearly empty. A group of four college-aged boys was talking loudly at a table near the door. Next to them were a couple of cops in uniform finishing up their breakfasts. Two women were eating burgers and fries at the table next to her. She imagined there'd be bigger crowds once Christmas was over, but this would remain an anonymous place with people minding their own business.

She paid the bill and set out toward the station. The bright restaurant and bar lights of Elgin Street tapered off as she walked south. The snow had stopped but the sky was grey and low. The station took up a city block on the tail end of downtown. Rows of glass block rimmed its base, giving it a modern look and relief from the grey block. She entered by the front door and said good evening to the desk constable, flashing her ID before continuing on to the office.

Grayson looked up from his desk when she entered. He raised his hand in a wave and continued typing.

"You're working late," she said.

"Just finishing the report on the day's search. Didn't expect to see you before tomorrow morning." He kept his eyes on the screen.

"If I slept any longer, I wouldn't be able to sleep tonight. I wanted to check what happened this afternoon." She crossed to her desk and shrugged out of her parka. "Any word on Whelan?"

He looked up this time. "You haven't heard?"

"Heard what?"

"His baby's sick in the hospital. Whelan won't be in until it's sorted."

"How sick?"

"Intensive care. Meningitis apparently."

"That's awful."

"Yeah. Touch and go. Looks like you won't have a partner for a while."

"That's the least of it." She sat in her chair and picked up the folder in her in-basket. She opened to the first page but couldn't concentrate. "He and Meghan must be frantic."

Grayson didn't respond. She watched him for a while, not sure how to take his silence. He appeared to have completely tuned her out, but just a little too intent on keeping his head down. *Asshole.*

She lowered her eyes and started reading. The typed report outlined what had been taken from Underwood's office and home. The last sheet updated the interviews. Underwood's partner and co-workers had given preliminary statements. There was a notation to follow up with J.P. Belliveau and Max Oliver the following day. When she finished reading, she clicked on her computer and checked her email. Her eyes scanned the list: a couple of messages from administration, one from Vermette wishing everyone happy holidays, and somebody named Connie Henderson in HR, telling her they were scheduling media training and she was on a waiting list — January spots were already gone. She sighed and looked toward Grayson. He'd stood up and was putting on his coat. She wondered how long he'd been watching her.

"Can I buy you a drink?" he asked.

She resisted the urge to look behind her. She started to say no, but reconsidered. She had nothing to lose and finding out what he was after could be worth knowing. "Okay. I have someplace to go afterwards so I'll take my truck and follow you."

———

She chose a table near the window and waited while Grayson got their drinks from the bar. It was a typical pub with wood panelling and nooks and crannies for private chats. Ottawa seemed to be full of them. The bar ran the length of one wall with glistening brass beer taps at its centre. A couple of men sat alone on stools facing the giant TV screen above the bar. She read the draft selection written on a chalkboard hanging above the beer taps. The names brought back memories of too many bars and the lost years before she signed up to be a cop.

Grayson set a soda and lime in front of her and slid a tall glass of beer across the table. He sat down and took a long drink before taking off his jacket. He looked around the room and back at her.

"Small crowd. This place is usually hopping."

"I imagine last minute Christmas shopping and parties are keeping people away." She took a sip of soda.

He pointed to her glass. "You don't drink alcohol?"

"No."

"Never?"

"Does it matter?"

"I guess not. You could be the only cop in Ottawa who never has a slug of booze after work."

"I can live with that. So what brought you to Rouleau's team?" she asked. The real question was why somebody with his ambition tied himself to a screwed unit.

"I came from the drug squad working undercover. I was getting burned out the same time as this was pitched as a new project that could change the way we operate. It was disappointing to find out we were set up to fail before we began."

"Vermette."

"Yeah, Vermette. He's as sneaky as they come and as nasty. If he doesn't want this project to succeed, it won't." His hand tightened around his glass as if he'd like to squeeze it until it shattered.

"He must have somebody protecting him."

Grayson smiled. "Well, he mixes in the right circles. His wife comes from a political family."

"Rouleau seems decent enough."

"He is, but it's a losing game and he knows it. I think he stayed on because he feels some responsibility to the team, but I don't think it will keep him much longer. It's been a waste of talent as far as I can see." He looked hard at her. "So what really brought you to Ottawa?"

She shrugged. "I wanted a break from small-town policing. This position came up and I figured it would give me experience and a chance to see if working in a city is something I want to pursue."

"I'd say you've wasted a trip if it hadn't been for the Underwood case coming along. Vermette will probably take it away after Christmas, but most of Major Crimes are taking the week off and he hates to get on their bad side, which he would if he called them in."

"Rouleau doesn't strike me as someone who would put up with this."

"It's hard to fathom, all right. He used to be a workaholic when he was married. He was a damned smart cop with a brilliant career ahead. Then his wife up and left and he lost his drive."

She looked at Grayson and wondered why he was telling her this. He caught her gaze and shrugged. "I'm just saying that you might want to head back north while the getting is good. This isn't a job you want to hang your career on. Rouleau would understand if you had second thoughts."

"That's good of you to think of my welfare."

"Not at all. Somebody has to give you enough information so you look out for yourself."

"Well, maybe I will head home. As you say, there's not much here for me." She watched his handsome face relax before he took another drink of beer. "So why do you stay on?" she asked as casually as she could. "I mean, you can't be satisfied with this job as you described it."

"Yeah, I know it doesn't add up that somebody with my qualifications would stay in a dead-end job, but I won't much longer."

She kept her face impassive. He leaned closer. "Rouleau has an offer coming and I'll be moving with him."

"Does Rouleau know, I mean, about the offer?"

"No, not yet, and I'd appreciate you not saying anything. I'm speaking out of school here." For the first time, he looked anxious.

She thought about stringing him along but knew he wouldn't take it well. "Whatever you and Rouleau have in the cooker is none of my concern." She took a long drink from her glass. "I'm curious though. How do you know about this offer when Rouleau doesn't?"

He smiled. "I've fostered a few political friends myself."

She set her glass down and reached for her jacket. "Well, thanks for the drink and conversation but I have to get to my appointment."

"Sure. I'm glad we had this chat." He leaned back in his chair. "Do you have Christmas plans? Family in Ottawa?"

"I have plans, thanks."

"That's good. You'll probably get the day off but will be on call. See you tomorrow then."

He picked up his glass and followed her as she threaded her way through the tables. She kept going toward the entrance after he turned toward the bar. He was just sliding onto a stool with a view of the sports channel when she pulled open the door to step outside.

———

The apartment building's door was still unlocked, giving Kala easy entry to the lobby. An out-of-order sign in shaky red lettering was taped onto the elevator door, but she'd planned to take the stairs anyhow. The same stale beer and cigarette smells rose up to greet her. The only change from her previous visit was the size of the dustballs on the steps.

On the third floor she pushed open the heavy door and hesitated. The hallway was darker than she remembered and her tingly sense went on high alert. It took her but a second to notice that the overhead light near apartment 305 had burnt out. She took a careful look around before shutting the door to the stairwell and crossing to the apartment. It was a full minute after she knocked before she heard footsteps.

"I'm not buying anything," a woman's reedy voice called through the door.

"And I'm not selling. I'm a friend of the woman who used to live across the hall. I'm wondering if you know where she went." Kala moved sideways so that she'd be clearly visible through the peephole.

The door opened but jumped back as the chain caught. A white-haired woman wearing thick glasses peered at her through the gap. A cat meowed at her feet. "Rosie left a few months ago. Couldn't pay the rent."

"You spoke with her?"

"We weren't friends if that's what you're asking. The landlord told her she had to leave."

"Did she say where she was going?"

"No, but I don't think she's gone far because of the kid."

"She has a child?" Kala didn't know why she was surprised. A lot of years had passed.

"I thought you said you were friends."

"Yeah, but we haven't been in touch for a while. I'm trying to make contact."

"Well, it must have been more than a few years if you didn't know Rosie has a kid. The girl is twelve years old. Name of Dawn, you know, like the sunrise. I'd watch for her to make sure she got home from school okay. Somebody had to. A couple of times she came over for cookies when her mother was passed out."

"Do you know what school she went to or have any idea where they could have gone?"

"Dawn took a bus to school is all I know. I'd guess they went somewhere cheaper to live." She laughed, showing nicotine-stained teeth. "Rosie didn't want to interrupt her drinking by working for a living." She started to close the door.

Kala lifted a hand to stop her but let her arm drop to her side. This woman wasn't going to share anything else. It didn't take a genius to realize that Rosie had to be living in a shelter or assisted living somewhere in the downtown.

Kala turned to walk down the hallway, a new resolve taking hold. She would find them before she left Ottawa. If it meant spending the whole year working for Rouleau, she'd stick it out. She wouldn't head north without Rosie and the child.

12

ROULEAU WOKE TO the sound of the wind rattling the living-room windows and whistling down the chimney. The room was semi-dark. Winter mornings took a depressingly long time for the sun to rise and get rid of the gloom. He sat up, scattering the newspaper and blanket onto the floor, and gingerly stretched his shoulders and neck. They felt tight but not too bad. He'd fallen asleep on the couch under a wool throw and the sports section of the paper just after eleven o'clock. The distance from the couch to his bedroom upstairs had seemed too far.

It was Christmas Eve in the beginning stages of a murder case. Unfortunate timing, especially this year with half the force booked off and the skeleton staff working in the labs processing only the most pressing cases. Tracking down Underwood's co-workers and family was also an issue. The autopsy was on track, however, and he should get a preliminary report first thing in the morning before the lab staff left early for the holiday. He was hoping for a fibre or some DNA from the killer.

He walked to the kitchen and got the coffee started. While it brewed, he put a Van Morrison record on the stereo and took a quick shower. Afterwards he sat at the kitchen table reading the paper that he'd started the night before. He raised his eyes to the window. The wind must have blown in a bank of snow clouds. Large flakes were swirling against the pane. It would have been a good day to hunker down and watch a movie. The idea of heading out in the storm to go to work when most people were enjoying a day off was infinitely unappealing.

He'd foregone a tree and decorations this year. It wasn't that he didn't like Christmas. The three weeks before Christmas had zipped past at unprecedented speed. It wasn't too late to mark the day though. He'd get his father's gift for his yearly visit to Kingston for lunch, then drop by the butcher and buy something special for his Christmas supper.

He swallowed the last of his coffee and set the cup in the sink. Breakfast was waiting for him at the drive-through on his way to the office. If all went well, he'd let the team off early. It was a hell of a shame that after weeks of not much going on they had to get this murder at Christmas time. It was almost as if Vermette had ordered the case to ruin the team's holiday plans.

———

Grayson, Malik, and Stonechild were working at their desks when Rouleau arrived with a box of doughnuts just before nine. He entered his office and checked his messages and the inbox on his desk. He spied the toxicology report sitting on top of the pile. It was already turning into a good day.

He grabbed the report and settled in at his desk to give it a thorough read. Twenty minutes later, he poured a cup of coffee and gathered the team in the makeshift meeting area at the far corner of the office space where they'd erected bulletin boards and charts. Bennett and Gage, two officers in uniform he'd wrangled on loan for the week, joined them for the debrief. Both were in their late twenties. Bennett was the taller of the two but both looked like they spent a lot of time in the gym. They'd been happy to accept the assignment.

"Right then. We have one new important piece of information from Forensics. Underwood was drugged before he was forced into the trunk. Possibly, the drug was administered in a cup of coffee or some drink. It was a street drug in the date rape family."

"It's often slipped into women's drinks in bars. He might have been having coffee with whoever killed him and they dropped it in when he wasn't looking," said Malik. "Makes sense it would be coffee since he went missing in the morning."

Rouleau nodded. "It also means that he didn't fight being put inside the trunk. Underwood is one hundred and fifty pounds and wouldn't have been too heavy for one person to handle. Even a fit woman could have gotten him in there. He would have woken up, realized where he was, and tried to get out. His car was parked outside and the cold got to him eventually. Not a nice way to end it."

He sat still for a moment while they all contemplated Underwood's end. His eyes circled the group and rested on Stonechild. She was staring straight ahead at nothing, her eyes unreadable. An uncoiled energy radiated from her at odds with her stillness. He'd pay to know what she was thinking.

Rouleau stood and picked up a magic marker and positioned himself in front of the white board. "Let's go over what we know so far. Family includes two adult children: Hunter Underwood, who's been estranged from his father for ten years and recently back on speaking terms, and Geraldine Oliver, pregnant with her first child and married to Max Oliver, who works for Tom Underwood's company. Then we have the first wife, Pauline, who still goes by the name Underwood, and the new wife, Laurel. She has a six-year-old daughter, Charlotte, with Tom."

"I rule out the six-year-old," said Malik.

"I knew there was a reason I brought you on the dream team," said Rouleau, toasting him with the marker. "Have another doughnut."

Malik grinned and selected a chocolate one from the box. "Don't mind if I do."

Rouleau finished writing the names on the board with their connection to the deceased. "That brings us to his work colleagues. J.P. Belliveau is his partner. Of course, we intersect again with Max Oliver, who has an assistant named Benny. We've yet to track down Underwood's clients, although we got a list from Underwood's wife Laurel at our first visit. She said most of them were more social acquaintances than friends, but worth checking out." Rouleau copied the names to the master list and then straightened. "Anybody else you can think of?"

Stonechild looked back through her notepad. "We met Pauline's friend Susan Halliday outside her house. They were going for a walk."

He added Susan's name to the board. "She might have some information about Tom, depending how long she's been friends with Pauline. Worth checking out. We can't rule out that this is a random killing, but I'd say the fact he was drugged means either he knew his killer or some person followed him and drugged his coffee in a restaurant or coffee shop. The bad news is we have no viable motive and no suspects."

"We might need to spin that," said Grayson. "Otherwise, Vermette won't be enjoying his Christmas turkey."

"Why should we be the only ones suffering?" asked Malik.

"Let me worry about Vermette," said Rouleau. "I'm going to send a few officers to check coffee shops in the area. Stonechild, could you take Gage and Bennett and begin the door-to-door in Underwood's neighbourhood? Start with his home and see if Laurel has turned up yet. Malik and Grayson, head back to his office and have a read through his files. Belliveau is going to be there at ten and you can interview him again. I'm going to be doing some media interviews to keep the press from coming up with gossip to fill in the blanks. Any questions?"

"Should I interview Susan Halliday if I have time?" asked Kala.

"Sure." Rouleau spoke to the team. "But it's Christmas Eve so I want each of you to quit by five and take tomorrow off. If I have to call you in, I'll need you to be in the vicinity, but likely that won't be necessary. Plan a full work day on Boxing Day."

They all stood. He motioned to Stonechild. "Can I see you a minute?"

She waited while the others spoke to Rouleau on their way back to their desks. He finished talking to Grayson and finally turned to her.

"I know this is a tough time of year to move towns, and now this case. I was thinking if you want a place to stay until you find an apartment, I have a big house with a spare room. It'll save you some money and give you a chance to find somewhere permanent." He saw surprise on her face and then hesitation as if she wasn't used to offers so freely given. She looked at him for a moment, weighing his offer.

She appeared on the brink of accepting when the openness in her eyes disappeared. "I'm okay where I am." She softened her words with a quick smile.

"Well, if you change your mind, here's my address and phone number. I'm in Kingston tomorrow for lunch but back by suppertime. You're welcome to come by any time if you change your mind."

She took the card and shoved it into her pocket. "Thank you, Sir."

"It's the least I can do. We've given you no time to get settled." He sensed that any more discussion on his offer would make her withdraw even further. "That was all," he said. "Check in later."

She made no move to leave. "Any word yet on Whelan's baby?" she asked.

"Nothing yet. The next few days are critical though."

"I hope it works out for them."

"I'll pass along your best wishes when I speak to him later this morning."

"Thanks."

He watched her join the others and then walked to his office. He'd done what he could to ease the guilt he felt for bringing her into this unit at Christmas time. It would be no big surprise if she headed home early in the new year. He could tell by the expression in her eyes that she'd already figured out the state of things. If he were in her position, he wouldn't be long leaving Ottawa either.

———

Kala shivered inside her leather jacket and leaned on the bell for a second time. She'd seen a curtain move inside the living-room window and wasn't going to leave until somebody answered the door. It took another three minutes but patience won out. The bald man in a tweed jacket and red ascot who slowly opened the door had rheumy eyes and no memory of who lived next door. She thanked him for his time and snapped her notebook shut as she strode over to Gage and Bennett on the sidewalk. Two hours of door-to-door and she'd come up with exactly nothing. It made her want to throw something.

The tips of Bennett's ears were cherry red and his moustache sparkled with white frost. "These people haven't got a clue who their neighbours are. God save us from people with money."

Kala shook her head. "One guy said if he wanted to know who lived next door, he'd move into a slum where they share diseases."

"The Christmas spirit kinda touches you right here, don't it?" said Gage, tapping his chest. "Wonder what it feels like to be this rich and able to tell everyone to take a piss."

"Damn satisfying, I imagine. There was one bit of information," said Bennet. He lowered his head to read from his notes. "Woman decked out in a gold lamé jumpsuit who lives across the street said she woke early the morning Underwood disappeared and is certain she saw him scraping ice off his windshield. Says it was around six thirty."

"It would have been black as pitch at that hour," said Kala. "How did she know it was him? Do you think she's reliable?"

"I'd say so. She got a look when he got into the car because the overhead light went on. Says it was definitely him."

"Did she see Laurel's car in the driveway?"

"No, just his. She said he was alone and drove off a few seconds later. Then she went for a shower and didn't see anything else."

"Well that's something at least. Establishes he left of his own accord. It would help to know where he was going so early in the morning since he never showed up at the office," said Kala.

"Did you check his phone messages and incoming calls?" asked Bennett.

Kala nodded. "He didn't have any incoming calls that morning on his cell or home phone. His daughter Geraldine called the night before the party, but nobody else." She began to shiver. "It's just past lunchtime and too cold to stand around here any longer, so why don't you both get home to your families and start enjoying the holiday? I'll go talk to the ex-wife's friend Susan Halliday on my way back to the station to file the report."

"You sure?" said Gage. "We can file if you like."

"It's okay," said Kala. "I've got nothing but time."

"Well, happy holidays," said Gage. "I expect I'll be getting a call to come back into the station just as I'm sitting down to a turkey dinner tomorrow."

"Criminals enjoy working through dinner hour," said Bennett.

"That'd change if they had to deal with my wife's anger when I get called into work. I haven't had one uninterrupted Christmas meal in five years."

Kala smiled. "Well, maybe this'll be your lucky year."

"Bloody unlikely, but thanks for holding out hope."

They separated and she got into the car she'd been assigned for the day. She jiggled the key in the ignition and turned the heater up high. She looked across the street to the Underwood front entrance. Still no sign of Underwood's wife and the little girl. For a woman who'd been so desperate to find her husband, their disappearance was odd. Worrisome, even.

She looked down the empty street toward the river. This would be a perfect morning to bundle up in her parka and Kodiaks and head for a tromp in the bush with Taiku. Last Christmas Eve they'd gone to the beach and walked its length while the sun rose above the churning waters of Lake Superior. Chunks of ice had been scattered like sculpture along the shoreline. She'd brought along her camera and taken pictures. One she'd even framed and put up in the office of her cabin. She closed her eyes and for a few seconds imagined herself there. The wind off the lake, miles of evergreens, and wild, haunting stillness. The smell of biting, cold air untouched by city traffic and the softness of Taiku's fur against her cheek as she squatted next to him to watch the sun's orange and pink fingers across the horizon.

Her lips parted in the beginnings of a smile. Three deep breaths and the tension left her shoulders and neck. When she opened her eyes again, the loneliness had lessened, tucked back into the well she carried deep inside. Her eyes surveyed the over-sized houses one last time as she set the car into drive and slowly pulled away from the curb.

13

THE MAN WHO led Kala inside the two-storey detached house on Eisenhower Crescent in Chapman Mills was not the husband Kala would have picked for Susan Halliday. He was younger, for one thing, and definitely military. Susan had struck her as artsy and bohemian. A quick inventory of his physical appearance included hair so sharp a person would cut their hand if they grazed a palm across the bristles, square shoulders, and a wide stance. He was Mr. Poster Boy for the armed forces. She'd felt like saluting when he opened the door.

She paused inside the doorway to the living room and looked around. French doors led into a room dominated by windows on the north wall and a ceiling-high stone fireplace on the wall facing her. A white leather couch and three mismatched chairs encircled a glass coffee table. A faded Oriental area rug lay in front of the couch with brass floor lamps flanking either side. It was a functional room, empty of clutter. It was a precisely ordered room.

Susan and Clinton lived in the same new subdivision as Pauline Underwood but several streets over in a slightly older home closer to a river. The houses on this street were spaced farther apart than those on Haileybury and had altogether a nicer feel.

"Susan will be down momentarily," Clinton said, directing her to the farthest chair near the windows. "Can I get you coffee, tea, or something stronger?"

"No, I'm fine thanks, but perhaps I could ask you a few questions while we wait for your wife."

"Certainly madam." He took a seat on the couch opposite her, his back rigid, arms folded across his chest.

Kala looked at him more closely. He couldn't be more than fifty with what she could see of his hair in the brown buzz cut. She guessed late-forties. Susan had to be the other side of fifty-five. His blue eyes held no softness. Muscular arms bulged out of the sleeves of his T-shirt that stretched tightly over his flat stomach. The guy was a weapon dressed up in a man's body. She shifted uncomfortably in what was surely the hardest chair in the room as his hard eyes flicked across her with just a trace of contempt. *He'd picked this seat for her on purpose.*

She took out her notepad and flipped to a clean page. "How well did you know Tom Underwood and his family?" She raised her eyes to meet his stare square on.

"I knew Tom through functions at his ex-wife's home. Susan and Pauline have been friends since high school. They both grew up in the west end of Ottawa. Bayshore, to be exact."

He'd managed to convey his distaste for her upbringing in the one word. Kala would ask around about Bayshore when she got back to the station.

"Do you know where Tom Underwood grew up?"

"He grew up in that neighbourhood. He and Pauline dated and married young."

"So they were childhood sweethearts."

"From what I understand."

"Did Tom visit Pauline often after they divorced?"

"I wouldn't know. I only met him at social functions, which usually involved their daughter Geraldine. Birthdays and the like. Susan would know more since she and Pauline are close as sisters." He looked toward the doorway. "I'm sorry my wife is taking so long. She hasn't been well this week. Some sort of flu that I've so far escaped."

"And where did you grow up?"

"Does that have any bearing?"

"Maybe not. I'm just gathering background information."

"Rockcliffe. My family was part owner of two pulp mills in the Gatineau. I went into the air force and have achieved the rank of major."

Kala jotted the details onto her notepad. She might not have heard of Bayshore but she had heard of Rockcliffe. It was the rich end of town where the prime minister and governor general lived.

They both turned as Susan walked into the room. Kala blinked. It was hard to believe this was the same rosy cheeked woman she'd seen only a few days before. Now, her skin was the colour of oatmeal and her eyes pools of exhaustion. She moved stiffly as if every bone in her body ached. When she stepped across the threshold, her eyes sought her husband's, before she looked toward Kala.

"I'm sorry to have kept you waiting. It took me a while to get dressed. Clinton?" She crossed the carpet toward her husband. "Did you offer our guest some coffee?"

"Of course. Sit here, Susan," he commanded as he stood to give her his seat. He remained standing at attention next to her.

Kala would have preferred to speak to Susan in private, but she could see he had no intention of leaving them alone, and she didn't have a good reason to ask him to leave. "I'm sorry you've been unwell. This shouldn't take long. I need to know where you both were last Thursday evening and Friday. This is just a routine question," she hastily added after Susan's face paled even more.

The major answered for both of them. "Susan was home and I was overnight in Trenton. Air force business. I got back mid-morning on the Friday."

"Did you meet anyone during that time, Susan?" Kala asked.

"No, I spent the night at home alone and did some Christmas baking in the morning before Clinton came home. I wanted to finish the shortbreads for a cookie exchange in the afternoon."

"What can you tell me about Pauline's relationship with her ex-husband?"

"With Tom?" Susan looked up at Clinton. "I'd say they were friendly but not true friends since their divorce. They knew each other a very long time. In fact, the three of us went to high school together. Pauline and I roomed together in university."

"Did Pauline forgive Tom for leaving the marriage?"

"I suppose. Pauline knew Tom wasn't happy with Laurel. I think she felt vindicated. Tom spent more time with Pauline this past year or so. I'd say their relationship had softened."

"Is there anything you can tell me about his relationship with his children?" Kala asked.

"Well, Geraldine and Tom were very close. She adored him and he couldn't say no to her. She was always awkward and self-conscious but Tom didn't see any of that. He was proud of her. He couldn't see how much pain she was in. The truth of it was that Geraldine had trouble making friends and was depressed all through her teen years." Susan's voice broke and she struggled to control her emotions. After a moment, she said, "I'm sorry. It's just been a shock. Tom and Hunter weren't close but it seems like they were starting to reconnect. We were hopeful, and now he's dead." Her voice trailed away.

"I know this is difficult," said Kala gently. "It might help if you could tell me why Tom and Hunter were at odds."

The major interrupted, "Again I must ask, is this of any value? A disagreement from so many years ago surely has no bearing on this case."

"I won't know that until all the facts are in," replied Kala. "The more I know, the better I can piece together what led to Mr. Underwood's death."

"I hate talking about them," said Susan with sudden vehemence. "It just feels like gossiping about something that happened a long time ago. I can't think that it will help find who killed Tom."

Clinton shifted his stance. "For Christ's sake, Susan, tell her. She's going to find out from someone."

Susan turned sideways to look at her husband before she glanced at Kala. Her eyes focused on a point above Kala's head. "You see, Hunter brought Laurel home from university to meet his family and Tom ... well, he slept with her. The dirty little secret is that Tom left his wife for their son's fiancée."

"The man had no sense of duty to his family. Some might say, his past trespasses came back and killed him. It was retribution," Clinton said.

"Really, Clinton, I don't think now is the time to start judging. What Tom did was a long time ago and everybody paid. Even Laurel."

A deep red suffused upward from his collar. "Why would you say Laurel paid? She married more money than she could ever spend and secured her fortune by giving birth to that kid Charlotte."

"Laurel was weak. She chose money over happiness with Hunter. In the end, her decision left everyone miserable. Now, if you'll excuse me, I'm still not well from the flu and really have to lie down. I should never have gotten out of bed."

"Of course," said Kala, standing at the same time as Susan. "I'm sorry to have come at such a bad time. If I have more questions, I'll phone or come by when you're feeling better." She dropped a card with her office phone number on the table, nodded in the major's direction before following Susan from the room.

Kala bent down to lace up her boots and watched Susan disappear up the stairwell, a feeling of excitement in the pit of her stomach. Susan's bombshell explained a lot about the tensions running through the Underwood family. It told a lot about Tom Underwood's character and the reason somebody might want him dead.

———

Susan Halliday woke from a dreamless sleep to a darkened bedroom. For a moment she couldn't remember where she was, but the confusion was fleeting. Lately, she was becoming more and more unsure of her surroundings upon wakening, often believing herself to be a young girl again in her parents' home. Once, she even thought her brother Roddy was sitting in the chair waiting for her, but it had been many years since they lived in the same house. She wondered if the confusion in her mind was a sign of things to come. Alzheimer's ran in her family and odds were not in her favour. So far she'd avoided speaking with her doctor about her vague symptoms. She was waiting for something more concrete before sharing her fears.

The bed springs creaked and her heart jumped. She kept her body still. She took a deep breath and turned her head toward her husband. He was a dark outline leaning against the headboard.

"Clinton. How long have you been sitting there?" she asked.

"Half an hour."

"I didn't hear you come in."

"I got lonely downstairs. It's Christmas Eve after all."

She heard him swallow and then ice cubes clink against glass. *Oh no. Keep him talking.* "I thought the officer was nice, considering why she came," she said. She turned on her side and propped herself up on the pillow, her head resting on her elbow so she could watch him.

He looked down at her. "You were home that night?"

"Of course. Why would you ask?"

"I called and you didn't answer the phone."

"What time was that? I was home all evening," she paused, "except when I went for a walk. But I wasn't gone long."

"Long enough. I tried calling for an hour and then gave up."

"I'm sorry, Clinton. If you'd said you planned to call, I would have waited at home."

He grunted and took another drink from his glass. She could smell rye from where she lay. His hand reached down and his fingers pulled a lock of her hair. She closed her eyes.

"I've got a present for you," he said. "Just a bit lower."

He tightened his hand in her hair and pulled her face toward his hip. Her cheek felt the skin of his leg and her mouth grazed his penis. She pulled away and pushed herself up with one hand until she was half-sitting.

"Clinton, I'm not feeling well. I'm not up for this tonight."

He laughed. "Well, I'm up for it. I'm sure you noticed." He laughed again. "It's your wifely duty to spread your legs more than once a month, or have you forgotten?"

"I just haven't been well this month. I need some time."

"And I need some ass."

He grabbed her head and pulled her level. His mouth found hers and he forced it open until his tongue filled her mouth. She tasted rye and garlic. She tried to push him away, but he had her against the headboard. His hand worked under her nightgown, snaking up her stomach and squeezing her nipples. The pain was sharp and tears started in the corners of her eyes. Still his mouth kept pummelling hers as his tongue darted in and out. He pulled away as suddenly and roughly pushed her lower in the bed. His breathing was raspy and excited. He forced her onto her side, her face away from him. She felt his erection pressing against her back.

"All I want is what you promised to give me when you signed the marriage contract," he said. "If you want it this way so you can pretend to be somewhere else, no fucking problem."

She felt the first thrust rip through her and couldn't stop the scream that rose up her throat. It excited him even more. His breath was hot in her ear.

"You like it rough," he whispered. "You like it this way, my little Suzy. Wake up little Suzy. Wake up my sweet … little … Suzy."

He flipped her onto her stomach and she bit with all her might into the pillow just as the full weight of him pushed deep inside her, again and again while she kept on screaming inside her head in a place so far down, nobody would ever hear.

14

Saturday, December 24, 5:40 p.m.

KALA FILED HER daily report late that afternoon before packing up her gear and heading downtown in her truck. She was becoming familiar with the rabbit warren of streets in the ByWard Market, but the Mission was just outside the core and close to Ottawa University. She easily found the three-storey, red brick building on Waller Street just before six o'clock. She followed an army of footprints up the snowy walkway to the front entrance. Red arrows posted on the walls led her to the packed hall.

The place was hopping.

Overhead speakers crooned Bing Crosby singing "Silent Night." His voice mixed with the noise made by the tables of street people and assisted living families who'd come in for turkey and mashed potatoes and pumpkin pie. She heard the clink of cutlery and plates being slid onto tables by volunteer servers, and people speaking in loud voices, trying to make themselves heard above each other. Cheap loops of silver tinsel hung from the ceiling. Multi-coloured lights flashed on a plastic Christmas tree near the washrooms. The room was as warm as a sweat lodge and steam blurred the inside of the windows. Moisture trickled down her back under her heavy parka.

She threaded her way through the long rows of tables and sea of people to the kitchen at the back. It took a few minutes to catch the attention of a large Black woman who looked to be in charge. She was dressed in a red skirt and shiny green blouse with a reindeer brooch pinned just below the collar. Rudolph's red nose flashed on and off like a turn signal. The woman held a clipboard and was directing volunteers with trays of food-laden plates.

"Yes, can I help you?" she asked, spotting Kala. Laugh lines creased around her eyes behind red-rimmed glasses.

"I phoned this morning about helping out. My name's Kala Stonechild."

The woman looked down at her clipboard. "Kala Stonechild. I was hoping you'd show up. A few of the volunteers are wanting to get home to their families. Welcome aboard. Take that apron over there and … you said you'd waited tables before? Then, that section by the door is all yours. This is the one day of the year our patrons don't have to line up for their food. If you have any questions, just ask. My name is Maya." She snapped her fingers in the direction of a heavily pierced girl with purple hair. "Tiffany! Show Kala here the ropes. She's going to help feed these hungry folks."

Tiffany smiled, said hello, and led Kala through the door into the kitchen. She set Kala up with a tray, notepad, and pen and showed her where to place orders and where to pick up the food. "You don't have to worry about clearing the tables," Tiffany said. "We have volunteers for that. If they finish eating, try to move them along to free up some tables. If we're lucky, we'll feed everybody by midnight. It's a madhouse this year."

"Everyone seems to be having a good time."

"Amazing, isn't it?" Tiffany laughed. "Even people with nothing can be happy at Christmas. Track me down if you need anything else." She waved and disappeared to deliver a tray of salads.

Kala looked around at the room of people and wondered what she'd gotten herself into. A few deep breaths and she headed to the first group of waiting people. Three tables later and she was in the thick of it. Taking orders. Back and forth from the kitchen with soup, salads, and plate after plate of turkey and dessert. Pouring coffee. Getting milk and juice for the kids. Everybody was in a good mood and laughter echoed off the corners of the room and down from the ceiling. After a while, she couldn't believe how much fun she was having.

She didn't forget the real reason she was spending her Christmas Eve working for the Mission. Every five minutes she scanned the room, looking for an Indigenous woman with a twelve-year-old daughter. Twice she thought she saw them, but both times she was disappointed.

People weren't coming into the hall as often now, and hadn't been for the past hour or so. She was finally able to manage her tables without rushing. It gave her time to notice how tired her legs and feet were feeling. She made one last trip to the kitchen for an order of turkey that she delivered to a table of three homeless men. She straightened from setting down the last plate and felt a tap on her shoulder. Turning, she found herself a foot away from Maya's beaming face.

"Well, now. You've done more than your fair share of serving people. It's starting to slow down. Time to have a plate of turkey and some pie and coffee," said Maya, taking her by the arm. "I've got it set up on the table over here. I could use a rest too."

"Now that you mention it, that pie does look good," said Kala. "I'm not hungry for turkey though. I ate earlier."

"It's fine pie. I baked them all myself."

They took seats across the table from each other. Kala added cream to her coffee and took a sip. She lifted her fork and took a bite of pumpkin pie. She rolled the filling around her tongue before swallowing. "Ah, I needed this. Thanks, Maya."

"You're welcome, girl. Now, tell me the story of what brought you to us on this fine Christmas Eve."

"What makes you think I have a story?"

"Everyone has a story. I've heard enough of them to fill a good number of books."

"I started a job here a few days ago. The reason I picked Ottawa was I got word my cousin was living here. I've been looking for her for a long time. We lost touch." She stopped talking and drank from her coffee cup. She looked up at the narrow window near the ceiling. "It's snowing again," she said.

Maya turned and lifted her head. She sighed. "Some folks'll be glad we're having a white Christmas. I'm not one of them." She turned back around. "So, you thought your cousin might be dropping in here for supper? It's a big city. We aren't the only place offering supper to people with no place to go."

"The address I had for her was downtown, near here, but she's moved on. I thought she might be in the same neighbourhood since her daughter's in school."

"That makes sense. How old is the daughter?"

"Twelve. Her name's Dawn and my cousin's name is Rosie. I'm wondering if you've seen them?"

Maya leaned her head sideways and studied Kala until she seemed satisfied. "A lot of people I see don't want to be found for one reason or another. Some are escaping their old lives that caused them pain. Some are sick or drinking too much and don't want anybody to see how far down they've fallen. If they change their minds, we do all we can to help them get back to their old lives, but that doesn't happen all that often. Sometimes we've had luck with teenagers, you know, getting them back to their families, but that's less often than you'd think. This Rosie girl, did she have it tough?"

"Yeah, she had it tough."

Maya's inky black eyes held Kala's so that she could not look away. "Looks like you might have had it tough too, child," she said softly.

"I'm doing okay."

Maya nodded. She chewed her pie while she considered the request. "A Native girl came in by herself when we first opened today. She looked to be around twelve. I went over to talk to her because it was so odd her being here all alone. She said her mom was too sick to come for supper, but she hoped she could bring some food home."

Kala's heart quickened. "Did she say where they were living?"

"No, but it had to be in the ByWard Market area somewhere. Somewhere nearby. We packed up two plates of food and sent her home with them."

"So close," murmured Kala. "I wonder if I could leave my phone number with you in case you see them again. It's really important that I find them." It was even more important if Rosie was too sick to come for dinner.

"You been looking a long time?"

"Yeah. A long time."

"I'll keep an eye out." Maya took the card Kala handed her and tucked it into her pocket. "I'll spread the word at the Ottawa Mission and see if I can find out anything for you."

"I'll be forever in your debt."

Kala walked out into the brisk winter night. She jogged back to her truck and started the engine while she scraped the snow off the windshield of her truck. Flakes sparkled like granulated sugar in the street light. She took a moment to watch their silent descent before tossing the scraper into the passenger seat and climbing in after it. The heater was on high but cold air was blasting into the cab. It would take a few more minutes to warm up. The street was all but deserted. She liked the calm of the night and the snow drifting down. What more did one need but a truck, homemade pie in the belly, and a warm bed waiting?

A man in a dark coat and Santa hat came out of a tavern and started walking toward her. He glanced in her direction as he passed her truck and nodded his head. His footprints left a crooked path through the snow.

You might have had it tough too.

Was her life's story written on her face or was Maya a witch who saw inside people's souls? Kala believed in a universe bigger than herself. Not in a god, exactly, but laws of nature that had to be respected. She thought that Maya might be more in tune with the rhythms of the land and water than most. In her home town, Maya would have been one of the Elders — one of the people in the community the others would go to for guidance.

I've seen things that no one should have to see. I've done things that I'm not proud of.

Images in her mind were coming back that she'd long closed away. It was this search for Rosie awakening past terrors. She didn't want to think about all the places she'd lived. The times she'd been scared and the reasons she lived alone. All the people she'd left behind.

You might have had it tough too.

The snow was coming down heavier. Flakes were sliding down the defrosting windshield while a coating of snow was piling on the hood of the truck. It felt safe in this wintery cocoon where sounds were muffled and the sharp bite of the wind was kept at bay.

She leaned back until her head was on the headrest and closed her eyes. It would be just fine to fall asleep like she'd done so many summers in her truck on summer canoe trips in the far North. Alone and safe with nobody knowing where she was. All alone, with Taiku, that is, with the exception of the summer before when Jordan had come with her. Two weeks canoeing the Fraser River as if they belonged together. Forgetting for fourteen days that he belonged to somebody else. She had nobody to blame now but herself for letting it go so far. She'd known better even as she kissed him back the first night they spent together after he'd told her that his marriage was over. She'd wanted so much to believe him that she'd ignored the warning signals going off in her head. *Stupid. Stupid.*

She forced her eyes open and pushed herself upright. This wasn't summer, and she wasn't alone on a bush road with nothing but wilderness stretched out in front of her. It was the middle of a big city in the middle of winter. If she didn't get moving soon, she'd have to get out and sweep the snow off the truck again. She checked the dark corners of the street one more time, put the truck into gear, and eased her way onto the road, thinking now only about laying her head on a pillow and closing her eyes for a night's sleep.

15

ROULEAU SAT ACROSS from his dad and watched him open the gifts he'd picked up the night before. The Brian McKillop biography of Pierre Burton was a stroke of genius and the book on North American birds received a fair bit of attention. His father opened the down comforter last.

"*Tiens, tiens,*" he said. "Now isn't this something?"

"Do you like it, Dad?"

"It'll keep me good and warm I should think. The apartment's been a bit drafty this winter."

Rouleau was pleased. It had taken him a long time to pick out the perfect duvet cover. His father never asked for anything but deserved everything. He always said the same thing before and after opening his gifts. "*Je suis un homme content.*" Rouleau automatically translated in his head, "I am a happy man."

The tradition was the same. After his father opened the gifts, they'd walk a block to his dad's favourite pub and have lunch. His dad would insist on buying both the turkey special and a bottle of burgundy. After the meal, they'd walk back to the apartment and a bottle of single malt would ceremoniously appear for a short tipple before

Jacques drove back to Ottawa in the late afternoon. The remainder of the bottle was his parting gift. Rouleau always locked it in the trunk of his car in case he got pulled over.

Today, as every Christmas Day, their lunch was served by Lottie McBride, owner and barkeep of the Bide a Wee Pub.

"Ye enjoyed the turkey, I see," she said before whisking away their empty plates. She returned with two bowls of trifle, coffee, and a plate of homemade shortbread cookies she baked for his father. Rouleau knew there'd be a full tin waiting for his dad on their way out the door.

Rouleau sat back and patted his stomach. He smiled at his dad. "You made a good choice of restaurant for once." The same joke every year. His father never considered going anywhere else. He looked down. "Your foot's more swollen, Dad. Are you in much pain?"

"Not really. They'll be operating in the spring."

"I'm glad. I'll get some time off and come stay with you."

"I don't want to be any trouble."

"No arguments, Dad."

"How are you doing, son? Last time you were down, you said you might have made a mistake taking that job. Do you still feel that way?"

"Most days. We have a murder case that's giving us some profile, but it'll likely be taken away after the holidays."

"You should find somewhere that makes you happy. Life's too short to have regrets."

"I wish it were that easy. How's your book coming? Do you still have your office at the university?"

His dad nodded. "They've even loaned me a research assistant. I've nearly completed the opening chapter. It's a fascinating subject, the making of the canal system. We've dug up some new material, if you excuse my pun. Even unearthed a murder to spice up the narrative."

"Solved?"

"No, unsolved. I hope you have better luck with yours."

"Solving this case could be the unit's only chance."

Lottie refilled their coffee cups, humming "Jingle Bells" under her breath while she swung the pot from Rouleau's cup to his father's. She patted his dad on the shoulder before slipping away.

His dad watched her go with a smile on his face. He sipped from his cup and set it down. "Frances came to see me." He paused and studied Rouleau from under his shaggy white eyebrows.

Rouleau was surprised at first but then not. Frances loved his dad and would have wanted to see him before she got too sick to make the trip. "Did she tell you …?"

His dad nodded. "How are you doing with this?"

"Not well. It'll be hard to imagine the time when she's not in this world."

"I know, but dying is part of life. I told her she should tell you that she was ill. I hope that was the right thing to say."

"Yes. We met a few days ago. I told her to marry Gordon."

"I'm sorry, son. That must have been difficult."

"The finality of her death is difficult. I already lost her to Gordon a long time ago."

———

He hugged his dad longer than usual before leaving to retrieve his car. His father stood in the doorway as he drove by, a tall man, stooped at the shoulders, with a shock of white hair and blue eyes that were brilliant still.

Rouleau waved and his father raised a hand before turning away.

The snow finally had stopped early morning and the roads were clear. Rouleau pushed in a Bonnie Raitt CD and set the cruise control. He settled back in the seat and let his mind wander. Traffic was light and he made good time, stopping once at a truck stop in Smiths Falls for coffee.

At close to four thirty he pulled into his driveway. The sun was already a silvery line on the horizon and his house a dark outline beyond the cedar hedge that cut across his property. Snow covered the bushes like a thick coating of frosting. It was good to be home.

He stepped out of his car and heard a door slam across the street. He turned his head and squinted through the darkness. A woman stopped to let a car pass by before running the distance to his driveway.

"Sir," she called, and he recognized Kala Stonechild. "I was going to wait ten more minutes and then leave. Good timing!"

He felt an unexpected lightness at the sight of her. "Kala," he said. "Merry Christmas."

She made it to where he stood and stopped in front of him. Her black hair was loose on her shoulders, making her look young and softening the angles of her face. "Merry Christmas, Sir. I want to run something by you about the murder if you've got a moment. I think it's important."

"Only if you come in for a drink and some supper. That's the deal."

She bowed her head. "Thank you, Sir."

"The other part of the deal is you call me Jacques, or Rouleau if you prefer. No more 'Sir.'"

He unlocked the side door and they stepped into the kitchen. He flicked on the light and was relieved to remember that he'd done up the dishes and taken out the garbage before leaving for Kingston. He took her coat and invited her to look around while he started cooking. "Maybe pick out some music. The record player is in the living room."

"You still play records?" she asked.

"I like the sound quality. I guess I'm a dinosaur."

"Not nearly as extinct though."

He could hear her walking around in the other room as he turned on the oven and started preparing the prime rib, rubbing a mixture of spices on the outside and spreading onions, potato wedges, and garlic in the pan. He was sliding the pan into the oven when Willie Nelson's voice poured through the speakers above the cupboards.

A few seconds later, Kala walked into the kitchen, a wide smile on her face. "Sorry I took so long. You must have five hundred albums. What a treasure trove! I think you have every Rolling Stones and Beatles album every made."

"I have five hundred and sixty-four albums to be exact, and those albums you mentioned are all first release." He gave the corkscrew a final push and the cork popped free. He held the bottle toward her. "Glass of wine?"

"I don't drink alcohol but please go ahead. Do you play any instruments?"

"Guitar. I used to be lead singer in a local band, but that is absolutely not to be repeated." He smiled. "The lads at the station would have a field day. How about some soda and orange juice?"

"Perfect. Thanks. So what was the name of your band?"

"You probably will wonder what we were thinking."

"Try me."

"The Gars."

"The Gars?"

"Short for Garçons. Two of us were French and we liked the fact that gars rhymed with cars, a band we modelled ourselves after." He finished mixing her drink and handed it to her. "Cheers."

"Did you sing as well?"

"I was lead singer more by default than anything, but that was all a very long time ago. Let's sit in the living room and talk about the case. I'll just pour myself a glass of wine and we're set."

They took seats across from each other, Kala on the couch and he in his favourite chair next to the fireplace. He set a match to the logs in the fireplace before sitting down. The wood was soon crackling and the smell of woodsmoke filled the room.

Kala lifted her eyes from the fire to his. "I wasn't looking forward to Christmas at all this year, but it's turned into a nice day after all. This is a comfortable room. It suits you."

"Thank you. I know the whole house needs a facelift, but maybe you're right. This old place does suit me." He smiled. "It's not a great time of year to move jobs. Do you know anybody in the city?"

"I'm tracking down an old friend."

"Well, it's nice to have you spend Christmas dinner with me. I had lunch with my father but he's a man of habit and can't be convinced to leave his home overnight."

"And your mother?"

"Ah, it's a long tale of love and sadness. Would you like to hear?"

"Only if you'd like to share it."

He didn't know if it was his recent visit with his father or the Christmas spirit, or Frances's heartbreaking news, but for the first time in a long time, he felt like talking. Kala was an intent listener and her eyes offered encouragement as he began his tale. He took a drink of wine and settled back against the cushions.

"My mother, whose last name I share, grew up in a little town on the Gaspé Peninsula. She spoke only French and was the apple of her parents' eyes, being the first born and having a gentle spirit. They had dreams of her becoming a nun, that is, until fate sent my father there for the summer to do some research. At the time, he was studying for his doctorate and specialized in Canadian history. Long story short, he met my mother walking on the bluffs near the sea and they fell in love. She was only sixteen.

"Her family didn't approve?"

"They didn't know. Marguerite, my mother, kept their relationship a secret. It was only after he returned to McGill in the fall that it became a secret she couldn't keep. She found out she was pregnant after he was gone. Her mother was devastated and her father ... well, let's say that it was just as well my father had returned to school."

"Your mother kept you?"

"She did, against the wishes of her family. In those days, it was a sin to have a child out of wedlock. The Catholic Church was the heart of the village and she'd broken the social order. My mother was very young, but she had a courageous heart."

"And your father?"

"He didn't forget my mother. The following summer he made the trip from Montreal to see her again. When he found out he had a son, he insisted on meeting her family. He wanted to marry her, but by then, she was just seventeen and her mother begged her to wait. My mother agreed because my father was on his way to France to carry out more research, and she was reluctant to leave her family and the village she'd known all her life. The plan was for him to return in the spring when they would wed."

"That must have been difficult. So much in love and so far apart."

"They wrote each other weekly and a few times he called. Over time, her mother softened to the idea of him and wedding plans began after Christmas. Tragically, my mother was struck by a car while out walking near dusk. It was a tourist passing through and unfamiliar with the roads. She died a few hours later."

"That is so sad."

"The entire village went into mourning. My father flew home and they waited for him before burying her. I was ten months old. He made an arrangement with my grandparents to let me stay with them while he finished school. He took me to Kingston when I was five and he was settled in the history department at Queen's University."

"And he's never left."

"No, he hasn't. He dedicated himself to raising me and to a life as an academic."

"Did he ever marry?"

"No. He never did. Now, what about you? Are you in the mood to tell your history?"

"My story isn't nearly as romantic."

"That's okay."

She stared into the fire. "Both of my parents spent time in residential schools from age six to fourteen. If you know anything about that period, the federal government in its great wisdom travelled far and wide to scoop up Indigenous children as young as six and placed them in boarding schools far from their homes. Many of the children died of tuberculosis in the schools or were abused in one fashion or another. They could go years without seeing their parents or families. The idea was to take the Indian out of the child, and the nuns and priests took their jobs seriously. The children weren't allowed to speak their native language or practise their culture. When my parents returned home, it wasn't long before both were alcoholics with no parenting skills to speak of. I was taken from them when I was three because of neglect. From there, I spent time in a succession of foster homes until I graduated from high school. I got a scholarship and went into policing." She looked at him and shrugged. "End of story."

"Do you know what happened to your parents?" he asked.

"Both died. I went in search of them one summer, and that's how I found out. I was fifteen years old."

"I'm sorry."

"It was a long time ago." Her black eyes focused on his. Whatever she'd been thinking about had been put away, like shutters sliding into place. "Perhaps we can talk about the case now, before supper."

He nodded. "Tell me what you've got," he said.

She leaned forward. "A neighbour saw Tom Underwood in his driveway around six thirty the morning he went missing. I dropped in on Susan Halliday and met her military husband, Clinton. Susan told me the reason Hunter and his father hadn't been on speaking terms for so many years, and it's a bit mind-blowing. It seems Hunter brought his fiancée Laurel home to meet the family, and his father decided to have her instead."

"You mean, Hunter's stepmother was supposed to marry him?"

"Exactly. If that's not a reason to murder, I don't know what is." Her voice rose slightly, the only way he knew she believed this was the key. She'd been so sure she had something, she hadn't waited until the next day to tell him. He tried to fit it in with what he knew. It didn't add up. Not yet anyway.

"That happened several years ago. Why would Hunter resort to violence now?"

"He and his father had just started speaking. It was a change in pattern."

"Agreed, but one might say a positive change. I know this family is neck deep in dysfunction, but we also have to consider Underwood's business dealings. Malik tells me there may have been some iffy transactions. He and Grayson are tracking down the man Underwood was making a deal with this week."

Her eyes lost some of their brilliance. "Are you saying his murder was a business deal gone bad?"

"All paths are still open. You've got a good lead here and I think you need to keep digging around his family. I'll have Malik and Grayson work the business angle. I think we're going to find it was somebody he knew and maybe trusted. Perhaps it was somebody who gains from his death financially."

"Laurel?"

"She's one to consider. Belliveau, his business partner, is another."

Rouleau's cellphone rang in his pocket. He took it out and held it to his ear. "Rouleau," he said. He listened and asked a few questions as Kala turned away from him to stare into the fire.

"Some good news," he said, putting the phone on the table. "That was Whelan. His son is out of intensive care and responding well to the antibiotics."

"Thank God," said Kala.

"Yeah, thank God. The other good news is that he checked his voice mail and found two messages he'd missed from Laurel Underwood from a few days ago. She was leaving town with her daughter to get away from the empty house and we were to call her if we found out anything. She phoned in to the switchboard and they sent her calls right to Whelan's voice mail."

"What were the odds of that happening?" asked Kala.

"At this time of year? Pretty good. Staff takes a lot of holidays and there isn't a lot of consistency on the front desk."

"Did she say when she'd be back in town?"

"Christmas afternoon, if we didn't contact her beforehand. She left a phone number in Quebec. Are you up for a visit before dinner? We have another hour and a bit before the roast is cooked."

Kala was already on her feet. "I'll bet she doesn't know that he's dead yet."

"This will be a horrible day to find out," said Rouleau.

16

GERALDINE SAT IN the car next to Max and stared out the window, imagining the happy families grouped around Christmas trees, kids playing with their new toys, and parents sipping red wine while Christmas songs played on the stereo. There'd be the smell of turkey that had cooked all day in the oven and a fire in the grate. Everyone behind the closed curtains would be having a happier time than she was having, that was for damn sure.

Max fiddled with the radio dial again, flipping through stations until he found one that played country music. He turned up the volume.

"I like this song," he said.

It was about a woman who caught her man cheating and destroyed his car. Carrie Underwood. Now there was a woman who wouldn't put up with a husband like Max.

Geraldine turned her head and looked at him. He was wearing a long black coat and mustard-coloured striped scarf like he was a GQ model. She used to like how he dressed. She thought he had style. Now she knew the clothes were just show. She waited for the song to end and reached over to turn down the volume. Max's eyes flicked across at her, but he didn't say anything. She settled back in the seat, uncomfortable with the way the baby was lying inside her stomach. A little body part, likely a foot, was pushing her stomach from within like a butterfly trapped inside. She patted the bump gently through her fur coat, then roused herself to make a comment.

"I was surprised Mom still wanted to cook a big meal with everything going on."

"Hunter didn't eat much supper. That's not like him," Max replied.

"It wasn't because of a guilty conscience if that's what you're implying."

"If you say so. Nobody mentioned your father once. Don't you find that odd?"

"We don't need to. He's everywhere I look."

Max took one hand off the wheel and reached over to touch her belly. "You have to stay calm for the baby. Try not to think about it too much."

She nodded, but didn't say anything. His unexpected show of tenderness had made her throat fill up with sobs that she would not let escape. She looked out her window again and was startled to see they'd turned the corner onto their street. A familiar black car was parked next to the curb across from their house. She squinted through the glass and turned to glare at Max. "You didn't tell me J.P. and Benny were coming over."

"I invited them for a Christmas drink. I didn't think you'd mind since you're always in bed by eight."

"Shouldn't the two of them be home with their families? This is supposed to be the one day of the year when families spend time together."

Max's voice took on the impatient note he was using more and more. "Come on, Geraldine. We've been working hard to pick up the pieces. Your father's death left a big hole and we're leaning on each other. It's a time people want to be together. Besides, if Christmas is just for families, what were Susan and Clinton doing at your mother's?"

"They are like family." She refused to let him sidetrack her. "I never got the feeling J.P. even liked Dad ... or you, for that matter."

"He's a means to an end. With your father gone, I have to keep on his good side so he keeps me in the business. You must get that?"

"Maybe you should get out of that business. I think it's what led to my father's murder. He was very unhappy lately."

"J.P. asked me to take over the deal your father was working on. When I get this inventor to sign, it's going to mean a huge bonus for us. It also might make me partner if I play this right."

Anger pulsed like an infusion of cold water through her veins. "You've wasted no time benefiting from my father's death. How long have the three of you been cooking this up?"

"I won't dignify that with an answer," Max said coldly. He pulled the car into the driveway and turned off the ignition. His face was half in shadow when he turned to her. "I've cooked nothing up with J.P. and Benny and would appreciate you keeping these accusations to yourself. You're distraught and hormonal and you're not thinking straight. Your father's death was tragic, but I have a window of opportunity here that I'm taking for you and the baby. This is about our future. Now, I'd appreciate it if you could be civil before you make your excuses and head off to bed. We have business to discuss and I don't need you there messing it up."

"Fine." She grabbed the door handle and gave it a wrench so that the door swung open. She faced him before she started the task of moving her bulk out of the seat. "But if I find any one of you had anything to do with my father's death, I will *not* remain silent. You can count on that when you're adding up how much money you're going to make off his murder."

———

"That's odd," said Kala. She turned and looked through the car back window at the green Jeep they'd just passed. She'd spotted it under a street light.

Rouleau glanced in the rear-view mirror. "What's odd? Should I go back?"

She glanced at him. "I've seen that Jeep recently." She ran scenes through her mind. "Hunter Underwood. Why wouldn't he park in Laurel's driveway if he came to visit her?"

"And what would make him visit her in the first place?" asked Rouleau. "If he really has come to see her, he's parked three blocks away. Most curious. You have keen eyes, Stonechild."

"Thanks."

Rouleau turned the corner onto Winding Way. A black Mercedes was parked halfway up her driveway. A thin layer of snow coated the roof and windows. He pulled in behind it and turned off the engine. "I don't think we'll be breaking the news of her husband's death if Hunter got here first. By the look of her car, she's been home a while."

"Too bad," said Stonechild. "I wanted to watch her reaction."

She and Rouleau followed a set of men's footsteps toward the front door. "Her company hasn't been here long though," observed Rouleau. "Snow would have filled in these prints. It started up again an hour ago."

He rang the doorbell and stepped back.

Laurel opened the door with the chimes still reverberating down the hallway. She was dressed completely in black, her red hair curled in long tendrils to her shoulders and her violet eyes red from weeping. Hunter stood next to her in the hallway, his duffle coat buttoned and gloves on his hands. He looked past Rouleau and found Kala's eyes. His were apologetic.

Laurel took a step closer to be directly in front of Rouleau. "How could you not have told me?" Her voice choked with anger. Kala thought the suffering in her face genuine. "I said if *anything* came up. *Anything!* I think my husband's murder would have been a no-brainer. All you had to do was call me. I was just a phone call away. You just had to call." Her voice trailed away to a whimper. Her eyes brimmed with tears. Hunter laid a hand on her back. She turned and collapsed against him, but only for a moment. When she turned to face them, her face was resigned. "I suppose if we need to talk, we can do it in the kitchen." She started down the hallway, not waiting for Rouleau to respond.

"Would you like me to stay?" asked Hunter.

Rouleau nodded before he bent down to slip off his boots. "I think that would be best." He started after Laurel while Hunter remained behind.

Kala looked up at him from where she'd leaned against the wall to pull off a boot. "Do you stop by often?" she asked quietly.

Red diffused upward from his collar. "No, but I've been checking because somebody had to tell her. Nobody else in the family would have made the call. I thought it would be a kindness if she heard about her husband's murder in person."

"Your sister wouldn't tell her?"

"Geraldine? Not bloody likely." His voice was as low as hers. The conversation felt too close and intimate. His eyes burned into hers as if he was trying to convince her that he was telling the truth. She swayed and he reached out and steadied her as she wobbled on one foot. His touch was unexpected. She pulled her arm away but not before his eyes looked hard into her own. She averted her eyes from his and took a step backward. She was uncomfortably aware of his closeness. He smelled of the outdoors and woodsmoke.

She followed him into the kitchen. Two glasses were on the table, one empty and one newly filled with amber liquid. Laurel lifted it to her lips. "Cheers," she said to nobody in particular. Hunter put the empty glass on the counter and sat in the chair closest to Laurel. He rested a hand on her wrist as if to calm her.

Rouleau glanced up at Kala and then back to Laurel. "Unfortunately, your messages went through to the voice mail of an officer who's been on sick leave," he said. "We've been by your home and called your phone numbers several times. We didn't find out until now that you'd left another number. We had no idea where you'd gone."

"But I phoned twice. Both times the officer who answered sent me through to the voice mail. I thought ... I thought my husband might join us if I was where we were supposed to be. We'd booked the chalet and I was hoping he would come to me. If he was in trouble, he would reach me there."

"Where is the chalet?"

"Mount Tremblant. Several hours from here."

"Didn't you have your cellphone with you?" asked Kala. "You gave us the number when we were last here. We called numerous times but it was turned off."

Laurel nodded. "After I left the number at the chalet, I turned off my phone. Charlotte and I only left the chalet to go for walks and I thought you would call me at the number I left twice on that voice mail."

"For which we sincerely apologize," said Rouleau.

Laurel turned toward Hunter, who had sat without moving through the exchange. "I just can't believe it. Who would kill Tom?"

"So you hadn't heard from your husband since you reported him missing," said Rouleau. It was a statement, not a question. "Do you have any idea at all who would have wanted to harm him?"

Laurel shook her head. Her eyes were closed and tears seeped from under her eyelids.

Hunter slid his hand down to cover one of her hands with his own. He turned to look at Rouleau. "I couldn't say either."

"What time did you arrive today?" Rouleau asked Hunter.

"A half hour or so before you."

"How did you know Laurel would be home?"

Hunter shrugged. "It was a guess. I was in town anyway and decided to take a chance. Nothing more covert, I'm afraid."

"But you parked three blocks away," said Kala. "Why?"

Hunter turned his gaze back to her. His half smile revealed nothing. "I felt like a walk in the snow. I'd been sitting a long time and wanted some exercise."

Laurel hit the table with the palm of her hand and they all looked at her. "All these intrusive questions when you should be out looking for who murdered my husband. Hunter had nothing to do with it and neither did I. I demand that you stop harassing us and find the person who did this!"

Kala glanced at Rouleau. He looked regretful but unmoved at the same time. She imagined it was an expression that served him well in other investigations. When he spoke, his tone was measured.

"We're only doing our job, madam. I'm sorry if you find the questions objectionable, but don't forget that your answers can serve to remove you as suspects. We only go where the evidence leads us, but to do that we must ask questions. I know your husband's death has come as a shock, but I assure you that we are doing everything possible to bring whoever is responsible to justice, including asking questions of everyone who knew him."

Laurel's shoulders slumped and she lowered her head so that a tumble of red hair covered her eyes. "I'm sorry," she said. "I just feel so ... devastated."

Kala studied her. Her submissive reaction struck a false note, but if Rouleau felt the same way, she couldn't tell.

He stood. We'd like to search your husband's home office and bedroom if you would be so kind. I have officers who will be looking for anything at all that will let us know who your husband was meeting the morning he disappeared.

Laurel raised her eyes. "I looked everywhere when he didn't come home but didn't find anything. I don't think you'll find anything either."

"But we will look. The team will be here within the half hour. We'll leave no stone unturned. Of this you can be assured." He motioned to Kala. "Perhaps you could show Officer Stonechild the library while she waits for the other officers to arrive."

Kala watched Laurel look at Hunter through the veil of hair that shielded her face. Whatever passed between them must have satisfied her because she nodded her head in his direction before standing.

"I'll do all it takes, to punish Tom's killer," she said. "If you need to camp out in our house and go through every goddamn piece of paper, you're welcome to it."

17

Monday, December 26, 11:35 a.m.

GERALDINE SPENT BOXING Day morning rattling around her empty house. When they'd gotten out of bed around seven, Max had made scrambled eggs, bacon, and toast for breakfast before saying that he'd put in a few hours at the office and be home mid-afternoon. She hadn't argued with him. In fact, she was glad to be alone.

All morning she'd tried to push away the grief and ignore the bottles of wine hidden in the upstairs cupboard — bottles that had started out as symbols of her inner strength that could quickly become her downfall. The baby was restless inside her, rolling and shifting position, trying to get comfortable, as if commiserating with her anguish. She'd spent an hour in the nursery rocking in the old oak rocker that had been her grandmother's. She'd been surprised to feel dampness on her collar, not aware of the tears rolling down her cheeks. At noon, she remembered that she hadn't eaten much of the breakfast Max made. She'd felt nauseous for the first time in ages when she first got out of bed, and the smell of frying bacon had made it worse. But now she was hungry.

She made her way into the kitchen and stood leaning into the fridge, feeling her stomach roll at the sight of bottles of gherkin pickles, mayonnaise, and defrosting chicken, pooling pinkish blood on a white dinner plate. Her eyes skimmed over the containers of yogourt and cottage cheese, apples and carrots. Healthy food that Max insisted she eat. He'd cleaned out the ice cream and Fudgsicles from the freezer. There was no point even opening *that* door. Nothing in the fridge appealed to her. She was ready to give up and check out the pantry when she spied an unopened brick of cheese under the carton of eggs. Cheese was something she might be able to keep down.

She cut thick slabs of bread and slathered butter on both sides. Then she sliced off wide pieces of cheese that she carefully arranged to cover the bread without overlapping. She set the sandwich into the melted butter in a frying pan she'd set on medium heat. When the bread was golden brown and the cheese oozing out the sides, she flipped the sandwich onto her plate and sat at the kitchen table, taking small bites and sipping on a glass of milk while she looked out the patio door.

The lilac trees were dressed in a coating of snow that sparkled in the brilliant sunshine. Two chickadees played on the railing of the deck, landing and taking off and sending sprays of snow into the air. She didn't know when blue sky had replaced the grey clouds, but the sudden brightness was a welcome relief. It felt like the snow had been coming down forever.

She set the second half of her sandwich onto the plate and pushed it away. She thought about taking a nap, but a nap would take her upstairs to the bottles she'd hidden in the cupboard. So far she'd managed not to give in to the need for a drink, but today she felt closer to the edge than ever before. She closed her eyes and imagined unscrewing one of the bottles and lifting it to her lips. The wine would be sunshine warm but tart like apples and sweet like peaches. She circled her tongue across her lips as if licking stray drops. *What could it hurt, really?* The baby was nearly formed. She'd allow herself one swallow ... just one little taste to slack her thirst ... and that was when she opened her eyes and cut off the daydream. The truth was that she would never stop at one swallow, or even one bottle. The urge to drink and drink until she filled the gaping hole inside of herself was like a monster begging to be fed. Once she started, she wouldn't be able to stop. She knew this with the certainty of her whole being. She looked down and patted her stomach. "You owe me big time, little one," she said. "Let's get our big ugly coat on and go visit Grandma."

Her mother was unexpectedly home. Pauline hugged Geraldine and helped her out of her winter coat, then sat her in a chair while she bent down to pull off her boots. She looked up at her daughter from where she knelt on the rug.

"Your feet are swollen. I hope you've been resting enough."

"I do nothing but rest. A month to go and it feels like an eternity."

"Enjoy these last days to yourself. It'll change very soon. Come, prop yourself up on the couch and I'll brew a pot of decaffeinated coffee. Are you hungry?"

"Not really, unless you have cake." Geraldine imagined Max's disapproving face and added, "With ice cream would be nice." She was tough all right, defying Max when he was nowhere in sight. "I'm okay to sit at the kitchen table." She followed her mom and gingerly lowered her bulk onto a chair while Pauline brewed coffee and cut a thick slice of gingerbread.

"I hope this cake and chocolate ice cream will do. It's all I have left from Christmas dinner." Pauline set the plate in front of Geraldine. "Cream in your coffee?"

"Mmm," said Geraldine.

Pauline returned with two mugs and sat down across from her. "Aren't you eating?" asked Geraldine.

Pauline shook her head and sipped from her mug. "I … ate earlier." She avoided meeting Geraldine's eyes.

Geraldine looked more closely at her mother. She'd turned into the workout queen in recent years but had appeared to be keeping her exercise sessions under control. If she'd gone off food again, they'd have to convince her to go talk to somebody. After their dad left, she'd been diagnosed as obsessive compulsive and had been in counselling up until a few years ago. Before that, she'd spent most of the day cleaning the house, but when that ended she had declared herself cured. Her cheeks were looking more gaunt than normal. Geraldine didn't remember her mother eating much at Christmas. She sighed. One more thing to worry about.

Geraldine ate the dessert slowly while she thought about how to bring up the subject of her father. Her mother hadn't said anything at all about his death, and that wasn't healthy. In fact, it was damn strange. She tuned in to her mother's monologue.

"So, I spent yesterday afternoon at Holt Renfrew looking for something decent to wear for New Year's. I finally found the perfect pant suit. It's silk and a winter white with silver beading. They're taking in the sleeves and waist. I pick it up tomorrow." Pauline turned her head toward the front door. "Was that the doorbell?"

"Yes," said Geraldine. "Were you expecting company?"

"No." Pauline stood but made no move toward the door.

"Should I get it?" asked Geraldine.

"If you wouldn't mind. I have to go to the washroom."

Geraldine pushed away her plate and got to her feet. So much for the motherly concern about her swollen ankles. She reached the door as someone banged the knocker hard three times. When she pushed the door open, Susan Halliday was standing on the landing. Without saying a word, Susan took Geraldine into her arms and hugged her gently before stepping inside. Susan linked her arm through Geraldine's as they started back toward the kitchen.

"I hope you aren't missing your dad too much," Susan said.

"I'm okay. You look tired though."

"I've had the flu but am definitely on the mend." Susan's voice was drained of energy and Geraldine wondered if she really was better.

"Mom's just gone upstairs for a minute. I'll get you some coffee."

"You sit," said Susan. "I can get my own cup."

Susan slid into the seat next to Geraldine after filling a mug from the cupboard. "This has been such a sad time with your father's death. How are you doing *really*?"

"Not so good." Geraldine took a deep breath. "I just can't believe he's gone, and what makes it worse is that Mom's acting like nothing happened. She won't even mention his name."

"Oh, dear," said Susan. "It sounds like she's taking it hard."

"Really? It seems to me that she's put it out of her mind completely."

"Your mother has a difficult time with loss. She's grieving in her own way."

"You're probably right. My only experience was when Dad left, and that was horrible. She pretended like he'd never existed, hosting parties and happy all the time. We didn't dare mention his name or let on that we missed him."

"She was trying to keep everything normal for you. It was very draining for her to put up that front."

"I guess. Maybe I should be more understanding. Has Clinton gone back to the base?"

"Yes. He left at lunchtime. He'll be back before New Year's." She chewed on her bottom lip. "He'll have the whole week off."

"Are you going to the same party as Mom?"

"At the Hunt Club, yes, with the same old crowd. I'm not in a party mood, but Clinton insists I keep busy."

"He's probably right."

Susan covered Geraldine's hand with her own. "I really am sorry about your dad. We'll miss him."

"Mom was happier lately ... you know, before this happened. She told me last week that Dad would probably be leaving Laurel soon and she seemed ... hopeful. I think she believed they stood a chance of getting back together. You're probably right about her grieving, but maybe she's just in denial. I'm worried about when she crashes."

Susan stood and turned to look out the window. When she turned back, her eyes were wet. "Don't worry, Geraldine. I'll be here for your mom. We've been friends a long, long time, and I won't let her go through this alone. I'm here for you too."

Geraldine stood and they hugged. She stepped back and said, "I wonder who told Laurel about Dad. I keep thinking that she won't be all that devastated by his death."

"Probably the police. She'll be planning his funeral I expect."

"The funeral. Damn. Will you go?"

"Of course. We should all go."

Geraldine glanced toward the door. "I'm not sure about my mother. It'll be awkward."

Susan lowered her voice. "Do you have any idea who could have murdered your father?"

Geraldine shook her head. "My first ugly thought was Laurel, but that might just be because I never liked her. Although I have to say, that for Laurel, killing Dad might have been easier than divorcing him."

Her first guilty thought had actually been Laurel and Hunter, but she pushed that idea as deep into her subconscious as she could. The Hunter she knew would not be capable. It was lunacy to even think it.

She paused, "My other fear is that it was someone Dad dealt with in his business. He told me once that he didn't like a lot of the people he negotiated with, and he'd become evasive lately. He was making deals with the military and an inventor in Montreal. I got the feeling this latest deal wasn't sitting easily with him."

"Did you tell this to the police?"

"They haven't asked me yet. I'm just not sure what was bothering him. Maybe it had nothing to do with work at all. What if I implicate somebody and they're innocent?"

"I think it's somebody from his business dealings. I can't truly believe any one of his family or friends capable of such a cold-blooded act."

Geraldine nodded. "Any of us except Laurel ... well, and maybe J.P. The man is slime. Oh yes, there's also Benny. The way he looks at me sometimes when he's visiting Max gives me the creeps."

Susan shuddered. "I never liked J.P. either. I have no real opinion about Benny one way or the other. I don't think he and I have ever had a full-length conversation." She paused. "I think your father was getting ready to leave the partnership. I'm not sure who else he told."

Geraldine looked away. Had Max known? He'd been acting strangely of late. She'd put it down to the baby, but maybe he'd been plotting to move up in the firm. If it was anything more than that, if he'd actually taken steps to hurt her father, she didn't know how she would do it, but if it took the rest of her life, she'd make Max pay.

18

Monday, December 26, 8:30 a.m.

KALA HAD FOUND it difficult to fall asleep. Her legs were aching and it was hard to get comfortable on the narrow bed. She remembered looking at the clock at three a.m. but must have fallen asleep soon afterwards because the next time she opened her eyes the room had lightened. She lay for a moment, trying to orient herself to her surroundings. Noise in the hall must have woken her because she heard something thumping against the wall and a man's voice. She sighed and rolled over to face the clock. Eight thirty. *No!*

She leapt out of bed and grabbed her towel and soap on her way to the communal showers. Luckily there was nobody in sight, and she showered in five minutes flat. She raced back to her room where she braided her hair and scrambled into clean black slacks and a wrinkled white blouse. She gave up trying to smooth out the creases by covering the blouse with a black pullover. There was no time to eat. She took the stairs to the lobby and jogged east the few blocks to the police station to pick up her truck. First, she'd check in with Rouleau.

One glance around the empty office and she cursed under her breath. She could hear the rise and fall of male voices and saw the team through the partially closed door of Rouleau's office. She shrugged out of her jacket, grabbed her notebook and a pen, and tried to slip in unnoticed. An unlikely feat. Malik looked up at her and smiled. Grayson was reading aloud from his notes while Rouleau was half-turned in his chair, looking out the window. Gage and Bennett, both in navy uniform, stood next to each other leaning against filing cabinets. They'd left a chair vacant for her and she nodded at them as she sat down.

Grayson lowered his notebook. "So we're done going through his office. Whoever he was meeting the morning he died wasn't recorded anywhere we can find."

"Phone records?" asked Rouleau.

"He called his wife Laurel around three the day before he went missing and she called him back on his cell. There was a call to his daughter Geraldine two days before. The other calls that week were work-related. He was dealing with an engineer named Pierre Archambault in Montreal. There were four calls, two in and two out, with Archambault. We followed up and he was in Montreal at the time of the murder. He was expecting Underwood to fax a contract the afternoon he went missing. It didn't arrive, obviously."

"What did you find out about that?"

"J.P. and Underwood own two munitions factories under the name Integrated Industries, one outside Ottawa and one in New Brunswick. They build heavy artillery and sell to the Americans and our armed forces. The deal in the works with Archambault was for the design of a vehicle that could withstand running over a land mine."

"Why were they contracting out research? Don't they have their own engineers on staff?" Rouleau asked.

Grayson nodded. "I thought of that too. Archambault designed a prototype but doesn't have the capital or resources to test and mass produce. He approached Belliveau initially. The deal was for financial backing and production if the prototype turned out to be as good as Archambault claimed. Underwood and Belliveau were gambling but they had to move fast. If the prototype turned out a dud, they still owed Archambault half a million just for sewing up exclusive rights. A company in the U.S. was interested, so they had to convince Archambault not to go looking farther afield for a better deal."

"Where was Belliveau in all this?"

"He set everything up. Word around the office was that Underwood wasn't thrilled with the deal because they could lose half a million and he wasn't convinced Archambault had invented anything extraordinary. Underwood wanted more time to test the product, but the Americans were willing to invest based on the specs. Since Underwood was the company's closer, he had to carry the ball and get the contract signed."

"Was Underwood right to be cautious?"

Grayson shrugged. "J.P. admitted that Underwood thought they should stick to research and design in-house and not gamble on an unknown. J.P. also said Underwood had changed lately. He didn't have the drive he once had. Said it worried him. I set up an appointment with Archambault at noon at his Montreal office."

Rouleau looked at Kala. "Malik will be checking out a lead on the missing homeless woman Annie Littlewolf. How's your French?"

"*Je parle*," she answered. "I spent a few years fully immersed."

"Good. You can go with Grayson."

"I can handle this alone. No need for two of us to go all that way." Grayson said.

Rouleau fixed his eyes on Grayson. "Stonechild has had the most dealing with the family. It's time she branched into the business end of his life so she can help us put the pieces together."

Kala listened uncomfortably to the exchange. What Rouleau said made sense but he wasn't making her any friends. Malik shifted in his chair and caught her glance. He seemed to be sending her a warning.

Rouleau looked around. "So what's everyone waiting for? You know what you have to do."

"Right, Sir," said Kala. She stood with the others and walked out of the room ahead of Malik. Grayson stayed behind.

Malik caught up to her as she was putting on her coat. "Rouleau asked me to give you this information on Archambault." He handed over a thick file. "I wrote a one-pager on top with the highlights."

"Thanks."

Grayson passed them with his head down, heading in a straight line to his desk. He dropped into his chair and picked up the phone, punched in a number, and swivelled the chair so his back was to the room. Malik followed the direction of Kala's gaze.

"He's a good detective but doesn't share well. Don't let him get to you."

She turned toward Malik to respond but he was already on the way back to his desk. "Great," she said to herself before she sat down and opened up the file.

She willed Grayson to get off the phone soon so they could get this trip over with. The two-and-a-half-hour drive to Montreal would eat up the day, but if they got back in time she could make another visit to the ByWard Market. The feeling she was running out of time was becoming so strong that it was all she could do not to just chuck this job and spend all her waking hours looking for her cousin. Yet a feeling of dread wasn't a good enough reason to let Rouleau down. She felt like she owed him something and the feeling didn't sit well. She never liked to be in debt to anyone — or attached either, but his sadness was a magnet. She could see the loss in his eyes when he thought nobody was looking.

—

Susan left Geraldine and Pauline after two cups of coffee and three homemade sugar cookies. It was the first food she'd eaten since Clinton made her poached eggs and toast the evening before. Her strength was returning but still fragile, feeling as if a good wind would blow her away.

She walked through the blocks of houses back toward her home, passing her street to reach the Jock River, a smaller river that fed into the Rideau. She started down the pathway that split off from the road, careful to set her feet in tracks made by others ahead of her.

She loved this city with its three major waterways, web of bike paths, and unexpected forests. During the coming summer, she'd walk the length of the canal, taking time to sit under her favourite oak tree at Dow's Lake before climbing the hill to the Central Experimental Farm. She'd linger in the gardens and sit on the stone bench by the shallow rectangular pool, watching the plump goldfish pass lazily through the veil of tangled plants. The police said they'd found Tom there. Not by the pond but close by in the visitor parking lot, hidden in the trunk of his car. She couldn't let the image take shape in her mind. The strength in his hands, the mind that never stopped, the energy that verged on hyperactive — she still couldn't believe the essence of him had been extinguished. Surely, he was just taking a break from the world and would call her one day when he was ready.

She let her feet take her down the slippery incline, the path trampled by cross-country skiers and dog walkers. Clouds were moving in fast, already hiding the sun. The shadows turned the river dark and dangerous. Farther out, she saw breaks in the ice where the current churned without end. She stood well back on the path, watching the shifting ice and bluish shadows in crevices of ice and snow.

She thought back to the first time she'd seen Tom Underwood. She'd been in grade nine, new to the west end neighbourhood. Her older sister Rhonda let her tag along to the Britannia Theatre to see a matinee. It was an Elvis Presley movie and she'd begged to be allowed to go. They'd only lived in their townhouse a few weeks but Rhonda already had a circle of friends and seemed to know everybody in the new school. She was outgoing and popular while Susan was ill at ease with people. She always thought they were judging her and seeing the flaws she saw in herself.

They'd paid for their tickets and walked into the lobby, a cavernous, noisy room decorated in red and purple with giant movie posters covering the walls. Tom was there with two other boys who walked over to say hello to Rhonda. He'd stood out from the others, even then. Black hair and blue eyes that saw everything, and a self-assured swagger that let you know he was going places. She'd felt something inside shift when she'd looked at him. It was a dazzling lightness in her chest that she'd never experienced before. The intensity of her feelings frightened her, but in a good way. He'd barely looked in her direction, but she couldn't take her eyes off him. She'd watched the back of his head three rows in front for the entire movie.

The boys had left while she waited for Rhonda outside the washroom. It wasn't until they were walking home that she'd asked Rhonda who he was.

"Tom Underwood. He's in my math class," Rhonda had said. "He thinks he's really something."

"Maybe he is," Susan had said without thinking.

Rhonda had stopped walking to stare at her. "He's not the kind of guy you should go for. He's too good looking and self-centred to be true."

"As if he'd ever look at me twice." She said it to keep Rhonda from guessing her true feelings.

Weeks sped by. She made friends with Pauline Green. They were both on the girls' volleyball team and walked home after practice together. They both liked sports, weren't doing well in school, and both wanted to be movie stars. Susan couldn't believe someone as popular and pretty as Pauline Green would want to be her friend. Up until then, she'd only been allowed on the fringes of the in crowd — not a full fledged member, but not one of the complete losers either. Pauline liked having her around for reasons known only to Pauline.

The first dance of the year was being put on by student council. It was the week before Halloween. Susan shyly told Pauline that she liked a boy in her sister's class and he'd probably be at the dance.

"What's his name?" asked Pauline. She was tall and slim with large breasts and dark hair that she wore long and straight.

"Tom Underwood," said Susan. Just saying his name made her feel hot and flushed. She immediately regretted sharing the name that made her heart beat fast; the face she saw just before falling asleep.

"I know Tom," said Pauline, linking her arm through Susan's. "I'll introduce you."

Susan hadn't known Pauline well enough to be wary.

She wasn't able to sleep the night before the dance. She kept running over and over in her mind what she would say when Pauline introduced her to Tom. She felt like she was going to meet her destiny.

The gods must have been laughing up their sleeves.

Pauline told her a month later on the way home from school that she and Tom started seeing each other the weekend before the dance. They'd met in the parking lot of Dunkin' Donuts on Carling Avenue, and he'd told her she was the sweetest thing he'd ever seen. She got into his car and they drove around until he found a dark spot in the empty Carlingwood Mall parking lot. They'd made out in the back of his car. She'd kept it secret until then to spare Susan's feelings. She was sure Susan would have forgotten about him right after the dance. She hadn't meant it to go like that, but Susan hadn't even met Tom so it wasn't like he was hers to steal.

Susan shivered inside her winter coat. Flakes of snow were drifting down from the sky. She lifted her face and closed her eyes. The cold was good on her cheeks and forehead. She still felt feverish from the flu. Her stomach hurt and she was tired. Perhaps she should have taken the car to visit Pauline. The walk suddenly seemed like more effort than she had to expend. She turned to walk back up the slope to the road, hunched over like an old woman. The walk home would take her twenty minutes. She'd reward herself with a soak in the tub before taking a nap. She'd wake up in time to wait for Clinton to call, as she did every night when he was away.

19

ARCHAMBAULT WAS TALL, stooped at the shoulders, and filled with apologies for keeping them waiting. He said he'd been stuck in traffic driving in from the west end. His entire family had gathered for Boxing Day lunch, and it had been hard to get away. They sat in his office on the third floor of a white stucco building on the outskirts of downtown Montreal. Kala could see the four-lane highway from his window. The sound of traffic was a constant low hum, rising up from the snow-covered pavement.

Grayson asked the questions while Kala took notes. She watched Archambault's eyes for signs that he was lying. He fidgeted with a pen that he sucked on between responses. He'd chosen to sit behind his desk as if he needed a physical barrier to separate them.

Grayson's face was skeptical and his voice held an undertone of disbelief that grew with each response. Kala wasn't sure if this was his interview style or if he was letting his annoyance at having her along show through. Whatever it was, he wasn't helping her figure out Archambault, who was growing increasingly on edge.

"This firm isn't in the armoury business," he repeated. "We build bridges and infrastructure. I worked on the design for the armoured car in my spare time. The study of war is my hobby. I became curious about a better way to protect our men and women in war zones. Most of those killed or maimed have run over land mines or homemade bombs. It seemed like a good idea to come up with something that would give them better protection, a chance to survive in one piece. I've been working on a design with the latest materials for three years. I used a recently invented product in the chassis but structured it in a new way. Then I went on to design the undercarriage and the body. I built a small prototype in my garage and ran tests." He leaned forward in his effort to convince them. "It looks very promising. Exciting, truly."

"How did you end up dealing with Tom Underwood?"

"It was through his partner, J.P. Belliveau. I approached Belliveau with my idea after I had it patented. He came to Montreal and we met. I'd researched their company and knew they supplied the armed forces with vehicles. Belliveau said he was going to get Underwood to set up the deal. He said this vehicle, if it was as good as I said it was, would make us all very rich."

Archambault kept adding facts to what he'd told them before. Kala jotted down the latest pearl.

"Was Underwood as convinced that this would make them rich?" Grayson leaned back in his chair as if he was listening to the biggest tall tale ever told.

Archambault's face paled. He looked toward Kala, his eyes begging for support. "Underwood was crunching numbers. I believe he arrived at the same conclusion as Belliveau. This was going to make us all some serious dough."

"You believe or you know?"

"I know. I'm sure. The contract was to come through that day. The day Underwood died."

"The day he was *murdered*," said Grayson.

"I had nothing to do with that. Why would I kill the man who was going to make me rich? I needed him."

"Maybe he saw through your design. Maybe he was going to scrap the whole deal and you couldn't handle that."

Archambault shook his head. "No. That's not how it was. Underwood had come around to believing in my product. He reviewed my credentials, all my material, the tests, everything. He knew my prototype could withstand a roadside bomb."

"Where were you the week before Christmas?"

"I was right here, in Montreal, when he was killed. I haven't been to Ottawa since last summer. You have to believe me. This is a good product. It will do what I designed it to do. Belliveau already was speaking to the brass at the Department of National Defence. They were *very* interested. We're all going to become wealthy men once this deal gets completed. It's a virtual certainty. I spent that day by the fax machine, waiting for the contract, but it never arrived."

———

"So you think he's responsible?" asked Grayson as they drove across a bridge on their way back to Ottawa.

Kala thought for a moment. "No, I don't think he had anything to do with it. He has no motive that I can see."

Grayson nodded as if in agreement.

"Unless …" Kala let the word tail away. She was thinking about all the money Archambault was so certain would come his way.

"Unless what?"

"Unless Underwood had found out something that could sink the deal. Was the contract ready to send?"

"Yeah. It was standard except for the clause about paying Archambault half a million for exclusive rights even if it tanked. No pun intended." He smiled at her, relaxed and confident. The charm had returned.

"What do you think of J.P. Belliveau?" she asked.

"Kind of a slippery character. Loud suits, big mouth. I think he's involved in the murder. He probably set it up."

"The problem with this case is that there are too many suspects. The murders I've dealt with before were clear cut: a jealous spouse or a bar fight gone too far. Underwood had several people in his private and professional life who could have been behind this."

"My money's on a business associate," said Grayson. "The kind of murder, stuffing him in the trunk of his car, that speaks mob to me."

"I'm not willing to bet yet," replied Kala. "But I do think it was someone close to him. Somebody he trusted."

"Not a paid hit?"

"No. I think he knew his killer."

"I wouldn't bet on that," said Grayson. "It looked impersonal to me, but maybe I just don't want to believe that a friend or family member could leave their loved one in the trunk of a car to freeze to death. Call me an optimist, but this is Ottawa, not a big American city where violence is a way of life."

Kala kept her eyes straight ahead. Grayson had grown up in the protected white, middle-class world. He had no idea the cruelties loved ones could inflict upon each other. What strangers could do to children. The violence a person could do if pushed.

"So what are you going to tell Rouleau?" she asked.

"That Archambault was nervous and hiding something. We need to look more closely at Belliveau."

She knew there was no point arguing with him. He might be right in the end, but her instincts told her they were missing something. The family had too much anger and too many secrets that began and ended with Tom Underwood.

———

Rouleau spread the crime scene photos of Underwood and the Central Experimental Farm parking area on his desk — various angles of Underwood lying in a fetal position in the trunk, his cheek resting on the carpet, his eyes open and staring. He'd filled the space inside the trunk without much room to spare. Somebody had stuffed him in, slammed and locked the trunk, and left him to die. What kind of person could do that? Whoever they were was cool enough to then drive him to the Central Experimental Farm and walk away. What kind of terror had Underwood felt when he regained consciousness and realized he was trapped and going to die? How long had it taken for his core body temperature to drop from mild to severe hypothermia ... for the extreme pain and shivering to give way to numbness, and his heart to slow to the point that oxygen stopped reaching his brain? He would have hallucinated at the end. If he'd had room in the trunk, he would have clawed off his clothes as his body raged with the feeling of burning up, the final paradoxical stage before death. Rouleau studied the waxy pallor of Underwood's skin. Hopefully the DNA tests would come up with something. They needed a break.

Rouleau raised his eyes and looked through his office window. Grayson and Stonechild were coming in separately, neither smiling or looking at the other. Stonechild took off her parka and wiped off a dusting of snow before she sat down and began typing at her computer, her eyes fixed on the screen in front of her. Grayson stopped at Malik's desk and the two men laughed about something. Grayson gestured toward Rouleau's office, then walked over to the coffee machine and filled a cup before ambling over.

"Well?" Rouleau asked. "How did it go with Archambault?"

"I think we're narrowing in on motive. The deal was going to be worth a lot of money. Either Underwood was going to upset the plans and Archambault put out a hit, or Belliveau wanted rid of Underwood so as not to have to share the profits. Archambault knew more than he was telling. I'll get the guys digging deeper on the paper trail on both ends. I'd also like to bring Belliveau in for more questioning."

"What does Stonechild think?"

"She hasn't come up with anything else. She's doing up the report now on Archambault."

"Okay then. Arrange an interview for first thing tomorrow."

"Will do. Any word from Whelan?"

"His baby is doing better. He'll be back just after New Year's."

"Good." Grayson turned to leave but stopped and looked back at Rouleau. He seemed reluctant to talk but then said, "I think Stonechild could use a partner. She needs a more experienced detective to guide her, help her to put the clues together."

"She's not connecting the dots?"

"I'd have to say no. I think she has potential, but she's in a bit over her head when it comes to interviewing and reading people. I wasn't going to say anything, but thought you should know."

"Okay, leave it with me."

Rouleau turned the words over in his mind. It was bad timing that Whelan had to take leave just when they were thrust into this case. It was hard on the team and hard on Stonechild. Whelan would be back in a few days and Stonechild would settle back into a secondary role. He liked her and didn't want to set her up to fail. Her inexperience in Homicide had been his one worry and he wasn't surprised Grayson had picked up on it. They'd just have to get by as things were for now.

20

ROULEAU LEFT FOR home before Kala finished typing her report. He told her just to file the report electronically in the records system and he'd read it after supper. Grayson and Malik soon followed, leaving her alone.

She looked up as they were getting their coats on and assured them that she wouldn't be far behind. She tucked her head back down so they wouldn't read her lie. She had no intention of leaving until she'd finished the work she'd laid out for herself. She'd already resumed typing before the door shut behind them and she didn't look up until she'd gotten through transcribing her notes. She kept the report factual, not forming conclusions as Grayson would have her do. Her name would be on the report, not his, and she wouldn't put her name to a theory she didn't believe … yet. She was deliberately ignoring Grayson's instruction to point the investigation in one direction. *Hell, let him write his own report,* she thought.

Once done, she saved the file, then poured a cup of coffee one step removed from sludge. After a few sips she accessed the system and opened the folder of reports submitted by Malik and Grayson over the course of the week.

She was looking for inconsistencies in statements, time-lines, and alibis. She occasionally jotted a note for follow-up on her notepad. Nothing jumped out except a feeling of unease at Laurel's disappearance just before Christmas. The tingling grew as she remembered Hunter arriving at Laurel's house just after she came home, his Jeep parked a good distance away. Tom Underwood had stolen Laurel from Hunter, but Tom and Laurel had slept in separate bedrooms. Their betrayal could be nothing. It could be everything.

Kala closed the folder and stretched. It was close to nine o'clock and her stomach was rumbling with hunger, but she wasn't done yet. She liked the silence of the office. Being alone was when she felt most comfortable. It was sad that Whelan's kid was sick, but she was just as happy not to have a partner. She'd always worked alone up North. Her favourite time was the night shift, driving the back roads with the moon and stars the only light in the ink black sky. She could deal with wolves and bears but this city might be another matter. The wild life here wore pants and drove fancy cars. The rabid ones weren't as easy to spot.

She searched through the records system until she found the file on the man who was groping women in apartment lobbies. She shared Rouleau's concern that this guy was escalating. They'd been pulled off the case, but somebody had to follow up. It might as well be her. She didn't have any family waiting for her to come home from work. This would keep her mind busy. It would also be a nice Christmas present for Rouleau if she broke the case.

She leaned in to read through every incident report and made notes as she went. She paid careful attention to the pattern of buildings where each attack took place He'd only ventured out of the Lincoln Fields area once and that had been the first time when he'd picked a high-rise tower near the Ottawa River. It must have been out of his comfort zone because ever since, he'd targeted women in high-rises along the Richmond Road corridor behind Lincoln Fields Shopping Centre. She was certain he lived between the two sectors, probably closer to the river where he'd made his first strike. He picked middle-aged women alone, grabbing them from behind. One woman said he'd wrenched her breast hard and left bruising. Two said that he'd called them a bitch and two said he muttered the word cunt in their ear before shoving them into the wall. For the latest victim Glenda Martin, he'd figured out how to grope and strangle at the same time. She was the only one he'd attacked early afternoon. The rest had been closer to suppertime. Everything that she read confirmed that Rouleau was right to be worried.

She closed the file. If the groper's pattern was predictable, he'd be grabbing another woman soon, maybe by the weekend, probably late in the day when the sun was beginning to set. She bit her lip and thought over what she should do. The perp was getting bolder and more violent. The next woman he grabbed might not be as lucky as the others.

She did a Google search and clicked on a map of Ottawa's west end on the computer screen and enlarged the area where the attacks had taken place. Then she hit print and crossed the room to pick up the copy to take back to her desk. She numbered each location with a red felt-tipped pen in the order they occurred and studied the results, tracing her finger along the route. He was working his way east and she could see a pocket of high-rises not far from his last outing. She jotted down the addresses in her notebook. The neighbourhood was unfamiliar to her but she would swing by and scout out the street and pick up some supper. She'd have to work quickly if she was to have a chance of catching him.

———

Richmond Road was an assortment of shops, restaurants, and condominiums in the area called Westboro Village. Heading west, the apartment buildings got older and higher. She knew the Ottawa River was somewhere to the north, not many blocks away. There were stretches of parkland, a large field, and tree-lined bike paths. If she was going to stay in Ottawa, she might look for an apartment in this neighbourhood. She slowed as she neared the high-rises behind Lincoln Fields Shopping Centre, scouting the streets and peering into lobbies. It was a quiet evening, not many people about, the snow beginning to fall like confetti tossed out of a shaker. There was no sign of a man dressed in black or anyone acting suspiciously. She spotted a pizza take-out restaurant and pulled into the recently plowed lot. The kid behind the counter sold her two slices of deluxe that she ate as she continued her drive east on Byron and south on Churchill to the Queensway. It was the quickest route back downtown.

The ByWard Market was becoming familiar to her now. She made another sweep of the side streets, looking down alleyways and checking intersections, but it was a quiet night in the city's downtown. A few people were walking, snow glistening from their coats in the street lights. She stared into the corners of buildings but couldn't find any Indigenous women or young girls who met the description of her cousin and niece. She checked the time on the radio. It was just past eleven and time to call it a night. She was tired and badly needed a few hours of sleep so she'd have a clear head when she began more Underwood interviews in the morning, starting with a visit to Hunter's property.

———

Kala put in an appearance at the station before her trip to Hunter's. Rouleau had been called to a meeting with Vermette and cancelled their morning brainstorming session. She poured herself a cup of coffee and asked Bennett if he'd seen Malik and Grayson. Bennett was busy reading through emails they'd confiscated from Underwood's computer. He shook his head but said, "They're bringing Belliveau in for questioning. I'll be going through his correspondence with my fine-toothed comb next."

"So are Underwood's business dealings the focus?" she asked, already knowing the answer.

"Looks that way for now. Gage went with the others to start looking through files."

"I'll be on my own today."

"I'd say so."

"No problem." She zipped up her parka. "I'm going to start at Hunter Underwood's place and will be back in town before lunch. I can always be reached on my cell."

Bennett nodded. "I'll tell the others to call you if they need anything."

"I'm sure they won't, but thanks."

She drove slowly out of the city toward Hunter's. The temperature had dropped steadily overnight and a frosty haze hung suspended over the fields like white smoke. The sky above the mist was pastel blue and cloudless. She felt herself relaxing the farther she got from the high-rises and shopping centres. Trees wrapped in ice and stretches of snowy flat land replaced the horizontal line of buildings on each side of the highway.

Hunter's turn off arrived too soon for her liking and she slowed the truck even more as she left the highway. Her eyes swept the road ahead. There wasn't much traffic this time of day heading east. Most cars were heading downtown. The schools were out and many had taken holidays between Christmas and New Year's. Today was also a stat holiday since Christmas had fallen on a Sunday.

A few miles farther on and she reached the junction that led her to Hunter's road. It was a narrower country road, not as well plowed as the highway or secondary road. The truck tires gripped without problem. She carefully pulled closer to the side of the road as a delivery truck flew past coming the other way. "Idiot," she said under her breath. She could see the turn off to Hunter's driveway up ahead.

A black Mercedes was just pulling out from Hunter's side road. As Kala watched, the car turned in a tight arc onto the road ahead of her, facing in her direction. She leaned forward to get a glimpse at the driver through the sun reflecting off the windshield. It wasn't until the car was alongside that she recognized the tumbling red hair and slender profile of Laurel Underwood. She passed by without glancing in Kala's direction.

The plot thickens. Kala craned her neck to follow the Mercedes until it was out of sight. It was curious how two people who said they had nothing to do with each other kept being caught in each other's company.

Kala parked in the same spot as her first visit. She could see the tire tracks from Laurel's Mercedes and her boot prints to and from the front door. Laurel couldn't have been there overnight or the prints would have been filled from the snowfall that ended early morning. Kala followed her own frosty breath up the walkway.

Hunter opened the door almost immediately. "Did you forget …?" he began, but stopped when he saw Kala standing in front of him. "Oh, it's you." He recovered quickly and stepped aside. "Come in out of the cold." He checked the parking area as he moved behind her to shut the door.

"Sorry to bother you so early," she said. "I just have a few more questions."

"Would you like coffee?" he asked.

She could smell coffee brewing and was suddenly thirsty for a cup. "Please," she said slipping out of her boots. She undid her parka as she followed him into the kitchen.

"I'll make a fresh pot. This one's been stewing for a while." He patted Fabio behind the ears on his way to the stove. The dog was lying near the hot air vent. He got up and stretched and made his way to Kala. She reached down scratched him behind the ears. Fabio thumped his tail against the table leg before retreating to the warmth of his corner.

She took a seat and watched Hunter pour water from a jug into a kettle. He measured coffee grounds into a filter that fit into a clear coffee pot on the stove. Then he poured milk from a carton into a small pitcher and set it on the table with teaspoons and mugs. His fingers were long and his hands strong and tanned. When the water boiled, he poured it carefully through the filter. The coffee dripped steaming dark and rich into the waiting pot.

"You're a coffee purist," Kala said. "I make it the same way at home."

"Anything worth having is worth extra care," he said, with his piercing grey eyes that had turned a charcoal shade in the kitchen light.

She smiled. Surely he didn't think she was that easily taken in by charm. She looked down and busied herself by taking out a notebook and pen while he poured the coffee into their mugs. She had to admit it smelled as good as she made at home. She set her notepad on her knee and added milk.

He watched her while she took a sip and smiled at her expression. "Good?"

"Wonderful." She set the mug down and picked up her notepad. "I want to get a better understanding of your father and his relationships with family members and colleagues. It's come to our attention that you were engaged to Laurel before she married your father." She paused and waited.

Something changed in his eyes. It was a flash of pain that crystallized into something unreadable. "I wondered how long it would take you to dig that up. Did my mother tell you?"

"The person who told me isn't important."

"I guess you're right." He sighed and stretched out his legs, then took a drink of coffee all the while watching her. "I met Laurel at university. She worked in the admin office. I thought I'd never seen a woman so beautiful but I didn't think about approaching her. I was a few years younger and she was out of my league. She actually introduced herself to me at the university pub one evening and we hit it off. I asked her out the next day, and we dated my senior year. I brought her home in the summer to meet my family after we got engaged. My father offered her a job, which she took. A few months later, she called off our engagement for no reason that I could understand. I found out why a few months later when she moved in with my father, who'd not so coincidently moved out of our family home into an apartment downtown."

"Do you blame Laurel for ending your parents' marriage?" Kala was still fishing for a reaction. He'd told the story as if it was about somebody else.

"I've thought about it recently with my father coming around to see me and asking to make amends. I think if it hadn't been for Laurel, he would still be married to my mother, or if he hadn't died that is. Laurel was the catalyst."

"So your mother and father had a good relationship before Laurel?"

"I'd say yes. They were comfortable with each other and always said they were in it for the long haul. They'd been together since high school."

"You must have taken Laurel's defection hard."

"I distanced myself from her and my father and soon got over it. I was blinded by her but came to realize that we didn't have anything in common. It wouldn't have been a good marriage."

"You say that like you're certain."

"Because I am. Laurel definitely is not my soul mate." He looked directly into her eyes. "You know how it is when you meet somebody and know right away that you fit? There's just something about them that feels like coming home. It wasn't that way with me and Laurel. I was infatuated and mistook it for something deeper."

Kala broke his stare and looked past him out the window. The depth of his gaze was disconcerting. Maybe he'd meant it to be. "Your mother and Geraldine. How did they take your father marrying Laurel?"

"About as you'd expect. My mother was a wreck for a few years. I think in hindsight that she had a breakdown, but we didn't recognize it then. She started seeing a counsellor and that helped her to recover her equilibrium. It also helped that Geraldine and I sided with her, and of course her best friend Susan was always there. Geraldine forgave our father after a little time passed and they've stayed close. He was excited that she was having a baby." Hunter smiled and spread his hands wide, "I didn't want to hear about my father at all, but Geraldine wouldn't give up. She kept telling me things and it got so I looked forward to her updates. When Dad asked to see me at the beginning of the month, I was ready to see him. More coffee?"

Kala looked down at her empty cup. "No, I need to get moving." She began packing up her notebook and began to stand. She stopped partway and sat back down as if she'd thought of one last question. It was the question she'd wanted to ask all along. "What was Laurel doing here this morning?"

Hunter grimaced. "I thought you might have seen her leaving."

"I'm finding it odd that I keep finding the two of you together."

Hunter stood up and crossed to the stove to refill his coffee cup. With his back to her, he said, "I didn't conspire with Laurel to kill my father. She drove here to tell me that there wasn't going to be a service. Dad wanted to be cremated with just his family to accompany his ashes to the vault. She wants me to organize Geraldine and Max, my mother, and Susan and Clinton."

"She could have phoned."

"Anybody who knows me knows that I rarely answer. I like my solitude."

His explanation was weak, just like the one about parking his Jeep far away from Laurel's driveway. Kala got up and walked to the front door. She bent to put on her boots and he stood leaning against the wall. When she straightened, Hunter was next to her. He waited until she was looking at him.

"I'm not involved with Laurel. If you start thinking that he was murdered because we wanted to get rid of him so we could be together, you are going entirely in the wrong direction."

Kala zipped up her jacket and opened the door. She turned to him before she stepped outside. "Perhaps you weren't involved, but I've only known you a little while and I have the impression that something is going on between you two. I wonder how many others thought the same, even if it's not true as you allege."

———

Rouleau looked across the table at J.P. Belliveau. His face was a purplish-red in the glaring fluorescent light of the interview room. He'd refused coffee or water and at the moment was glaring at Grayson, who was tinkering with the recording device in preparation for the interview. Rouleau leaned back in his chair and looked at the ceiling. This was Grayson's show.

"Let's begin," said Grayson. He leaned into the microphone and named the people in the room, date, and time. Malik sat next to him ready to play good cop if needed. "How long were you and Tom Underwood business partners?"

"Going on twenty-five years. We built the business together. If I'd wanted to off him, I wouldn't have waited so long."

"For the record, we're not suggesting you killed him at this time."

"Good to know." J.P.'s eyes let them know he didn't believe it.

"What was Underwood working on when he died?"

"He was setting up a contract with an engineer in Montreal to test a design with an eye to manufacturing a vehicle that could withstand land mines. He was getting the contract ready to send the day he died."

"Who takes over the file?"

J.P.'s eyes narrowed. "Max Oliver. He's leaving for Montreal as I speak to reassure the client and work on getting the contract signed. You can't seriously think Max or I had anything to do with this. We needed Tom. He was our closer."

"So you keep saying, but it looks like you've managed to carry on without him." Grayson paused and looked down at his notes. "Did you know that Tom Underwood was planning on getting out of the business?"

"Who told you that?" J.P. looked at Grayson, but when he didn't respond, J.P. shrugged. "Tom mentioned a few times over the past year that he was tired and considering a career change. The problem was he had an expensive young wife and kid to worry about and a certain lifestyle to maintain. I don't know where else he'd make the kind of money he was making in our firm. He wasn't serious."

"What would have happened if he was?" Rouleau interjected.

J.P. took his time answering. "From what I know about Laurel, she might have taken the kid and left him. She'd fight him for a big chunk of change. He couldn't afford that drop in fortune."

"That doesn't say much for his marriage," said Rouleau.

J.P. let out a harsh laugh. "Anybody with eyes could see that she was just sticking around for the money. He had a lawyer come by to discuss a separation. His concern was having the kid half-time."

"You know this for a fact?" Grayson asked.

"Yeah. I was there a few weeks ago when this woman in a fancy suit showed up asking for Mr. Underwood. I told her that he got called away and asked if I could help. She asked that he call her to set up another time later in the afternoon because she had to be in court. She left her card. It said 'Sandra Woosley, divorce lawyer,' plain as day. I asked Tom about it when I passed on the message and he said he was investigating his options."

"You never mentioned this before."

"You never accused me of killing my partner before."

"For the record, we have not accused you of killing any-one. So that would fit in with Tom deciding to leave the business," said Grayson. "Ditch his wife and make a lifestyle change."

"You might think so," agreed J.P., "except that after Tom spoke to the lawyer, we went out for a beer and he told me that he'd decided to get a few things in order before he made a move. He told me the best thing he could do was hire a hit man and be done with her. He said it all jokey like, but with everything that's happened, I wonder if she got to the hit man first."

21

KALA TOOK ROULEAU'S phone call on her way back into the city. She was to interview Geraldine in Kanata before coming into the station. She pulled over and took down the address and directions.

"I know it's a stat holiday so take the rest of the afternoon off," Rouleau said before hanging up. "Fill in your reports tomorrow."

"Yes, Sir," she answered into the dial tone.

She merged onto the Queensway and continued past downtown taking the split toward Kanata. She took the March Road exit and turned left on Campeau Drive and right on Knudson, past the Kanata Golf and Country Club to Goulding Crescent — a road that circled around eight large detached houses with tiny front yards and garages sticking out toward the street like eyesores.

She found the house number and pulled into the empty driveway. It looked like nobody was home, but she rang the bell a few times anyway before returning to her truck. She drummed her fingers on the steering wheel and thought about her next move. It was a long way to head back downtown and return. Better to grab some lunch and try again in an hour or so.

She backtracked to Campeau Drive and followed it south until it crossed another major road. It didn't take her long to find a commercial area and a diner that was open on the holiday. She was one of five customers.

She took a table near the window and ordered coffee and the full breakfast special. While she waited for her food to arrive, she pulled out a file she'd been keeping on the investigation. She jotted down notes about her encounter with Hunter. The fried eggs, hash browns, sausage, and toast arrived before she'd gotten through the first paragraph. She loaded the food with ketchup and ate quickly, cleaning her plate with the last of the toast. The waitress returned to clear her plate and Kala asked for a coffee refill. There was lots of time to finish her notes and to reread Hunter's previous interview before she set out to try his sister again. She'd give Geraldine an hour at least to return home from wherever she'd gone. In all likelihood, there was a family gathering somewhere and she'd have to wait until the next day to see Geraldine, but she'd give it one last try.

When she returned to Goulding Crescent, a van was parked in Geraldine's driveway. Kala left her truck on the street and walked toward the house. She peeled off a glove and felt the hood of the van. It was still warm from its trip home.

Geraldine took a while to answer the door, but Kala could see that Geraldine recognized her.

"Sorry to bother you on a holiday, but I wonder if you have a few minutes to talk?" She took a step back as Geraldine swung the door open further. "I guess you know by now that I'm with the police."

"Sure, why not? Come on in."

"Is your husband at home?" Kala asked before stooping to pull off her boots.

"No, Max is working."

They sat in the family room off the kitchen. Geraldine offered tea but Kala declined. She'd drunk enough coffee at the diner to keep her buzzing the rest of the day.

"This is a nice room," said Kala, looking around. The mid-afternoon sun warmed the wood panelling around the fireplace and gave the Persian carpet a golden hue. They sat on a leather couch with aqua satin cushions.

Geraldine's eyes swept around the room and back to Kala. "This is where I do all my thinking. I'd light a fire, but the wood is in the basement and it would take a while."

"Don't trouble yourself," said Kala. "Are you up to telling me what you know about the evening of the party?" She took out her notebook and pen. She added, "I know this has been difficult for you."

Geraldine wrapped both arms around her bulging stomach. "It's been a nightmare. I'll tell you what I know though. I want you to find who did this and send them away forever."

"How did you father appear the last time you saw him?"

"My father hadn't seemed like himself for a few months. He was distracted and unhappy with work. He'd become distant."

"Do you have any idea what was bothering him?"

Geraldine shook her head. "Perhaps the contract he was working on. The rest, I shouldn't say."

"The rest?"

"Well, I have no proof."

"It's okay to share your thoughts with me. They could give me avenues to pursue."

Geraldine squirmed in her seat, trying to get comfortable. She hesitated before saying, "My father wanted out of his marriage with Laurel. He'd known for some time that it was a mistake."

"Did he tell you this?"

"About a month ago, he told me that he wished he could go back and redo some of the decisions he'd made. He didn't say his marriage exactly, but I know it's what he meant."

"How can you be certain?"

"Afterwards, he said that regardless of his bad decisions, he wouldn't change Charlotte's birth for anything. It wasn't a day or two later that he went to visit Hunter. I know he was also seeing my mother more often. She ... seemed hopeful that they would be back together."

"Even after all this time?"

"She never stopped thinking of him as her husband. They were high school sweethearts and more suited than he and Laurel could ever be."

"What about his business? Did he get along with his partner?"

"J.P.? I couldn't say."

"Your husband Max has taken over your dad's files."

"So he tells me."

"How long has Max worked at your father's company?"

Geraldine's eyes slid away from Kala's. "Right after university. About six years. Benny Goldstone was a friend of his from university and Max eventually brought him into the company as his assistant."

"Did Max and your father get along?"

"To be honest, I don't think my father thought Max was the right man for me. Dad tried to get along with him though because he loved me and wanted ..." Geraldine's voice broke and she lowered her head. "I'm sorry. This is just so difficult. The doctor told me not to get upset because of the baby. I'm trying to stop thinking about how my dad died."

"I understand. I have just one more question. You mentioned that your father and Hunter were on speaking terms. How did Hunter feel about having your dad back in his life after not speaking for so many years?"

"I think he wanted a relationship. He'd realized long before that Dad did him a favour marrying Laurel. Hunter deserves better."

"You think highly of him."

"He's the only one who's been able to leave and lead his own life. My father and Laurel couldn't hurt him anymore. He had no reason to want my father dead."

Kala studied Geraldine's head, tilted to the left so that her eyes were fixed on something outside the window. She sounded sincere, but Kala would have been much happier if Geraldine had turned to face her when insisting on her brother's innocence. It was a lot more difficult for someone to lie when they were looking you in the eye.

———

Rouleau hung up the phone and walked toward the fax machine in the outer office. Grayson was working at his computer, but everyone else had gone home early.

"Any luck?" asked Grayson without looking up.

"Yeah. The lawyer's sending a copy of the will from a secure server."

The machine whirred into action and six sheets of legalese appeared in the tray. Rouleau picked them up and skimmed their contents, having already gotten the highlights from Tom Underwood's lawyer. He crossed the floor toward Grayson's desk and sat down in Malik's chair. He spread the papers on the desk and reread the key paragraphs.

"So?" asked Grayson. "Anything worth killing for?"

"Depends how badly somebody wanted their money. Underwood gave his kids Hunter and Geraldine each a million and put another million in trust for his youngest. He left his ex-wife Pauline two million and his current wife Laurel two million as well as the house and contents and stock options in his company."

"That's crazy he left so much to his ex."

"And to Hunter. They'd only spoken once in ten years. When I talked with Underwood's lawyer, he said that Underwood revised his will a couple of weeks ago. Before that, Laurel got most of the money. He upped what he left the kids and added Pauline."

"Two million." Grayson whistled. "If I was his current wife, I wouldn't be too happy about that."

"No," said Rouleau. "I don't imagine any woman would." He stood and stretched. "Any plans for the evening?"

"I've got a date and should push off. What about you?"

"Home to leftovers and a movie."

"Too bad I made this date or we could have gone out for a bite."

"I don't mind a night in. Go enjoy your evening. I'll put these papers away and will be right behind you."

"Night then," said Grayson. He turned off his computer and reached for his coat.

Rouleau returned to his office and sorted through the papers on his desk. His phone rang as he was locking the filing cabinet. A number flashed on the screen that he didn't recognize, and his first thought was to let the answering machine take a message. Then he remembered that Stonechild was on her own, interviewing the daughter, and he had no idea of her number. He picked up. "Rouleau here."

"Jacques, it's Frances. I almost didn't recognize your voice."

She'd surprised him twice in one week. He looked out the window. The lower half of the glass was patterned in frost and blurred his view of the buildings across the street. What he could see of the sky had darkened into early evening.

"How are you, Frances?"

"Not too bad. I wanted to wish you a Merry Christmas. Did you make the trip to Kingston?"

"I did. Dad sends his love. Merry Christmas to you too."

"Give him my love back when you next talk to him." She paused and he didn't try to fill in the silence. He could hear her deep intake of breath. Her words came out quickly. "I know this is short notice, but I decided to take your advice. Gordon and I are getting married at city hall four days from now, on New Year's Eve. Around three o'clock. I was hoping you could come."

It took him a moment to speak. "I'm happy for you, Frances, for you both, but I can't promise anything. We're in the middle of a murder investigation." Even as he said the words, he knew they were inadequate.

Her voice lost some of its bounce. "I know it's unusual, but it would mean so much to me to have you there. Maybe you could come to the Westin for the reception afterwards if you can't make the ceremony. We'll just be thirty or so and you wouldn't have to stay long. Will you think about it, Jacques?"

"Are you sure you want me there?"

"Yes, we're both sure. We'll be leaving the next day for Paris. We're planning a few months away, or as long as my health holds up and the doctors let me. Remember how I always wanted to visit the south of France and swim in the Mediterranean? I'm excited for this trip."

"I'm glad for you, Franny. I truly am. I can't promise to make the ceremony but I'll try to get to the reception."

"Thank you. It would mean a lot to me ... to us. You can bring someone if you like. It would be nice to meet the person in your life."

"Thanks, but I'll probably come alone." The silence lengthened. "Take care, Fran," he said before hanging up the phone. He stood for a long while afterward without moving, his eyes fixed on the frosted window pane.

He'd failed her in so many ways over the course of their marriage. She'd wanted to travel and see all the exotic places she'd read about in the novels she inhaled like fresh air. She'd minored in art history at university and spent many Sunday afternoons visiting Ottawa's museums and art galleries, returning with pamphlets, maps, and dreams of foreign lands. He'd used his job as an excuse for not taking her the places she'd wanted to see and convinced himself that her increasing silence about distant places was a sign she'd lost interest in going. He'd allowed his work to colour his personal life, rationalizing his neglect by falsely believing that Frances had accepted the routine of their lives. Those days, he'd been overwhelmed with the toll of long work hours and the weight of murder cases. He'd wanted nothing but to be home with her on his time off. Home where they were safe from the ugliness of the world. He knew too late that he should have tried harder. They should have bloody well gone to Europe. He could have taken her dancing before she went looking for another partner.

He turned and crossed the floor to take his coat from the hook on the wall. He flicked off the lights and started down the hall on his way out to the parking garage. A few uniforms were around but most were on patrol or home with their families.

When he crossed the Pretoria Bridge and stopped at a red light across the street from the Royal Oak, he looked at his face in the rear-view mirror and grimaced at his appearance. He'd aged a lifetime since Frances's first call.

A woman in a short white coat and frizzy hair stood at the corner turning tricks. Three men spilled out of the pub and walked past her without a second look. Hopefully they were going home to their wives or partners and ending their evening of drinking. The light turned green and Rouleau pressed on the gas pedal harder than he'd meant to.

He didn't want to see Frances married to someone else or to raise a glass at her reception, but it wasn't about him anymore. God knew he'd made enough wrong moves while they were together. He would do what it took not to add to them now.

22

SUSAN SLEPT IN as she had every morning since Clinton went back to the base, happy that he was miles away. She'd stopped feeling bad about wishing he'd never come home. Sometimes the thought of never seeing him again was what kept her going. The trick was to keep him from finding out.

As she made her way downstairs to the kitchen, she mused on how her life had turned into a cliché: older wife, living in a loveless marriage with an abusive military husband. How had she allowed her life to turn out so horribly wrong and why couldn't she stir herself to get out of it?

She sat at the dining-room table in front of the bay window to eat her toast and yogourt. Her interest in food still hadn't returned, but she was forcing herself to eat to get her strength back. She had to be at full power when Clinton returned home for New Year's Eve. He revelled in any sign of weakness.

She looked out the window toward the back of the property. The sun should have been well up by now, but the sky was grey with clouds that blocked the light. Gloomy. The world was in tune with her weary thoughts. The first snowflakes drifted past the glass as she watched. She smiled at this reminder that beauty was waiting to show itself when least expected.

The sparkling white flakes spurred her into action. She'd wait to have her tea until she'd returned from her morning walk. Normally she would have called on Pauline to walk with her down to the river on the well-worn pedestrian path, but Pauline had refused any offers of exercise lately. Susan understood this need for solitude and wouldn't press. A part of her welcomed the break from her friend's self-absorbed view of the world. Pauline was all about Pauline, and while Susan accepted her secondary role in their friendship, sometimes she was happy for a reprieve.

She took her dishes into the kitchen. Maybe she should think bigger than a walk. She'd put off skiing since Tom died and her body was getting sluggish. She had more than enough time to go farther afield across the border into Quebec to her favourite trail. A change of scene in the big outdoors was just what the doctor ordered. First a shower and a start on the housework, and then she could enjoy the afternoon outdoors without thinking about the chores she had let slide. She'd drink her tea when she was drying her hair and would bring a thermos with her on the excursion.

It was just past one o'clock when she loaded her cross-country skis into the back of her Mazda van. She climbed in and backed out of the driveway, aiming toward downtown. The snow was light and wouldn't be an issue on the woodland trail. She crossed the MacDonald-Cartier Bridge into Quebec and continued west on the road that ran parallel to the Ottawa River until she reached the Gatineau Parkway. The parkway wound north into the Gatineau Hills and the preserved parkland. Already, the tightness in her chest was loosening. She joined in with

"Rudolph the Red-Nosed Reindeer" on the radio, a silly song that always made her smile.

She pulled off on a side road that she knew about from previous visits and travelled a few kilometres to a parking lot sheltered deep in the woods where she unloaded her skis and poles. A car and van were there ahead of her. New ski tracks disappeared down the trail into the forest. The wind was ruffling the tops of the conifer trees back and forth and soughing like a cello. One of her favourite things was to lie in bed before falling asleep and listen to the wind howl around the house. Today's wind gave her the same feeling of comfort.

She strapped on her skis and started down the path. Her plan was to ski for a half hour or so before stopping to eat the apple she'd brought. She'd find a spot to hang the suet ball she'd grabbed from the pantry for the birds and then return to the car. She'd make it home in plenty of time for Clinton's six o'clock call.

She passed two women who were skiing back to the parking lot half a kilometre in. She stepped off the path to let them pass and they called a greeting. Another fifteen minutes and she met a young man and his dog, a husky that bounded ahead through the deeper snow. They were also on their way back to the parking lot. The man wished her a good journey before disappearing around the bend in the trail.

She skied another hour once her arms and legs found their familiar rhythm. She realized how much she'd missed the outdoors and this sport. Fatigue seemed a thing of the past, but she knew that she mustn't overdo it. She found a shelter of pine trees and ventured off the path to sit on a fallen log where she could comfortably eat her apple and drink some sugared tea. It was a peaceful spot with animal tracks crisscrossing into the woods and birds playing in the branches overhead. The trees cocooned her from the wind and cast dark shadows across the snow. She threw the apple core onto the path for a deer to find, then skied over to a tree with drooping branches. It took her a few minutes to fasten the suet ball to a lower limb. She moved back onto the trail and stood silently for a while, watching the birds land on the bough to eat from her offering.

She hadn't realized how tired the exercise had made her until she started the long trip back. A headache was throbbing just behind her eyes, reminding her that her energy reserves were still depleted. Perhaps she shouldn't have been quite so ambitious when setting out on the trail. She'd ski back slowly and not overexert herself, even if it meant having to listen to Clinton rant about missing his call.

It took almost two hours of repeatedly skiing a short distance and stopping to rest before she finally broke into the clearing. The woods had darkened as the sun had begun to set, and her van was a welcome sight. It was the only vehicle left in the parking lot and dusted with snow that would only take a moment to clean off. She was surprised to see tire tracks close to her car and partially covered boot prints that didn't look like hers. Somebody else had come and gone while she was skiing in the woods.

She took off her skis and loaded them onto the rack, fatigue and cold making her movements cumbersome and slow. The air was getting chillier now that she'd stopped moving. It was with relief when she made it into the front seat. Her gloved hands fumbled with the ignition key. The engine didn't start the first time, which was odd. Normally, the engine turned over without hesitation. By the fifth try, she knew she was in trouble. She squinted at the gas gauge and her heart sank. The needle rested below the red line. Why hadn't she heard the warning bell go off?

She banged the steering wheel with her palms. Why hadn't she brought her cellphone? It didn't matter that she rarely used it; she should have taken precautions travelling into the wilderness. What was she going to do now with the afternoon light already starting to fade and the temperature dropping? Please let somebody come along soon, or there'd be no choice but to set out for the main road to flag down someone to help her. She just hoped her strength didn't fail her before rescue arrived.

———

Kala finished her reports late morning, just before Rouleau's daily team meeting. Rouleau gathered them in front of the crime scene photos pinned to the wall. His mouth was set in a grim line. She knew he'd spent the last hour on the phone with Vermette, an activity that would knock the sunshine from anyone's face.

"Listen up," he began. "We have several lines of investigation going but no firm suspect or motive. I don't need to remind you that the clock is ticking. Let's be sure to keep each other in the loop about our separate strands of the investigation in case one piece of information can be pieced together with another to give us a new slant. I'll be going through all your updates this afternoon. Make sure to include every detail in your daily reports, no matter how insignificant it might seem." He turned toward Grayson and Malik. "Go back to Underwood's workplace and interview all his co-workers and partner again. See if they remember any detail about Underwood's last movements and his state of mind. Watch for contradictions. Stonechild, focus on the family. We've received some interesting information about Underwood's will, particularly the fact that he left a chunk of money to his ex-wife and son. It's time to interview Laurel again. Take Bennett with you and see if you can rattle something out of her."

"A confession would be nice," said Malik.

"I'll see what I can do," said Kala. She smiled at him.

"Gage, continue going through the computer documents. We need to know if there's anything buried in his files," continued Rouleau. "So far, our search has been wide open, but we need to start narrowing in. We've got a list of suspects but no stand outs. Motive? There are lots if you read between the lines. Money, power, jealousy, hatred. We don't even know for sure if his killing was personal, business, or stranger. As for forensic evidence, we haven't got much. There's nothing in Underwood's car that links the killer to him. Either they were incredibly smart or incredibly lucky."

"It points to a professional," said Grayson. "They lured him to a private place and killed him without witnesses or physical evidence left behind. My money's on a hit."

"Then get me some proof," said Rouleau. "We need an airtight case and not just a gut feeling."

Grayson shrugged and smiled as if Rouleau's words hadn't held an unspoken rebuke. Kala stood to leave with the others. Rouleau motioned for her to stay behind.

"Sir?"

"Here's a copy of the will. Read it through before you head over to Laurel's. Underwood changed it a week before he died. Try to find out if Laurel knew beforehand. She says she was sleeping when he left that morning. See if anyone can confirm that. Interview the staff."

"You're not convinced about the hit?"

"If it was, Laurel could have hired someone as easily as his business partner. She stood to lose a lot in a divorce. I'd say she's still in the running."

"It's often the spouse."

"I know. Find out if she was seeing anyone on the side."

Kala's stomach dropped. She nodded before walking away from Rouleau toward her desk. She sat down and began reading the will, but her mind wasn't on it. Hunter's face kept interrupting her train of thought. She had to find out how involved he was with his stepmother even though she wanted to believe him when he said nothing was going on. She gave herself a mental shake, squared her shoulders and forced him from her mind. This was a murder investigation and she could not afford to look at any one of them as anything less than a potential killer. If Hunter and Laurel were in on this together, she would find out and bring them to Rouleau without hesitation. Regret would be kept for another day. She stood and packed up her file, certain she'd read enough of the highlights to prepare for Laurel's interview.

Laurel had lost weight. The skin around her eyes was bruised from lack of sleep, but her beauty was heightened if anything, not diminished. Kala waited while Laurel organized Charlotte at the dining room table with cookies and juice before she came into the family room and sat at the other end of the couch. Bennett had shown tact by selecting an armchair out of Laurel's line of vision. Kala sent him silent thanks.

Laurel leaned forward toward Kala. Her violet eyes brimmed with suffering. "Have you found who killed Tom?"

Her hushed voice trembled as if she could barely control her tears.

"No, but we will," said Kala.

"I won't rest until they pay for what they've done. Charlotte will grow up without a father."

"Did you know about your husband's new will?"

"I'm sorry?"

"Your husband signed a new will about a week before he died. Were you aware of this?"

Laurel shook her head, but not before Kala saw hesitation in her eyes. "Tom looked after us. I know that. He was always generous where Charlotte and I are concerned." She grasped her hand around a thick gold bracelet on her left arm and slid it up and down her wrist. She looked down. "Tom wrapped this for me before he died. I found it in his drawer after ... after I knew he would never be coming home."

"It's lovely. Were you aware he left Pauline two million dollars?"

Something in Laurel's eyes shifted. "I knew he planned to leave her something. I wasn't aware how much."

"He spoke with you about it?"

"Of course. I was in complete agreement."

"And yet earlier you said that you and Pauline didn't get along. It's hard to believe that you wouldn't be upset that Tom was leaving her money, let alone so much."

Laurel shrugged. "I know he left me a lot too and this house. I'm going to sell it and move into something smaller. Charlotte and I won't starve."

"Why did he tell you that he was changing his will?"

Laurel hesitated. When she spoke, her voice was harder. "I didn't know that he'd actually gone ahead and signed anything. He wanted to make amends for pain he'd caused, but he told me that Charlotte and I wouldn't suffer. I believed him."

"Even though he was making amends with his ex-wife?"

"I had no idea how much he planned to leave her. I would have fought him on that, but I wasn't opposed to the idea of giving her something if it eased his conscience. To be honest, I thought it was to be less than a hundred thousand. How much did he leave Hunter?"

"You knew about that?"

"As I said, he was making amends. I'm not the money-grabbing wife some in the family paint me."

"I'm told that you were engaged to Hunter before you married his father."

"So?"

"You must know how that looks."

"People fall all over themselves to judge me, but I loved Tom. I was infatuated with him soon after we met. He saw to that. They might do better to ask how a man my father's age would set out to seduce *me*. I was young and naive, and yes, foolish. I gave up my soul mate for a transitory feeling."

"Hunter is available."

"And now, so am I. Just what are you implying, Detective?"

Kala waited silently, her eyes never leaving Laurel's face. The corners of Laurel's mouth lifted in a self-mocking smile.

"Hunter doesn't want me, and that should make everyone in this hypocritical family happier than wolves chewing on a dead deer. He's been kind to me but nothing more. He's a decent man, which I know is rare in this cynical time. I wasn't mature enough to know what I was throwing away. I've had other lovers since I married, yes, but none that threatened my marriage. Tom and I had reached an understanding."

"Did you know that your husband contacted a divorce lawyer?"

Laurel leaned back heavily against the couch. She covered her eyes with her hands. "No. I had no idea. He never told me." When she lowered her hands and looked Kala in the eyes, hers weren't as defiant as they'd been. She managed a shaky laugh. "I always believed that I would be the one to leave him. I knew something had changed in him recently, but I didn't know how much. Perhaps, if you find out what that something was, you'll find out why he was killed."

"Can you describe what had changed?"

"He didn't seem interested in work like he had been and he was moping around. I got the feeling something was gnawing at him, but he never spoke about it. I thought it had to do with his latest project, although going to see Hunter and changing his will … I don't know. It was as if he was making restitution." Laurel turned her body toward Kala and turned her palms heavenward. "It's almost as if he knew he was going to die."

Kala believed that some people had premonitions of their impending death. It wasn't clear if Tom Underwood knew the universe was turning on him. Perhaps he'd been threatened. Had he known someone was planning to murder him?

"Is there anything else?" Laurel looked through the doorway at Charlotte, who'd finished her snack and was trying to catch her mother's attention. "What is it Charlotte?"

"Can I go watch my video now?"

"Just for a bit. I'm taking you to play at Amber's as soon as we're done here." She turned toward Kala. "Any more questions?"

"You and Tom were at a party the night before he disappeared."

"Yes, but he left some time before me. He was tired but asked me to stay since he was co-owner of the company."

"Who was looking after Charlotte while you both were away from home?"

"Winnie. She's our live-in nanny and has a room in the east wing."

"Is she here today?"

"No, she's gone to visit her family for the holidays. I spoke with her when I found out Tom died, but she said that she hadn't seen anything that morning. She didn't hear him come home from the party either."

"We'll need to confirm that. Can you provide us with contact information?"

"Of course."

"Do you have other staff?"

"I have cleaners come in twice a week on Mondays and Thursdays, but that's it. Tom was never home when they came so they didn't know him."

"Officer Bennett will take their contact information too. Thank you again for your time today."

"I just want you to find who killed Tom."

———

Bennett turned toward Kala, his hands on the steering wheel. "Where to now?"

She checked her watch. "It's almost four o'clock. Let's go back to the station so I can fill in the report. Thanks for taking notes, by the way. You can track down the nanny and the cleaning staff and see if they have anything to add. I doubt it, but we need to cover those bases."

"Phone calls okay?"

"I'd say so, yes."

Bennett put the car into gear. "Wolves chewing on a dead deer. Nice."

"Paints a picture. Who knows how much of what she said was true? At certain points, she seemed honest enough."

"She was startled by the news her husband had contacted a divorce lawyer."

"Yeah. Interesting since they obviously weren't a close couple even though she's been trying to make us believe otherwise. Rouleau and I learned about their separate bedrooms on our first visit."

"She's got the grieving widow thing down."

Kala looked over at him. "Do you work on many murder cases, Bennett?"

"No, but I always thought I'd like to." He grinned at her. She hadn't noticed his dimples before. "I don't even mind the grunt work. You know, door-to-door and surveillance. I could get into it."

"Good to know. You'd also have to like writing reports." She sighed. "Seems like I've spent most of my time at the computer since I got here. Whoever said being a detective was glamorous hasn't got a sweet clue. You did well in there too, by the way. I think she forgot you were sitting behind her."

"Thanks. We make a good team." He took his eyes off the road to glance at her.

Kala smiled back. She turned her head to look out the side window, her thoughts already on Laurel, sifting through the things she'd said, the flashes of emotion in her eyes. What was the significance of the will additions and why had Underwood made them? The answer to his murder had to be tied to his changed behaviour in the month leading up to his death. If she could just find the trigger to his recent need to seek restitution with his son and ex-wife, she might have the piece to break the case open.

23

IT WAS NEARLY eight o'clock and dark and cold as any northern night in the dead of winter — a starless night with heavy cloud cover. Kala shivered in her red wool coat and decided to give one more pass around the apartment building before heading for her truck. It was her second evening patrolling the entranceways of two identical towers, the buildings next to the one where Glenda Martin had been assaulted. Kala was doing it on her own time without telling anyone, but only because she agreed with Rouleau that the guy was getting more dangerous. She didn't want to think too deeply about the reason she wasn't telling Rouleau about her after hours surveillance. He wouldn't understand her need to work alone, to avoid being controlled. It was easier just to get on with the job until she had something to share. This way she could focus on the puzzle and not have to deal with the eternal bureaucracy. A couple of coats and hats from the Sally Ann gave her different disguises in case the perp was staking out the buildings. The trick was not to look like she was hanging around because that would tip him off that she was on the hunt.

A man exited the building ahead of her, and she tensed, ready for his approach, but he took an immediate right and got into a car idling in the visitor parking lot. The dropping temperatures appeared to be keeping nearly everyone indoors, even Grab 'n Go, the nickname Malik had given the suspect.

Kala walked slowly up the sidewalk, holding a grocery bag in her left hand and leaving her right hand free. He normally attacked from behind and her senses were on high alert. Somebody was coming up the path behind her. She entered the lobby and pretended to fumble with the bag, keeping herself turned away from the door.

"Need help?" a man asked.

She looked over her shoulder at him. "No, I just forgot something in my car and have to go get it. But thanks."

She stepped back outside and checked her watch. Grab 'n Go didn't appear to be on the prowl tonight. It was disappointing to have a second night coming up empty, but she wasn't deterred. Stalking an animal quarry sometimes took days in the woods. Human targets demanded equal patience. The advantage she had over this serial predator was knowing he preferred hunting in his own backyard. He'd be back to his familiar hunting ground sooner or later.

She started toward her truck parked across Richmond Road in the Lincoln Fields parking lot. Finding Rosie was going to be a trickier business and she'd have to rely on a certain degree of luck. There was still time to cruise around the ByWard Market before packing it in for the night.

———

Kala spotted Grayson and Malik on her way in to the station at seven the next morning. She parked her truck and hurried after them. Malik held the front door open and waited for her to catch up. Grayson had already disappeared inside the building.

"You're up bright and early," she said to Malik, slightly out of breath.

"Rouleau called us at home around five a.m. to get over to the General and interview Susan Halliday." He yawned. His breath came out in a stream of white frost. "I could have used another hour's sleep."

"The General?"

"Hospital. Halliday was found unconscious in the Gatineau Hills late yesterday afternoon."

Kala stopped. "Is she okay?"

"She's doing better than she was last night. We were able to speak with her for about ten minutes before the doctor told us we had to leave. She's suffering from hypothermia and has some frostbite to her feet and hands."

"Is this tied to Underwood's murder?"

They'd begun walking down the hall toward the office. Malik lowered his voice when they stepped inside the main office.

"Not likely. Her Mazda was out of gas and had to be towed. She said it wouldn't start so she started walking toward the main road. She was lucky a park ranger was on patrol or she wouldn't have lasted the night."

"What in the world was she doing out there?"

"Cross-country skiing. She said it was her favourite trail. She likes to go there during the week when there aren't a lot of people around."

Kala shook her head at the insanity of someone heading into the woods without checking their gas tank. "Craziness," she said.

She left Malik and sat down at her desk. Something didn't feel right. Susan hadn't struck her as a stupid woman. She'd appeared logical and organized, not the type who would leave the city without checking if there was gas in the car.

Rouleau called them over for the morning briefing just after eight. They filled up their coffee mugs and gathered around the crime scene photos posted on the wall.

Grayson stood first to give the report on Susan Halliday. He read the details and ended with, "So no connection to Underwood's murder. She was still a bit out of it this morning but blamed herself for going into the park without checking her gas gauge." He shut his file and started back to his seat.

"Where was her husband when this happened?" Kala asked.

Grayson hesitated and looked around the group as if waiting for a better question. Finally, he looked toward her. "On his way home from the base in Trenton for a surprise visit. He arrived at their house shortly after six p.m. and was concerned to not find her there. He started checking around. The hospital called him less than an hour later. He was in her hospital room when we spoke with her."

"Your thoughts, Stonechild?" asked Rouleau.

She forced herself to look away from Grayson's stare. "It seems odd to me that a woman close to Underwood and his family has this kind of accident."

"Shit happens," said Grayson. "She's an old woman who forgot to check the gas before heading out. She said as much in the hospital. You can't go looking for a conspiracy theory when accidents happen."

"Do you have anything to add?" Rouleau asked Kala.

"No."

"If Susan Halliday admitted she was careless, we haven't got reason to believe someone was trying to hurt her." Rouleau smiled at her. "By the way, I've told Whelan he can have until the new year off. His wife has come down with the flu and with the baby in the hospital and a toddler to look after, he can't be spared at home."

"No problem, Sir," said Kala. "Bennett and I can cover."

"Good. I'd like you both to give Gage a hand going through the phone records and the documents on Underwood's home and office computers. There's a lot to go through and I'd like that wrapped up today."

She nodded even though she'd just been demoted to the drudgery work.

Grayson shifted in his seat and crossed his legs. He said, "Gage found one email from Underwood to J.P. asking to meet the day before he died. Malik and I are going back to their office to talk to him about it."

"I'm in meetings all morning but you can reach me on my cell if anything breaks. Stay in touch," said Rouleau. He turned to Malik. "Any sign of Annie Littlewolf yet?"

"No, but the cops patrolling the ByWard Market are keeping an eye out. She's not in her usual haunts. I'd like to think she's visiting family for the holidays, but it's not likely. We can swing by the Rideau Centre later if you like."

"Let's hope we get a lead on something today. We could use a break."

———

Just before one o'clock, Kala stretched and turned her chair toward Bennett. "I'm going to an appointment and might have a slightly longer lunch hour than usual. If you and

Gage can keep at this, I'll stay late and finish up what you don't get through."

Bennett looked up from his computer screen. "Take your time. I'll cover. I'll stick around to help if it goes late."

"You don't need to do that."

He looked up and smiled at her. "I know, but I want to."

She found herself smiling back. "Call me if anything comes up." She grabbed her coat and a stale doughnut from a box sitting on the filing cabinet as she headed out the door.

Twenty minutes later, she parked her truck in the General Hospital parking lot. She followed the trail of visitors through the sliding glass door at the front entrance and asked the woman at reception for Susan Halliday's room number. She walked toward the elevator and watched the people streaming out of the open doors as it reached the ground floor. Clinton Halliday stepped off behind a woman dressed in green scrubs and a man in a wheelchair. Halliday was a hard man to miss with his buzz cut and wrestler body. He appeared to be alone and immediately snapped open his cellphone. Kala stepped back from the doors behind the other visitors until he'd passed by. For now, she'd rather he didn't know she was there.

She got off on the fourth and slipped past the nurses' station. The two nurses on the desk were busy working on charts and didn't look up. She located the number to Susan's private room halfway down the corridor and entered after a quick knock on the door that she hadn't expected to be answered. She approached the bed. An I.V. bag hung on a pole dripping a clear liquid through a needle into Susan's arm. Her hands lay on top of the sheet and were wrapped in gauze. Her eyes were closed.

Kala stood for a moment, uncertain whether to wake her. She was likely doped up on pain killers and it might be better to return later. Just as Kala decided to leave, Susan opened her eyes and blinked at the ceiling. She turned her head slowly sideways and focused on Kala. Her lips moved with effort.

"You're the detective who came to our house."

"Yes. I wanted to ask you a few questions about your accident. Do you feel up to it?"

Susan gave a small nod and Kala drew a chair close to the bed so that her head was at Susan's eye level.

"Had you checked the gas gauge before you went into the Gatineau Hills?"

"No."

"I find it odd that you would have set out on your own without making sure there was gas in the car. You don't strike me as disorganized."

"I get ... confused sometimes. Forget things. I thought I'd filled it up last week. I must have been mistaken. I can't even remember the warning bell go off."

"Did you use a credit card?"

"I'm not sure." Susan reached a bandaged hand toward the bedside table, then carefully placed it back onto the bed. "Clinton took my purse home for safekeeping. If I charged the gas, the receipt would be in my wallet."

"Does Clinton drive your van?"

"Yes, but he's been away all week."

"Could someone have siphoned off the gas?"

Susan's eyes widened as if she remembered something. She closed them quickly and her breathing became more laboured.

Kala stood and filled the water glass from a jug on the tray next to the bed. "Sip this," she said. She helped to prop up Susan's head so that she could swallow from the glass. Susan leaned back against the pillows.

"Do you feel better or should I ring for the nurse?"

"No, I'm fine."

"What bothered you just now?" asked Kala, sitting back down in the chair.

Susan's forehead furrowed in deep lines. "Tire tracks. There were tire tracks in the snow next to my van and footprints. I wondered who'd been there because I didn't meet them on the trail."

Her strength was weakening and Kala touched her shoulder. "You should sleep now. I'll be back to talk when you feel better."

Susan's eyes had already closed as Kala backed away toward the door. She'd wanted to ask about Clinton and where he was that day but would have to wait until tomorrow for Susan's response. In the meantime, she would try to find out on her own.

Kala pushed the door open and almost collided with Hunter Underwood as he pulled the door open from his side.

"Officer Stonechild," he said, taking hold of her arm to steady her. "I think it's time we talked."

24

THEY LEFT THE hospital separately and met up at the New Edinburgh Pub on Beechwood. Hunter arrived ahead of her and secured a table near the back. The lunchtime crowd had thinned and they had a degree of privacy. She stood in the entranceway for a few moments and studied him. He was dressed in jeans and a navy sweater, his curly hair blown about from the wind. He'd begun growing a beard since she'd seen him last and it made him look even more appealing. She mentally kicked herself for noticing.

Hunter spotted her and waved her over. A pretty blond waitress was at the table as soon as she sat down, her smile all for Hunter. She flipped coasters onto the table and asked what they'd like to drink. She stood close to Hunter as she waited for Kala to order.

"Coffee please, and a club sandwich on brown," Kala said.

"I'll have the Irish stew and a Guinness," Hunter added.

The girl took their menus and smiled one more time at Hunter before leaving.

"You know her?" asked Kala.

"I've seen her in here before, but not waitressing. She must have just started." He shrugged and grinned back at her. He leaned forward, his smile disappearing. "So, it looks like Susan is doing okay. I could hardly take it in when I got the news. First my father and now her. I'm having trouble believing the two events aren't linked somehow."

"Why do say that? Susan admitted that she forgot to check the gas before leaving home."

"Susan is one of the more competent women I know and it's out of character. She's had to be on her toes, married to Clinton."

"You don't sound like you think much of him."

"Because I don't. Susan's changed the last few years. She's less sure of herself and always rushing home for his phone calls. He keeps tabs on her like he owns her. She's become scared of making him mad. I've seen it. We've all seen it."

"So what are you suggesting?" Kala waited while the waitress set down their drinks. She stirred cream into her coffee while Hunter took a sip of beer. He set his glass on the coaster and rubbed his fingers up and down its side.

"I think someone did this to Susan. My first thought was Clinton. It makes me wonder if he killed my father too."

"Do you have any proof?"

"No, but if it's him, I'll find the proof."

"You have to leave that to us."

"Yeah." He grimaced before taking a long drink from his glass.

She waited until he was looking at her again. "Did you know that your father was leaving you a million dollars?"

Hunter laughed. "Is that what he did? First I've heard."

"Really?"

"Really. He needn't have bothered."

"I think he was trying to tell you that he was sorry."

"He told me that the last day I saw him. It was enough. You look like you want to say something."

Kala shrugged. "It's just that you seem so bitter after all these years. Ten years is a long time to stay angry."

"Not angry so much as indifferent. I got over being mad that he married Laurel. It wasn't even about her in the end. The thing that's kept me from welcoming my father back into my life, if you really want to know, was the knowledge that he totalled my world without an ounce of remorse. I'm not a parent, but I would never want to make my own happiness at the expense of my child's. I'm sure your parents wouldn't have done that either."

"I never knew my parents."

His eyes filled with a compassion that surprised her. He began to apologize but she held up a hand and cut him off.

"I'm sorry. That just came out. You couldn't have known," she said. "Besides, my life has nothing to do with you."

"I deserved to be put in my place. I was the one who made an assumption."

Their lunch arrived at that moment and they stopped talking, sitting awkwardly while the waitress set down their plates.

"I'll have to get back to the station so I have to eat quickly," she said as soon as the girl left, "so I apologize in advance. Another officer is covering for me, but it means we may have to work late." She bit into her sandwich and hoped that he took the hint. She wasn't going to talk about herself and didn't want him asking.

He paused. "I know this isn't on at the moment," he said finally, "but maybe when this is over, you might like to go out for dinner or something. I'd like to have a chance to talk under less constrained circumstances."

"I'm not sure that would be a good idea."

"Yeah, maybe you're right."

The disappointed expression on his face made her smile. "I didn't say we couldn't keep the possibility open, but I think you might feel differently about socializing with me when this wraps up. Murder investigations have a funny way of changing how people see each other. You might not be too fond of me when all is said and done."

Especially if you had a hand in killing your father.

He lifted his head and smiled back at her. "Fair enough. You haven't shut and locked the door, and that's about all I can ask."

Her phone rang as they were paying the bill. She listened with her eyes on Hunter. She shut off the phone and said, "Your sister Geraldine has gone into labour. She's at the General. Your mother's been trying to track you down."

"God, she's three weeks early. Did they say how she is?"

"No, but that's probably because she's okay. You go and I'll settle up here."

"Thanks." He jumped up and grabbed his jacket from the hook. "I don't know whether to be excited or worried for her."

"Would you call me to let me know how it goes?"

He stopped and looked down at her. "I'll call the station. Hopefully, for Geraldine's sake, this isn't going to be an all-nighter. We could sure use some good news to end this miserable year. Keep your fingers crossed."

———

Kala arrived at the office twenty minutes later. She plunked down across from Bennett and looked toward Rouleau's office. Grayson and Malik were standing just inside the doorway and she could see Vermette sitting across from Rouleau.

"What's going on?" she asked.

"We found some documents on Underwood's hard drive in a subfolder entitled 'exit strategy.' He was going to make big changes in his life, beginning with pulling out of the business. The morning he disappeared was the morning he planned to tell J.P. He typed it up in his master plan. Remember Gage found the email from Underwood to J.P. asking for a meeting? Well, J.P. denied they had anything set up for that morning when he was interviewed earlier this week. Underwood's file combined with the email say otherwise. It's as if Underwood's pointing a big finger at J.P. from the grave. Grayson and Malik are about to bring him in for questioning again. The team is in there, planning the interview strategy."

She turned and looked again into Rouleau's office. "How come Vermette's part of the posse?"

"Grayson met him in the hall and told him what we found on the computer."

She turned back to Bennett. "Rouleau looks like a thunder-cloud."

"It's because Grayson jumped the gun telling Vermette. Puts Rouleau in a bad place. How'd your appointment go by the way?"

"Fine."

She turned on her computer and leaned on the desk with her chin cupped in her hand while she waited for it to boot up. J.P. had motive and opportunity. He'd been caught in a lie that would have him with Underwood around the time he was killed. It all fit. What didn't fit was the possible attempt on Susan Halliday's life. If but for the park ranger, Susan would likely be dead. Why would J.P. go to all that trouble to harm a woman who wasn't connected to his business if this was about greed? Were

Underwood's murder and Susan's emptied gas tank even linked?

"Looks like we might have New Year's off when they wrap this up," Bennett said. "You got any plans for New Year's Eve?"

"Yeah." She looked closely at him. He was busy with some papers on his desk and avoiding her eyes. That's all she needed. Some young, earnest cop getting ideas about her. What the hell was up with Ottawa men anyhow? "If you can finish going through this stuff, I'll go watch them interview J.P. through the two-way glass," she said.

"Leave me to the slogging bits while you go have all the fun."

"Well, find something juicy about one of our suspects and we can hold our own interview."

"You don't think J.P. is our man?"

"Let's just say my mind is still open to other possibilities."

"Don't let Grayson or Vermette hear you say that. They've already ordered the party streamers."

"They really like to set themselves up," said Kala.

"How do you mean?"

She sighed. "Just seems to me like they're too eager to go with one theory."

For the first time, Bennett looked uncomfortable. It was as if he remembered that she was the outsider and he was part of the old boys' club meeting in Rouleau's office.

"They're working with the facts. It seems logical to me that they'd want to question Underwood's partner, especially since he lied about the meeting."

Kala smiled. "I agree that he's up there on the list of suspects. It's just good to remember that we have other people who could have murdered Underwood."

Bennett nodded before turning back to the paperwork, but she could tell he wasn't convinced. She hesitated. She'd been running the idea of inviting him to her next stake-out on Richmond Road around in her mind, but now it didn't seem like a good idea. He was likely to go running to Rouleau with the news. Besides, she preferred working alone.

25

GERALDINE HELD HER new baby girl and smiled up at her mother and Hunter. The newborn had a shock of Max's black hair and an elfin red face that resembled an old man's. To Geraldine, she was the most beautiful baby in the world. Only three hours of labour and out she'd popped like a jack in the box. Geraldine had fully expected to be one of those women in labour for forty-eight hours and the quick release of pain was euphoric. The surge of love she felt for this tiny being was unexpected.

"If I'd known it would be this easy, I'd have gotten knocked up in high school," she'd joked to Hunter when he entered her room ahead of their mother.

"Can I hold her?" asked Pauline, dropping her purse and coat on the nearest chair.

"Of course." Geraldine handed over the bundle. She immediately missed the weight of the baby in her arms.

"She's just beautiful. Have you picked a name?"

"I was thinking Amy Rose. Max said I could pick if it was a girl."

"Amy Rose," said Pauline as she kissed the tiny forehead. She rocked the baby as she walked toward the window.

Hunter grabbed Geraldine's hand and smiled. "Can I get you anything?"

"No, but I'm wondering where Max has gotten to. He left for that coffee half an hour ago."

"I could go look if you like."

"Would you?"

"Sure."

She watched him go and then looked over at her mom. "Have you been to visit Susan?"

"I plan to later. I haven't had time with you in labour."

"I know you must be worried sick about her, so go now if you like. I'll be okay."

"Hunter checked and she's fine. Frostbite on her toes and fingers but nothing too serious. The rest is doing her good. She'll be home tomorrow."

"What a relief. Are you going to look after her with Clinton away?"

"You haven't heard? No, I suppose not. He's been back since yesterday and will stay home until after New Year's. Apparently, he was en route to Ottawa from Trenton even before Susan's accident."

"That's odd. Susan said he'd be gone until New Year's Eve, and that's a few days away."

"I know. He's usually a slave to his routine. I don't know how Susan puts up with it, but I suppose she works around him when he isn't here. To be honest, I don't feel like running into him."

"Are you okay, Mom? You seem upset about something." Perhaps this wasn't the time to ask, but there never was a good time with her mother who could flit around deep conversation like a butterfly.

"I'm fine. I just wish your father could have been here to see his first grandchild." She crossed to the bed and handed the baby back to Geraldine. "It just all makes me so angry … and sad."

"It's good to talk about this, Mom. You need to let out how you're feeling."

"And Susan. It's as if she was asking for something bad to happen, all alone out there in the woods like that."

"She was lucky the park ranger found her when he did."

"The pair of them were foolish and we're left to pick up the pieces." Pauline grabbed her coat and purse from the chair in a jerky movement. "I'm going to meet a friend for a late supper. I'll be back first thing tomorrow to take you home."

"I'll be ready." Guilt flooded through her. Their mother was truly suffering from their dad's death and Geraldine had been too immersed in her own pain to give support. "We can spend all day together after I check out."

"I'll make lunch and will help with the baby while you sleep," said Pauline, smiling.

Hunter stepped into the room as Pauline reached the door. "Where's Max?" she asked, slipping an arm into her coat sleeve.

"He had to go check on something at work," said Hunter, glancing past her. "He said he'd call you later, Ger."

Geraldine saw the look that passed between her mother and brother and humiliation made her drop her face into the soft down on top of the baby's head. Their pity was worse than anything Max could do to her. God, what she'd give for a stiff Scotch. Hold the ice. Hold the soda. "Well, I told him that I'd like to sleep so I guess that's why he decided to go back to work. If the two of you don't mind, I'm going to rest now that the baby's asleep."

"We'll see you later, then," said Hunter. "I'll be back tomorrow."

She couldn't raise her head to look at him. Her neck felt as heavy as a tree bough weighted with snow. "I just want to sleep."

She waited for the door to snap closed before she opened her eyes. The baby was blurry and she blinked to clear her vision. "If you'd held off a bit, Amy Rose, you could have been the first born in the new year and made the paper. You could have started your life famous and made your daddy proud. You might have made him stick around if you'd made the six o'clock news."

She tried to erase from her mind the disappointment in Max's eyes when they'd told him he had a daughter; the split second of dislike in his expression when the nurse placed Amy Rose in his arms. She'd watched the mask slip deftly back into place, but knew she hadn't imagined his reaction. The truth had caught like a fist in her stomach.

Her husband had no use for a daughter — or for her.

This was the meaning she'd seen in his eyes and chosen not to believe for so long. She'd been nothing more than a stepping stone for his ambition. Her mother had warned her before the wedding, but she'd stubbornly clung to the belief that he loved her. She'd put her mother's cynicism down to bitterness and jealousy. The question now was just how far she was prepared to go along with his lie. Could she live with knowing her marriage was a sham?

"What should I do, Daddy?" she whispered into the softness of her baby's hair. She ran her fingers across the rosy cheek and kissed her smooth forehead. She reached for the buzzer to bring the nurse. She'd have them keep the baby for the night in the nursery and get some sleep. She was glad now that she'd decided not to breastfeed. It was one thing not to have a drink when she was pregnant but if she had to refrain from alcohol for a year or more of breastfeeding, they may as well book her a room now in the loony bin.

———

Susan let the day slip away, grateful that Clinton left after lunch to work from home for a few hours. The doctor was due in mid-afternoon for a final check before releasing her. He'd poked and prodded and then prescribed pain killers to get her through the week. Her hands and feet throbbed when the pills began to wear off, but she'd been assured this was a good thing. It just didn't feel like a good thing.

She turned toward the door as it slowly opened. A momentary surge of fear disappeared at the sight of her goddaughter Geraldine in her hospital gown. "Come give me a hug," she called. "What a surprise to see you up so soon. Is the baby with you?"

"No, she's sleeping, but I had to come see you. I'm here the night and home in the morning. How are you? What an awful scare you gave us."

Geraldine crossed to the bed and reached down to hug Susan. They released and Susan studied Geraldine's wan face and darting gaze that seemed so out of keeping for a new mom. Anger rose up from her stomach. What was that self-serving prick Max up to now?

Geraldine grimaced. "Your poor hands."

Susan shook off a sense of foreboding and laughed. "They'll soon be right as rain. I was so foolish to go into the Gatineau Hills alone. I don't know what I was thinking."

"We all do things without thinking them through now and then." Geraldine lowered herself into the chair and straightened her hospital gown.

"I seem to be doing that more and more. But tell me, how is the baby?"

"She … Amy Rose, is wonderful. Perfect. Labour was easy, only three hours. I just wish my father could be here to see her."

"He'd be so proud and I know he's somewhere up there smiling down on you both."

"I hope." Geraldine took Susan's bandaged hand in hers. "I'm sorry. I didn't mean to make you cry."

"No, it's just that so much has gone on this week. I'm not feeling like myself." Susan dabbed at her eyes with the end of the sheet. She hated to cry in front of Tom's daughter. It should be the other way around, her offering comfort.

"I wanted to ask your advice on something, but now isn't the time. Maybe I could come visit you when we're both home," said Geraldine.

"I'd like that. I'm sorry that I'm so weepy these days. I really don't know what's come over me."

"Well, we have one thing to be thankful for. Laurel isn't having a service for Dad. He asked in his will to be cremated and no funeral. She's decided to respect his wishes. I think that considering the state of our family, it'll be for the best if we aren't all in the same room."

"It might have been nice if his death brought everyone together."

"Nice, but a reach. It will take more than Dad's death to get Mom and Laurel to be civil with each other."

After Geraldine returned to her room, Susan got out of bed and began slowly packing her few things into the overnight bag Clinton had brought earlier. Her bandaged hands made movement awkward, but not impossible. Clinton had been solicitous and hovered around her as if he had nowhere else to be. She'd finally sent him home to get some work done and to give her room to think.

Should she believe his story about being in transit when she was stranded in the Quebec woods? Why hadn't he called to say that he was coming home? He'd never been one for surprises or deviations from a schedule. Why was he being so damn nice all of a sudden?

She looked at the empty chair next to her bed and thought about Geraldine and the change in her eyes the last few times they'd met. It could have to do with Tom's death, but it wasn't just grief she was seeing. Something had shaken her. She should have asked Geraldine what was on her mind when she came into her room. Instead, she'd cried about Tom and lost the chance. She wasn't a woman who believed in wicked beings, but it felt like something evil was brewing. It had begun even before Tom's murder, like a palpable malevolence encircling them.

They had been so careful. *Surely, nobody knew?*

A shiver travelled up her spine just as Clinton stepped into the room. She lifted her head to smile at him.

"All set to go home?" he asked.

26

"HE'S NOT SOMEONE I'd pick for a business partner," Rouleau commented, glancing sideways.

"He seems somewhat shady," Kala agreed.

They stood side by side, watching J.P. Belliveau through the one-way mirror. Belliveau's stocky body was slouched in the chair across from Grayson and Malik, his mouth set in a belligerent line, his eyes narrowed inside pouches of loose skin. They could hear the interview thanks to a strategically placed microphone. Acoustics were crystal clear.

"Grayson's circling around him, preparing to zoom in on the lie," said Rouleau.

Kala was grudgingly impressed with Grayson's technique. He'd gotten Belliveau to repeat that he hadn't met with Underwood the morning he went missing, then lulled him with innocuous questions about the division of work between the partners. Both Kala and Rouleau leaned closer to the glass, as if that would speed things along. After a pause, Grayson slid a piece of paper across the table and Belliveau picked it up. He read what was on it and shrugged.

"Yeah, we were *supposed* to meet, but I talked to him at the party and said since it was a late night, we'd reschedule for another day."

"Did anyone hear you reschedule."

"Not that I know of. We were alone at the time and it wouldn't have interested anyone else. Is this why you called me in? Over a postponed meeting?"

"Why didn't you tell us about this meeting when we asked earlier this week and again a few minutes ago?" Grayson's voice was puzzled, non-believing.

"Because we'd cancelled it. There was nothing to tell, and to be honest, it slipped my mind. It was almost Christmas and we were rescheduling meetings all week. If you hadn't just shown me the email, I would never have remembered. Do you know how many meetings I attend in the course of a week? At least thirty. Do I need a lawyer?"

"That's up to you. You're not under arrest."

"Good." Belliveau's voice rose. "'Cause for a minute there, it sounded like you were getting ready to make an accusation."

Kala looked at Rouleau. "They're not going to get anything out of him, are they?"

Rouleau fixed his stare on Belliveau a while longer before turning to look at her. "No. He's sidestepped the lie with something impossible for us to disprove even if it is hard to believe he wouldn't have remembered they were supposed to have a meeting the morning Underwood went missing."

"He knew how it would look. His word against a dead man's. He probably thought we'd never find out."

"And he'd already planned what to say if we did."

"Well, I'll push off then. It's been a long day." Kala stepped away from the glass. Rouleau stopped her at the door.

"How're you doing with the Underwood clan? Anyone standing out?"

"They all seem to have a secret or two. I may never learn the full truth of their tangled relationships."

"If you had to guess?"

"Susan Halliday ... not that I think she killed Tom Underwood, but I think she knows something. I also worry that her empty gas tank wasn't an accident."

"I'd like you to interview her again. Tomorrow, if possible."

"She's going home from the hospital today. I'll swing by in the morning." She took a step closer to Rouleau. "Does this mean you don't think Underwood's death is work-related?"

"At this point, I have no idea. I agree though that Susan's near-death experience could be linked and you should pursue it."

"I heard that Vermette's hoping to close the file today."

"He's not alone, but we haven't got enough to charge anybody, let alone go to trial. Keep in touch tomorrow and enjoy your evening."

Kala nodded and left before he could ask how she intended to spend it.

She returned to the YWCA and put on her navy parka, jeans, and knee-high Sorel boots to stake out the apartment buildings. She was dressing in dark colours to stay hidden tonight. It would be bad if the target spotted her hanging around, looking like a victim too many nights in a row.

While waiting for the elevator, she rechecked the map she'd printed with the locations of the previous assaults marked in red dots. "This has to be the building," she said aloud, resting her finger on the last high-rise in the string. She looked guiltily around to make certain nobody else was in the hallway. Living alone, she'd taken to talking to herself. It was a bad habit in the city. Grab 'n Go was working his way down Richmond Road, skipping buildings but always heading east. There were only two apartment towers left in the row and she was betting on the last. She wondered what he would do when he was finished with this row of apartment buildings. Start over or pick a new area? Hopefully he'd never have the chance to begin in a new location.

Twenty minutes later, she parked in the Lincoln Fields parking lot, choosing a different end of the mall to leave her truck. She crossed Richmond Road on foot and headed toward the nine-storey sprawling apartment building with the black-tinted windows. It was a more modern structure than its neighbours and tucked farther back from the road next to a line of trees and a field. A string of globe lights on top of black poles led up the walkway. Two of the lights were burnt out near the entrance, creating a promising section of darkness on the path.

The night was partially overcast, the moon hidden behind a pocket of cloud. Now and then it reappeared and cast a shimmering light onto the snow. The air wasn't as frigid as it had been that morning, for which Kala gave silent thanks. She'd been warned that Ottawa weather was capricious and changed on a dime. The meteorologists had said often enough that global warming would make weather go crazy around the world. The Ottawa Valley might be the canary in the coal mine.

She surveyed the path and parking lot, looking for a sheltered place to stand where she wouldn't be easily seen. She settled on a spot behind an oak tree ten feet from the path, even with the darkened section of the walkway. The position was a good vantage point for seeing a section of the sidewalk and the path leading to the front door of the building. It also protected her from the gusty easterly wind. She pulled her hood up over her head and squatted down in the snow to wait.

Cars and city buses periodically passing on Richmond Road broke the evening's silence. Pedestrian traffic was light, and those few who passed by on the sidewalk walked quickly, heads down, buffeted by the wind and swirling snow. Each time someone came into view, Kala raised her head and followed their progress as long as they remained in her line of vision. The rest of the time she let her thoughts wander.

Rouleau's request for her to name her prime suspect for Underwood's murder had triggered her to reconsider the suspects. She'd been treating each with equal suspicion and hadn't rated them one against the other. Now she lined them up in her head.

Laurel definitely had a lot to gain from her husband's death, especially if she had gotten wind that he was planning to change his will and divorce her. Kala believed the surprise in Laurel's eyes when she found out the will had already been changed. Perhaps, she thought that by killing him she'd prevent a loss in fortune. Even more damning was her seemingly secret, close relationship with Hunter. They could have murdered Tom together or separately.

Then, there were Max and Geraldine. They gained financially and Max gained business-wise. From what she'd seen of him, he wasn't exactly a doting husband. He actually appeared effeminate, something she hadn't put in any report since it was only a personal observation. Besides, being effeminate didn't necessarily mean he wasn't interested in women. One had to be careful of stereotypes. He'd just fathered a baby, after all. Maybe he'd talked Geraldine into killing her father. She'd known of men who had that amount of control over their wives.

Then, there was Pauline, the ex-wife who appeared to be a loose cannon. If she believed Laurel, Pauline had never recovered from Tom's desertion, but did she have the wherewithal to kill, and why after all this time?

Kala liked Susan Halliday as a person but had serious concerns about her army husband Clinton, who seemed to hide a well of nastiness behind a rigid facade. Susan's near-fatal accident put Clinton top of the list in her mind. If only she knew why he would kill Tom Underwood — did Tom know something about Clinton that got him killed? Was it even a family member who committed the murder?

Kala sighed. She really couldn't rule anybody out yet. In fact, the list kept growing longer, not shorter. J.P. Belliveau had just as much motivation as did the inventor Archambault in Montreal as far as she could see. God only knew what other business associates had it in for Underwood. It was becoming a big muddle, but she knew that one piece of evidence would make all the bits fall into place. The trick was patience. She'd have to start making the rounds again, trying to sift out the lies and secrets.

She stood and stretched, jumping in place to keep the circulation flowing in her legs. Stakeouts were something she'd come to enjoy in her old job. She liked the chance to be alone outdoors. One foster father she'd lived with when she was thirteen had taken her hunting for deer in the fall and they'd spent hours huddled in the thickets, silently waiting for their prey to appear. She'd liked it because she'd liked him. Jock was the only one who really took an interest in her. She was sad when they had to give her back.

A woman in a fur coat walked past on the sidewalk, her shaggy black Maltese tugging on its leash. They started up the walkway to the apartment building. A man in a black ski jacket and white toque appeared from the other direction and started up the walkway after her. Kala took a step forward. The woman turned as he reached her and called him by name. Kala settled back into her hiding spot, her heart beat gradually returning to normal.

The next half hour passed slowly. Kala was warm in her winter clothing but her face was raw from the wind. She'd give it another half hour and then take a drive around the ByWard Market to look for Dawn and Rosie. She might even stop in at the Ottawa Mission to visit Maya. She wished she could take a leave of absence and spend her days searching. Once they found Underwood's murderer, she'd do just that. This job meant nothing to her, even though she felt a growing attachment to Rouleau. He was like the father she wished she'd had. Her real father had been nineteen when she was born. He'd be in his forties now, younger even than Rouleau, if he were still alive.

An unusual noise carried by the wind from the direction of the woods and field made her stand again and cock her head to listen. It sounded like branches breaking, likely a fox or other city wildlife. She relaxed and took one final look around. It was time to pack it in. The groper had taken another night off.

She stepped from her hiding place. She almost reached the sidewalk when a muffled scream came from the direction of the wood. Her body froze as she turned her head toward the noise, listening intently. At first she thought she was hearing things, but knew this might be all she got. She knew to trust her instincts.

She ran across the plowed sidewalk into the line of trees a couple of meters back. The snow there was soft and deep, but years in the bush made her sure-footed and quicker than most in the shadowy darkness. It took but a few minutes to break into the clearing. She scanned the field, trying to make out shapes. If only she'd brought her flashlight from the truck, but she'd never thought he would attack someone away from the lighted apartment building.

The moon slipped from behind the clouds and the field was suddenly bathed in soft light. A movement caught her attention near the bushes directly across from where she was standing, the width of a soccer field away. She lurched forward, her eyes on the dark shape in the snow. Several steps closer and she recognized a man's back and his raised arm, striking down at something lying at his feet. Adrenaline propelled her forward. His arm raised again.

"Stop! Police!" she called. "Stop what you're doing and put your hands where I can see them."

He half turned, his back humped like the Hunchback of Notre Dame — a Quasimodo shape to awaken night terrors. She was close enough to see the dark, lifeless form at his feet, to glimpse the flash of his white teeth in what might pass for a smile. He turned his face away from her. His hand dropped to his side and he took off through the bushes toward the far road.

She chased after him, making the split decision to leave the person in the snow a moment longer. He was trying to run, but the snow was deeper, a drift caught in the line of bushes. She gained precious steps and flung herself across the remaining distance to tackle his legs at thigh level. The impact knocked him to the ground. She kept her arms squeezed around kicking legs. He rolled under her, twisting his body so that he was sitting up. His arms came down around her head, a bare hand grabbing on to her neck. She released his legs and squirmed away, dodging kicks and somehow managing to get her hands free to push herself to her feet. One blow landed on her back before she steadied herself. She felt searing pain across her shoulder but managed to push herself back from his boots. He was standing now, kicking wildly in her direction. One kick landed on her collarbone but she pulled back in time to deflect the full impact.

"Cunt," he said. "Stupid bitch."

She scrambled to her feet and faced him, panting. "Police. Get down on the ground."

"Not on your life, bitch. Come closer so I can teach you a lesson."

"Don't say I didn't warn you."

She jumped back from another kick and then leapt forward, catching him off balance. She had her feet spread in a wide stance, bent at the knees. She pushed off with her feet and lunged, slugging him in the stomach with her fist. He doubled over and gasped for air as if he'd just finished running a marathon. She raised both hands and chopped him across the back until he dropped onto his knees in the snow. She knelt on one knee in the snow next to him and wrenched his arm back, twisting it with enough force to hear a snap. He screeched in pain. Her knee came up and dug into his back as she used her body weight to force him face down onto the ground. In one quick movement, she had her handcuffs out of her jacket pocket and cuffed both hands behind his back. She clicked them shut.

He writhed in the snow, but all resistance was gone. A stream of profanity spewed from his mouth. She leaned close to his ear, exposed where his hat had twisted nearly off. The rank smell of greasy hair filled her nose. His hair was white, just as Glenda Martin had reported. His face was clean shaven and barely lined. He couldn't be more than thirty-five years old.

"Whoever you were hitting back there better be alive," she said, "or I might just forget to come back for you."

She took off her rope belt and wrapped it around his legs below the knees. She pulled it tight and tied a knot. Even if he managed to crawl somewhere, he wouldn't get far.

His eyes were feverish with rage and pain in the moonlight. "You broke my arm, you fucking bitch. I'm going to have you put away." He rocked back and forth on his stomach, moaning and trying to flip onto his side without success.

"No point struggling," she said. "You'll just make it worse."

He howled as she stepped away from him. "Undo me! I said undo me! I'll make you pay if it's the last thing I do."

"I very much doubt that."

She pulled out her cellphone to call 911 as she started running back through the snow to find the victim, his screams and curses following her through the darkness.

27

ROULEAU REPLAYED THE interview from earlier that morning on the flat screen television on his office wall. His head was weary but he forced himself to focus. Kala Stonechild stood at attention next to Vermette while he congratulated her for getting a dangerous offender off the street. Her hair was tied back and she wore a navy jacket over a black turtleneck sweater. She'd borrowed the jacket and it fit loosely, a few sizes too large. Her face was unreadable, her eyes staring straight ahead, and her bandaged shoulder hidden by the over-sized coat.

What were you thinking? he wondered as the camera zoomed in on her. *What the hell were you doing out there?*

He turned at a knock on the door.

"Stonechild just came in," said Grayson. "Thought you'd want to know."

He withdrew and Rouleau crossed to the door. His team had surrounded her like she was a homecoming queen. Malik was hugging her and Bennett was waiting his turn. She had her back to Rouleau but appeared to be willingly accepting the attention. He heard her laugh at something Malik said. He waited a few minutes before calling for her to come into his office.

She turned to look at him and the smile left her face. She broke away from the group and walked toward him, her back as straight as an army cadet's. They entered his office.

"Sir," she said as he motioned for her to sit.

He settled into his desk chair across from her. "How are you feeling, Stonechild?" He'd noticed the line of sweat across her forehead and the grimace of pain as she sat down.

She shifted slightly. "I'm fine. Thanks for sending Bennett to drive me home from the hospital last night. Any word on the victim?"

"She's stable. A broken nose and cheek bone. Two broken ribs. The damage to one eye could be permanent."

"Damn," Stonechild muttered under her breath.

"Even though you were off duty, Vermette would like a full report. Are you feeling up to it?"

She nodded. "I had a few hours of sleep and should be good until tonight."

"I meant your shoulder. Can you type?"

"We'll soon see." She smiled for the first time.

His instinct was to smile back but he refrained. "It was a fortunate coincidence that you were at the same place as the man who'd been assaulting women along that stretch of Richmond Road." He waited while she collected how much she would tell him. The evasion in her eyes gave her away.

"I might have misled you about my living conditions. I never actually found an apartment yet and have been staying just down the street at the YWCA. There were vacancies in the apartment building on Richmond Road and I decided to check them out. I remembered the area from when we interviewed Glenda Martin after her assault." She shrugged.

"I heard a scream from the trees as I was walking back to my truck." She met his eyes and didn't look away this time.

After a few seconds, he looked down. "Richard Kennedy says you busted his arm on purpose."

"He resisted arrest. I had to control him quickly and get back to the victim."

Rouleau nodded. "You'll need to be clear in your report."

"I will. What have they found out about him?"

"Richard Kennedy's wife left him last year for his best friend. The two worked construction. They were framers for Chalmers Housing. After his wife walked out, Kennedy upped his coke habit and dreamed about getting even. He was practising taking out his anger on middle-aged women. You were right, by the way. He lives closer to the river but in the same general area."

"His rage probably didn't start after his wife left him. Will he press charges, you know, about the arm?"

"Won't matter if he does. As you say, he resisted arrest. The photos of your injuries confirm this."

She nodded, her eyes relieved. "Did he give a reason for beating this particular woman?"

"He said this morning that he hadn't planned to hurt her but she reminded him of his ex-wife."

"So he's admitted to all the assaults?"

"No, but we've got Glenda Martin coming in to see if she can pick him out of a photo array."

"Good."

"You can take the rest of the day off after you finish your report. Vermette's thrilled, by the way. You might have breathed life into this unit."

"Thank you, Sir, but I'm going to visit Susan Halliday before I go home."

"Take Bennett."

"I will."

She was nearly at the door when he said, "I don't want you doing this again."

"Sir?" She turned and was about to say something but stopped after reading something in his face.

"I know we understand each other," Rouleau said. Her eyes were bottomless black flint, and for the briefest of moments, defiant. He stared her down until she slowly dropped her head in a nod. He softened his voice. "You could have been seriously hurt. If you do something like this again, I will have to let you go. I can't have you out there putting yourself in danger. I'm responsible for you and everyone in this unit."

She kept her head lowered so that he couldn't see her eyes. "Yes, Sir. It won't happen again." She turned away from him again and opened the door.

"Thank you, Stonechild," he said. "For stopping him. You saved that woman's life. There's no doubt in my mind."

She paused with her back to him and nodded, but she said nothing. He watched her cross the room and sit down at her desk chair. She leaned down to turn on her computer. For the first time, he thought he might have made a mistake in hiring her.

He looked across at his navy suit in the drycleaner bag hanging on the wall hook behind his door. He'd had it cleaned and pressed down the street for Frances's New Year's Eve wedding. Just a day away. One day before his wife became somebody else's. What kind of gift did you buy for this occasion? Did they make cards to mark ex-wives' remarriages? Probably. They made them for everything else.

—

"So how does it feel to be a hero?" Bennett caught up to her at the main entrance. "You've become a legend in the department your first week here."

"Watch and learn, little grasshopper," Kala said, holding the door for him with her good arm. "Watch and learn." She grinned at him. "Just the right place at the right time, that's all."

"I think it was more than that. You took the guy down. Impressive. How's your shoulder?"

"Nothing major. He managed to crack it but I'm a fast healer."

"He's not so lucky. You taught him what for."

"Thanks." She liked that he'd forgotten the old boys' club for the moment. Maybe she was teaching him something after all. She followed him outside.

Bennett zipped up his jacket. "Where to now, boss?"

"We've got to figure out what's going on with Susan Halliday. First we'll drive up to the spot she got into car trouble in the Gatineau Hills. Do some old-fashioned detective work. Then we'll go talk to her and her husband Clinton. Somehow, we'll have to get her alone and I'll need your help with that."

"Right. Aren't you tired after last night?"

"I'm getting my second wind." The key was to keep moving. If she stopped for long, the exhaustion would catch up. She reached into the inside pocket of her parka. "I printed the map and marked the spot where she parked to go skiing."

He took it from her. "I know the place. I bike up there in the summer."

"Good. You can drive then."

Bennett headed north through downtown and crossed the Portage Bridge at the end of Wellington Street into

Quebec. He followed Chemin d'Aylmer for a few kilometres before turning right onto the Gatineau Parkway. The road wound steadily skyward into the wooded hills blanketed in glistening snow under the crystal blue sky. Kala felt the tightness in her chest ease. Even the pain in her shoulder was lessening as they progressed into the wilderness.

"It's been a few days since her accident. What do you expect to find?"

"Don't know. I just want to get a feel for how it happened."

"Fair enough." He fished around in his pocket and pulled out aviator sunglasses. "Shit, that sun is bright. This must take you back home, being out here."

"Yeah."

"Do you miss it?"

"You could say that."

He glanced in her direction and she saw her face reflected back in his glasses. "So did you leave any family or boyfriends behind?"

She stared at his profile. "Just the usual."

"Must be nice. I'd give anything to get a break from my family, not to mention my ex who still thinks we're going to get back together. Some women just won't take no."

"Why don't you ask for a transfer?" She was genuinely curious why he would stay in Ottawa if he wanted to leave so badly.

"I don't know. I've never lived anywhere else. Sounds like you've moved around a bit."

She squinted out the side window. The light felt like pinpricks in her eyes. They were passing a sign that said Pinks Lake. The turn off wasn't far. Just a few more minutes and she could focus on something besides the uncomfortable turn this conversation had taken. She had no intention of thinking about her past just now, let alone share it with Bennett.

They reached the empty parking lot. Bennett pulled into a spot near the entrance and they both got out. Kala looked around, then crossed the lot with Bennett following behind her. She crouched down, looking for tire marks. She was disappointed but not surprised that any evidence was long gone.

"Do you see something?" Bennett squatted down in the snow next to her.

"Susan Halliday told me she parked here at the north end and another vehicle parked next to her while she was skiing. She never saw the driver."

Kala looked around the flat expanse of open space. It was bordered by a wooden fence of rough logs tied horizontally that held back the thick woods. A packed cross-country ski trail snaked into the trees from an opening in the fence. Looking up, the blue sky was a dome hinged by the tops of conifer trees on all sides. Heavy, grey clouds had begun gathering over the western perimeter and she sensed more snow coming, likely by nightfall. She thought again of how the weather changed quickly in the Ottawa Valley, not like in the North where storms took their time coming and going. She tried to imagine Susan out here alone with evening falling.

"There's nothing left to see from her visit. The lot was plowed since she was here." Kala stood and looked toward the woods. "Why would someone park right next to her when the lot was empty? Why would they even be up here if they weren't going skiing?"

"Do you think she was followed?"

"Maybe. Someone could have taken the opportunity to strand her out here. She doesn't strike me as the kind of woman who would drive into the Gatineau Hills and not notice she was out of gas. She said that she's been forgetful, but how many people really let the tank get that low? It's something you check automatically. Especially if you're the only driver. You gauge how much time between fill ups." Kala looked back at the entrance to the parking area. "You'd have to know this spot was here or have followed her. Maybe somebody was waiting outside her house. Why would they do that is the question. Why would somebody set out to hurt her?"

"It's easy enough to siphon gas if you have the time. Somebody would have had the privacy to do it unseen up here in the middle of nowhere."

Kala took another look around. "It's a peaceful place but there's something ominous about it too. The spirits aren't all happy here."

Bennett looked at her oddly. "There was a rape just over there by the path a few summers ago. It made a lot of people scared to use the bike paths."

"Did they catch him?"

"No."

Kala suddenly couldn't wait to get away from this isolated place. "You ready to leave?"

Bennett pulled the keys out his pocket. He took a final look around. "Yeah. Looks like we're not going to learn anything here unless one of those spirits decides to start talking."

28

THIS TIME, SUSAN Halliday was the one who answered the door. She'd made an attempt to fix her hair and had applied make up that gave an artificial rosiness to her cheeks and lips. A bright red mohair sweater hung loosely on her thin frame, topping tight black pants. Kala was impressed with Susan's natural grace although she doubted Susan was aware of her beauty. Women approaching sixty were made to feel unattractive because of their lined faces and aging skin. There was an apologetic air about Susan as if she was afraid of offending by her very presence. However, it wasn't enough to extinguish the inner light when her tawny eyes found Kala's. A self-effacing smile spread across Susan's face.

"I know why you've come, but I'm fine. I'm embarrassed for causing so much trouble. Clinton has made me promise not to go anywhere again unless I first check the gas level."

"Speaking of your husband, is he home?" asked Kala.

"No, he's gone to get his hair cut and to pick up a few things for supper. I expect him back in a few hours."

Kala glanced at Bennett and he nodded.

"I'll just go make those calls if you don't mind me in your kitchen. That way I won't disturb you," said Bennett.

"Of course," said Susan. "Help yourself to tea. I just made a pot and it's on the stove." She looked at Kala. "Would you like some?"

"Tea would be lovely."

A few minutes later, they were sitting across from each other with mugs of tea in hand as if they were girlfriends having a chat. Susan tucked her feet under her.

"So you're feeling better?" Kala asked.

"Yes. My hands and feet are fine. I wasn't in the woods long enough for any lasting damage. I was very lucky that ranger came along when he did."

"Have you recalled any details of that afternoon?"

Susan shook her head. "I'm sorry."

"Did you find the credit card receipt for your last gas purchase?"

"I was mistaken. I paid cash the last time I bought gas."

"Do you normally pay cash?"

"Not as a rule, but I'm very sloppy about my record-keeping I'm afraid. I remembered after leaving the hospital that I paid cash because I'd forgotten my credit card at home. I just got careless about keeping track. I was driving more than usual, getting ready for Christmas, and then I became distracted with Tom Underwood's death."

"Any receipt of the cash payment?"

"No. I must have tossed it." She laughed lightly. "You must wonder how I've managed to survive this long."

"On the contrary. Has Clinton shared with you where he was that day that you went into the Gatineau Hills?"

"He left the base in Trenton mid-morning and was on his way home. He wanted to surprise me."

"We checked and he left close to seven thirty. It's a four hour drive so he would have been home before noon. You told us that you set out for the park after one o'clock."

Susan took a sip of tea. Her hand shook slightly when she lowered the mug but her voice was firm. "He stopped for breakfast in Gananoque. He told me that service was slow because a tour bus arrived just before he ordered. Really, officer, I know what you're getting at, but you are completely mistaken."

"Mrs. Halliday, I need to ask, how are things between you and your husband? Has he ever been violent with you?"

Susan forcefully shook her head. "He would never have done this to me. Never. I was just careless."

"If not your husband, perhaps you know of someone else? They may be the person who murdered Tom Underwood."

"I don't know of anyone. Tom had to have been killed by a stranger or someone from his work life. I don't know which would be worse." She drew her fist up to her mouth and closed her eyes.

Kala studied her. Should she continue to push? Susan was shielding someone and her money was on Clinton. She reached into her pocket. "I'm going to give you my cellphone number. You can call me anytime, day or night, and I'll come. If you feel like talking, I'm a good listener. I want to help you."

Susan opened her eyes. They were filled with pain but also resolve. "Thank you, officer, but I'm certain I'll be fine." She took the card and tucked it into her pocket. "Now, if that is all, I would like to rest. It's been a long, tiring week."

"Of course. Please contact me if you remember anything else. I'm just a phone call away."

———

Kala left Bennett at the station and trudged through the snow to the Y. She was ready to spend the rest of the day sleeping. Her legs and arms felt weighted down with cement. Fatigue had settled into her brain like cotton batting. Her cell vibrated inside her pocket just as she pressed the elevator button in the lobby. She got the phone to her ear before the caller hung up. She hadn't recognized the number.

"Hello?"

"Is this Kala Stonechild?"

"Yes. Who's calling?"

"It's Maya from the Mission. How are you doing, child?"

Kala smiled. "Good. I'm good." The tiredness lifted for the moment. "You have news?"

"I saw that young girl, Dawn, last night. She came in with another woman, not your cousin, but the homeless woman the police are looking for. Anyhow, I called the other officer who asked me to keep an eye out for her but the girls had both gone before the police arrived. I would have called you sooner, but I'd misplaced your card."

"What's the name of the homeless woman?"

"Annie Littlewolf. She's five foot nothing, about forty years old. An Ojibway from out west. I hadn't seen her around since her friend was found dead in that alley. Poor soul."

"Did the little girl, Dawn, did she look okay? She wasn't with this woman against her will?"

"As far as I could tell, they were friendly with each other. They got some food and disappeared before I could get to them."

"And they haven't been back?"

"No, but now that I've found your card, I'll call you right away the next time I see either of them."

"I'd appreciate that, Maya."

"No problem, child. You take care."

"You too … and thanks."

Kala rode the elevator to her floor. She unlocked the door to her room and stepped inside. The air was stale and dry. She crossed to the window before she remembered that it was sealed shut. She was going to have to hope that the heat shut off soon since she also didn't have a thermostat control in her room. She dropped her clothes on the floor and climbed naked under the sheets. The throbbing in her shoulder reminded her that she needed to take another pain-killer. She sighed and got up again to rummage through her bag. It was an effort to walk back to her bed and lower herself onto the mattress. She had a voice mail message from Shannon that she'd meant to return before going to sleep, but it wasn't going to happen. Whatever Shannon wanted to tell her would keep until morning. Kala stretched her aching legs and rolled onto her side, careful to protect her bandaged shoulder. Ten seconds later, she was sound asleep. She didn't stir until dawn.

Benny sat on Max's desk, one leg crossed over the other at the knee, a burning cigarette in his hand. Max leaned back in his desk chair, his head at crotch level but his eyes on Benny's face. Benny's blue eyes reminded him of sparkling aquamarine stones. They were his best feature by far. Max absentmindedly reached over and rubbed his fingers lightly along the crease in Benny's pant leg.

"It's getting harder to put up with this domestic crap, Benny. I never thought it would be this exhausting. At least the kid should keep her occupied."

"You're a trooper. Just keep your eye on the money."

"I don't know anymore. When you cooked up this scheme, it felt like a sure thing, but the longer it goes on, the less good I feel about deceiving Geraldine. She's going to cotton on if she hasn't already."

"That's why you have to start investing more time in keeping her happy. You have to make it look like you really want to be married to her." Benny took one last puff and dabbed the cigarette in the ashtray next to him on the desk. "We knew going in this was going to take time."

"Why was I the one who had to get married again?"

"Because you're better looking and you have way more charm."

"I'll bet you say that to all the guys." Max's fingers moved lightly up Benny's leg. "It's just not as easy to keep up the pretence as time goes by. Believe it or not, I feel sorry for Geraldine."

"Well, use your empathy to start treating her better. We're too close to the jackpot for you to grow a conscience now."

"You always could talk me into ... stuff."

"We're going to have to be careful about meeting for a while. With the cops poking around, it could get dicey. After this evening, you need to spend more time at home. Act like you and the missus and your kid are one happy family."

"Great. For how long?"

"After they stop investigating Tom's death, we'll start moving money again. If all goes well, you can extricate yourself by summer. We'll winter somewhere warm. What do you think about next Christmas in Cuba?"

Max nodded slowly and looked at this man who'd had a hold on him since high school. Benny was too short and slender and his black hair too bristly to be called handsome, but it was the blue eyes that won him over — that and Benny's wild side. Benny took chances that maybe bordered on reckless. When they first met, Benny had needed some-one to dominate and Max had been happy to oblige. A Bonnie to his Clyde. What had he let this obsession lead him into?

"I'll hold you to that," Max said. His fingers had reached Benny's zipper. "So this could be it for a while?"

"Sadly, we have to be careful," Benny said. His face changed and he held up a hand. "Did you hear that noise?"

"What noise?"

"I thought we were the only two in the building." Benny jumped off the desk and crossed to the partially open door. He pushed it all the way open and looked both ways down the hall. He shut and locked it, then walked slowly back to Max. "I guess I'm just getting jumpy." He leaned against the desk and cupped Max's chin in his hand. "You really are a delicious-looking man, you know that Maxy? And if we stick together, you'll soon be a rich and single delicious-looking man."

"Don't worry. I won't blow it." Max looked up at Benny and batted his eyes. "Although you are another matter." He growled deep in his throat and they both laughed.

Max placed his hand on Benny's thigh. "If this is going to be it for a while, let's stop wasting time."

29

CARLA RODRIGUEZ WOKE up earlier than usual when her husband Phil grunted like a bull moose and rolled over to toss a beefy arm across her back. His mouth came to rest next to her ear. The ripple of snores coming from deep in his chest sounded like a small plane engine preparing for takeoff. Carla opened her eyes and tried to focus in the small bedroom's dim light. Phil mumbled something in his sleep before a new snort broke the sound barrier. Well, that settled it. There would be no more sleep for her this morning.

She slipped out from under his arm and stood looking down at this great hulk of a man she adored more than life itself. His black hair had turned grey above his ears and the deep lines in his forehead were no longer softened by sleep. Two children grown and gone — the last off to find himself six months ago — and they were acting like newlyweds. They couldn't get enough of each other. It was funny how life went in circles. For years, they'd barely had breathing space to be alone together, let alone have sex. Phil was sure making up for lost time. It was as if he hadn't realized they were sixty-two years old and should be past all the physical lust. For this, she lit a candle of thanks every Sunday before mass.

She placed a kiss on his shoulder and grabbed her robe from the foot of their bed as she made her way to the downstairs shower. A quick rinse and she'd stop at Andy's Diner for coffee and a muffin on her way to the office. If she got in an hour early, she'd have the floors washed before everyone started trooping into the building. Christmas holidays and the moguls barely missed an hour of work. Well, next year at this time, she and Phil would be retired in an adult-only community in Florida and she wouldn't give a hoot if these people wanted to work themselves to death. She'd been a careful saver and with Phil's bus driver pension from OC Transpo, they'd do okay. It would be a relief to get out of the rat race.

A half hour later, Carla pulled into the staff parking lot at the back of the five-storey office building at the corner of Kent and Somerset. The street lamps were still on with the sun rising late on these winter mornings. Her employer had sent her to this building three weeks earlier to look after the cleaning on the first two floors. John Schiemann had the top three floors, but his medical clients had the decency to close over the holiday. Her client had put in a request for their cleaner to work regular hours through the holiday season. Just her luck. She'd gotten into the habit of finishing her two floors and helping John with the third. It had been a surprisingly lonely week with him on holidays.

She removed the blueberry muffin from the brown wrapper and bit into it. Still warm from the oven. It took effort to rip the plastic from the coffee lid with her teeth but she managed. A few sips and she felt ready to face the cold outdoors. The temperature had dropped from the day before and it had taken forever to warm up her car. It was a shame to have to leave it to make a dash to the back door.

She glanced to the north end of the lot. Who was working this early? She tried to remember the man who drove the black Impala that was backed into one of the spaces. Did he have no life at all? She glanced at the clock on the dashboard. It was just going on six thirty. Even this crowd usually didn't make it in before seven thirty.

She wrapped the muffin back up and stuffed it into her bag. Then she opened the door while holding on to her coffee cup. As she locked the door with her key, she again glanced across the lot at the car. Snow had blown over the windshield and piled onto the hood on the driver's side. The car must have been there a while. She shook her head. What in the world could get someone into work so early over the holiday week? It was New Year's Eve for goodness sake. She'd be going home at noon no matter what the other workaholics planned to do. Phil had tickets to the Legion dinner and dance and she needed a few hours to get ready. He'd even had her book a hair appointment and buy a new dress. She'd picked a cherry red number with silver sparkles around the neckline. A bit tighter than she usually wore, but the salesgirl said it made her look good. She could live with good.

Carla started walking across the parking lot toward the back entrance. The fresh layer of snow from the night's snowfall covered the walkways. It hadn't been snowing when she got up at quarter after five and something didn't feel right. She slowed her steps. Where were the footprints from the person who'd beaten her in to work? She turned and looked back at the car, her brow furrowing into puzzled lines. The parking lot was empty and the strengthening dawn sunlight cast long shadows. The sun wouldn't be completely up for another hour or so.

She started back toward the car. They'd had a problem with people parking in the lot who didn't work in the building. It wasn't the case this time though. She recognized the car. It belonged to one of the men who liked to work overtime. He was usually in the other one's office with the door closed. In the mornings she'd find empty pizza boxes and sometimes beer cans from late night sessions stacked beside the garbage can.

A memory worried itself into her mind. There'd been a murder connected to the company recently. Phil had read the article out loud in the paper, but she'd only been half listening. It wasn't like she felt any connection to this place. Phil liked to read stuff to her because he knew the effort it took her to work through an article. Then she'd go back and reread what he'd just read out loud. He knew that it helped her make sense of the jumble of letters on the page if she already had an idea of their meaning.

She remembered now. One of the big shots was found in the trunk of his car a few days before Christmas. She'd been instructed not to clean his office until further notice. She'd never met the man who died and hadn't felt anything more than passing sadness for a stranger. She slowed her steps. What if there was a body in the car?

She stood still, trying to convince herself not to be foolish when John Schiemann's blue truck pulled into the lot a bit faster than necessary. He parked it next to hers and got out, jingling a row of keys as he approached. He was just a kid in his late twenties with green and black tattoos winding up his arms and the back of his neck. He usually covered his Mohawk haircut with a baseball cap at work. Today, he wore an unbuttoned duffle coat and runners, the sight of which made her shiver inside her down coat.

"What're you doing just standing there? Locked out?" he asked.

"No. I was wondering ... well, it seems silly, but that car has been here a while and I was going to make sure it was ... empty." She laughed self-consciously.

He turned and studied it. "You're thinking of the old dude they found in the trunk."

She nodded.

"Let's check it out."

She followed him to the car, trying not to slip as she hurried to keep up with his loping strides. By the time she caught up, he'd cleared off the front driver's side of snow and was cupping his hands to look inside. She moved next to him and rubbed a spot on the glass to look in the back seat. They shrugged at each other before he circled around the back of the car. He thumped the trunk a few times before coming back to stand beside her.

"Doesn't look to be anything weighing down the trunk. I think whoever owns this already split."

"Well, thank the Lord for that," she said, feeling relieved but oddly disappointed at the same time. The empty car made her look like a fanciful, old woman afraid of her own shadow.

They crossed to the office building and she unlocked the door. Her fingers were numb through her gloves and it took a few tries.

"I'm supposed to work New Year's Day, but screw that," John said. "I came in to do the floors and nobody'll know the difference."

"They won't hear it from me," said Carla.

They cleaned the snow off their boots before starting down the hallway.

"You want to take a break around ten?" Carla asked. She frowned and pointed. "What's that mess on the floor by the storage room? I didn't leave it like that yesterday."

John glanced over then back at her. They stared into each other's eyes as comprehension dawned, then looked back at the closed door. A pool of dark liquid had seeped from under the opening.

"I'll go see what it is," John said. His voice had risen to the shrill range. He cleared his throat. "You stay here."

"No, I'm responsible for this floor." They both stood for a moment without moving. "I'll do it," Carla said with more determination than she felt.

John nodded encouragement.

She marched over to the storage room and took a deep breath before yanking the door open. Immediately, she heard somebody screaming. It took her a few seconds to figure out that it was her.

She remembered now who owned the car in the parking lot. He was lying scrunched up in front of her with the back of his head beaten into a bloody pulp. She backed away and bumped into John who'd followed her to get a better look.

"I'm ... I'll ..." His face was as white as toilet paper and he couldn't get his words out. Carla felt as rocky as he looked. Her knees buckled and she took a step sideways to lean against the wall. John opened his mouth before turning to flee, almost making it to the men's room before he vomited down the hallway.

—

Geraldine woke from a deep sleep and rolled onto her side. Amy Rose was in the bassinet a few feet away, sleeping peacefully at last. They'd been up most of the night. Amy

Rose had fussed and cried for no reason Geraldine could figure out. She'd finally taken half a bottle at five a.m. and mercifully fallen asleep. It hadn't taken Geraldine long to follow suit.

She stretched and looked at the bedside clock. Ten after eleven. She did a quick calculation in her head; just six hours of sleep, but it would have to do. Her breasts were engorged and uncomfortable. She'd missed her pills to dry up the milk and needed to get up and find them. She felt like hell. She'd risk a shower and hopefully would have time to make a cup of tea. It was highly unlikely that Max would take over if the baby woke and she was in the shower.

She sat on the side of the bed for a few moments to watch her baby sleeping. It was hard to believe this perfect little person came out of her. Giving birth could make you believe in miracles. It could make you want to stop drinking. She looked at Max's tidy side of the bed and sighed. He'd called just after supper the night before to say that he'd be home late and would take the guest bedroom. He'd said it was so that he wouldn't disturb her. He'd accomplished that feat because she hadn't heard him come in. He planned to take today off. She wondered how long before he went out somewhere.

She sighed again and looked back at Amy Rose. It was amazing that she'd been conceived at all. Max's initial interest in the bedroom had died off completely once she became pregnant. He'd said it was because of all the extra hours he was putting in at the office to prove himself. They'd laughed once about his body becoming like a worn out old tire. She knew deep down that he'd been pulling away from her. He'd spent more time with his assistant Benny than he had with her.

Geraldine stood up too quickly and swayed against the side of the bed as a wave of dizziness spread through her. It took a few seconds to regain her balance. It was as if she was drunk, but not on alcohol. She moved closer to the bassinet and looked down on Amy Rose. So innocent. So undeserving of this cruel world. She leaned forward so that her hair trailed onto Amy Rose's blanket. The baby startled in her sleep, her eyelids fluttered as if she was dreaming. Geraldine held her breath and counted to ten. Amy Rose didn't wake up. It was a good sign. She would still had time to shower and make tea before Max put in an appearance downstairs.

30

ROULEAU RANG THE doorbell and took a step back. He drew his coat tighter around his neck and cursed himself for forgetting his hat and scarf at the office. He hadn't realized how low the temperature had dropped. He saw movement through the bevelled glass and it wasn't long before Geraldine opened the door. She held a nearly empty cup of tea in one hand and a baby bottle of milk tucked under her arm. Her wet hair had left dark splotches on the shoulders of her bathrobe. She looked at Rouleau with a puzzled expression on her face.

"Yes, can I help you?" she asked.

He realized they'd never met even though he knew so much about her. She'd inherited more of her mother's facial features than her father's, but somehow in the new mixture, the beauty had been lost. Even her body was slightly out of proportion and too large to be feminine. He could imagine the childhood cruelties she had endured. He held up his ID. "Geraldine Oliver?"

She nodded.

"I need to speak with you. It's not good news I'm afraid."

"Of course, come in out of the cold."

She didn't wait for him to remove his boots but walked down the hallway as if his last sentence hadn't registered. She called over her shoulder, "I was expecting my mother. She's supposed to be coming to help with the baby today."

He followed behind her into the kitchen. It was a newly done-over room, quite welcoming with pine cupboards and a sitting area arranged in front of patio windows. The smell of Earl Grey tea and baby formula mixed sweetly in the air. She slipped past him toward the hallway.

"I'll just get Max, shall I? It's almost lunch time and he should be up." She disappeared from the room before he could respond.

Rouleau walked over to the window and looked out at the mounds of snow on the deck and the birds circling a feeder atop a pole farther down in the yard. A squirrel was entrenched in the middle of the feeder, fending off his competition. He slowed his breathing and tried to get into the zen place Malik told him helped with stress. So far, he hadn't mastered it.

Max Oliver took his time coming downstairs and into the kitchen. His hair was uncombed and his eyes were bleary from sleep but he'd put on jeans and a cable knit pullover. He held out a hand to Rouleau.

"Sergeant. Sorry, I was up late with the baby and took the opportunity to sleep in. I understand you have news?"

"Yes, sad news I'm afraid. You have an assistant, Benny Goldstone?"

"Yes."

"When did you see him last?"

"We worked late last night on the project I was handed because of Tom's death. The contract needed some tightening up and it took us until about eight o'clock. What's this about?"

"Did you come home right afterwards?"

"No, I went for a few drinks and got home around midnight. Look, detective, I have no idea why you're asking me this but ..."

"The cleaners in your office building found Benny Goldstone dead this morning."

"No." Max's face drained to the colour of paste. He clutched his chest and staggered back a step. "I ... can't believe ... this."

Geraldine appeared in the doorway. "What is it? Max, are you all right?"

"I'm fine. It's just that Benny ..."

"Benny what?"

Rouleau heard the exasperation that had crept into her voice. She crossed her arms across her breasts.

"He's dead," said Max harshly. He turned back toward Rouleau. "Benny left the office before me. I don't understand how this is possible."

"Did you leave by the parking lot exit?"

"No. The main doors. My car was closer to the front of the building."

"How far behind him were you?"

"About half an hour. I had a few calls to make."

"So you left work around quarter to nine?"

"That's right." Max glanced at Geraldine. "I called Ger around seven to say I'd be late."

"You never mentioned the part about going to a bar," said Geraldine.

"I just needed to unwind after the baby and work. It's been a busy week."

"You didn't hear or see anything unusual?" asked Rouleau. He directed his question to Max but kept his eyes on Geraldine. He found her rigid stance odd.

"Nothing. The front door was locked but I set the alarm before exiting. It's always the last one to leave that sets it."

"I thought you shared the building with doctors."

"We do, but they leave by six. Plus they weren't in over the holiday week. It's understood that we set the alarm since we're always there later. If we happen to leave early, we let one of their receptionists know. There's never been a problem. Christ. How did he die?"

"It's early to say, but it wasn't an accident. Somebody killed him."

"Just like Tom. My God."

Geraldine moved closer to Rouleau. "It must mean their deaths are work-related. Perhaps it's that project you're working on. Daddy was working on the same one before he was murdered. Do you think it's the same killer?"

"Again, it's early yet to speculate," said Rouleau. "Were you alone all evening?" he asked Geraldine.

"Yes, except for my baby."

"J.P. Belliveau identified Benny," Rouleau said.

"Benny's mother lives in Sandy Hill on Stewart Street." Max's voice broke.

"Yes, we notified her half an hour ago. She should be at the police station now."

"Could I ... see him?"

"Just family at this point, I'm afraid."

"Max is like Benny's immediate family, isn't that right, Max?" asked Geraldine. "They were as close as brothers."

"I suppose I could take you to see him."

Max straightened his shoulders. "I'll just get dressed and will follow you in my car. My wife needs to stay here with the baby."

"Take your time," she said. "I can manage just fine on my own."

—

Hunter opened the door and hesitated at the sight of Kala on his doorstep. He held a tea towel and dried his hands as he invited her in. His eyes were wary.

She took off her boots and followed him into the kitchen. Fabio padded over to the doorway to nuzzle her leg. She bent down to pet him and then straightened. She was startled to see six-year-old Charlotte Underwood sitting at the table, a forkful of pancake on its way to her mouth. Her violet eyes, so like her mother's, fixed themselves on Kala's face. She chewed with her mouth open.

"Coffee?" asked Hunter, lifting the half-full pot and pointing it in Kala's direction. The brew smelled deep-roasted and strong.

She pulled her gaze away from the child and looked at Hunter. "No, thank you. I'm afraid I'm here with more bad news, although not as directly related to you as your father's death."

Hunter turned and set the coffee pot on the stove. "Not again," he said quietly.

"Should we ... perhaps it's better if we go into the other room."

He nodded. "Charlotte, I'll be right back."

Her red curls bobbed up and down. Fabio's toenails click clicked as he made his way across the floor to flop down next to her swinging feet.

In the living room, they stood near the window that looked out over the side yard. Kala was still trying to absorb Rouleau's early morning call. First Tom Underwood and now an employee from his company. She didn't believe in coincidences. Did Laurel and Hunter's burgeoning friendship still fit into the puzzle?

"Well?" Hunter asked.

"We got a call around seven a.m. Benny Goldstone was found dead this morning by the cleaning staff at your father's office."

Hunter looked out the window then back at Kala, his face empty of expression.

"Do my sister and Max know?"

"Sergeant Rouleau has gone to tell them. He sent me to let you know the news."

"And to see how I react."

"That too."

"This is … unbelievable. If it's okay with you, I'll pack up Charlotte and we'll go over to Geraldine's. I'll try to reach Laurel from there."

"Where is Laurel?"

"A spa in Chelsea. She needed some time away and I offered to take Charlotte. She is my half sister, after all." The corner of his mouth rose in a mocking grin.

"Where's Chelsea?"

"In Quebec on the way to Wakefield. It's about forty-five minutes from Ottawa." He shook his head as if trying to shake away the craziness of her news. "Do you know how Benny died?"

"He was bludgeoned to death, it looks like with an Inuit art sculpture from the lobby. J.P. Belliveau identified him."

"What time was he killed?"

"It's too early to tell, but he'd been dead a while when he was found. What time did Laurel drop off Charlotte?"

Hunter frowned. He stared into her eyes as if searching for something. "It was nearly nine o'clock last night. Laurel decided on the spur of the moment around eight that she had to get away. She called me and made a reservation after I agreed to take Charlotte. Charlotte was ready for bed when

Laurel phoned so she bundled her up and they arrived an hour later."

"This didn't strike you as odd?"

"The entire holiday season strikes me as odd. Laurel is grieving. I didn't question her need to get away."

"Did you know Benny Goldstone?"

"I'd met him a few times at my sister's. Max would bring him around to family dinners."

"What did you think of him?"

"He was socially awkward, always in the background and not saying much. I had no opinion about him one way or the other."

"Did Geraldine have any issues with Benny spending so much time with her husband?"

Hunter glared at her. "Look, are you trying to say Geraldine had something to do with Benny's death? Or maybe you'd rather I just admit that I killed him. Sounds like he died at work. Maybe that's where you should be looking for the killer."

He avoided her eyes as he pushed past her to get to the kitchen. She could hear him calling for Charlotte to finish the last few bites of her pancake so they could go visit her new baby niece.

Kala turned down the hallway to put on her boots. She told herself that the heaviness in her stomach had nothing to do with the coldness in his voice. Wasn't it she who had warned him that he would feel differently about her by the end of the investigation? She turned as Charlotte came skipping down the hallway.

"Hunter says we're going to Geraldine's house. He's just got to take Fabio outside for a minute. I'm to put on my snowsuit and wait here."

"I'll wait with you then. Is this your suit on the hook?"

"The pink one."

"Of course. I've got it." She handed the jacket and ski pants to Charlotte and smiled. "Let me know if you need help tying up your scarf."

"I can do it myself." Charlotte stood motionless in front of her, eyes solemn. "Daddy's not here to help me anymore and Mommy's tired. She told me that I need to learn to do more things for myself. We're going to move away soon."

"Oh?" Kala leaned forward.

"Mommy doesn't like our big house. Daddy didn't like it either. He was going to move away too."

"He told you that?"

Charlotte nodded. "He said he would always love me even if he and Mommy didn't live together."

"When did he tell you this, Charlotte?"

"When we went out with the lady he was going to live with. I wasn't to tell Mommy."

"You kept the secret."

"I promised."

"Was he going to move in with Pauline?"

Charlotte's forehead scrunched up in a frown. "Who's Pauline again?"

Kala looked up. Hunter was standing in the doorway to the kitchen. "All set to go, Charlotte?" he asked. "We don't want to keep Officer Stonechild from her work."

Kala straightened. "I'm sure I'll be seeing you soon."

She smiled at Charlotte and opened the door, noticing for the first time a milder wind blowing in from the south. The deep freeze was on its last legs as a mid-winter thaw began stealing into the Ottawa Valley. Kala stepped outside, happy to feel the shifting wind on her face as she thought about Tom Underwood and the woman he was prepared to leave home for.

31

THEY GATHERED MID-AFTERNOON in Rouleau's office. The sunlight poured like weak tea through slats in the venetian blind. It was the dead of winter, but the rising temperature was giving a brief respite from the frigid temperatures. The warmer air mass wouldn't last long, but it was enough to raise their spirits.

Kala took the chair near the wall away from the others. She was overheated in her turtleneck sweater and thermal undershirt and felt sweat dampening her armpits. She took a sip of coffee and let the mug rest on her knee. The coffee was bitter and had likely been made just after lunch. No wonder she was the only one with a cup. Grayson and Malik were going through their notes and commenting to each other. She half-listened to Bennett and Gage's animated discussion on whether or not to trade the Senators' goalie. Rouleau appeared a few minutes later from a meeting with Vermette.

"Right," he said, slapping a couple of files on the desk and dropping into his battered leather chair. "One bit of good news in this miserable week. We can stop looking for Annie Littlewolf. Her partner died of natural causes, a heart attack to be exact. He wasn't murdered, so Annie has no reason to be in hiding because we have no reason to believe she's in danger."

"Shouldn't we still be trying to locate her though?" asked Kala. If they didn't locate Annie, her lead to Dawn and Rosie would be lost.

"Social Services is on the lookout now. They'll look after her when she turns up." Rouleau looked at each of them in turn. "Initial forensics is in on Benny Goldstone. He was hit repeatedly with a blunt object from behind, which I can now confirm is the Inuit art sculpture from the showcase in the lobby. He was then dragged into the closet where most of the bleeding took place. It's likely death occurred on the second blow, which crushed the back of his skull. He was standing near the exit door when struck. Whoever did it, superficially wiped up the blood in the hallway and dumped the paper towels into the trash inside the closet. The security camera in the parking lot didn't record anybody coming or going around the time he was killed, but someone could have gotten around it if they knew how it's angled. There were no prints so the killer likely wore gloves. Goldstone was a small man. Five seven and one hundred and thirty-five pounds; a man or woman could have moved him easily enough. He'd been with the firm five years, the last two as Max Oliver's assistant. What have you found out about Goldstone's home life, Malik?"

Malik flicked open his notebook. "Lived in a one bed-room in Hintonburg near Wellington for the last ten years. Graduated from Algonquin College with a business degree and worked for a high-tech company for several years before it went belly up. Took a job with Underwood and company a few years ago. Mother lives in Sandy Hill. Father deceased. No siblings. Never married." Malik looked up and paused.

"Benny curled in the rainbow league at the Ottawa Curling Club."

"He's gay?" asked Grayson.

"Looks that way."

"Boyfriends?" asked Rouleau.

"Officially, no. However, there are rumours that he and Max Oliver had something going on. He frequented gay bars on Elgin and in the ByWard Market."

Kala kept silent even though it was validating to know she'd pegged Max correctly.

"It can't be a coincidence that both Oliver and Underwood were working on the same project. I still say all this has something to do with work," Grayson said.

Rouleau looked at Kala. "Thoughts?"

"Work is a possible reason. The family connection is another."

"Can you narrow that down?"

"Not yet."

"Great," said Grayson, letting them know it was not. "I say we pull in Oliver and Belliveau. The link has to be there."

"Okay," said Rouleau. "Malik and Grayson, you start redoing the interviews in their office, although most of the employees will have gone home by now since it's New Year's Eve. It'll mean some driving around to find them, but see what you can do. Start with Max and J.P. and do the rest tomorrow. You might need to go back to Montreal to talk to Archambault. Bennett and Gage, start going through Benny Goldstone's files and computer. Stonechild, stick with the family angle. Whelan will be back in January to give you a hand."

They nodded and stood. Rouleau held up a hand. "One more thing. We have until January fifth before Major

Crimes takes over the cases. We'll move back into the supporting role."

"That means we'll still be doing the legwork but without
the credit," said Grayson.

Kala looked more closely at Rouleau. The tiredness in
his eyes went deeper than this case. She'd noticed his suit in
the dry cleaning bag hanging on the hook next to the door.
Whatever New Year's Eve party he was supposed to attend
would likely be a miss. She wondered if it was important to
him. "We should be wrapping this up before Major Crimes
gets involved," she said.

Rouleau smiled. "I'm not organizing a parade yet."

Grayson said something under his breath to Malik. They
sent Kala darting, sideways looks. Bennett and Gage ex-
changed equally disbelieving glances. The old boys' club was
closing ranks. Kala ignored them and went to get her coat.
She knew where she had to go to get answers. It was just a
matter of putting the pieces together.

———

She pulled over in front of a townhouse and picked up her
phone from where she'd tossed it on the passenger seat. She
checked the incoming call. It was Shannon trying to reach
her again. She pressed talk and held the phone to her ear.

"Shannon? Everything okay?"

"You're harder to reach than the Pope. I've left messages
for two days already."

"Sorry. I've been on a case. What's up?"

"Jordan came by again. I told him you wouldn't be coming home. That you took a job out of town and wanted him
to forget about you. That it was over."

"And?"

"Your plan worked. He moved back in with his wife. I hope that's really what you wanted."

"It is." She shut a door in her mind.

"I honestly thought he'd hold out for you."

"You're a romantic."

"Yeah. He didn't say anything after I told him you'd gone for good. Just stood there for a minute, then nodded and walked away."

"It's for the best, Shan."

"I guess. It's just sometimes … you never let anyone in. Not really." A pause. "Any news on finding your cousin?"

"I'm close, I think. It's just a matter of time."

"I hope you come home soon, Kala. We miss you like crazy."

"I miss you too. How's Taiku?"

"He's moping around but eating."

"I'll try to call again soon."

"Don't forget about us. We aren't going anywhere."

Kala closed her eyes. "I promise I'll call. You know I always keep my word."

"I know."

Kala snapped her phone shut and stared straight ahead. *Or at least I try to.*

———

Susan answered the door and led Kala into the living room. They sat at opposite ends of the couch.

"You've missed Clinton again. He had some errands to run."

"It's you I've come to see," said Kala. "You're looking better." Susan's colour had returned. Her eyes were clear amber. Kala felt the warmth of her smile.

"I am better. So, how can I help you, Detective?"

"You've heard about Benny Goldstone's murder?"

"On the news, yes. It's just awful. I didn't know him particularly well, but it's a horrible tragedy nonetheless."

"I understand Max brought him to dinners and social events with the family."

"Yes, but he was so quiet that I can't say I knew him except to say hello and talk about the weather. He really was just a colleague of Max's. I'm planning to go over to Geraldine's later today. They must be reeling." Her elegant ruby-ringed hand pushed back a lock of hair from her forehead.

"Do you have any idea why he would have been killed?"

"I think it must be work-related. Both Tom and Benny were working on the same file, weren't they?" Her hand settled on her chest just above her heart. "My God, I hope Max isn't in danger."

"We'll be keeping a watch if this is work-related. Tom and Benny also had something else in common."

"They did? And what would that be?" Susan turned her tawny eyes on Kala; her eyebrows were raised, her expression perplexed but cautious.

"They were both having affairs."

Susan was the first to look away. "This is a serious accusation to make against two people who cannot defend themselves."

"Most people would have asked who with, but you already knew, isn't that right?"

"I just said that I don't know Benny Goldstone. I can't pretend to know who he's sleeping with."

"But you must have figured out that he and Max are more than just colleagues."

"I wasn't certain, but I had a feeling."

"And Tom Underwood. How long had it been going on?"

Her eyes flickered like candles. "I don't know what you mean."

"I think you do."

Susan stood abruptly and walked toward the window. She cradled her arms across her chest. Kala waited. It was almost a minute before Susan spoke without turning.

"I loved Tom from the moment I laid eyes on him. We were made for each other, but Pauline got to him first. Laurel was an infatuation. Neither was his soul mate." She walked back to the couch and looked down at Kala. "We were lovers, yes. It began six months ago when Clinton was at the base. We had plans to move away together. Tom was going to get a divorce ... or not. It didn't matter to either of us. I was going to separate from Clinton in the new year, and no, Clinton didn't know. As you may also have guessed, he is controlling. We worried about his reaction."

"I'm not here to judge you, Mrs. Halliday. I'm only seeking the truth. How can you be sure that Clinton didn't know?"

"I don't know how he could have. He was always away and we were extremely discreet. I told nobody and neither did Tom."

"But you've wondered."

"Yes," she whispered. "The car running out of gas. Clinton said he was driving home from Trenton when it happened, but I just couldn't be sure."

"I've asked before. Has your husband ever been violent? Do you have reason to fear what he might do to you if he found out?"

"He likes to control. I suppose you might call it violence. I really don't know what he's capable of doing. Why would he hurt Benny though? Me and Tom yes, but why Benny? It makes no sense."

"No reason that we know of … yet. I have the same question if the murders are work-related. Why were you also targeted? I have no doubt you could have died out there alone in the woods with night coming on."

Susan shuddered. "There's a part of me that wishes it had happened."

Kala stood. "Is there someone you could stay with until this is over?"

"We're out tonight at a dance at the Hunt Club and then Clinton is returning to the base in Trenton by lunchtime. I'll be fine."

"You still have my cellphone number. Call me any time, day or night. You can also call 911 if you feel threatened. Keep your phone with you at all times. If you find any evidence that Clinton was involved, don't confront him. Call me and we'll handle it. Unfortunately, we haven't any concrete evidence on which to bring him in for questioning, but I'll be pursuing this new line of enquiry."

Susan laughed. "I'm not as convinced that I'm a target as you seem to be. I promise to be careful though. I'll even key your phone number into my phone." Fear froze her features. "You can't let Clinton know about me and Tom. Promise you won't say anything."

"The last thing I would do is put you in more danger. I'll keep this confidential. In the meantime, I'll see if I can arrange for an officer to patrol by your house until we have more to go on."

"I hope you're wrong about this."

"I hope so too."

32

ROULEAU WAS ALONE in the office when Kala knocked on his closed door. She stepped inside upon his call to enter, leaving the door ajar. He stood near the window dressed in the suit she'd seen hanging next to the door.

"Going to a party tonight, Sir?" she asked as she joined him at the window.

"Something like that. I have to put in an appearance. You're in the office late. Any plans this New Year's Eve?"

"No. I might take a trip to the ByWard Market and walk around. It's milder than it's been."

"I could meet you for a drink after this reception. I'll be in the vicinity."

She studied the rigid line of his shoulders. He was preparing himself for something he didn't want to do. "I'd like that. Name a time and place and I'll be there."

"Is there something you want to discuss about the cases now?"

"It can wait until we meet up if you don't mind talking work on a night that should be dedicated to partying."

"I'll look forward to it. Let's meet at Vine's wine bar around ten. Do you know where that is?"

"I'll find it."

He looked at his watch. "I have to be going. You should take off too."

"I just want to check a few things. I won't be long behind you."

"Good. See you in a bit then."

Kala poured through the reports, beginning with Tom Underwood's disappearance. His affair with Susan Halliday and their plans to leave their spouses gave the information a different focus. Who would lose the most if they carried through with their plan? Who would be angry enough to kill? Had Benny Goldstone known something the murderer wanted covered up? It was possible the murders were unrelated, but it wasn't likely. Odds were they were killed by the same person. Logic dictated there was a link. She might have believed the murders were work-related but for the attempt on Susan Halliday. Someone was making them pay. Clinton? Max? Hunter? Laurel? They all had reason. She just had to find the missing piece to make everything tumble into place. Maybe discussing it with Rouleau would give new insight.

At nine, she wearily turned off her computer and put on her coat. She found her phone in her pocket and checked for messages, relieved to find that nobody had tried to reach her. Perhaps, it would be a quiet night. She stopped at the main desk on her way out and spoke to the sergeant about having an officer patrol by the Hallidays' overnight. He said that he'd see what he could do.

She thought about heading back to her room to change, but she didn't have anything better to wear than what she had on. Instead, she made a stop in the washroom to loosen her braid and comb her hair. Rather than tie it back again, she left it loose around her face. She washed with the soap from the dispenser and patted her skin dry with paper towel, then dug around in her bag until she found lip gloss. Next to Rouleau, she'd be underdressed but he probably wouldn't care. For certain, she didn't.

The ByWard Market was busier than she'd ever seen. People were in a party mood, spilling onto the sidewalks in front of the bars and milling around in groups talking and laughing. Blasts of music assailed her ears whenever a door opened. The restaurants were brimming with customers sitting in tables of four or more; Christmas wreathes and strings of lights decked the buildings like party favours.

She spent a half hour walking down side streets, looking in windows and keeping an eye out for a young Indigenous girl. A few minutes past ten o'clock, she reached the Fish Market restaurant. The Internet had shown Vines in the basement. She climbed downstairs where she was greeted by a hostess in a red dress. The room was dimly lit with candles at the tables, dark wooden bar running the front width of the room, booths and intimate tables. People filled each table and a buzz of talking punctuated by laughter almost drowned out the guitar player in the corner.

"I see my friend," she said.

Rouleau was sitting with his back to the wall and rose at her approach. She noticed that he'd taken off his tie and suit jacket and rolled up his sleeves. He smiled as she slid into the chair across from him.

"I phoned and reserved a table, otherwise, we never would've gotten in."

She looked around. "The whole market is crazy with people. New Year's Eve at home was never like this."

"I imagine not. I took the liberty of ordering a few appetizers. What would you like to drink?"

"Soda and cranberry."

He signalled for the waitress and placed her order. He already had a glass of red wine in front of him. "So it looks like we're spending the major holidays together."

"Our paths do seem to be crossing." She smiled. "How was the reception?"

"Good." He paused. "My ex-wife remarried this afternoon. She asked me to attend and I did it for her." He drank deeply from his glass.

"That must have been hard."

"It was the least I could do."

"You still care for her."

He shrugged. "I had my chance. If I could pass on any advice, it would be not to let the job take over. You can lose too much." He smiled wryly although his eyes were sad. She found herself liking him at that moment, a wounded man who didn't wallow in it.

They both leaned back as the waitress set down a plate of steaming mussels and crusty bread. They nodded at each other and dug in.

"These are wonderful," said Kala. "I love seafood." Wine and garlic broth dripped from her lips onto the napkin. She reached for another mussel.

"I was just hoping you weren't allergic. I have some paté and finger food coming just in case. So what did you want to tell me about the case?"

"I discovered something interesting today. Tom Underwood and Susan Halliday have been having an affair for the past six months. They were planning to leave their spouses."

Rouleau stopped with a piece of bread in mid-air and looked at her. "Who else knew?"

"That's the thing. Susan believes nobody, but I can think of a few who would be very displeased if they did."

"Their spouses."

"I went back through the interviews. If Laurel believed Tom was leaving her, no matter for whom, she might have wanted to ensure her lifestyle by getting rid of him. It gets confusing though when you add in the attack on Susan as well as Benny's murder. Why would Laurel want to hurt them? If she knew about Susan and Tom, she might have wanted revenge. But Benny? I just don't know."

"What do you propose to do next?"

"I've thought all along that Susan Halliday is key, and I still think so. This may be nothing, but when we last interviewed Laurel, she said that if we found out what made Tom change his behaviour the last while, we'd find out who killed him. If I believe what Susan told me, it was because they'd fallen in love and he was going to change his life for her. I'd like to keep her under surveillance. Whoever emptied her gas tank and left her in the Gatineau Hills to freeze to death will probably try again. There's so much going on beneath the surface with these people, I just don't know who to trust." She thought of Hunter and Laurel and the times she'd found them together, the awful feeling she got being around Clinton, Max and Benny and their obvious connection.

"We don't have a big enough team."

"Bennett, Gage, and I can cover. Whelan will be back in a few days. Grayson and Malik can continue with the work angle."

"I wish it were that simple. Vermette's not going to okay protection on Susan. I can guarantee it. Grayson has J.P. Belliveau in his sights and won't give that up easily, especially to go on surveillance. I'm not even certain that he should because Belliveau remains a prime suspect. We need to keep pursuing the work angle, especially since Underwood and

Goldstone were in the same office, working on the same project."

Kala kept her eyes on the food and didn't say anything.

"I know this isn't how you like working, but red tape takes priority, and that includes answering to Vermette and those above him. Believe me, there are days I'd like to go maverick too." Rouleau sounded tired.

She looked across the table at him. "I just think we're missing an opportunity. Clinton is leaving for the base tomorrow and if it's him, the window is small."

"You mean, for Clinton to do something to Susan? But we don't even know for sure that it's him."

"But he's also a very real candidate. I just feel that something bad is going to happen to her. She's keeping secrets. I think she knows more than she's saying."

"Take Bennett and go see her early in the day. Let Clinton know we're watching. That's the best we can do without some evidence."

"Thanks, Sir."

"Whelan will be back on the second and life will get back to normal. We'll resume our supporting role for Major Crimes and you'll have a chance to settle in for real."

"Beginning with media training."

"Beginning with media training." He smiled and his green eyes lightened a shade. "I think I'm going to be apologizing for that for quite some time." He looked over her shoulder. "I see more food coming. Hope you're hungry."

"Always."

"Then let's eat our way into the new year."

"That's the best idea I've heard in a long time."

33

SUSAN HALLIDAY LOOKED across at Officer Stonechild and her sidekick, the young good-looking officer with the cleft chin. She met their gazes head on, no flinching or dropping of eyes. She knew why they'd come. Eleven o'clock on New Year's morning and they acted like it was a routine call. She wondered if Clinton would realize they were here to make sure he returned to Trenton base without doing her in. They were already too late to make sure he didn't hurt her. She instinctively raised her left hand to rub her arm but kept her hand moving up to her hair, which she pretended to pat into place. She hoped they didn't notice how little she was using her right arm. The shoulder was swollen and hurt to move from where Clinton had gripped her in a rage the night before.

Clinton stood from his spot next to her on the couch. "Well, if you don't have any more questions for me, I have to pack. I'm expected back at the base this afternoon."

"Your uniforms are pressed and hanging in the spare room, darling," said Susan.

"Thank you," he said smiling down at her. "You're the best wife a man could ask for." He bent and kissed the top of her head.

She smiled up at him, playing the role he expected. She'd learned it was better to pretend to forgive him than to let him know how much he'd hurt her. If she stood up to him now, he'd make her pay later, in private.

They watched him leave the room with his stilted military gait. Officer Stonechild waited a few beats before asking for the tea Susan had offered at their arrival. Susan wondered how she was going to manage a tray as she agreed to put the kettle on.

"Sit," said the young officer. "I'll go make it while you two have a chat. That is, if you don't mind?"

"That would be lovely. The teabags are in a blue canister next to the stove and the sugar bowl is on the table." He made it sound like she and this detective with the black eyes that saw everything were girlfriends having another gab. Nothing could be further from the truth.

He left the room and Officer Stonechild turned toward her. "I believe you're hiding something that could help us figure out who murdered Tom and likely Benny. It's time to share what you know."

"I'm sorry, but you're mistaken. I'm not hiding anything."

"You told me that you and Tom began seeing each other secretly about six months ago, is this correct?"

"Yes. I met him by chance on one of my walks and he came back here for coffee. It began then." She remembered the day with a longing so sharp that Tom might be sitting across from her now. "Tom was going through a personal crisis. He was despondent about work and his life with Laurel. We found we had a lot in common."

"You also said that you stopped seeing each other. You'd decided to wait until you were both free before moving away together, is this correct?"

"Yes, we agreed not to see each other until we'd taken steps to leave our marriages."

"Had you begun proceedings before Tom was killed?"

"No. I planned to tell Clinton I was moving out after the Christmas break. I believe if he knew about me and Tom, he would have told me by now."

"Are you still planning to leave the marriage?"

"There doesn't seem to be much point now."

"Has anyone in Tom's family let on that they knew about your relationship?"

"No. As I told you, we were discreet. I'd also like to thank you for not telling anyone. You know, Detective, I never believed that our affair had anything to do with Tom's death, or Benny's for that matter. Their deaths had to be linked to their work."

"You may well be right." Kala turned toward the door. "Here comes Officer Bennett with our tea."

Clinton followed Bennett into the room. He walked over to Susan. "I'm on my way then. I'll see you in a few weeks." He bent down to kiss her cheek. "I'll call tonight."

"I'll be waiting by the phone at the usual time," she said.

———

Susan watched the officers leave from behind the curtain in the den. She didn't know why she'd kept secret that she and Tom had met the night before he went missing. It just felt like the last precious memory she had to hold on to. She didn't want their last time together to be defiled by the police or to be investigated. Nobody else knew about that night. How could it possibly have anything to do with his murder? She let the curtain drop back into place and stepped back from the window.

Clinton must be halfway to Trenton. It was a clear winter day and he should make good time on the highway. She'd planned to clean the house today, but her shoulder ached too much to do any lifting. She'd have a hot bath and curl up with a book. If she felt like it later, she might walk over to Pauline's to see if she wanted to go to a movie. It would cheer them both up. Then she remembered that it was New Year's Day. Pauline would be doing something with her family. Normally she was included, but there was nothing normal about this holiday.

Perhaps she'd just slip back into bed for a nap. They'd had a late night at the country club and then Clinton had gone into that tirade after she'd been reluctant to have sex. She should have just given in without telling him she was tired. This time it had been her fault.

She started walking slowly upstairs, undoing her blouse as she went. She winced as she pulled the sleeve down her arm. *A sleep and then a bath.* The detective seemed awfully concerned with her welfare no matter how many times she told her not to be. Susan stood at the entrance to the bedroom she shared with Clinton and looked at the king size bed for a moment before continuing down the hall. The bed in the smallest spare room was made up and the place she slept when Clinton was away.

The detective didn't need to be so concerned with her welfare because she wasn't. If someone wanted to kill her, she'd welcome it. A quick death was preferable to the empty life that lay before her without Tom. It would be considerably better than the miserable existence she was going to have with Clinton if she didn't work up the energy to leave him. If she could close her eyes and never wake up, she would choose to do so with no regret, no looking back. Death would be a blessing.

34

"'THIS TIME, SAY the lines as if you're talking to a superior who's also a girlfriend. Aim for officious but caring.' Can you believe the nonsense?" said Kala. She picked up her milkshake and took a slurp. "I would never tell my girlfriend that financial constraints are the reason the department's murder-solving stats are low. Besides, more resources aren't the problem. We have to go into investigations with an open mind and screw the politics."

Whelan grinned. "You're the only one I know who's actually questioned the canned message in media training. The important thing though is to pass."

"Oh, I'll pass. This afternoon we get our final feedback and a certificate. Then I'll be the brown face of the department."

"Well, you'll be a more refreshing face than the old guy doing it now."

"That sounds like ageism, Whelan, which is about as pretty as racism."

"Guilty as charged. We're a shallow lot, me and my male friends. That includes men of all ages and races. Personally, I'm hoping they put you in a miniskirt."

Kala laughed. "Are you going to finish that burger? It *is* your second."

Whelan lifted it from the table and took a bite. "I'm keeping up my strength. I'm back on the beat, interviewing cab drivers this afternoon."

"It's not looking promising, is it?"

"No. We need someone to come forward."

"No developments on the Underwood and Goldstone murders?"

"Nothing concrete. Of course, I'm just doing grunt paperwork now and not one of those in the know."

"Almost March already. The trail is cold."

"The latest theory is that J.P. Belliveau hired someone to kill them. We're close to arresting him if you believe Grayson."

"I'd still like to know how Grayson weaseled himself onto the lead team."

"Grayson will always land on his feet. He's a self-serving animal. So, have you found an apartment yet?"

"Nope, I'm still at the Y. The place is growing on me. I've started using the gym after work now that overtime has ended."

"Don't forget we're having you and the Maliks over for supper Sunday."

"I'm looking forward to it. The kids are good?"

"Yes, knock on wood. Our lives are back to normal for the moment. I'm just sorry I missed all the excitement over the Christmas holidays. It would have been something to be part of the murder investigations, if only for a week. Lousy timing."

"I wanted to solve the murders so Rouleau would get credit."

"Yeah, I know what you mean."

Whelan scrunched up the wrappings from his hamburgers and stood. "Well, time to get back to the office, and you'll be needing to get your TV star certificate. See you Sunday around six. Don't bring anything but yourself."

"I'll be there. You go ahead. I'm just going to go buy another chocolate shake to take back to the classroom."

"The camera puts on ten pounds, don't forget."

"Whatever gets me out of wearing a miniskirt."

Kala watched Whelan walk away, then joined the line up in front of the cashiers. This might put her a few minutes late, but it wasn't like she was learning anything earth-shattering. She reached the front of the line when her cellphone rang. The number was vaguely familiar. She hit the button and held the phone to her ear.

"Stonechild. Can I help you?"

"Kala? It's Maya. I'm at the Ottawa Mission serving lunch. Now I know they called off the search for Annie Littlewolf, but I remembered that last time we spoke you were still interested in talking to her. If you still are, Annie just walked in."

Kala's heart started pounding faster. "Yes, I am. Is she there now?"

"She's just come in for something to eat. If you hurry, you might catch her. The young girl's not with her though."

"I'm on my way. Try to stall Annie if you can, but don't tell her I'm coming. I don't want to spook her."

"You got it, child."

Kala waved off the kid behind the counter and started running toward the exit, zipping up her jacket as she ran. A line of cabs was always parked outside the Westin Hotel and would save valuable minutes. The media relations guru would have to wrap up the class without her.

Maya met Kala as soon as she stepped inside the hall. She waved a dish towel toward the door, nearly out of breath. "You're too late. Annie just left with some food, but I think you can catch her if you hurry. She crossed the street and started heading north. You can just see her green jacket, there, past those two men on the corner."

"Thanks Maya. I owe you."

Kala exited quickly and dashed across Waller Street, keeping her eyes on the retreating green jacket. She slipped on a piece of ice and stumbled against the curb but managed to stay upright. She regained her footing and stepped over the snowbank onto the recently plowed sidewalk. Patches of ice glistened in the sunlight.

They'd had a two-week thaw but the temperature had dipped below freezing again overnight, making ice patches out of melting snow. The Rideau Canal was closed to skaters and people were being warned to stay off the ice on the rivers and lakes. The temperatures had been swinging like a pendulum in the Ottawa spring. Whelan had warned her that cold and storms could blow in on a minute's notice, but he'd also said the wild weather wouldn't last long.

Annie disappeared around the corner and Kala started jogging. When she turned right onto Daly, she caught sight of Annie again and started walking more cautiously on the slippery sidewalk. She held back a little to keep Annie from knowing that she was being followed.

Annie continued up Daly and turned left on Cumberland. She continued past Rideau Street into the ByWard Market. Kala stayed close enough not to lose her if Annie veered off course unexpectedly. At York Street, Annie made a right and walked halfway down the block. She stopped in front of a two-storey, box-shaped house that looked to be divided into apartments. The exterior walls were covered in white vinyl

siding stained yellow and the yard was the size of a postage
stamp. Pigeons huddled on the roof where heat was escaping. Annie walked up the sidewalk and climbed the front
steps. She kicked the door open with her foot.

Kala waited a few minutes before following her. The
front door was unlocked and she stepped into a dingy
hallway with doors to two apartments directly ahead. A
staircase led to apartments upstairs, two more if Kala had
to guess. The air was heavy with cooking grease and stale
cigarette smoke. She hesitated, unsure which door to try.
Finally, she knocked at the one on the right. Nobody answered. She listened at the other door but heard nobody
within. She climbed the stairs, her feet seeking clean spots
on the stained carpet. On the landing, she stopped and
strained to hear noises inside one of the two apartments.
A woman was talking inside the door on the right. Kala
knocked and stepped back to wait. After what felt like an
eternity, the door opened. Annie Littlewolf's suspicious
black eyes met hers.

"Yeah?"

Seventeen years had led to this door. Kala took a deep
breath. "Annie Littlewolf?"

Annie's eyes filled with suspicion. She started to close the
door as she asked, "You a cop?"

"That's not why I'm here. I'm looking for someone. My
cousin Rose and her daughter Dawn."

"Really? 'Cause I don't know nobody by those names."

"Please. I've been looking a long time. We grew up
together, on a rez. Birdtail Creek." She caught a movement
inside. Annie turned sideways and looked back into the
apartment.

"Let her in." A husky voice thick with phlegm came
from behind her.

Annie stepped aside without a word and motioned for Kala to enter. Her eyes stayed hostile.

Kala walked into the darkened apartment. Blankets covered the two windows in the living room but there was enough light to see a woman lying on the couch in the centre of the room. A pink blanket covered her legs. The coffee table in front of her was empty except for a coffee mug and a tinfoil ashtray at arm's length. The ashtray held two half-smoked cigarettes. The place reeked of cigarettes and stale beer. The only other furniture was two plastic garden chairs and a table used as a stand for an old-fashioned television. An afternoon drama flickered without sound on the screen.

Kala approached the woman on the couch. Time had hollowed out her cheeks and dried her skin. The black braids were laced with premature grey. Her exhausted black eyes stared at Kala without recognition.

"Lily," Kala said softly. "It's me, Sunny."

"Christ, Sunny Stonechild? I never thought I'd hear that name again." Lily's voice echoed in the nearly empty room. "Little Sunny. I called you that because you always had this shit-faced smile, like you was waiting for something good to happen."

Kala grinned. "We were a club of two back then. Remember the ceremony when we cut our arms and gave each other those secret names?"

"Yeah. When we made ourselves cousins. You'd read some book where the white kids had a clubhouse and secret password. You wouldn't stop badgering me until we made up a secret group with names for each other. Never could figure out why you picked the name Lily for me."

"I loved lilies. The first time I saw a bay full of them I wanted to pick every one. You reminded me of a lily."

"Would have been a waste to pick them. Lilies don't last out of water once you cut the root. Roses do for a while anyhow. I chose the name Rose when I moved to Thunder Bay because the idea of being a flower grew on me." She shifted positions on the couch. "Have a seat and take the load off. What're you doing in Ottawa?"

Kala moved the plastic chair closer so that she was in Rose's line of vision. "I've been looking for you for a long time. Last summer I went back to Birdtail Creek. Roger's still there. He's nearly sixty but keeps up his trapline. He had an address for you in Ottawa, but you'd moved by the time I got to it."

"I move a lot. Roger kept in touch with me for a while after I left Birdtail. He was the only one. We lost contact for a lot of years, but I sent him a postcard when we moved here, when it seemed I had a decent place. I wasn't happy living in the Peg but I got my grade nine at least. I boarded with this family and the father used to come into my room at night and look at me when he thought I was sleeping. The day after he decided to do more than look, I took off for Thunder Bay. I wanted to kill him but one body was enough on my conscience." Her lips raised in a sideways smile. "That's where I met Paul."

"Is he Dawn's father?"

"Shit, how do you know about Dawn?"

"Your old neighbour across the hall told me when I went there to find you.

Rose shook her head. "That old bat was one nosy piece of work. I made up stories to keep her from coming over and bugging me. She thought I was a raging wino, which suited me fine. Yeah, Paul is Dawn's daddy. We moved to Toronto to look for work. Nobody was hiring."

"So what did you do?"

"We got real good at B and Es." She laughed and broke into a fit of coughing that racked her body. Annie appeared with a glass of water and some pills. Rose managed to swallow a tablet and the coughing stopped.

Annie straightened the blanket around Rose's legs. "Let me know if you want anything else," she said before leaving.

"You're sick," said Kala.

"Tail end of pneumonia. Plus I got run down and have something called anemia. I'll be fine when the warmer weather comes."

"Have you seen a doctor?"

"There's a free clinic. I've been a couple of times. Dawn and Annie are looking after me just fine."

"We were searching for Annie after her partner died."

"She used to panhandle near the restaurant where I worked. I ran into her one time when I left the clinic and she helped me home. I told her to stay if she wanted. She was kind of broken up because her old man up and died when they were drinking together and she hated being alone. Also, she thought she might get blamed. I told her just to lay low with us."

"Where's Dawn now?"

"Today's a PD day but she went to the youth centre for the afternoon. She likes to play basketball and they have an arts program that she likes more than breathing. She's real good at drawing. She should be home soon."

They were quiet for a moment. Rosie leaned back against the cushion. "Whatever happened to Rascal, your little dog? You sure were crazy about that mutt."

"A few weeks after you left, one of the boys where I was living let Rascal off his leash. He was hit by a car on the highway and died." Kala faltered. "I ran away right after and hid in the bush, but Roger found me just before dark.

They let me live with him for a while but then found another family for me in Regina. I lived with them for a few years and they moved to a town in Ontario. I went to school in Sudbury and became a cop." She didn't mention the years in between.

Rose's eyes studied her. "A cop. I guess that makes sense. We both had to make up for what we done somehow."

"It was my fault. I got in the van. If it hadn't been for me, we never would have killed that man. I needed to find you to make sure you were okay. I need to make it right." It was the guilt she'd had to live with her whole life, the sorrow she'd never been able to say out loud.

Rose half rose from the couch. She shook her head. "Nah, it was *his* fault. We were just two kids who didn't know any better. It took me a long time to realize that. It took me having Dawn. You have to let it go, Sun. I have."

"You should blame me, Rose. I got us into that trouble."

"You don't get it, do you? *That man* got us into that trouble. He set his own fate when he drove us up that dirt road and did what he did to us. You and me, we were just victims. We did *nothing* we need to be ashamed about. *Nothing.*"

The door opened behind them and a cold draught of air pushed in from the unheated hallway. Kala turned. Dawn was in the foyer, hunched over taking off her rubber boots. When she straightened, she spotted Kala. Dawn hung her jacket on a hook and walked into the living room carrying a rolled up paper. She sat on the couch by her mother's feet.

"I made you a picture, Mama," she said and handed over the gift. She kept her eyes on Kala. They were Rose's black eyes partially hidden by straight black bangs. The rest of her hair was pulled into two braids. She was tall and slender in jeans and a faded black sweatshirt with a rip in the sleeve.

Rose unrolled it and held it so Kala could see. Dawn had drawn a sunset over the river in pen and ink. It was detailed for a girl of twelve.

"This is different than your paintings, but I love it too," said Rose.

"I have a new teacher."

"Thank you, my sweet child. Meet my cousin Sunny. You were named after her."

"Hi Dawn. My name is actually Kala, but your mom and I decided to be cousins with new names when we were about your age."

"What was your new name, Mom?" Dawn's eyes danced at the thought.

"Lily."

"Lily. I like that name. I wish I had a cousin or a sister," said Dawn. "Maybe I can find one like you two did. How are you feeling, Mom?"

"Better today. Annie brought some supper home. Why don't you go eat and get your homework done?"

"Okay. You only smoked two today?"

"Yup. And only half of each."

"Good. That's real good. Nice to meet you, Kala."

"Nice to meet you too, Dawn."

"Honey, take the picture and tape it up with the rest."

Dawn took the rolled up paper. "Okay, Mom. Are you going to eat too?"

"Not yet, but save me a few bites." Rose watched Dawn walk away from her, then looked over at Kala. "You didn't ask about Paul and me but you probably wonder. Paul's doing a stretch at Kingston Penitentiary. He got six years for armed robbery but should be out soon. We're waiting for him." Her eyes challenged Kala to judge her. The defiant Lily from their childhood had returned.

"Your daughter is beautiful. She looks like you did at that age."

"She's why I cleaned up and went straight. Paul wouldn't though. He liked stealing stuff from people who wouldn't miss it. I had a job in a restaurant until I got sick. I'm going to find another one when I get my strength."

"Can I come see you again?"

"Are you sure you want to? A lot of years have passed and we were just kids."

"You're still my blood cousin. You're the only family I got."

Rose looked at her with the old mocking smile. "Yeah, come by. We're not going nowhere for a while. It might be nice to have some family again."

Kala stood. "I'll come see you tomorrow." She already had plans to go shopping for food. The old Lily would never ask for her help, but she was going to give it anyhow.

35

SATURDAY MORNING THE sun broke through at close to eight o'clock. Streaks of pink light gradually strengthened in brilliance until the winter sun climbed to its lookout over the Ottawa Valley. Temperatures had plummeted during the night and continued to fall during the early morning hours until they reached a frigid minus twenty-two degrees Celsius at ten a.m. when Kala made her way to the Elgin Street Diner for a late breakfast. She'd already spent an hour in the gym, showered, and done a load of laundry. Finding Rose had left her energized and eager to get started on improving their lives. This was what she'd dreamed of from the moment she'd watched Lily walk away from her for the last time that fall day on Birdtail reserve.

First she'd get some breakfast before shopping for food to bring to Rose's apartment on York Street. She hoped to take Dawn later for new boots if Rose would let her, but knew she had to go carefully. Rose wouldn't like being treated as a charity case. *Rose.* She was still Lily in Kala's mind, but she could appreciate Lily's need to carve out a new identity with a new name. Hell, she'd done much the same herself.

The restaurant was full and she had to wait ten minutes for a table. She followed the hostess to the back of the noisy room and sat at a table for two, facing the front windows. The waitress came right over with coffee and Kala ordered her usual breakfast fare — eggs over easy, homefries, sausage, and brown toast. Kala settled back in the chair and lifted the white mug to her lips. Her eyes scanned the room and doubled back. She squinted over her coffee cup, then her heart jumped like she'd had a hit of adrenaline.

Hunter Underwood was sitting directly across from her at a table with a blond-haired woman dressed in a tight red sweater and silver chains around her neck. They were leaning into each other, deep in conversation. Hunter's eyes were fixed on the woman and he was listening intently to whatever it was she was waxing on about. He'd tied back his hair and wore a pressed blue shirt, so she must be important to him.

Kala squirmed inside, remembering how attracted she'd been to Hunter the few times they met. It would never have gone anywhere, but she was sorry how they'd left things. It was unsettling to think he was still angry with her.

The murders seemed far removed from her now. It was two months since Vermette had effectively taken her team off the investigation except for research support. She'd continued to think about the case, but she'd let it go after Rouleau had made it clear that she was not to pursue matters on her own. He'd kept her busy taking courses so that she couldn't have even if she'd wanted to.

She continued to watch Hunter, but he didn't look her way and she told herself it was just as well. When her breakfast arrived she lowered her head and began eating. She'd been too excited to eat much the night before and was famished. The food was greasy cholesterol ambrosia.

The waitress came by a second time with the coffee pot and the bill as Kala was finishing up the last of the toast. She mumbled thanks with her mouth full and nodded for a refill. The girl poured and set down more creamers then moved back and let out a yelp as she stepped into the person standing behind her.

Hunter steadied her arm and apologized. He waited until she was well clear before dropping into the empty chair across from Kala. He set his gloves on the table but left on his coat, his smile warming her, his grey eyes lingering on her face.

Her initial surprise over, Kala continued chewing her toast. She didn't return his smile.

"Haven't seen you around for a while," he said.

She swallowed. "No, busy with other cases."

"And here I thought we were the biggest case in town."

"It got turned over to Major Crimes after the holiday. We're still assisting behind the scenes."

"That's a shame."

She couldn't tell how he meant her to take that so she said nothing, just stirred cream into her coffee and waited. The silence stretched awkwardly.

"I wasn't sure it was you at first," he said. "I was sitting at that table with a woman who owns an art gallery on Elgin just up the way. She wants me to put on a show this spring, but I'm not sure it gives me enough time to get the pieces together. Did you see us?"

"Yes."

"You should have said hello. There've been a few changes in my family that might interest you."

"Oh?"

"Geraldine gave Max the boot."

"Because of Benny?"

"That was one reason, but she also found he'd been taking money out of their joint account, and he had no explanation as to where he spent it or why. It was Pauline who suggested my sister look at her accounts after we found out about Benny and Max's relationship."

"How much money?"

"Geraldine thinks close to two hundred thousand. She had a small inheritance when our grandmother died and kept it in a separate joint account. She admits now that she was naive to trust him with paying the bills."

"She should file a complaint, although if he had signing authority it could be hard to prove."

"The thing that worries her the most is that he'll be entitled to half of her inheritance from our father even if they divorce."

"She needs a good lawyer. They weren't married that long and there are extenuating circumstances. You said there were a few changes in your family that would interest me. So far, you've only named one."

"Laurel and Charlotte are moving to Calgary where Laurel grew up. She's put the house up for sale and hopes to be gone by summer."

"How do you feel about that?"

"Her presence in Ottawa is hard on my mom and Geraldine. It keeps things complicated." He fixed his eyes on hers. "There really was nothing going on between us," he said.

"Then why did you act like there was? I keep wondering about that night when you told Laurel about your father's death. Your Jeep was parked conspicuously out of sight some distance away. Laurel also appeared quite familiar with the road to your place."

"I didn't park in her driveway in case my mother happened by and saw the Jeep. Silly as it sounds, my mother hated Laurel and wanted me as far away from her as possible. I figured my family had enough grief without them worrying if I was taking up with Laurel."

"Why would your mother happen by, as you put it?"

"She didn't live far away. She often walked those roads and down by the Rideau River."

Kala lifted her cup and finished the last of the now tepid coffee. It was a sign she'd stayed too long. She set the cup on the table and said, "Well, I have things to do, but it was good running into you. I hope everything works out for you and your family." She reached around to grab her jacket from the back of her chair.

Hunter stood and looked down at her. His eyes didn't give much away, but she could tell he'd wanted more from her. "Thanks, I'm hoping so too. Maybe I'll see you around."

She waited until he'd disappeared out the front door before fishing the money out of her jacket pocket. She didn't know whether she believed Hunter or not, but he'd put up a convincing front. Happily, the investigation wasn't hers to worry about any longer.

She left a ten on the table with the bill and made her way to the washroom, pulling out her cellphone as she went. She'd share what she learned with Grayson anyhow, and hopefully he'd follow up on the missing money in Geraldine's account and Laurel's plans to leave Ottawa. She wasn't convinced that he would, but her conscience would be clear. As for Hunter, it would never have worked out between them. She was smart to have just let the whole thing go.

—

Kala made two trips up the stairs to Rose's apartment. The first was to bring a couple of bags of groceries and the next was for the cake and bagels she'd picked up from the bakery. Rose and Dawn were alone. Annie had gone out early in the morning to panhandle near the Rideau Centre.

Dawn took the groceries from Kala into the kitchen while she made the second trip. On her return, Kala set the cake on the coffee table and smiled at Rose who was sewing a button on one of Dawn's shirts. She could see Dawn through the doorway putting them away.

"How're you feeling today?"

"Much better. I was only up twice in the night coughing and my strength's almost back to normal." Rose called to Dawn, "Make two instant coffees and bring them in with a glass of milk for yourself. We'll also need plates, forks, and a knife to cut the cake." She motioned for Kala to sit and pointed at the cake. "You didn't need to do this."

"I know, but I wanted to celebrate your birthday, even if it's a bit late."

"Yeah, but we could do that without all this food."

Kala took off her coat and sat down. She looked Rose over carefully. "You do seem better today. Are they holding your waitressing job for you?"

Rose shook her head. "Nah, but I'll find another."

Dawn entered with two coffees and Kala jumped up to help. Dawn's black eyes widened when she saw the cake box on the table.

"Cake, Mom! We haven't had cake in forever."

"I hope you like chocolate fudge," said Kala, smiling. The sight of the girl in ripped jeans and a moth-eaten sweater tugged at her heart. She looked back at Rose who was staring at her with an odd expression on her face. A childhood memory flashed through Kala's mind. Lily looking down at her hiding in the tall grass, getting ready to lay a trail for the man who was chasing them. Lily's black eyes hardening at Kala's pleas not to leave her. Kala shivered and looked back at Dawn as she sat and served up a large slices of cake. She tried to shake off the feeling of foreboding.

They took their time eating the cake, listening to Dawn talk nonstop about school and how much she liked her teacher Mrs. Johnson and all the art projects they did in class. They were going on a field trip to the art gallery on Monday and she couldn't wait. Rose let her talk without interrupting, glancing at Kala every now and then with pride in her eyes and something else Kala couldn't read.

It wasn't long before Kala could see that Rose was getting tired. She'd eaten all of the cake though, so that was a good sign. When Dawn took a drink of milk and was momentarily quiet, Kala said, "Why don't I take Dawn for a walk and you can have a nap? We'll come back by four o'clock and make supper."

"That'd be good. I think I need to sleep for a bit because I did the laundry this morning. Annie should be back by then too."

Dawn and Kala scooped up the dirty dishes and remainder of the cake and brought everything into the kitchen. Kala hadn't been in this room before and took her time looking around. The floor was yellowing linoleum, curling at the edges, and the cupboards were fifties-style plywood painted apple green. The stained counter and ancient appliances were spotlessly clean. A small table and wooden chairs filled the spare space. Her eyes travelled to the art gallery on the wall and she stepped closer.

"Dawn, are these your paintings?"

"Yes, all except for this one. My last teacher at the community centre gave it to me for Christmas." Dawn danced in front of her and pointed to a framed watercolour of daisies in a vase. "She said I was her best student ever. See how pretty? I want to paint like that some day."

Kala looked from the painting to Dawn and then back at the painting. Her heart quickened. She leaned closer and squinted. "What was the name of your teacher?"

"Pauline. She was nice. See, her name is on the bottom corner."

It was exactly as Kala had thought. *Pauline Underwood.* "You said that she quit before Christmas? Can you remember when exactly?"

"Two weeks before. She said that she was going away to get married. She had to get things ready because it was a big surprise."

"Pauline, your teacher, said that?"

"Uh huh. We used to talk because I stayed late to work on my art projects. She knew my dad was away and said that her husband left her and her kids too for a while, so she knew how hard it was. She was happy we were both going to have them back soon."

Kala stood still. Something cold and dark travelled up her spine. The curtain had blown back for the briefest of instants, but it was enough. She never doubted the silent, mysterious workings of the universe. Signs were fleeting and intangible. You had to be open to them when they appeared.

She knew that murder could happen when people were pushed too far — when a loved one betrayed a person beyond what they could endure. Betrayal could throw someone who was off-balanced to begin with into a tailspin. She ran the facts of Tom Underwood's and Benny Goldstone's deaths and Susan's near-death in the Gatineau Hills through her mind, and all that she remembered about Pauline Underwood. Comments that family members had made about her inability to cope with Tom's desertion slotted into place like puzzle pieces. The clues had been there all along, but Pauline had kept herself a quiet presence in the background, hiding her rage behind a facade of normalcy. Pauline had fooled them all and might have still, but for the secret she'd confided in this innocent girl whom she'd had no reason to believe would ever tell anyone of importance. Pauline had shared her fantasy world with Dawn before she learned of Tom's final betrayal with her best friend.

Kala knew she would have to go carefully and methodically if she was to trip Pauline up. A theory wasn't enough. She was going to have to find hard proof that Pauline was a cold-blooded killer.

She looked at Dawn standing so quietly beside her. They'd go shopping for new boots and then she'd return to the station to start sifting through the evidence one more time. The night ahead would be a long one, but it felt good to be back on the trail.

36

SUSAN WAITED BY the back door, getting overheated in her down winter coat. She could hear Clinton upstairs walking from the bathroom to their bedroom and back again. He must be almost done packing his toiletries and the last of his clothes. A few more minutes and he'd be on his way downstairs.

She waited until she heard him leave the bedroom to cross to the landing at the head of the stairs before opening the front door. She stepped outside into the dark, cold morning, which was all the more painful after two weeks of above seasonal temperatures. Her nightgown under the knee-length coat clung to her legs as she darted down the steps and the icy walk to Clinton's Toyota. Her breath was a cloud of frosty mist in front of her. She fumbled with the electronic opener and hoisted herself into the front seat, leaving one leg to dangle outside the open door. The engine took some coaxing but turned over on the third try. Clinton had forgotten to plug in the block heater the night before, and it was the coldest morning they'd had in quite a while. She adjusted the dial to turn the heater on full before stepping down to scoot back inside the house.

A white paper fluttering under the windshield wiper on the driver's side of the frosted window of her van caught her attention. She smiled and carefully removed the paper, tucking it into her pocket.

At last.

Clinton met her just inside the door, putting on his green coat. He'd already laced up his black army boots.

"Cold out there?"

"Very," she shivered and decided to keep her coat on a while longer.

"A few minutes earlier next time, aye? It won't have warmed up before I hit the 417."

"Sorry." She forced herself to frown as if she really was.

"That's okay. I'll call tonight at the usual time."

"I'll be waiting. Drive safe," she said as an afterthought.

He grabbed the sleeve of her coat and pulled her to him. Panic fluttered in her chest for the briefest of moments before she felt his hot lips on hers. He forced his tongue into her mouth. She forced herself to relax and fought down the urge to gag.

He smiled as he pulled back from her. "Stay out of trouble." He patted her rear end hard enough to leave a mark, if she hadn't been wearing a layer of down.

"Always," she responded.

She locked the door after he left and watched through the curtain in the living room until she was certain he'd gone. She drifted into the kitchen. As usual, Clinton's dishes were rinsed and neatly stacked in the sink. She'd made him bacon and eggs but hadn't eaten any herself. It was odd this feeling of never being hungry.

She took a coffee mug from the cupboard over the sink and poured herself a cup from the coffeemaker. The first few swallows washed away the taste of him in her mouth. She pushed the hair out of her eyes, catching sight of her reflection in the window. When had she become this old woman with tangled hair and haunted eyes?

She crossed the floor and sat down heavily at the kitchen table. She stared into her coffee cup and tried to find the energy to drink. A flush of heat travelled up her neck and cheeks and she remembered that she still wore her down coat. She wiggled one arm out of a sleeve and paper crinkled in the pocket. The note! She reached inside and pulled it out, smoothing it on the table as she shrugged out of the other sleeve. A smile tugged at her lips. *Pauline.*

She was always leaving notes for people in unexpected places. An obsessive walker, she'd drop messages in the mailbox or under windshield wipers if it was too early or too late to visit. This one was short and unsigned. The letters were jerky as if Pauline'd leaned the paper against a tree while she scrawled the message. *The usual place? Nine a.m.*

Susan sighed deeply. Maybe her friend was back from the deep well inside herself where she'd retreated to grieve. They'd hardly spoken since Tom died, but now Pauline seemed willing to revive their daily walks down by the Rideau River. Not for the first time, she was glad that Pauline had never found out about her and Tom. It would have strained their friendship, perhaps irreparably, and Susan would be bereft without this link to Tom and her past to hang on to, especially now.

As their relationship had blossomed, Tom had confided how bad he felt about Pauline and their divorce and what it had done to Geraldine and Hunter. The weight of it had become a burden of guilt exacerbated by his failed second marriage and what he knew lay ahead for Charlotte.

He'd gone to visit Hunter at her urging and had spent time with Pauline after she told him that making restitution would help to heal Pauline's wounds — and his own. He'd been mending fences and had been finding a measure of peace before his death. This knowledge gave her solace now.

That last night when he'd come over, he'd told her that he was ready to move out of the house he shared with Laurel to find an apartment in downtown Ottawa. He'd wait for her there to break free of Clinton. He didn't care if they stayed in Ottawa, but if he fought for joint custody of Charlotte, it would be best if they remained somewhere in Ontario. He didn't want to do to Charlotte what he'd done to Geraldine and Hunter, but she knew he was worried about how Clinton would react to her departure and would leave this city for her. She hadn't told Tom how bad it had gotten at home, but she wondered now if he'd guessed and that was why he'd been willing to make a move. She'd been stronger that last night, determined to face Clinton and tell him that their marriage was over. Tom had given her strength. Now ... well now she could barely muster the energy to lift this full cup of coffee to her lips.

The sun had risen enough so that Susan could see the dark outline of trees beyond the patio doors. Cloud cover would keep the day a sullen grey but it would be plenty light enough for a tramp along the riverbank in Chapman Mills Conservation Area, a ten-minute drive across Prince of Wales Drive south of Winding Way. Normally, she'd walk the distance, but today she'd be too cold by the time she reached their meeting spot.

Susan stirred herself to stand up and get moving. If she hurried, there would be time for a quick bath and a bowl of granola before she set out to meet Pauline. Fresh air and a walk with her oldest friend could be all she needed to get her energy back. It would be two weeks before Clinton returned home from the base. Time enough to pull herself out of this dangerous funk. Time enough to decide the best way to leave him.

37

THE SNOW CRUNCHED underfoot as if she was walking on shattered glass. Susan inhaled the sharp edge of cold air and surveyed the stretch of Rideau River cradled in pine, Douglas fir, scraggly cedar, and snowy banks. The current was strong in places, with eddies of black water visible under the thinning layer of ice that snaked up-river toward the rapids. This sudden cold snap couldn't hold back the approaching spring. Already, the ice had been weakened by the two weeks of unprecedented warmth.

Susan spotted Pauline standing in the shadow of a giant pine at the beginning of the path. From spring to fall this was a walking trail with heavy traffic morning to night. Not so in the winter on a frigid morning. It was unusually cold, but Susan had dressed warmly in her down coat and lined nylon pants. She'd put her hood up and wrapped a wool scarf around her neck so that the stinging wind only found her cheeks and forehead. Pauline looked to be dressed as warmly as well and completely in white — ski jacket, ski pants, hat, gloves, and boots. Dark, wrap-around sunglasses were the only bit of colour.

"I could hardly see you standing there," Susan said, puffing as she approached the meeting spot. "You blend right into the snowy day."

They hugged. Pauline laughed and held up a thermos. "Glad you could make it. I brought sweet tea for our break on the trail."

"I think we might be alone on our walk. This north wind will keep people inside."

"I don't mind if you don't. We can just walk to the big bend in the river. It's only twenty minutes in."

They started into the wood side by side. The path paralleled the river, winding through pine, cedar, tamarack, birch, and stretches of bulrushes. Leafless sumac and honeysuckle bushes lined the river bank in places, their branches poking out from under a coat of snow. The canopy of branches had kept the snow from the path for the most part. Cross-country skiers and hikers had flattened down the rest so walking was not difficult. Inside the woods they were protected from the harshest bite of the wind. When the trail wound into openings next to the river, the wind bit into their cheeks, but just as quickly they'd be back amongst the trees. Susan could hear the wind soughing through the pines, a lonely, animal sound, and yet she found it comforting. It reminded her that the wind was powerful energy that nobody could control. When she leaned way back, she saw the tree tops swaying like skirted women dancing a languid samba. She smiled at the image and let the peace of the day replace the unsettled thoughts that were with her now every waking moment. She turned toward Pauline.

"I didn't see your car in the lot."

"No, I had an appointment and came directly from there. I parked on a side street off Winding Way because I was early and wanted to stretch my legs. I've been sadly neglecting my exercise regime with all the turmoil. I'll take a lift back to my car if you don't mind."

It was the closest Pauline had come to mentioning Tom's death. Susan linked her arm through Pauline's. "It's been a tough time but we'll get through it together."

Pauline's head swivelled so that she was looking at Susan through her dark sunglasses. They completely hid her eyes. Her mouth was a thin, tight line, and for the first time Susan felt a twinge of unease.

"Yes, together. It's the only way for friends to get through," said Pauline.

Susan smiled and relaxed. This was the Pauline she'd known since high school. The friend she sometimes didn't like very much, but the one she always loved. "How are Max and Geraldine coping with the new baby?"

"You haven't heard? Max moved out."

Susan stopped walking. "I had no idea. Is Geraldine all right?"

"It was for the best. Max stole money from her and he was unfaithful." Pauline turned and looked at Susan and then kept walking. Susan hurried to catch up.

"Poor Geraldine. I remember how in love she was when they married."

Pauline barked a laugh. "If I've learned one thing, it's that you never really know anybody. People act one way but will stab you in the back first chance they get."

Susan couldn't think of a response.

They walked single file across a walking bridge and then along a narrow curve in the path that wound through a tangle of prickly bushes. Small birds flitted from limb to limb on the branches overhead. The deeper woods were like a cocoon, sounds from the river muffled, the air still and damp. Susan wondered what was going on in Pauline's head. They'd all worked hard to protect her after Tom deserted her for Laurel. Even still, Pauline had gone through a manic period of pretending her life was glorious before she'd crashed into a state of not eating and depression. Could she have fallen back into that place? Susan caught up to her when the path broke into a clearing and widened so that they could walk two abreast.

"I'm so sorry Geraldine and Max couldn't work it out."

"Yes, but it's better this way. Geraldine finally saw him for what he is and now he's out of her life."

Pauline picked up speed as they entered the wood again. The trees were old growth and towered above them, plumy branches casting shadows on the path. Susan hurried to keep pace. Even with the cold temperature, a trickle of sweat dampened the back of her neck inside the down coat.

"Did you tell anyone we were walking today?" asked Pauline.

"No. I got your note when Clinton was heading back to the base but didn't mention it. I'm thinking about leaving him." Susan said the words aloud for the first time. They felt leaden on her tongue but also freeing.

Pauline turned her head and stared at her through her dark sunglasses. Susan wished she could see Pauline's eyes to know what she was thinking. Probably I told you so. Pauline had never liked Clinton.

"You have a black eye," said Pauline.

"I fell."

Pauline stared at her for a few moments and then shrugged. "If you say so."

They kept walking in silence. Susan wanted to break the wall that had grown between them, but felt helpless. Pauline pointed to the river ahead. The path curved left and a park bench sat in a clearing a few metres from the river.

Bulrushes and reeds filled the space between the path and the waterline. It was a pleasant place to sit in the summer when the heat and humidity were too much to bear in the concrete suburbs.

"How about a cup of tea and then we can head back?" Pauline asked.

"Lovely."

Pauline rushed ahead and wiped the snow from half the bench. "You sit and I'll stand," she said. "I've been having trouble with my legs and don't want them to seize up."

"Is that new?" Susan asked, concerned.

"The doctor gave me a new prescription that seems to be helping with the circulation. Here, I'll pour some tea." She took off her glove and unscrewed the thermos lid, filling the cup to the brim and handing it to Susan. She took out another plastic cup from her jacket pocket. "I came prepared." She poured some of the tea into it and raised it to her lips as she set the thermos on the bench next to Susan.

"Lots of sugar," said Susan. "Sweet but good," she added so as not to offend.

"I figured we'd need some energy." Pauline watched her drink before turning her back and looking out over the frozen river. "I like it here. It's so peaceful."

"Have you been spending much time with Geraldine and Amy Rose?"

"Oh yes. There's something about a baby that makes everything seem worthwhile. You haven't been to visit?"

"No. Clinton was home and it was hard to get away."

"He never seemed like a good match for you. Why ever did you marry him?"

"Loneliness, I guess. He was attentive and persistent at the beginning." Susan laughed. "He still is, come to think of it, but now his behaviour just seems controlling."

"Well, drink up. Would you like a bit more before we head back?"

Susan drained the last of her cup. "No, this is fine, thanks." She handed the cup in Pauline's direction, but Pauline had suddenly gone blurry.

"Wow, I feel dizzy all of a sudden." She could make out Pauline staring at her from behind those damn sunglasses. Susan started to stand but fell back onto the bench. "Everything is spinning. What … was in … that tea?"

"GHB, which the kids tell me stands for grievous bodily harm," Pauline said, matter-of-factly. Her voice was as cold as the frosty air. She poured the tea from her own cup in a long golden stream into the snow. "Causes dizziness, trouble moving, and loss of consciousness. If I'm lucky, seizures and problems breathing. It takes about fifteen minutes to take full effect."

"Why?" Susan gripped on to the underside of the bench with both hands to steady herself. Even the fear coursing through her felt off balance.

"To kill you. Why else? Tom fell for the same trick. Oh, don't look at me like that. The two of you played me for a fool, but I've shown you both that I won't accept your betrayal. I was out walking that night he spent in your bedroom. I saw him go inside and then the two of you embracing through your bedroom window. I went home and got my car and waited outside until he went home. How long had the affair been going on? Did you think you were Charles and Camilla, screwing around behind my back while we were married? You both must have found it so funny, putting one over on me all these years and laughing at how pathetic I was. Well, she who laughs last …"

Susan tried to shake her head. Lights trailed like shooting stars across her vision. *Pauline had drugged Tom?* Horror kept her hanging on to the shreds of reality already slipping away. "Benny," she mumbled, "too?"

"I overheard him with Max in the office. They were screwing around on Geraldine and had been for years, just like you and Tom were on me. Sinners, the whole lot of you." Pauline took a step closer and wrapped a hand under Susan's arm. She bent down and whispered through clenched teeth into Susan's ear, "Somebody has to make you pay for your sins, you see that, don't you? The beauty is that Clinton will be blamed. I've left enough clues to put him away for a very long time. Three murders' worth. That ought to bring you some cold comfort. Geraldine, Amy Rose, and I are going to start a new life free from the lot of you, and you, my *dear* friend, will find out how it feels to have your life destroyed just as I did." She cocked her head sideways, "Of course, you won't remember any of this so you probably won't know. But whatever."

Susan screamed, but her throat barely got the sound out. The wind carried her fear into the woods with nobody to save her. She tried to grip more tightly on to the bench as Pauline yanked her forward. Her arms were as floppy as a rag doll's. She stumbled to her knees and looked up at Pauline's bright red face, so familiar and so grotesque. It kept fading in and out like an image distorted by mirrors in a fun house. Panic shot up from her stomach.

"I don't want to die," she screamed with all the fear of a woman who knew the end was near. The words were garbled when they finally made it to her lips.

Pauline kicked her in the side. "You should have thought of that before you slept with my husband."

38

ROULEAU TOOK STONECHILD'S call in his kitchen. "You're up early for a Sunday," he said while shuffling eggs with a spatula around the frying pan. He glanced at his watch. "Not even nine yet. Eager to put your media training to work?" Her excited voice at the other end made him smile. "No, but I am psyched about something I found out yesterday. I've been up most of the night going through the files and I think I have proof."

"Proof of what?"

"Who killed Tom Underwood and Benny Goldstone."

"It's not your case anymore, Stonechild."

"I know, I know, but this fell into my lap. I was with friends I hadn't seen in a long time yesterday and the little girl goes to the after four program at the community centre downtown. Guess who her art teacher was?"

Rouleau shifted left to pop down the bread in the toaster. "No idea. Who?"

"Pauline Underwood. Tom's ex-wife."

Rouleau paused, the spatula suspended above the frying pan. "And?"

"Pauline told this little girl before Christmas that she was leaving to get married. Her husband was coming back to her at long last. As you recall, her husband was Tom Underwood, and he was planning to marry her best friend Susan."

Rouleau lowered the spatula and began scraping the eggs from where they'd begun to brown. "If this is true, it's bizarre behaviour. Maybe even delusional."

"Isn't it? Anyhow, I spent the night going through all the documents and Pauline could have done the murders. In fact, she's the logical choice when you look at who was killed. Also, don't forget Susan's near-death experience in the Gatineaus."

"Why's it logical?" The facts of the case filed through his brain.

"Let's say Pauline found out about Tom and Susan and their affair. Here's a woman who thinks she's about to be reunited with her ex-husband, only to find out he's sleeping with her best and oldest friend. Pauline's family mentioned a few times her desperation and odd behaviour when Tom left her for Laurel. She stopped eating and visited a counsellor, likely a shrink if you read between the lines. It makes sense she would have tried to make them both pay for what she must have believed was their betrayal. For an unstable woman, it wouldn't matter that years had passed since she and Tom were married. Tom's murder was personal. I think she got him to drop in for coffee early that morning and drugged him. She could have parked his car in her garage and left him in the trunk. He might have even been there when we were first looking for him. She must have brought the car to the Central Experimental Farm one night and jogged to a bus stop where nobody would remember her. It wouldn't have taken him long to freeze to death. As for the attempt on Susan Halliday, the two of them routinely went cross-country skiing together on that trail in the Gatineau Hills. It was just a matter of Pauline following Susan up there and waiting for an opportunity. Susan said there were tire marks near her van."

"What about Benny Goldstone?"

"He was cheating on Geraldine with Max and stealing from her. Pauline must have caught them. The fact it was a piece of sculpture from the office used to kill Benny makes it appear the killing was done spur of the moment. Pauline's whereabouts for the time he was killed are vague at best. She'd already made Tom pay. She must have thought the men in her life were all cheating scum."

"Where would she get the drug she used on Underwood? It was a street drug."

"Pauline worked at a couple of youth centres. Stuff is floating around, and she was well liked by the kids. It wouldn't take much for one of them to sell her something."

"Where are you now?" he asked.

"On my way to Susan Halliday's. I think she was lying about the last time she and Tom got together. Something tipped Pauline off. I'm going to see if I can make her talk to me."

Rouleau turned off the stove. "Wait for me in front of her house. Don't talk to her until I get there. I'm on my way."

"Will do, Sir."

———

Kala kept the motor running in her truck and watched Susan's house from a discreet distance across the street. She was quite certain that it was Susan's Mazda in the driveway.

A few minutes later, as if Kala conjured her up, Susan stepped onto the front steps, bundled up in a red down coat and nylon pants, scarf, hat, and mitts. She fumbled with the front door lock before striding toward the van and climbing into the front seat.

Kala started to open her truck door to intercept her, but remembered Rouleau's instruction to wait until he arrived before approaching Susan. She thought about ignoring his order. While she hesitated, she figured it might be a better idea to see where Susan was heading. Kala grabbed a map from where she'd tucked it under the passenger seat and held it up near her face. She lowered it enough to keep an eye on the driveway.

Susan let the van warm up for a good minute before slowly backing onto the street so that she was pointed west. Acting on instinct, Kala ducked down and averted her head just before Susan cruised past. Kala checked in the side mirror, but Susan hadn't looked in her direction. Kala straightened and kept watching in the mirror. The van was rounding a curve in the road and heading north, still on Eisenhower.

Kala didn't have a good feeling. Susan was dressed for the outdoors. Was she meeting Pauline somewhere, or was she foolish enough to be going somewhere isolated alone? She tossed the map onto the passenger seat and put the truck into gear, making a three-point turn and following several metres behind the van. Kala stayed back but close enough to see if Susan turned off onto a side road. She felt in her coat for her cell and hit the speed dial button to Rouleau's phone. He answered on the second ring.

"Susan's on the move, dressed for the outdoors. We're heading north on Eisenhower Crescent. Any ideas? Should I intercept her or just keep following?"

"It might be an idea to see what she's up to. She could be going to meet Pauline who lives farther into Chapman Mills. Her place is not too far from Susan's house, but far enough that she might drive. I've sent Bennett over to Pauline's to see if she's home. I'm waiting for him to check in."

"Oh wait, she's making a right onto Cortleigh, heading east, so she's not going to Pauline's. She just drove past Davidson Park and I see a larger park up ahead on the right."

"Heart's Desire Forest Park. I've brought up a map on my cellphone. Is she stopping?"

"No. She drove right past."

"I'd bet money she's heading to those nature trails."

"You could be right. She's turning south on Woodroffe toward the Rideau River."

"There're a couple of places along there to walk. I'll start in that direction. Call me when you know her exact destination. Perhaps she'll lead us to something interesting."

"Will do."

Kala dropped back. She'd been gaining on the van and didn't want Susan to spot her. Traffic was light. She checked her mirrors to make sure Pauline wasn't also on Susan's tail. All looked clear.

Five minutes later, Kala turned south on Woodroffe and followed it for a few minutes until she reached Prince of Wales. Susan was a few cars in front. They idled at a red light for several beats before it turned green. Susan pulled out slowly and headed north on Prince of Wales. Traffic was heavier and Kala was able to drop back and put more cars between them.

A few kilometres farther on, she spotted the red flash of Susan's right turn signal and slowed the truck even more. Kala watched the van pull off the road into the wooded area called Chapman Mills Conservation Area. Kala put on her turn signal and pulled onto the shoulder not too close to the turn off so Susan wouldn't notice her if she looked back toward the roadway. Susan's van took the side road down an incline into a plowed parking lot.

Kala called Rouleau again while taking off her seat belt. She shut down the engine and did a shoulder check, careful not to open her door into oncoming traffic. Two cars sped past doing over the speed limit. There was never a traffic cop around when you needed one.

"She's gone into the parking lot at Chapman Mills Conservation Area. I parked on the shoulder on Prince of Wales and am going in on foot." Kala watched in her side mirror for a break in traffic.

"I'm almost there. I can see your truck on the shoulder. Sit tight. I'll do a U-turn and will park behind you."

"Okay."

Kala spotted Rouleau driving toward her less than a minute later. The minute felt like an hour. Her instincts told her not to wait, but she didn't have any reason for this sense of urgency. Susan might just be on a nature walk by herself with no danger present. Pauline hadn't followed her, of this Kala was certain.

Rouleau made the turn and slid his car in behind her truck. Kala opened her door and stepped onto the snowy shoulder. She shivered and pulled up the hood of her jacket as cars sped by, blowing up gusts of snow.

Rouleau walked toward her, his phone cupped next to his ear. He was dressed casually in a dark blue parka, jeans, and Sorels. He closed his phone and stopped next to her. "Pauline's not at home. Her car's not in the driveway."

"She might be at her daughter's. It'll be a shame if I got you out here for no reason. Pauline didn't follow Susan here but she could already be in the parking lot."

"I told Bennett to keep checking for her. Shall we take a walk to see if Susan's alone?"

"Sure."

They trudged from the main road to the parking lot. It took a long five minutes. The lot had been recently plowed, but the snow had blown into drifts that were knee-deep outside the tire tracks.

"Hard to believe the temperature fell so suddenly. I was thinking about getting my golf clubs out a few days ago," said Rouleau.

"Just Susan's van over there. That's a relief," said Kala. She felt a drop in adrenaline. "I guess I really did get you out here for nothing."

Rouleau's phone buzzed in his pocket. He looked around as he answered. He said a few words that Kala couldn't hear and shut it again. "That was Bennett. Geraldine's expecting her mother within the hour. They're catching a plane to Florida for a two-week holiday."

"Geraldine and Pauline?"

"And the baby. Geraldine told Bennett that they need a break from all that's been going on."

"Understandable," said Kala. Disappointment washed over her. She'd really believed she was onto something. She looked at Rouleau. "Are you heading out then? Likely there's nothing to worry about here if Pauline is on her way to Florida. Will you be bringing her in for questioning?"

"We haven't enough evidence."

"I'll just go have a look at Susan's van before we go. I'll get some lunch and then head back to her house for that interview. She should be home by then. Clinton looked to be away."

"I'll come with you."

They trudged through the snow and circled the van. Kala squatted down next to the footprints. "Looks like she was alone. She headed that way toward the path."

Kala stood and began following the footprints. They were difficult to see in the crusty snow but no harder than tracking animals through the woods. Rouleau followed a few steps behind her. They reached the first line of trees. Kala searched the ground under a big pine. She crouched down for a better look, then looked up at Rouleau, not as relaxed as she'd been a moment before.

"There's two sets of footprints. I think she met someone and they went down the path into the woods together." She pointed toward the river. "They have a good fifteen-minute head start. We should follow."

"Could the two of them have come in the same van?" Rouleau asked.

"No, it was definitely just Susan in the van."

Rouleau looked back at the parking lot. "Then where's the other vehicle?"

"We'd better hurry," said Kala. "That bad feeling has just come back."

—

Kala was jogging close behind Rouleau and nearly crashed into him when they rounded a curve in the path some twenty minutes into the woods. Rouleau reached back to steady her. He half turned and looked at her with eyes that reminded her of hard green stones.

He spoke quietly. "They're up ahead talking. I'm not sure if it's Pauline in white. What was Susan wearing?"

"Red coat. Knee length." Kala's chest heaved as she tried to catch her breath.

"Susan's sitting on the bench. The other woman is standing. They might be strangers who met by chance. It looks like Pauline's height and weight."

"How do you want to play this?"

"We can pretend we're just out for a walk."

"They won't buy it."

Rouleau thought for a moment. "If it is Pauline, we don't want to tip her off before we have some evidence that she killed Underwood. Let's stick to the original plan and interview Susan alone. We can start back and hope they don't catch up to us."

"You think Susan's safe?"

"Looks safe enough to me." Rouleau watched the two women another moment "They're just talking." He turned and started walking back the way they'd come.

Kala hesitated. Rouleau stopped and looked at her. "Coming?"

"Yeah, I guess." She took a step toward him, but a noise that sounded like a strangled scream made her turn and look back. She motioned to Rouleau to stop.

"Susan's fallen off the bench into the snow. Something's wrong," she said.

He walked back and moved around her. "The other woman just kicked Susan."

Rouleau ran faster than she could have imagined and she was right behind him. Unfortunately, they couldn't hide their approach. The woman in white looked up at them from where she was crouched, undoing Susan's coat. Dark sunglasses hid her eyes but Kala recognized Pauline. Her lips were clasped tightly together, her face determined. She looked from them back down at Susan, bending to grab under her arms. Pauline's back heaved with exertion as she pulled the dead weight backwards through the reeds bowed with ice. She was making slow progress closer to the river's edge.

"It's too late," Pauline screamed. "You're too late."

Rouleau held out a hand. "Let us help you."

"Then help me pull this bitch onto the ice." Pauline's hysterical laughter travelled across the eerily frigid landscape to where they stood motionless. They were a hundred metres away and there was nowhere for Pauline to go. She wouldn't be able to drag Susan far. Pauline gave another frantic pull at Susan's arm and then straightened up and looked at them. She let Susan's arm drop into the snow. She stared at them for a moment longer before turning in one swift movement and stomping through the reeds toward the river.

"Stop!" yelled Kala, but she knew Pauline was past listening. She was picking up speed and running full tilt toward the deeper part of the river. As Kala watched, Pauline zigzagged around sections, trying frantically to find ice thick enough to bear her weight.

Rouleau reached the river bank first and took tentative steps onto the ice before Kala reached him. She looked down at Susan lying awkwardly just above the frozen water line then across the white expanse of river to where Pauline was making her way. Rouleau kept calling for her to come back but had stopped following.

Pauline turned and must have seen that nobody was coming after her. She slowed her pace, now testing her steps more tentatively on the ice. She wasn't even a third of the way across.

Kala shouted to Rouleau not to follow. It was too dangerous. He looked back at her, his face filled with indecision. She waved her arms for him to come back.

Suddenly, a cracking noise filled the silence, carried by the wind back to where they stood. Rouleau turned back toward the river in time to hear Pauline scream, her arms flailing above her head, her legs slipping out from under her. She seemed to skid several feet before she disappeared into a gaping hole. Dark, jagged fissures in the ice snaked toward the shoreline. Rouleau took a step forward.

"Don't do it." Kala yelled into the wind. "Pauline can't be saved." She knew it was true. Her last glance at the river had witnessed Pauline's head disappearing into the darkness of the black hole. He wouldn't have time to reach her even if the ice held his weight.

Rouleau hesitated and Kala held her breath. She willed him back to shore. Rouleau's shoulders dropped in defeat. He slowly turned and started back toward her. "She's gone," he said. He scrambled up the incline and squatted next to Susan, zipping up her coat. She writhed in the snow and moaned, her eyes still closed.

"She's been drugged. Let's get her moving before she freezes and we lose both of them," Rouleau looked up at Kala. The papery lines in his face were deeper than they'd been seconds before. He stood and pulled out his cellphone. He looked out across the river while he called for an ambulance and police backup.

Together they grabbed Susan under the arms and started down the path the way they'd come, carrying her limp body between them. The path was barely wide enough for three and the going was awkward. Susan was a dead weight between them. Nearly half an hour later, they reached the opening to the parking lot. A siren wailed from somewhere close by.

Kala looked over Susan's head at Rouleau. "It's better this way, Sir, for everyone. You couldn't have saved her."

"Maybe."

"We had no way of knowing what she was planning," Kala said. She felt a sudden urgency to convince him. "She had everyone fooled."

"Not everyone," said Rouleau, meeting her eyes. "I should have trusted your judgement and moved sooner back on the path."

"It could easily have gone the other way."

"You were closer to the case than I was. You have good instincts and I should have remembered."

"And I should have pieced it together sooner. We did the best we could."

39

THEY MET AFTER work in the Royal Oak on Bank Street, another pub furnished in the British tradition. Grayson and Malik were already well into their first quart of beer when Kala and Whelan arrived. Kala took off her jacket and sat across from them while Whelan went to the bar to order their drinks. He returned a minute later, carrying a Guinness and a club soda. He lowered his bulk with a grunt in the seat next to Kala and slid her drink over to her.

Malik raised his glass in her direction. "To our new colleague who broke the case. You're a credit to the Ottawa Police force and to mankind in general."

"Here, here," said Whelan.

They clinked glasses and drank.

"The paperwork and interviews made it almost not worth solving this thing," said Kala. "You should have warned me."

"You'd have been better off if Pauline Underwood hadn't drowned while you were trying to apprehend her. Otherwise, you wouldn't be under the scrutiny her death has subjected you to," said Malik. "Has it been rough?"

"Rough enough. SIU has zero personality and they take themselves extremely seriously."

She looked at Grayson. He was hunched over his beer as if the amber liquid was keeping him warm. He met her eyes and lifted his glass in her direction. "Good work, Stonechild."

"Thanks." He almost looked like he meant it. She glanced around the table. "Any word on how Pauline's family is doing?"

"Yeah, not every day your mother murders your father and then gets killed trying to kill her best friend," said Whelan. "Might make you question your genetic pool."

"I know I'd think twice before having kids," agreed Malik.

"Geraldine Oliver put her house on the market yesterday," Whelan commented. "She and her baby have moved in with the brother."

"Hunter?" asked Kala.

"Yeah. Apparently she's giving up the high life." Malik pointed at Grayson. "Tell Kala about the big business deal her father's company was working on."

"It fell through. While the murder investigation was going on, an American company offered the inventor Archambault a better deal and he went for it. From what I hear, J.P. Belliveau and company are in a great deal of financial trouble."

"It just doesn't get any better for that family, does it?" said Kala.

"Say, did anyone invite Rouleau?" asked Whelan, looking toward the door.

"He's working on something back at the office," said Grayson. "He couldn't make it."

"That's a shame," said Kala. She took a long drink from her glass, suddenly eager to get away. "I wanted to ask him something."

An hour later, she knocked lightly on Rouleau's office door and stepped inside. He was reading a typed page that he turned over before motioning her to take a seat.

"I thought you'd be celebrating," he said with a smile. "It's been a rough few days with SIU studying us from all angles." His green eyes were tired, his face pasty in the fluorescent lighting. She wondered if he'd eaten. SIU had been harder on him than her, and she was drained, not sleeping well and forgetting to eat.

"Grayson said you were still here and I wanted to talk to you about Susan Halliday. Clinton is abusing her, I'm sure of it."

"And what do you propose we do?"

"I know a woman has to make the decision to leave an abusive partner, but couldn't I go visit her and let her know about the support that's available?"

"It would be a tricky conversation."

"I just don't think I can ignore what I see in front of me."

Rouleau considered her words. "As investigators, we enter into people's lives and find out things about them that would never come to light otherwise. We have to learn tunnel vision. People are entitled to their privacy unless it has an impact on the case at hand. That said, I'm certain you'll find a way to see her even if I say not to." His eyes held hers. "It wouldn't hurt to make her aware of her options, but tread carefully. Is she still in the hospital?"

"She went home yesterday."

"Take Bennett. He can amuse the husband while you chat with her. Tell Clinton you're there as follow up to the murder investigation."

"Thank you, Sir."

"You know, life and relationships are never the tidy packages we'd like them to be. Sometimes, they don't end well no matter our best efforts. People can disappoint."

"I know." She paused not sure if he expected more from her. Her eyes lighted on a card with a picture of a French café at the edge of his desk. "Is this a postcard from Paris?" she asked. "May I?" He nodded and she picked it up. "I've always wanted to go overseas." She kept the photo side up, careful not to turn it over to read the message.

"It's from my ex, Frances. She and her husband are having a wonderful time. They're heading to Italy at the end of the month."

"What a great trip." She raised her eyes and studied Rouleau. He'd shifted his chair so that he was looking out the window. Darkness had fallen between the time she'd left the pub and entered his office. A soft snow was feathering the pane. When he turned back toward her, the curve of his mouth had lightened. He leaned across the desk and took the postcard from her.

"I'm handing in my resignation tonight," he said. "I've accepted a job in the homicide unit in Kingston. They have another opening, if you're interested."

She felt a jolt through her stomach. "Is it because of Pauline Underwood's death? Because if it was …"

He interrupted her. "No. I've been thinking about this for a while. My father lives in Kingston, as you know, and I want to spend more time with him. I also want to get back into the field. That's where I feel the most at home."

"What will happen to this unit?"

"I'm recommending Grayson take it over. He has his faults, but he's a good detective. He's agreed that I put his name forward. I know he'd like you to stay on. We've discussed it."

Kala slouched back in her chair. "It's a lot to take in."

"Well, think on it and let me know your decision."

"I will." She stood and looked down at him. "I understand your need to move on, but I think I might stay here a while longer."

"I figured you might." He smiled. "I'll tell them to hold the Kingston position another few weeks just in case you change your mind."

———

The lights were off on the second floor. Kala angled her wrist to catch the light from the street lamp through the window. Only eight o'clock. They shouldn't be in bed yet.

She stepped out of the truck and dodged traffic crossing York Street. The sidewalk was shovelled but the walkway wasn't and the snow hid patches of ice. One near fall and she slowed her steps. The front door was still unlocked and this time the smell of fried fish filled the hallway. It almost covered the smell of cigarette smoke, but not quite. She climbed the staircase slowly, ribbons of shadow darkening the walls. The only light came from a bulb dangling on an exposed wire from the ceiling at the bottom of the stairs. This was no place to raise a kid, but she'd lived in worse.

She knocked on Rose's door, knowing in her gut that nobody would answer. A sense of loss was already filling her like an old friend returning from a short vacation. She shifted sideways. It was the sound of a lock turning and a chain sliding across metal that alerted her. The door to the next apartment creaked open. She took a step toward it.

A white-haired head poked out, black current eyes in a wizened face. His teeth were probably soaking in a glass. "They left two days ago, all three of 'em. Rent coming due, I guess."

"No forwarding address?"

"They won't be keen to have anyone find them, now will they?

"I guess not. Did Rose leave a note or anything? I'm her cousin."

"They left nothing." He pushed the door shut with a bang. She could hear the lock click into place and the chain sliding back.

So, that's how it will be.

Kala looked at Rose's door one last time, willing it to open before she started down the stairs. She reached the bottom step and leaned heavily against the wall, her energy suddenly drained away. She watched a woman and young girl pass by on the sidewalk, snow dusting their heads like icing sugar.

Relationships are never the tidy packages we would like. People can disappoint.

Rouleau could have been talking about her life. Kala's jaw tightened. She'd invented a relationship that was as dead as that man they'd thrown into the river when she was ten years old. She'd been crazy to believe the bond between her and Rose was real. Rose was only a childish fantasy that kept her going through years of having nobody.

The old man's door creaked open again and she sensed him on the landing. She looked at the stained carpet and suddenly couldn't wait to get out of there. It was time to keep moving. She pushed herself away from the wall and caught her blurry reflection in the glass. She straightened her shoulders and pulled her hood up over her head before stepping outside into the night. Checking both ways for traffic, she ran through the falling snow toward her truck.

It would take her where she needed to go.

ACKNOWLEDGEMENTS

BRINGING A BOOK to its final form takes a great deal of work and vision by many dedicated folks. First, thank you to Sylvia McConnell for reading the original manuscript and championing it for publication — your support and encouragement have always been invaluable. Thanks also go to Allister Thompson for his continued support these many years. *Cold Mourning* was patiently and carefully edited by Jennifer McKnight, and Karen McMullin coordinated publicity — thank you both for all of your guidance and hard work. Thanks also to Jesse Hooper, Carmen Giraudy, and Laura Boyle for the splendid cover designs. My deep appreciation goes to the entire Dundurn team, led by Publisher Kirk Howard and Vice-President Beth Bruder, for your belief in Canadian authors and our work.

Since the release of my first mystery novel in 2004, I have belonged to a supportive crime-writing group called Capital Crime Writers. I've benefited from a wealth of subject specialists who've visited our monthly meetings. Retired Sergeant Damien Coakeley from Ottawa Police Services was one such guest speaker, who went on to read my manuscript and to guide me on details of the crime and investigative techniques. I owe Damien a huge debt of gratitude for his first-hand knowledge and wise advice.

I also would like to acknowledge the supportive crime-writing community in Ottawa and across the country. In particular, I would like to express my deep respect and appreciation to my Ottawa writing buddies Mary Jane Maffini, Barbara Fradkin, Linda Wiken, R.J. Harlick, Tim Wynne-Jones, Rick Mofina, Thomas Rendell Curran, Alex Brett, C.B. Forrest, Jeff Ross, Michael J. McCann, Dave Whellams, and Peggy Blair. You each make this writing gig a lot more fun.

Many friends and readers, old and new, have supported me along the way. Every kind comment, Facebook "like," and retweet have made me smile and kept me motivated. You are the ones who show up at my book launches and signings, send words of encouragement across the miles and, most importantly, read my books — I thank each and every one of you.

Finally, thank you to my family, near and far. Ted, Lisa, and Julia Weagle, you are much loved and appreciated — and welcome to our family, Robin Guy. A special word of love and affection to my sister-in-law Phyllis Goucher, who has always been one of my strongest cheerleaders.

Read on for a preview of the next
Stonechild and Rouleau Mystery, *Butterfly Kills*

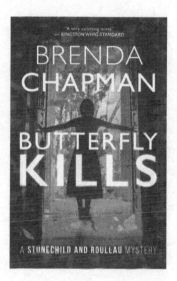

I

LEAH SAMPSON COULDN'T wait for the day to end. Twelve straight hours on the phone talking students through school jitters, boyfriend troubles, and suicidal thoughts was enough to make anyone go mad. Whoever said this generation had their shit together was dreaming in Technicolor. The problems she'd worked this lot through today had left her drained. A glass of Pinot, bowl of chocolate ice cream, and soak in a hot tub were long past due.

She turned her head as Wolf skirted past her desk to flop onto the couch positioned under a line of grimy windows. Darkness pressed against the glass and she glanced at her watch. *Ten to nine.* Ten more minutes and she'd be on her way home.

She tuned back into the girl's voice droning into her ear and waited for her to take a breath. "If he threatens to hit you again, call me back," Leah said. "We'll talk further about your options. It'll be time to decide whether you want to make a change. Yes, call anytime. We're always here to help you through."

She wearily hung up and looked across at Wolf, his long legs stretched out on the floor in front of him. His eyes were closed.

"What have you got on for tonight?" he asked.

A question inside of a question. He was really asking if she'd ended the affair. Had she stopped slinking around behind his back?

She couldn't risk him finding out what she'd done. Not yet.

"I'm going home, *alone*, and putting my feet up," she said, using both hands to refasten the clip that held her long hair away from her face. "And I'll be in the library writing a paper tomorrow, so no chance of getting into trouble."

Wolf's eyes flashed open; expressive green orbs flecked with gold. They were half of the reason why he'd been nicknamed a member of the animal kingdom. The other half lay in his mane of brown hair and full beard. She could have added his animal fierceness in bed, but that was an observation she'd attempted to seal away in her memory bank. Some days with more success than others.

He nodded, a smile tugging at his lips. "I'll walk you out if you're ready."

She glanced at her watch again. Four minutes after nine. "Where the hell is Gail? She's taking over the line from me and late as usual."

"Getting a coffee. She'll be back in a few."

"I can't leave until she gets here."

"I'll wait."

With blessed kindness, the phone remained silent until Gail traipsed in at a quarter past. Leah grimaced in her direction, but Gail ignored the rebuke just as she ignored most subtleties in life. Spiky red hair, round face, and rounder body littered with cartoon character tattoos and piercings, her style was as unapologetic as her character. Yet, Leah had to admit that Gail had a way with the callers; an empathy one couldn't fake.

Gail balanced a coffee cup in one hand and a biology text and iPad under her arm. "How're our loonies doing today?" she asked. "I hope they had the grace to call you and didn't save up their anxieties for my shift."

"Nice," said Wolf, rubbing a hand through his beard. "If callers knew the sensitive face of Queen's University at the other end of the help line, they might think twice about sharing their secrets with you."

"I'm just talking about the repeat loonies who wallow in messes of their own making." Gail dropped into the swivel chair newly vacated by Leah and scattered her possessions across the desk. "Thank God for the rule never to meet any of them. Can you imagine?"

"The regulars have all phoned in this afternoon, I think," Leah said. "Some more than once." She grabbed her cellphone from the desk. "We're off then." She turned her head so that Wolf didn't see her face. He'd know she was hiding something. He had a sixth sense when it came to her and lying.

They exited their office in the limestone house sandwiched next to the student centre on University Avenue. A cool breeze had come up from the direction of Lake Ontario and the air smelled of rain, dank, fecund vegetation, and earth worms. The fall semester had only begun four weeks ago, but the student problems never took a break. Summer, fall, winter, spring — each season had its own emotional issues. Leah noticed the asphalt was wet in the circle of light under a streetlamp. She shivered in her light T-shirt and denim skirt. Late September had brought in a welcome Indian summer. It had been a hot day when she left for work that morning. She hadn't thought to bring a jacket.

Wolf walked on the road side. He told her one night in bed that they'd been taught how to treat a girl in gym class:

walk closest to the oncoming traffic, hold the door open, wear a condom. He'd taken it all to heart.

She'd been hurt at first when he ended their relationship. Hurt that he'd doubted her, then anger that finally resolved itself into acceptance. She'd been shocked when he told her the month before that he knew she was having an affair. It was exactly the wrong time for him to accuse her. He'd pressed for a name and she'd refused. Predictably, he'd made the leap that she was protecting a married man. She hadn't denied it, not even when Wolf told her they had to take a break from each other. It still made her chest constrict and her eyes burn to think he didn't want her anymore, that he could doubt her so easily. They reached a truce after a few weeks of not speaking. Now she was grateful for his brotherly presence in her life. It meant he might still come around and become something more. She just needed a bit more time.

"I've handed in my notice to Mark," he said.

She stopped walking. "I hope it wasn't because of my …"

"No," he interrupted quickly. "Our breakup had nothing to do with my decision. I just think it's time I got into the field. I've accepted a job with the Kingston Public School Board that starts next semester. I'm heading out west for a few weeks first."

She caught up to him. "Then you'll come back to Kingston." For a moment, she'd feared losing him altogether.

"For now." He turned his head sideways and grinned at her. "I'll have an office, but will travel to different schools to work with the kids."

"You'll be terrific. I'm jealous."

"When you finish next year, I can put a word in for you too."

"I'm not sure this kind of work is for me. I've had doubts lately."

"It's the first you've said."

"It's just all the pain, you know? People and their problems that never get resolved. I think they've finally worn me out."

Wolf reached an arm around her shoulders and pulled her into a hug. She let herself relax against him for a moment before pushing him away.

"I'm just thinking about it, okay? No decision yet."

"Don't do anything rash. You're good at helping people, even if the results aren't always obvious. You have empathy."

"I just can't distance myself." Some of their troubles hit too close to home. She wanted to tell him about what she'd done, but couldn't bring herself to yet. She'd crossed lines, but wouldn't drag in anybody else. Still, her actions proved she wasn't professional enough for this field of work.

Wolf looked down Sydenham Street toward the house where she had an apartment. It was dark along the road, a street lamp burned out near her driveway. "I could walk you to your door if you'd like."

"I thought you were meeting someone at the pub."

"Yeah, but they can wait."

"I'm fine, Wolf. You go."

"You sure?"

"I'll see you in a couple of days."

"Get some rest, then." He gave her a quick kiss on the cheek. She held on to his arm for a moment before he turned away. She would have liked to wrap her whole body around him and make things right. From the look in his eyes, she believed he wanted the same.

Leah walked briskly down Sydenham toward Johnson, chilled in her light clothing. At the walkway to the front door of the two-storey red brick house where she'd lived for the past two years, she stopped and looked back toward the corner. Wolf still stood in the shadows where the streets intersected, watching until she made it safely inside. Another gym class lesson well learned.

She smiled and waved at the same time he looked down to check his phone. She slowly lowered her hand. A feeling of sadness welled up unexpectedly. One day Wolf would find somebody else and this fragile friendship would slip away. Some things could never go back to what they were. It always went like that with the people who meant the most to her. *Sometimes you don't know what you've got till it's gone.*

She started up the short walkway toward the house and surveyed the apartment windows. Lights on the main floor were off, but Becky appeared to be home on the second. Leah's spirits rose a bit. It looked like there'd be some company around for the weekend.

The house was built in the 1930s when front porches and bay windows were in vogue. Leah liked the old style elegance of the structure, even if time had worn the brick and peeled the paint on the wood detailing above the windows. Her one-bedroom apartment in the basement was cozy but definitely student digs. She'd filled it with IKEA furniture and her parents' cast offs. As soon as she finished her thesis, she planned to move into a nicer place and have a yard sale. The Queen's Help Line had promised her more hours whenever she had more time to give them. It would do until she made up her mind about the future.

The front door creaked open and she entered the hallway. An envelope lay at the base of the stairs, stark white against the grey carpet. She walked over and stooped to pick it up, flipping the envelope over to read the name as she straightened. Becky must have dropped it on her way upstairs.

Leah walked up the creaky stairs to the second floor landing and knocked on Becky's door. She could hear music and Becky talking on the phone when she leaned her ear against the wood. She listened for a while to see if Becky would hang up. After a minute or so, Leah knocked a second time before bending to slip the letter under the door. She would have liked to share a glass of wine and a chat, so she lingered a while longer before giving up and heading downstairs. For some reason she didn't feel like being alone this evening.

She flicked on the light switch at the head of the basement stairs and cursed as the light remained off. It was the second time the bulb had burned out within three weeks. She'd phone the landlord as soon as she got inside and get him to check the wiring. She should have insisted last time.

She stepped carefully down the steep stairwell, the light from the landing just enough to make out the outline of the steps. A mustiness seeped up from the basement concrete floor that no amount of air freshener could disguise. She'd bought a dehumidifier that helped slightly and lit a lot of incense, but it was time to start looking at apartment ads in the *Whig Standard*. Hopefully she'd find a better place not already rented for fall term.

At the bottom of the stairs, she felt in her pocket for her keys, then slid her hand down the door to the lock. She stopped with her hand on the knob and turned her head toward the laundry room. Was that a noise she'd heard or was fatigue making her jumpy? She listened for a moment more, her heart pounding like a jackhammer. Silence filled the space and she exhaled slowly. A braver person would have gone to look, but that would not be her. She had no desire to face a rat or other vermin in the dark.

It took three fumbling tries before she unlocked the door and opened it into her apartment. She stepped inside and felt along the wall to the light switch. She smiled when the room burst into brightness. At least the wiring problem hadn't entered her inner sanctum as she'd feared it might.

She reached back with her foot to shove the door closed. Instead of clicking shut, it swung back toward her. Her first thought was that dampness had warped the wood and the lock didn't catch as it should. "Dammit," she said aloud.

She turned and took a step toward the door before her legs stopped working. Her eyes widened as her brain scrambled to make sense of what she was seeing. A person dressed entirely in black filled the opening like a character out of a slasher movie. Her first thought was how absurd they looked, but horror quickly followed. The hand she'd extended toward the door handle found her mouth. She let out a shriek.

The figure stepped inside her apartment and pushed the door shut. Their eyes stayed on hers. "Did you think this was a game?"

She shook her head but comprehension dawned. Her mind was scrambling, searching frantically for toeholds. The chance of Becky hearing her scream two floors above was remote. There was no chance of pushing past the person in the narrow hallway and even less chance to make it out the closed door without being grabbed.

"I have no idea what you want," she heard herself beg. "Please just leave." She stumbled backward, her leg banging against the wall.

The person took a step closer, leather-gloved hands reaching toward her. Leah turned to run into the living room, knowing she was trapped with no way out.

Knowing she was in very big trouble.

ABOUT THE AUTHOR

BRENDA CHAPMAN GREW up in Terrace Bay, Ontario, and earned an English degree at Lakehead University and a teaching degree at Queen's University. She spent fifteen years teaching in the field of special education followed by an eighteen-year career in communications with the federal government.

Brenda's first series of middle-grade Jennifer Bannon mysteries garnered critical acclaim, including the Canadian Library Association's nomination for the 2006 Book of the Year for Children Award. In addition to standalones and short stories, she penned the acclaimed Stonechild and Rouleau police procedural series and the Anna Sweet novella series for adult literacy, both nominated for numerous awards, including four Crime Writers of Canada Awards of Excellence. *Blind Date: A Hunter and Tate Mystery*, released in 2022, is the first in an exciting new series.

Brenda, husband Ted Weagle, and daughters Lisa and Julia are all avid curlers in the winter months. Brenda also enjoys working in her garden, travelling, biking, and reading. She is active in the crime-writing community, having served two years as president of Capital Crime Writers and two terms as regional director for Crime Writers of Canada. She and her husband make their home in Ottawa, Ontario.